Days of
Wonder

KEITH STUART

sphere

To Mum, Dad, Catherine and Nina

SPHERE

First published in Great Britain in 2018 by Sphere
This paperback edition published by Sphere in 2019

1 3 5 7 9 10 8 6 4 2

A CIP catalogue record for this book
is available from the British Library.

ISBN 978-0-7515-6330-6

Typeset in Electra by M Rules
Printed and bound in Great Britain by
Clays Ltd, Elcograf S.p.A.

Papers used by Sphere are from well-managed forests
and other responsible sources.

MIX
Paper from
responsible sources
FSC® C104740
www.fsc.org

Sphere
An imprint of
Little, Brown Book Group
Carmelite House
50 Victoria Embankment
London EC4Y 0DZ

An Hachette UK Company
www.hachette.co.uk

www.littlebrown.co.uk

Praise for
Days of Wonder

'Fans of Jojo Moyes' *Me Before You* will love
Days of Wonder, which packs a similar emotional punch.
Made me laugh and cry in turn'
GOOD HOUSEKEEPING

'So powerful, yet incredibly gentle and poignant.
Utterly and completely beautiful'
JOANNA CANNON

'A story of life, love and hope –
the perfect antidote to today's world. Phenomenal'
CLARE MACKINTOSH

'A lovely, funny and very moving novel'
SUN

'This is the most emotionally powerful book
we've read all year'
HEAT

'*Days of Wonder* is a heartwarming
and magical story. A wonderful read'
LIBBY PAGE

reader love

'Spectacular' 'Truly wonderful'
★★★★★   ★★★★★

'Deeply moving, beautiful book. I didn't think
Keith's novel *A Boy Made of Blocks* could be topped,
but he's done it'

★★★★★

'I adore   'I loved
this book'   every character'

★★★★★   ★★★★★

'Full of joy, loyalty, heartache and love'

★★★★★

'Keith Stuart is fast emerging as one of the
UK's great emotive writers when it comes to
finding the beauty in everyday life'

★★★★★

'A joy to read'
★★★★★

Tom

There is such a thing as magic. That is what I always believed. I don't mean pulling rabbits out of hats or sawing people in half (and then putting them back together: otherwise it's not magic, it's technically murder). I don't really mean fairy-tale magic, either, with its princesses and witches and frogs that turn into handsome guys – although fairy tales will certainly play a part in our story. I just mean the idea that incredible things are possible, and that they can be conjured into existence through will, effort and love. That's how it started. That's how we got through everything in the way we did.

I suppose I really ought to begin with Hannah's diagnosis, but no, we're not going there, not yet. This is a story about magic, and therefore I will start somewhere magical. Or kind of magical. Oh look, it'll make sense, trust me. Let's begin two weeks after the diagnosis, on Hannah's fifth birthday – because this is what life is like sometimes: you're planning for a big day and then suddenly – *pow!* – have some shocking news about your daughter, no, go on, I insist. Of course, I didn't explain things fully to Hannah, how could I? But she was already wise, wiser than me – wise enough to look into my eyes and understand the essence of what the doctors had told me, and what was coming. We stood at the bus stop outside the hospital, the cold sun glinting off the scratched Plexiglas shelter. I tried hard to swallow, but it felt like I had a bowling ball in my throat. She looked up at me.

'It's okay,' she said. 'It's okay.'

And she put out her tiny fist for me to bump. I bumped it.

Anyway.

Anyway.

Where was I?

So yes, I thought, I have to do something special for her birthday – something to take us out of this place. I asked her what she wanted, and she shrugged and said, 'I just want to play Lego with my friend Jay.' That's easy enough, I thought.

'And fairies,' she added. 'Can I have real fairies?'

She had this book she absolutely loved – a fairy tale collection that had been handed down through my mum's family. It was incredibly ancient, so had none of the neurotic delicacy of a modern translation: kids died in the forest, dwarfs were eaten by witches, wolves butchered woodcutters – just horrible stuff. Hannah adored it. But she especially loved the idea of fairies – not the supermarket fancy-dress fairies with their pink sparkly wings and crystal wands, but the old-school fairies; the mischief-makers, cavorting in the woods and trapping humans in magical glades. Whenever we got to the end of a story, she'd always sigh and say, 'But fairies aren't real, are they?' and I'd tell her they definitely were, but that only special people got to see them. It was just a joke, a little routine to end the day. But on that night, the night of her fifth birthday, she asked as usual, only this time I said to her, 'Look out of the window later and you may be lucky.' She laughed at me dismissively, and buried her head in the duvet

2

until I got up to go. But I knew she was curious, because she was always curious.

So I kissed her on top of her head, her curly hair bedraggled and knotty because neither of us were any good at combing it; then I walked out of the room, closing the door behind me – except I left a gap, just enough to peek through. And sure enough, when she thought I was gone, she pulled back the duvet and crept towards the window . . .

I should explain at this point that I was a theatre manager, and before that an actor. When I was eight my parents took me to see *Dick Whittington* one Christmas and that was it, I was hooked. I begged them to take me back the next night, and the next. As a teenager, my friends were following Bowie, Pink Floyd and the Clash, while I was obsessed with the RSC, the Royal Court and the Old Vic. The magic I always believed in most was the magic of the stage, the miracles that take place when you put performers in front of an audience. You should bear this in mind for what comes next.

Outside Hannah's room, the night was almost completely black, the stars obscured behind a layer of distant cloud. Our house backs onto a field and during the day we'd sometimes see horse riders pass by, following the bridleway up to the woods. But at night there was nothing but darkness and then the distant twinkling lights from the next town miles away.

I could see that Hannah was now on tiptoes at the window, her small body silhouetted against the darkness outside. Suddenly, her head flicked to the right. From behind the tall hedge at the rear of our neighbour's garden there was a curious glow, orange and warm, like a bonfire – except there was no crackling, just the sound of very gentle music, almost lost in the buffeting wind. Then, indistinct at first but gradually louder, there were voices too. They were singing.

I heard Hannah take a sharp intake of breath, and then she rubbed furiously at her eyes with the sleeve of her pyjamas, before staring out again. She didn't move away, she didn't shrink from the window – she stayed still, as though entranced, as though connected to whatever was happening outside. Then as the music got louder, she somehow stirred from her reverie.

'Daddy!' she shouted. But there was no fear in her voice; it was not even shock or surprise. It was delight.

'Daddy,' she said again. 'I can see them, I can see them!'

'See what?' I said. And I was bounding into the bedroom, pretending that I had no idea what was going on. She grabbed my hand and dragged me to the window.

'The fairies,' she said. 'There are fairies here!'

And sure enough, dancing along the bridle path at the end of the garden, waving and smiling as they passed, was a line of beautiful figures in luminous white dresses and giant fluttering wings. Some held lanterns suspended from long staffs, the candlelight flickering as they moved; others were wrapped in shawls of flashing fairy lights. Hannah watched, at first transfixed, then banging on the window, waving delightedly. When one figure stopped, leant on the garden gate and blew a kiss up towards the window, she gasped. It was the first time in a week I'd seen her forget herself and everything else. If only for an instant, it wiped away the darkness of the preceding days. The figures danced and sang, the light from the lanterns forming a halo around them. Gradually, as the caravan of fairies passed, the music faded and the glow dispersed. The darkness returned, but not as deep or as black as it had once seemed. Something of the fairies had been left behind for ever.

I'll let you into a little secret. Technically, they weren't fairies. If you listened carefully you would recognise that the music was not some enchanting lullaby or mystical ballad – it was 'When Two Become One' by the Spice Girls, playing on a ghetto blaster. The thing is, when you manage a theatre, one of the perks of the job is twenty-four-hour access to enthusiastic amateur actors, who respond positively to the request, 'Will you come and dance past our house on Sunday night dressed in glowing leotards?' We also had a reasonably stocked props department so getting hold of Victorian lanterns at short notice wasn't as much of a problem for us as it would have been for someone relying on Homebase.

Anyway, I'd found this silly way to lighten the darkness, and it had worked. Eventually, Hannah bolted from the window and made for the stairs, determined to see the show up close. But by the time she got to the back door, the fairies were long gone (as we had arranged), scarpering into the alley a few houses down. I still don't know if she believed they were real or knew it was a show, but when I caught her up, she was standing in the open doorway, the breeze blowing her hair around her shoulders. She glanced up at me, then grabbed my hand.

'Again,' she said. 'Again.'

I suppose it was clear from that point that Hannah would be a sucker for escapism, for theatrical wonder – it was in her genes after all. As for me, I knew I had a way, however trivial and momentary, to help her cope with what had happened, and what was to come. I knew make-believe would be important.

So every year I arranged something like this for her birthday. A little play, a little surprise. It became something of a ritual to ward off the reality of the health tests and assessments that closed in every autumn.

The years passed, faster than I could ever have imagined, and when she was thirteen she decided she just wanted to spend her birthday with her friends. A walk into town, pizza, videos. It was always going to happen. All the make-believe in the world will not stop time.

Three months before her sixteenth birthday, I began to wonder if there was time to put on just one more show for her. It felt important – as though a little part of the future depended on it. I had this persistent feeling that something terrible was coming – we needed to be prepared and this was the only way to do it. I was a big believer in the magic of the theatre, you see. Did I mention that?

Summer 2005

Hannah

Don't die on stage. Don't even think about it. I'm completely fucking serious.

This is the rip-roaring motivational speech drifting through my head as I walk out beneath the theatre's glaring spotlights for the first time; for the first proper time, at least. As an actor.

I've been here before of course, lots of times. When your dad is a theatre manager, you quite literally grow up on the stage – which sounds incredibly glamorous until you learn that this particular stage is in a small market town in Somerset, and not, say, New York. I am also making my debut for the local drama group, not for the RSC, and while we're being totally honest, the play isn't *Hamlet* or *A Doll's House*, or anything else I've been pretending to read for GCSE Drama. The play is a 'bawdy farce', written in the seventies by some guy I've never heard of – my dad calls it *Carry On Being a Sexist Prick*, but that's not its actual name. Anyway, this sort of thing still goes down well with audiences, so we're stuck with it. Sally, the drama club creative director, has at least adapted the script for the modern era – which has meant taking out the racist jokes. The sexist ones have stayed in though, because apparently they're fine as long as we perform them with irony. I have learned a lot about what adults consider acceptable since joining the drama club last year. I don't get out much so I take my life lessons where I can.

By the time I'm due on stage, things are already in full swing. The set is a seventies suburban living room, complete with a lime-green sofa, shagpile carpet and a bamboo coffee table. Ted is putting in a brilliant performance in the lead role as a neurotic and flustered accountant, staring retirement in the face and having to deal with a moribund home life. It was genius casting by Sally, because he is, in real life, a neurotic and flustered accountant staring retirement in the face and having to deal with a moribund home life. Natasha is playing his wife, even though she is twenty years too young and about a hundred times too cool to be married to Ted. She used to do PR for an art gallery in London, but she and her husband decided to escape the rat race when their daughter Ashley was born. She set up a 'micro agency' for galleries and artists in the West Country, but now she's on maternity leave with their second child and it's driving her a bit mad. She told me that living in Somerset feels like being trapped in a cross between *Groundhog Day* and *Deliverance*. I looked up *Deliverance* on Google – I don't think it was a compliment. Dora, our costume designer, found her a grey wig in a costume hire store, and Margaret – the drama club's oldest member at eighty-one – said it makes Natasha look like a French harlot. Margaret is the rudest, most cynical person I ever met, and also one of my closest friends. Did I mention I don't get out much? Anyway, I also had to look up 'harlot' on Google and it is now my favourite word.

So that's the scene I am about to step into: a neurotic middle-class couple in seventies Britain, about to host a dinner party for the new neighbours, who seem extremely posh and respectable.

But then the hosts' drunken teenage daughter – that's me – comes home from a party and they have to hide her in the understairs cupboard. I am wearing a garish dress made entirely out of polyester and static electricity, and it's while I'm trying to flatten out the skirt that Sally nods at me from the small shadowy backstage area. My cue is coming.

Deep breaths.

I feel my heart thudding, and I don't want to think about that right now. There is the sound effect of a doorbell, and then I'm on, out through the black curtains at the edge of the stage and into the open auditorium in front of rows of people who have paid actual money to be entertained.

Oh shit, here we go.

The first thing I notice is that the air has this weird crackle to it, a kind of all-enveloping tension that seems to tingle all over my skin – it's either the anticipation of the crowd or the electricity being generated by this polyester fire hazard I'm wearing. I try to block it out and concentrate on what I'm doing, which is giggling and shrugging apologetically when my parents ask what the heck is wrong with me. Then I stagger past Natasha, whose wig has sort of slipped over her right eye at a jaunty angle. Then I pratfall onto the hostess trolley. I hear some laughs from the audience, which is a relief because I have zero personal experience of alcohol. In drama, we're learning about the theatre practitioner Konstantin Stanislavski who said all the best acting comes from the 'emotional memory' of the performer – you have to call on things you've experienced. However, the only emotional memory I have of alcohol is seeing my dad fall off a pub bench at his thirty-seventh birthday party and cracking his stupid head open. So I watched a lot of *Hollyoaks* and also typed 'drunken teenage girls' into an image search engine. That was a mistake I won't make again.

So now I'm on stage, collapsed across the ugly furniture. Ted and Natasha are splashing me in the face with vase water to try and sober me up – and the audience is chuckling along. It's fun, it's actually going well.

Then out of the corner of my eye, I spot Dad – or Tom as he is known to everyone else – watching me from the side of the stage. He is wearing his usual outfit of black jeans, shirt, tie and blazer. His hair is all spiky, and the gel glistens in the light. My friends Jenna and Daisy say he looks like an ageing pop star – sort of handsome, but filling out a bit, and a few grey hairs here and there. Whatever he looks like, there's not much family resemblance between us. Judging by the photos, I'm much more like Mum – kind of skinny, kind of okay-looking, grey eyes, mega-sharp cheekbones that look swollen if I put on too much blusher. Oh and crazy curly hair that Jenna refers to as an 'explosion in a corkscrew factory'. (It's pretty useful for when you're playing a drunk.) Anyway, Dad's expression is the familiar mix of deranged pride and encouragement that I have become accustomed to. That's another thing my friends say about him: he's not like other dads because he always looks happy, he isn't obsessed with sport and he actually listens to them when they talk. He *invests*. These are apparently rare commodities in fatherhood, which seems sad to me.

He has been bringing me here ever since I was a toddler, when he first got the job as manager. He'd lift me up onto the stage and act out stories for me. He practically taught me to read sitting up here, a single spotlight on us, working our way through fairy-tale books (which I was obsessed with and still am) as well as the standard young thespian syllabus: *Swish of the Curtain*, *Ballet Shoes*, *The Town in Bloom*. Those were the best days. He'd pick me up from school and bring me straight to the theatre and while he sat with some touring company planning their show, I'd prance about the stage or leg it along the aisles, yelling and singing. Then, for my birthdays, we started to plan these little plays together, and we'd put them on with the drama group, for all our families and friends. It became a sort of tradition. It meant so much to me when I was younger. It feels like a long time ago.

Of course I was desperate to be in a real actual play, but Dad always tried to put me off. 'We can't let people believe there is nepotism in the arts,' he'd say. 'The critics will tear us apart like wild dogs.' I seriously doubt the theatre reviewer at the local paper would be capable of tearing anything apart, let alone a person – being as she's a gentle seventy-year-old woman with a penchant for Noël Coward. But Dad was adamant. Last year, he refused to let me play Cecily in *The Importance of Being Earnest* because he said there were some dangerous stunts – I mean, that's such bullshit.

When they'd decided on this particular play, and it had a part for a fifteen-year-old girl, I literally begged Sally for the role. She said it was fine but I'd have to ask Dad for 'health reasons'. I thought it was hopeless, to be honest. I know it's because he worries about me and not because he thinks I'll be crap at acting and bring shame and disrepute on his theatrical empire. Ideally, he'd like to keep me locked up in a small room and never let me out. No wait, that sounds weird. Ideally he'd like to roll me up in bubble wrap and . . . oh god, whatever, you get the idea. And it's not like I have grand ambitions to be a big goddamn movie star. I don't have any ambitions at all; ambitions are *so* not my thing.

After a whole skit about a soufflé that hasn't risen (which somehow segues into a really gross mother-in-law joke), Margaret makes a cameo appearance as a nosy next-door neighbour, standing at the front door in a nightgown, her wild grey hair in curlers. She usually tints it in lurid colours and got it done like a rainbow for London Gay Pride last year, where she somehow had her photo taken with

Sir Ian McKellen. In the play, she comes round to complain about the noise and threatens to call the police until Ted gives her a bottle of sherry. For the dress rehearsal they used an actual bottle of sherry but she drank the lot before the interval. This time they've filled the bottle with cold tea – to her obvious distress.

Next, Ted's character has to hide me from the neighbours by dragging me to the understairs cupboard at the rear of the stage. This is no shoddy piece of sub-IKEA furniture, by the way; it was purpose-built by Kamil, the drama club's props manager, who teaches a woodwork diploma at the local college and takes the theatre very seriously. He worked on it for weeks then proudly unveiled to us an actual wooden staircase, complete with cupboard and built-on casters for easy deployment. It's so solidly constructed that you could conceivably throw it off a cliff and it would still be in one piece at the bottom. Which is probably more than could be said for the person locked inside.

Sorry, I get a bit dark sometimes. Especially when I am being hauled across a stage. It's sort of weird to be manhandled in front of a roomful of laughing people, but Ted is very professional and also extremely careful not to hold me anywhere that could conceivably get him arrested.

'How are you doing?' he whispers as he shoves me in the box. His thin, slightly haggard grey face is a mask of concern and his glasses are slipping off the end of his nose. I nod imperceptibly. Seemingly assured, he tries to slam the door shut, but my arm is still sticking out. Ouch, thanks Ted! He lifts my bruised limb in and slams the door so hard the staircase wobbles. Cue general hilarity.

Now I have to sit here for twenty minutes, which is not great because it's dark, it's cramped and there's no air . . . this is a crappy combination for someone with my health issues. I'm also feeling extremely hot. Earlier on, Margaret claimed she was on the verge of freezing to death and stormed off to the boiler room to try and kick-start the heating. Maybe she turned it up to warp factor nine. Maybe that's why I am drenched in sweat. I try to ignore my rapidly increasing heart rate. Deep breaths. Deep breaths. This is the theatre and the show must go on, even when you're locked in an oven. Fortunately, Kamil has drilled a small spyhole into the door so I can see what's going on. I spot another couple of actors from the drama group, Rachel and Shaun, enter the stage as the neighbours dressed in ridiculous Oxfam approximations of upper-middle-class seventies casual wear. But that's not all I notice. Around the entrance to the backstage area there appears to be a large pool of water. Little streams are working their way along the wall towards me. For a second, I wonder if this is a last-minute special effect that my dad has introduced without telling me – but then I notice Shaun nervously eyeing the flood and elbowing Rachel in the side. Something is wrong. Tendrils of water are slithering towards the main stage area, and I'm thinking, is this a hazard? There are all these lights and cables around. Oh god, it's like an opening scene from *Casualty*. The whole cast is about to be electrocuted.

Meanwhile in the play, it turns out that the neighbours think they have been invited to a swinging party, rather than a polite dinner soirée. As soon as Ted and Natasha leave the stage to 'fetch the crudités', Rachel and Shaun decide this is a code and start removing their clothes. The audience is really into it, guffawing unselfconsciously. Inevitably, the local vicar arrives, played by James, who is twenty-seven, really fit, and also the most devout atheist I've ever met. He sees the semi-naked couple and passes out on the sofa. Natasha shouts, 'I'll get you a stiff drink, this is not what it seems', and then opens the cupboard door, at which point

I sprawl out, swearing loudly. Everything is happening so quickly and there seems to be no way to subtly communicate to anyone else that we appear to be sinking. The vicar tries to help me up, but I fall on top of him (my favourite part of the play) and we sprawl together on the stage floor unable to extricate ourselves from each other. I try to whisper to James, 'I think we're sinking,' but Natasha drags me up, almost yanking my arm out of its socket, and James crawls out through the door.

Our big finale has my parents chasing me around a table as the embarrassed neighbours get dressed. They finally restrain me, dumping me on a chair at the dining table, just as two police officers turn up, responding to reports of a possible orgy or violent murder. I pass out with my face in a strawberry pavlova. The generously constructed stunt dessert fills my nose and eyes with squirty cream, which has gone rancid under the lights.

And then, the play is over. There are a few tense moments of silence as the lights fade, but they are followed by rapturous applause. I bound to the front of the stage, taking Ted and Natasha's hands and swinging them extravagantly. For a few seconds, I feel like a proper part of this bizarre little team. Later at the pub, the drama club actors will relive every line, every audience reaction, as they always do after a performance, whether it is good, like this, or bad, like that ill-advised attempt to stage *Equus* at a local horse and pony show.

I look into the crowds of people, hoping to spot Jenna and Daisy, or perhaps my drama teacher. But all the faces are similar and hard to make out beyond the clapping hands. Ted is hugging me and so is Natasha, and they pat me on the back, and then Natasha is very close and saying something, and I have to lean in to hear it. 'Can you hear me, Hannah?' she's saying. 'Are you still with us?' I want to say, 'I'm great. I'm a STAR.' But then I realise I can't really feel

16

my legs, and a swirling black fog has gathered at the edges of my vision. I stagger backwards a bit.

From a long distance away, I feel a hand on my arm, and another on my back, but it seems as though I am falling through them. The world is a woozy carousel of blurred shapes. Suddenly, I worry that the audience can see what's happening. Oh god, how mortifying. I have a strange hallucinogenic vision of Dad standing at my graveside delivering a eulogy: 'She died as she lived – like Tommy Cooper.' Now I *know* something is very wrong because that's just fucking weird.

Finally, I manage to say, 'Oh this is bloody typical.' Because it is not the first time I've done this, not by a long way.

The theatre lights look like stars above me. They swim about in the darkness. Then there is absolutely nothing.

Welcome to my world.

Tom

When Hannah was four, she started to complain about feeling tired all the time. It wasn't just in the early evenings, or after nursery, but all day. She'd stopped bounding about with her friends; she looked pale. I thought it was some sort of virus, or growing pains or something. I made a GP appointment fully expecting to be told what parents are always told: to keep an eye on it, that it's nothing to worry about. Our doctor was very much of the old school – balding, tall and dour, with the welcoming air of a medieval executioner. You'd gingerly enter his room and he'd sit back in his chair, arms crossed tightly, a reproachful glare etched into his craggy face that said, 'Come on then, out with it, convince me you're not another blithering hypochondriac.' You would list your symptoms and he would shake his head as though you had imagined the whole thing, and then he would tell you that it was perfectly survivable, and you would leave duly chastened. This is what happened when I went in to see him at thirty-one years old, with my lower back in such painful spasm that I couldn't stand straight for three days. This is what he did when I went in with chest pains when Hannah was three and I was having difficulty coping with parenthood alone all of a sudden. A shake of the head, a few bluff words of castigation, and then an abrupt return to his computer, which was your cue to immediately vacate the room.

So the day I took Hannah in and listed her symptoms, I was expecting the usual brush off and I almost didn't bother to sit down; but then, after glaring at me for several seconds, he did something I didn't expect. He put Hannah onto a chair, reached for his stethoscope and listened to her chest. He listened for a long time, dotting it about her torso seemingly at random. 'It's cold!' she complained, squirming away. He said nothing.

Finally, he sat back, took the plugs from his ears, and turned to his computer. Here we go, I thought. I was already standing up, ready to scarper for the door.

'I'm going to refer you to the cardiology unit at North Somerset Hospital,' he said. I stopped and sat back down in the chair next to Hannah's. She sidled onto my knee.

'Why? What's wrong?' I asked.

'Do you have any history of heart disease in your family?'

The wall clock ticked loudly; I could smell instant coffee above the faint ever-present odour of surgical spirit. I did not fully take in what I was being asked.

'I don't think so. I don't know. Why?'

He started tapping at his keyboard.

'She has a heart murmur. Usually, it's nothing to worry about, but I want it to be checked. Just in case.'

'Just in case of what?'

Suddenly bored, Hannah was trying to writhe off my lap.

'Well, as I say, it's probably nothing. I wouldn't want to make any diagnoses at this stage. You should get a letter with an appointment within a fortnight.'

I let Hannah escape from my grip and she ran towards the door, her thin fingers pulling at the handle. I rose from my chair slowly, too confused and intimidated to ask for more information. As I walked towards the door, I heard him turn towards us. I looked back with dawning concern.

'Goodbye, Mr Rose,' was all he said.

But the look on his face, the sound in his voice; they were as close as he'd ever come to sympathy. He'd never even said goodbye before.

As we walked away, Hannah's tiny hand in mine, I felt an awful weight on me, like being suddenly enveloped in a heavy black cloak.

It took me a few seconds to realise it was terror.

All this came back to me as I knelt by Hannah's side on the stage, the others gathering around as I got close enough to see her breathing. It's fine, I was thinking, this had happened before, it was just something boring that we had to deal with – like the British weather or televised motor sport. What most concerned me was thinking of something amusing to say when she came round. Something about corpsing on stage? I didn't know. The important thing was, we'd joke about it. It wouldn't be frightening. It would be all right.

Somewhere I heard Ted shouting at the audience, assuring them it was just all the excitement and the heat of the lights. He asked if everyone could file out and he thanked them for coming.

So yes, it had been an interesting night at the Willow Tree Theatre. On the plus side, all the actors turned up, we had an audience and the majority of that audience stayed awake until the end of the performance. The absolute dream scenario. On the negative side: Hannah fainted and we had a biblical flood. That, as they say, is show business.

My mind kept tracing back through the previous minutes. What had happened? The play ended well, the entire cast came out on stage. Ted was relaxed and smiling for once, gesturing to his wife Angela in the crowd. Natasha was waving that ridiculous grey wig at her husband who had brought their daughter along, even though I'd explained it might not be a suitable play for a seven-year-old. ('Ashley is a very mature seven,' Natasha had assured me. 'And she's learned all about swinging parties from her grandmother.' I did not enquire further.) In the centre was my own daughter, Hannah, on this little stage as a proper actor for the first time, greedily sucking up as much credit and applause as she could get away with. And then suddenly, she stopped moving, her face pale and blank. The noise of the audience seemed to fade, and I watched, unable to move, as she fell. It seemed as though we were both in some sort of dream.

'I've got some water,' said Shaun, wafting a cup in my direction. 'And um, talking about water . . .'

But I wasn't listening.

'Hannah,' I said. 'Come on, baby, stop hogging the limelight.'

'Should I call an ambulance?' asked Natasha, her hand gently resting on my shoulder.

'She'll be fine,' I said quietly.

I saw the slightest movement around her eyes, just a twitch, yet something unmistakable.

'Hannah,' I said. 'Hannah, come back.'

Sally, my closest friend, had seen this before. She knelt down beside me, and quietly brushed Hannah's hair away from her face.

'We could just call a doctor?' she said, her voice soft and reassuring.

I waited a few seconds for something else to happen, some kind of movement – a jolt of the arm, her fingers clasping mine – but there was nothing.

'Maybe,' I said. 'Maybe.'

Sally was just getting up and I was about to explain what she should say to the paramedics, when a clear voice, caught in the weird acoustics of the stage, resonated around the auditorium.

'You are such *drama* queens,' it said.

And I looked down to see Hannah awake, her head raised slightly, her eyes glazed but becoming focused, her mouth turning into a groggy smile. She tried to sit up and I helped, her ridiculous dress crackling with static against my blazer. She flopped backwards a little and I supported her; Sally was there too, her hand behind Hannah's back. There was an audible sigh of relief from the other members of the company. Shaun gently offered the cup of water to Hannah and she took it with a drunken waft of her arm, spilling almost half of it but lifting the rest to her mouth and glugging noisily.

'What happened?' she said.

'You passed out,' replied Ted. 'During the ovation.'

She looked at me, pushing her wild curly hair out of her eyes.

'Oh shit,' she said. 'I'm sorry, Dad. I'm really sorry.'

'What are you talking about?' I said, taking the empty cup from her. 'The audience loved it! Fainting was a masterstroke. They'll be flocking back in their droves.' But I knew she wasn't thinking about the play. Whenever this happened, wherever we were, she'd always apologise. And I'd always say don't be silly, and we'd just put it behind us. We had become adept at it. We were theatre people after all. The show must go on.

'I need to get changed,' said Hannah. 'Before this dress explodes.' She clambered to her feet and Sally and I gingerly drew our hands away from her as though removing a really risky block in a game of Jenga.

'I'll come with you,' said Sally.

'Is Phil not waiting for you?' I asked her. Phil was Sally's husband, a cheery red-faced rugger-bugger and much-admired local property developer.

'Oh, you know,' said Sally. 'He's not one for the theatre.'

'But he was here earlier, wasn't he? I saw you and him after the dress rehearsal.'

She looked like she was about to reply, but then turned back to Hannah.

'Come on, let's get you back to the dressing room.'

It was curious – Sally and I had been very close friends for years, but she barely ever mentioned Phil, and I barely ever saw him. I knew he was old-fashioned, that he didn't want Sally to work after their son Jay was born; perhaps he frowned on platonic friendships between men and women. Perhaps he thought the drama group was a maelstrom of sexual passion. He'd only have to attend one meeting to have that notion soundly quashed.

Hannah and Sally walked slowly down the corridor to the green room. The others stood around quietly looking at me, but trying not to *obviously* look at me. I could feel the fear and uncertainty radiating off them. I knew I needed to do something to diffuse the tension.

'It's fine everyone,' I said finally. 'It's fine. She'll be all right. It's just one of those things. Ted, you were hilarious tonight. Natasha, wonderful wig work, keep it up. Rachel, brilliant flirtatious scene with the vicar, well done. Shaun, excellent arse-grabbing, as usual. Oh and . . . I don't want to add any more drama to the evening, but does anyone know where all the water is coming from?'

'Ah yeah, I was trying to tell you about that,' Shaun said. 'The boiler's had a leak. Well, more of an eruption really. It looks like a pipe burst. I've switched off the water, but the back room is a lake.'

As an ex-builder, Shaun always came in especially handy

whenever part of the theatre broke or collapsed or flooded, which was increasingly often. With his cropped hair, tattoos and Fred Perry tops he looked like the sort of person who would beat up theatregoers in a pub, but thanks to his innate intelligence and a brilliantly determined English teacher he'd cultivated an unlikely interest in British post-war drama. He's still the only person I know who can quote *Look Back in Anger* while insulating a loft space. When his brother set up a taxi firm, Shaun persuaded him to call it 'Godot Cars', with the advertising catchphrase, 'What are *you* waiting for?'

'How does it look?' I said to him, trying to draw him ever-so-subtly away from the others.

'Hard to say, I'm not a plumber. I've opened the back doors so a lot of it is draining out. I've got a mate who can look at it but not until the morning.'

'Will we be all set for tomorrow night?'

Shaun shrugged. 'Ask me tomorrow.'

It was time to get things back on track. I turned to the rest of the cast. 'Come on,' I said. 'You should all change and get to the pub.'

'Are you coming for the debriefing?' asked Natasha.

'No, I'll take Hannah home. Sally will do the honours. It was a great performance; it's going to be a successful weekend.'

As the cast filed out towards the green room, Ted patted me gently on the back. 'We're here,' he said. 'If you need us.'

In the car on the way home, Hannah sat silently beside me, staring through the window at the empty evening roads. She was back in her own clothes, clutching her mobile phone. I patted her on the knee and when she looked back we smiled at each other.

'Are you sure you don't want to stop by the hospital?' I asked. 'Or McDonald's? Or the pub?'

'Get me *home*,' she said. 'I just ...' But her voice faded away into the night.

'What?' I said.

She shook her head. When she pushed her hair back behind her ear, I noticed she was wearing the hooped earrings I bought for her fourteenth birthday, the ones I got in a little jewellery shop in Bath while she was in hospital one time. Finally, she looked back at me.

'Nothing's ever going to be normal, is it, Dad? Let's be honest.'

The road was empty, and we drove through the quiet streets unnoticed. On either side of us were rows of Victorian houses, their lights warm against the encroaching darkness. We passed the church, its cemetery extending out behind it, far out into the field beyond. Hannah shuddered to herself.

'Let's do something tomorrow morning,' I said. 'Let's go down to Dorset, get breakfast at some ramshackle beachside café, read newspapers and comics, eat our combined bodyweight in fish and chips.'

Hannah smiled at me, and I recognised the expression so well – it was sympathetic and indulgent, sort of how a parent might smile at their child if they'd just asked to have their birthday party on Mars. Then she turned back to her phone and started tapping away. Kids today.

When we pulled up outside the house, our chubby cat was sitting on the wall, seemingly waiting for us.

'Malvolio, you fat little bastard!' cried Hannah as she got out of the car. He padded towards her lazily and I noticed that when she stroked him, she discreetly balanced herself against the gatepost with her other hand.

I had delayed her theatrical debut for a number of years, but the truth is, she had always been an excellent actor.

Hannah

This morning, still feeling slightly mortified about passing out on stage during the encore, I did a Google search for 'great theatrical disasters'. I found out that during a 1948 production of *Macbeth*, the actor Diana Wynyard attempted the Lady Macbeth sleep-walking scene with her eyes closed and fell fifteen feet into the orchestra pit. This made me feel slightly better about myself.

She was fine, by the way.

I feel like I should explain why I fainted. As an exciting subplot to my main medical condition, which I'm not going to go into right now because it's Saturday, I suffer from an arrhythmia. This means that sometimes my heart skips a beat or two; in fact, sometimes it skips several, like the drummer in a shitty indie band. Then I feel woozy, and sometimes I faint. It hasn't happened in ages, so it's bloody annoying that it should happen while I'm on stage. I also know that it freaked Dad out – even if he pretends it didn't. I expect he's been lying in bed, working out the best thing to do to protect me and I'm fairly certain that will mean the end of my starring role in *Carry on Being A Sexist Prick*.

Sure enough, the little director–daughter chat I've been waiting for happens at 9.38 a.m. I'm sitting at the kitchen table eating a thick slab of toast and listening to Regina Spektor. Dad slopes in, switches off the CD and sits down opposite me.

'Hannah,' he says brightly, slapping his hands down on the table top. 'I've been thinking ...'

'You've been thinking that I shouldn't do the play tonight,' I say, taking a bite out of the toast and pretending to study text messages on my phone. 'Or tomorrow night. You know, just to be on the safe side.'

'It's just ...'

'Dad, don't.'

' ... it's hot up there on stage, and it's stressful, and there's a lot of chucking you about and locking you in cupboards, and there's the bit where we shove your face in a pavlova.'

'I know,' I say, glancing through endless incomprehensible messages from Jenna who has evolved her own form of txt speak in order to confuse her parents. 'I was there.'

He reaches out and gently takes my phone out of my hand and puts it on the table. I hate it when he does that.

'The next production is autumn. We'll make sure you get a bloody good role – just one that's a little less manic. How's that?'

I sigh heavily, and look at him. I used to do what he said when he gave me his concerned-parent look, but lately it was beginning to grate.

'No,' I say. 'No deal.'

'Huh?'

He is not expecting this. He even does a comedy double take.

'I'm doing the play. You cast me and I'm doing it.'

'But Hannah ...'

'Dad, I fainted in the curtain call – that's all. I'll drink more water tonight, I'll take it easy. But you can't just pull me out. Don't you get it? You can't do that any more.'

He looks crestfallen. We don't argue often, hardly at all. And I mean, this guy has just seen his daughter take a nosedive in front of eighty-five people – that's got to be tough. Also, I haven't told him this, but lately I've begun to feel tired a lot. I struggled through the last few weeks of the school term, almost drifting off to sleep in the afternoons, stabbing myself with a compass to stay awake in double maths (although I'm not alone there, to be honest). But I'm not budging. I'm too pissed off. I've got to take a stand.

We're both opening our mouths to speak at the same time, when another text comes in. I grab my phone, relieved at the distraction. It's from Jay, Sally's son, asking if he can come round. I've known Jay since I was four; we went to nursery school together, and then every educational stage since then, trapped into a friendship we couldn't escape. Sally and Dad are BFFs and when your parents are friends, you tend to get lumped together whether you like it or not. Fortunately, Jay is all right. He's this big, dumb teenage boy, bounding about the place like a Labrador. We're not as close these days, but we still hang out. He plays video games, I read comics and we're both comfortable occupying the same sofa for hours on end. Lately though, he's become really sensitive and I don't know why. He spends waaaay too much time worrying about whether or not he is a gross social leper. I mean, he could definitely work on his personal hygiene at times, and his ridiculously long grunge hair is about ten years out of style, but people like him – they like him because, in this deeply cynical world, he's a bundle of energy and enthusiasm. He's also sort of good-looking I suppose, but I have trouble thinking of him in 'that way' – partly because, well, we've grown up together, so yuck, but also because he has this tendency to treat me like some sort of sickly heiress in a Victorian melodrama. There is literally nothing sexy about that – unless you have some sort of weird fetish for petticoats or consumption. Which I don't.

'Jay wants to come round,' I drawl.

'That's great!' says Dad, glad of the change in topic and already pinning his hopes on the restorative power of hanging around with boys. 'I'm going out to Sainsbury's so I'll get you two some snacks!'

I decide I'm not going to let him off the hook that easily.

'Did you know,' I say, 'that during a 1948 production of *Macbeth*, the actor Diana Wynyard fell fifteen feet into the orchestra pit during the sleepwalking scene? She was back on stage the next night. Just putting that out there.'

'The Scottish Play,' replies Dad.

'Huh?'

'You called it *Macbeth*, you must call it the—'

'Oh piss off,' I say.

He smiles and, despite myself, so do I.

I decide to have a bath, and while I'm lying there, trying not to feel or listen to my heartbeat, trying not to obsess over its staccato rhythm, I hear Dad yell goodbye and the front door slams behind him. For almost an hour, I stay submerged beneath heavily perfumed bubbles, wondering about the summer ahead and what I'll do. Dad will probably insist on a series of ad hoc road trips, usually to places of theatrical interest. While other families are off to Spain and Italy, we'll be visiting Aldwincle in Northamptonshire to see the birthplace of John Dryden, or watching the York Minster Mystery Plays. It's fine, it's the way things have always been. But it's not ... normal, I guess. I wonder when I should start telling him to go on his own.

I'm getting dressed when I hear Dad return from the supermarket. For twenty minutes he clatters around the house doing god knows what, and then he's gone again. When I wander downstairs I find a note:

Hidden a few treats around the house for you and Jaybo. Have fun.
See ya later – I am at the theatre, investigating the flood with
Shaun – don't worry I have goggles and a snorkel. Papa x.

Treats? 'Jaybo'? 'Papa'?! He's such an unbearable dork.

A few minutes later the doorbell rings, then there's a loud series of knocks, then two more rings. It's Jay. I trudge through our tiny living room with its wobbly coffee table covered in newspapers and its sagging shelves filled with Faber and Faber play texts and Penguin Classics. The gaudily patterned sixties-era wallpaper is peeling off, and there are spots of mould in the corners, but Dad never gets round to doing anything about it. 'It's Joe Orton chic,' he says. So I remind him that Joe Orton was bludgeoned to death by his flatmate.

When I open the door, there is Jay, dressed in cargo shorts and a Blink 182 T-shirt, with his NY baseball cap on backwards. I usher him in quickly to spare him further public humiliation.

'Heyyy,' he says, holding up a tattered backpack. 'I've brought my PlayStation 2 – let the games commence!'

'I am not playing "Medal of Honor",' I say. 'Or fucking "FIFA". Dad says he's left "treats" around the house for us. I don't know what he means, but I suppose we should have a look.'

'Wicked,' he says. 'Your dad is cool. Weird but definitely cool.'

'I guess so.'

'The only things my dad ever leaves around the house are these little Post-it notes reminding Mum about chores that need doing.'

'Nice.'

'How are you feeling, anyway? God, that must have been pretty scary last night.'

'I'm fine, Jay. Don't ask again.'

'Got it.'

We search through the living room, upending sofa cushions and peering behind the books and under the armchair. We find two tubes of Pringles, a giant bag of Haribo Tangfastic and a two-litre bottle of Cherry Coke. We run into the kitchen, yanking open the cupboards and rummaging through the packets of pasta and jars of passata that make up our staple diet. In the fridge we find a huge meat feast pizza and some garlic bread – and also a DVD copy of the eighties movie *Mannequin*. Jay spots a bag of Revels in the washing machine, but when he leans into the drum to retrieve them, a stray pair of knickers drops onto his hand, causing him to scream and yank his arm out, flinging my rogue underwear across the room. We burst out laughing.

'Jesus,' he says. 'Your pants were all over me.'

'You wish,' I say.

And then it's really awkward for a few seconds.

Once he's recovered, I put the disc in the DVD player and we sit at opposite ends of the big saggy sofa, the coffee table loaded with our ultra-calorific spoils. I must admit, I'm not really that into films; they're too fast and noisy for me. Maybe it's something to do with my condition. But *Mannequin* is a goddamn masterpiece. We discover to our considerable surprise that it's about a guy who falls in love with an Ancient Egyptian princess who is trapped inside the body of a shop window dummy. It is totally random. The princess is played by Kim Cattrall from *Sex in the City*, which I used to watch with Daisy when her parents weren't looking – largely as a form of sex education.

'They don't make films like this any more,' says Jay, between handfuls of sugar-coated dummies.

'That's because we're not *completely* deranged,' I say. 'What the hell was happening in the eighties? What was wrong with these people?'

'Mum was like a punk or something. I've seen photos; her hair was stuck out everywhere – it was mad.'

'Did she look cool?'

'She looked like a zombie.'

'Jesus. The eighties were terrifying.'

We're having fun, making all these bitchy comments about everyone's clothes, which are really hilarious, and I put my head on his shoulder laughing. But when the film's over, Jay plugs his console in, and ends up playing this new military shooting game, which is exactly like every other military shooting game I've ever seen. While he's throwing grenades at a seemingly indestructible helicopter, I storm out into the kitchen to put the oven on for pizza. Straight away, I hear him pause the game, and he follows me through like a sad puppy.

'Is anything wrong?' he says, with a grating tone of genuine concern.

'No, I'm just not into that game.'

'But *Official PlayStation Magazine* gave it nine out of ten.'

'I don't care, Jay.'

'I've almost beaten the helicopter boss battle.'

'Jay, seriously. I don't want to just sit there and watch all that … death and dying.'

The words hang in the air like a curse.

'Oh god,' he says. 'I'm sorry. I'm so sorry. I didn't think.'

I slam the fridge shut in frustration.

'Oh for fuck's sake, Jay, I didn't mean *that*! It's got nothing to do with me, I'm just not interested in gung-ho army guys blowing stuff up and shouting "I've got your six" at each other, whatever the hell that means.'

'All right,' he says, 'just calm down.' He goes to touch my shoulder, and I recoil from him, furious.

'Don't!' I seethe.

'What?!' he yells, clearly hurt.

It's just a tiny insignificant exchange, but Jay's cloying, suffocating concern reconfirms to me that nothing is ever going to happen between us. Not in that way. It's acceptable to get that crap from Dad, he's contractually obliged to look after me, but I really do not need *two* men treating me like a china ornament – especially when they can barely look after themselves. I walk away from him, into the living room, where I slump across the whole sofa so he can't sit next to me.

As if on cue, the front door opens and in walks Dad. He's wearing an old hoodie and some torn jeans – both are covered in oil and grime. I remember that I'm still pissed off with him about the play, so offer an unsmiling wave instead of hello.

'Hey,' he says. 'Where's Jay?'

'In the kitchen. What happened to you?'

'Ah, just working on the boiler with Shaun. It's bad news I'm afraid.' He looks like he has been rehearsing this all the way home. 'It needs some new parts that we can't fit until Monday, so the water is off, which means we can't open to the public – it's against health and safety. We're having to cancel.'

'Oh really?' I say. 'How fucking convenient.'

'Hannah!' This time he's not apologetic, he's mildly angry – which for Dad, is actually very angry indeed. 'This is an expensive decision. I haven't done it because of you.'

'Of course not.'

Jay appears at the door.

'Hello, Mr Rose.'

'Ah Jay! How are you?'

Silence and tension. The guys are trying to read each other, and also me, in a crossfire of awkward stares. It's like that scene at the end of *Reservoir Dogs* when they're all pointing guns at each other – except we're middle class and British so it's just a lot of unspoken anxiety. For a few seconds I really wish there was an adult woman around to sort the pair of them out.

Finally, I sigh loudly, restart Jay's game and blow the absolute shit out of the helicopter.

Tom

On Monday morning I drove to the theatre, singing along with a Bobby Darin CD. Pulling into the empty car park, I got that familiar frisson of excitement. Even after a flooding disaster, the sight of that place lifted my heart.

If I'm completely honest, it is not a beautiful building. In fact, it's a 1970s concrete monstrosity of almost spiteful ugliness. If a multi-storey car park shagged an old people's home, the Willow Tree Theatre would be their hideous love child. Nevertheless, there is something magical and transformative about a live performance – even in a carbuncle like this. The proximity of actor and audience; the tension in the air between them – no flat-screen TV or broadband-connected computer can contend with it. People used to come to be shocked, challenged and educated. Now they mostly come for Disney adaptations and modern musicals, cobbled together from the greatest hits of long-gone pop acts. But that's fine. If people want to see *Reflex: The Duran Duran Story*, we'll put it on. And every time I walked into our little auditorium, whether we were showing Shakespeare or a Shakespeare's Sister tribute act (there isn't one, obviously, but if there was I'd probably have booked it) I felt the sheer buzzing potential of the empty space.

Tonight would see our over-thirty-fives breakdancing master-class with MC Neat Trix, who is actually called Greg and works in a refrigerated warehouse in Shepton. Lovely guy. Later in the week, as long as the boiler could be repaired, we would be welcoming Broadway Bonanza, a selection of favourite scenes from classic musicals performed by a local dance company. Box office gold. Once in a while we'd do a classic or some acclaimed masterpiece of modern theatre, especially if it had cropped up on the GCSE syllabus – that always got us a wodge of funding – but we'd never be sure anyone would turn up beyond thirty bored teenagers snogging or text-messaging their way through the evening. It was getting harder to book interesting theatre companies. The county council was slyly cutting its support for the arts, so we had to keep our heads down and do the best we could. Apparently, when this place was built in the 1970s, they had actual famous actors here. Margaret told us she'd been in a production of *Mother Courage and Her Children* with Brian Blessed. It sounded unlikely, but then most of her showbiz anecdotes did. She claimed to have appeared in several television shows of the late sixties and seventies, but I looked up Margaret Wright on Internet Movie Database and there was nothing. We didn't know if she was sharing actual memories or making really dirty jokes. She'd say things like, 'Dennis Waterman once slapped me on *The Sweeney*' and then pretend to be mystified when we all dissolved into laughter.

I headed through the sliding glass doors into the lobby. With its garish plum-coloured carpet and bare grey walls it looked like a leisure centre reception area circa 1978. On the walls there were framed photos of previous performances, including an abridged *Hamlet* (nonsensical but all over in seventy-five minutes) and a disastrous musical version of *The Woman in Black*. There was a little bar area with a few cramped tables; it doubled as a café on the days we had enough staff to run it. The box office, which resembled a nuclear bunker, housed a Cold War-era computer that could just about handle internet bookings. My office was upstairs, along from the toilets. It was effectively a physical representation of my brain: a chaotic jumble of theatrical paraphernalia and family memories. Every surface was piled with touring company directories, well-thumbed copies of *The Stage* and lever-arch folders stuffed with I don't even know what. I kept eight framed photos of Hannah on my desk, tracking her life from toddler (sitting on the stage in a tutu) to teenager (sitting on the stage in a Joy Division T-shirt). I felt very comfortable here, partly because of all the memories, and partly because of the expensive back-supporting swivel chair the council bought me when I convinced them I had acute lumbago. That was two hours of form-filling well spent.

My contact with the council was actually minimal. As long as I attended budget meetings and didn't put on any all-nude productions of *Romans in Britain*, they let us be. The Willow Tree was a tiny theatrical outpost on the other side of the galaxy – like *Star Trek: Deep Space Nine* but with a slightly lower make-up budget.

As my laptop powered up, I looked out of the small window by my desk, just in time to see Ted cycling up to the entrance in his corduroy trousers and checked blazer like a local Labour politician or Open University lecturer. He had been an accountant at a plastics firm in Bristol for his whole working life before retiring three years ago. His two sons had long since grown up and left home, and he harboured grand plans to travel through Europe with his wife Angela. In his garage, draped under sheets, he kept an old Triumph motorbike and sidecar that he'd always intended to restore; the dream was for them to ride it up into Finland to see the

Northern Lights. But Angela's sister developed dementia and they needed to be nearby. So, instead of zooming towards the horizon on a classic piece of British engineering, he started volunteering for the theatre, keeping the books in some semblance of order. It got him out of the house, he'd say. When Henry David Thoreau wrote 'The mass of men lead lives of quiet desperation', I'm certain he was picturing Ted in his bicycle clips.

'Good day,' he said as he bumbled into the office and sat down, immediately retrieving a laptop from the battered leather satchel that his father had bought him forty years ago. Ted is good at saving worthless artefacts – that's why he's proved so useful in local theatre.

'So,' he continued in a let's-get-down-to-business sort of way. 'What did Shaun say about our biblical flood?'

He was acting casually, but I knew he was not expressing polite curiosity. This was very much Serious Accountant Ted. This was Money Ted. And I knew that what I was about to say would disturb him.

'Well,' I started. 'He and his mate managed to pump the excess water out on Saturday, then set up dehumidifiers, so most of the water is gone. But the boiler is out of action for now, and there's water damage to the flooring in the corridor and on the stage.'

'I'll get the insurance claim forms started,' he said. 'Did they say what caused it?'

'Well, Shaun's plumber friend said he was no expert on 1970s industrial boilers – which sounds like the worst *Mastermind* specialist subject of all time, doesn't it?'

Ted was not having any joviality.

'But,' I continued, 'he said it might have been a build-up of pressure. He asked if it had been knocked or if anyone had been fiddling with it, but I said no of course not – who would fiddle with a boiler? I mean, does it matter?'

'The insurance company will ask,' Ted said.

'Really? Won't they just pay out?'

He looked at me with a mixture of strained patience and pity. 'No, Tom. They never just pay out. They're looking for reasons *not* to pay out. That's how insurance works.'

'Really? What a swindle!'

'Tom ...' He removed his glasses and rubbed his eyes, like a frustrated parent trying to explain quadratic equations to a slightly dim child. 'We need as much information as we can get. I mean, is it possible that someone went in and tried to change the setting? Margaret was complaining that she was cold during the technical rehearsal. I wouldn't put it past her to go at the boiler with a wrench.'

'Let's not turn this into an investigation. I don't want to start drawing up a list of suspects, for heaven's sake.'

Now there was a weird tension in the air so I switched on Radio 4. Ted reached for his satchel and lifted out a packet of chocolate digestives. He was just putting them down on the desk when he noticed a small Post-it note stuck to the packet. It said *Love you, Teddy. A x.* He blushed and removed it selfconsciously.

'It's from Angela,' he clarified, somewhat needlessly. 'We've been having some issues lately. We're making an effort.'

Ted seemed to be on the verge of uncharacteristically opening up about his marriage, so I reached over to turn the radio down in case he was put off by Melvyn Bragg asking a historian about the 1833 Factory Act and its effect on Victorian industry.

'Marriage is a form of accountancy isn't it?' he said. 'You balance the good and bad, and everything works out. We're definitely in profit.'

I waited, expecting more detail, but apparently none was forthcoming.

'That's good, I'm glad,' I replied. 'And also, well done for leveraging in an accountancy metaphor.'

We turned back to our computers. Ted tapped away at his keyboard for a few seconds, but then looked up with a quizzical expression.

'Do you miss her?' he asked. 'Elizabeth, I mean.'

To be honest, the question caught me by surprise, coming out of nowhere like that. It was uncharacteristically direct of him. I had to think it through.

'I don't really miss *her*,' I said. 'But, you know, I miss . . . something. I miss *someone*. Does that make sense?'

Just then, Hannah burst in, a backpack slung over one shoulder and a gigantic pair of headphones around her neck.

'Hey losers,' she said. 'What's going on? Ooh, chocolate biscuits.'

She made a grab for the packet but Ted playfully swiped them away.

'Have you eaten lunch yet, young lady?' he said.

'I have, but *he* hasn't,' she said, pulling a sandwich box from her backpack and sliding it onto my desk. 'That's why I'm here. You forgot your packed lunch again. You're completely useless. I swear you'd starve to death if it wasn't for me.'

'I'll go and fetch us some tea,' said Ted

He went off to the little kitchen area next door and Hannah grabbed three biscuits then slumped into the worn armchair in the corner of the office. She often stopped by on her way into town, usually concocting some excuse for her visit, but secretly, I think, just wanting to be here for a while. She'd start reading comics or text-messaging her friends until she got bored, then she'd go. Today though, she sat there staring at me. I tried to ignore her, pretending to read some emails, but while the kettle boiled and Ted noisily gathered mugs and tea bags, she kept staring. And munching on biscuits. And staring.

'Hey, Dad,' she said finally. 'Are you okay?'

'Yes, fine. Just trying to get this flood business sorted.'

'No, I mean, are you *okay*?'

At last, I knew what was going on. I swivelled my executive chair to face her, my hands clasped together like a Bond villain.

'Did you hear what we were talking about just then?' I said.

'Just when?'

'Just before you burst in. You heard Ted ask about Elizabeth and I.'

'Elizabeth and *me*,' she corrected. 'But yeah, I heard it all.'

'Everything is fine,' I said. 'I was just humouring the old swine.'

She screwed up her face into an expression of disbelief and was clearly about to interrogate her sad dad further when Ted returned with three cups of tea. He then got straight on the phone to the insurance company. It was a long and interminable conversation, in which the subject of human error and liability, and the exact nature and extent of the damage seemed to keep coming up – but at least it halted Hannah's inquisition. She eventually left in a huff.

'Thank you for bringing my lunch,' I called after her.

'This conversation is not over,' she yelled back.

Ted spent the rest of the day silently labouring over the online claim documents. I had a recurring mental image of water cascading through the stage doors like that scene in *The Shining* with the blood coming out of the elevator. I was not thinking about Elizabeth. Not at all. And I knew that by the time I got home that night, Hannah would have forgotten about it too.

Hannah

So later that evening, Dad and I are at home, picking away at a Chinese takeaway in front of the television. He clearly thinks I've forgotten the whole thing about Elizabeth, but he is wrong. There's something playing on my mind. It's been there for a while, nagging away at me from the shadows, but what happened to me on Friday night, and then overhearing that conversation with Ted . . . I need answers.

My only memory of her is a single scene. A tearful goodbye. I'm holding Dad's hand and we are standing at the front door; there is a taxi outside. Someone is saying sorry a lot. That's all I've got. I wonder what he remembers. I wonder if he has moved on.

'We should do something tomorrow,' he says suddenly in a really loud, bright voice. 'Do you have any plans?'

'Hanging out with Jenna and Daisy, I guess. Dad, you're not answering my question.'

'I've got an idea: we will play I Dare You To Wear.'

'Oh my god, really?'

'Yes! It'll be fun!'

I Dare You To Wear was a favourite game of ours when I was

younger. The rules were simple: we had to go to charity shops and buy the most ridiculous outfits we could find for each other; then we'd have to go out to a restaurant wearing whatever had been selected. It was because of this game that Dad once took me to Bath's finest French restaurant wearing lime-green jogging bottoms and a very tight pink S Club 7 T-shirt, while I sported a boy's three-piece wedding suit and a Pokémon bobble hat (model's own).

'Dad no, I'm too old for that dumb game.'

'Come on, we need to exorcise the disappointment of the flood and mark the beginning of the summer holidays with a flourish. Also, if you don't play I Dare You To Wear with me I'm going to insist on discussing your A Level options with you every single morning for the next six weeks. In excruciating detail.'

Oh shit. He found the letter from school.

'Yes, I found the letter from your school,' he says.

The letter was from the head of year, telling students to spend the holiday thinking about our A Levels. It came with a questionnaire asking us to name the subjects we thought we'd take, and also – and this is the fun part – where we thought we'd be in five years' time. God, whatever. I thought about scrawling 'pushing up daisies'. As I may have mentioned, I get a bit dark sometimes.

'Mr Devon wrote that you are about to make one of the most important decisions of your educational career,' he says. 'What I want to know is, why was the letter screwed up in your waste-paper bin?'

I scowl at him. A 1.21 gigawatt scowl. A scowl that could launch a thousand ships – in the opposite direction.

'I'll play your damn game,' I say.

He smiles a triumphant smile. The thing is, it was a foregone conclusion anyway – we have a rule: you can't turn down the I Dare You To Wear game. If one of us proposes it, the other has to accept. It's all about being there for each other no matter what – even if 'being there' just means humiliating yourself in a public place. You have to do that sometimes, I guess.

But his joy is misplaced. I shall get my revenge for the cancelled play and for that A Level letter. He treats me like a precious little princess. But I am not Snow White any more. I am the goddamn Snow Queen.

Tom

Stupidly, I thought I'd been very clever in swerving the whole conversation away from Elizabeth. But I saw something in Hannah's eyes – a look of quiet, thoughtful determination – and, oh the dramatic irony, I'd never seen her look so much like her mother. It reminded me of a look I'd seen twenty years ago in a university library in Manchester.

Hannah was clearly devising some sort of scheme, like a chess master planning several moves ahead. I did not know whether I was to be a pawn or the opponent.

The next day, we were on the high street, trying on clothes in charity shops. I found her a pair of stonewashed dungarees and an extravagantly shiny salmon-pink blouse, which looked like something Penelope Keith might have rejected from *The Good Life* wardrobe department for being too kitsch. It was my usual gambit – daft and loud, but pretty harmless.

But for her, this was war. When we got to the Pet Rescue shop, she was rifling through some tops, when her face lit up. She looked around to check I hadn't seen, then pointed to a pair of tight silver jeans hanging on a rack nearby.

'Try those on,' she demanded.

By the time I waddled out of the changing room, she was holding up her coup de grâce: a white sweatshirt with the words BITCH, PLEASE written on the front in very large gold sparkly letters. I was about to protest, but she interrupted.

'I've already bought it,' she said.

We went to a café because Hannah said her feet were hurting and I spent the first ten minutes asking where we were going to eat that night, but she wouldn't tell me. While we were there two girls of Hannah's age approached the table. They were both in velour tracksuits in different pastel colours.

'Hey Hannah,' yelled one.

'Oh hey,' said Hannah without enthusiasm. 'Dad, this is Emilia and Georgia.'

'Hello there,' I said, immediately trying to assess the social dynamic. Were these friends? Rivals? Casual acquaintances? In moments like these, fathers of teenage girls must learn to read subtext, body language, tone and mood in order to most amusingly humiliate their children. Look, after *that* top, it was game on as far as I was concerned.

'Hey,' said Emilia, shrugging nervously. Georgia was on her phone, lost to the conversation. 'So are you going to Nath's party tonight? It's going to be well good.'

'Probably not,' Hannah sighed.

'But *Callum* will be there,' drawled Emilia. Hannah gave her a look that, although lasting barely a millisecond, very obviously communicated the words, '*What the fuck are you doing? My dad is sitting right there. Shut up, or I will murder you with my bare hands.*'

'Oh right,' said Emilia, backing away.

I wondered if I should interject in a sensitive and mature manner. I thought about asking, 'So, who's Callum?' while

46

nudging Hannah and winking lasciviously. But I didn't. I figured I could use this generosity as leverage.

There was a long awkward silence.

'Right. Anyway, see ya!' said Georgia.

And the girls shuffled away.

'They're from school,' said Hannah. 'They're not really my friends.'

'I understand,' I said. 'Now, where are we going tonight? Or do I need to run after them and tell them you can't attend Nath's party because you have a Girl Guide meeting?'

'Do your worst,' she replied.

She didn't break.

It was only half an hour before our dinner reservation that she finally relented. We were going to a place called Virago. A feminist café, named after the famous feminist book publisher. I looked at my new sweatshirt and thought to myself, I will have to keep my arms folded all night or I will be going home in an ambulance.

Wedged between a florist and an artisan apothecary, on a narrow cobbled lane leading off the high street, Virago was the place to be in our little town. Slate floors, exposed wooden beams, walls lined with bookshelves (filled with Virago books, naturally). It was a muggy hothouse, crammed with chattering couples and noisy groups eating steaming bowls of pasta and huge vegetarian pizzas. At the counter, people gathered on bar stools or stood in dense clusters, drinking and laughing, most of them from the town's faintly alternative community of affluent thirty- and forty-somethings. The women were in boho dresses and flared jeans, the men mostly opting for vintage waistcoats, pointy boots and flat caps, like extras from a Sunday evening costume drama about a slightly camp mafia family. A few I recognised as theatre regulars – but only from the nights we put on proper plays or folk music gigs, rather than mouthy comics or Bananarama tribute acts. Just as we walked in, we spotted Natasha and her husband Seb getting up to leave, and as we all saw each other they gestured to their small table.

'It looks like your legs are wrapped in tinfoil,' said Natasha. 'And why do you have your arms folded like that? What are you trying to hide?'

I moved my arms down fractionally.

'Holy shit. Did Trinny and Susannah get really high and give you a makeover?'

'No, Hannah did.'

'You two,' she said, shaking her head at us.

'Can you stay for a drink?' I asked. 'Or are we too cool for you?'

'I'd love to, darling,' said Natasha, wrapping an expensive-looking shawl around her shoulders. 'But Seb's mother called. The baby is awake and so is Ashley. Absolute chaos. Being a mum is just like doing PR: you're never off duty and you have to be nice to everybody.'

When they left, we squeezed into our seats and gasped for breath, wedged like sardines between other diners. Hannah handed me one of the menus, which were pieces of brown paper on which the dishes were listed in a typewriter font. It was all clever modern takes on Italian and American classics, with local produce and no meat. I wasn't reading it though, I was propping it up against my chest to form a defensive barrier so that no one could read my sweatshirt. I was still very worried about being lynched by furious beatniks and metrosexuals. I surveyed the room, checking for any looks of horror or disgust, but then somehow my gaze fell on a woman in an Iron Maiden T-shirt leaning against the rear wall. She was looking bored but also disarmingly beautiful, and seemed to be with an older man and a younger woman, but they were deep in conversation, closing in toward each other. Suddenly she caught my eye, smiled, then gestured at her friends, rolling her eyes conspiratorially. I looked away at once, hoping Hannah hadn't noticed me eyeing someone up.

'Who's *that*?' my daughter said. 'She's hot.'

Hannah had noticed me eyeing someone up.

'I don't know. What do you want to eat?'

'No way, we're not changing the subject – you two had a definite moment there.'

'What? No we didn't! I don't know her. I don't want to know her. I just want to eat and not let anyone see this shirt.'

I pretended to furiously study the menu, but at the periphery of my vision I could see Hannah bending round to get another look at our new acquaintance.

'Go and talk to her!'

'Hannah, no.'

'Go on, she's the only woman here not dressed like a Jimi Hendrix groupie.'

I decided to pretend this wasn't happening. The room had begun to feel very hot. It must have been all the candles, I thought to myself. I perused the menu with what I hoped was a look of clinical concentration – I figured if I did this for long enough, Hannah would get bored.

'Hmm, I might go for the macaroni cheese,' I said, finally. 'Or maybe the nutburger. What even *is* a nutburger? Have you—'

'Actually, sorry Dad, could you get me a glass of water, really quickly?' said Hannah.

I looked up and she was fanning herself with the menu, breathing fast, her other hand to her chest.

'Please,' she said.

'Yes, yes, right away,' I said, leaping to my feet. I slalomed as quickly as I could towards the bar, forcing my way through the clutter of chairs and bags, excusing myself between conversations. Memories of that night at the theatre came jolting back.

Finally, I clambered past the last table and reached a comparatively quiet part of the bar just behind a woman who was arriving slightly before me. A woman from the rear of the room. A woman in an Iron Maiden T-shirt. Ah, of course. I had been set up. I looked back towards our table, and saw Hannah getting up and waving at another girl who was heading out to the patio garden at the side of the café. As she ran after her friend, she shrugged apologetically and gave me a double thumbs-up sign. I turned back to the bar and resolved to order some food and then quickly sit back down. I did not have to talk to anybody. I didn't even have to . . .

'That's quite a top,' said Iron Maiden lady, who was now nestled in beside me at the bar. 'A brave choice for this place.'

I looked down and immediately crossed my arms over BITCH, PLEASE.

'Ah yeah,' I said. 'It was sort of a bet.'

She smiled and looked away to her friends.

'This was supposed to be a work night out,' she said. 'But, half the office didn't turn up and the rest left early – now it's just me and Romeo and Juliet over there.'

'Right . . .'

I tried gesturing at the bar staff, but they were all taking food orders and pouring drinks for the tsunami of thirsty punters at the other end of the counter. My mouth was suddenly dry. I could feel pinpricks of sweat on my forehead. She swayed slightly into me.

'Oops, sorry,' she said. 'We've been drinking since 5 p.m. What time is it now?'

'Eight-thirty.'

'Oh crap. I'm Kirsten, how are you? No, *who* are you?'

'I'm Tom.'

'Nice to meet you, Tom, I . . . Whoa, hang on, are you wearing silver trousers? Wow, you *really* lost that bet. Maybe it's time to think about not gambling any more?'

'I think you're right.'

I was now trying to use The Force to will a member of staff over so I could get our drinks and food and run away. I'd have to guess at what Hannah wanted because she'd fled the scene of the crime. Probably pizza. Kirsten didn't seem to be in a hurry. She lazily pulled her hair into a bunch and tied it back with a scrunchy. Her skin was honey-brown. She smelled faintly of White Musk. I could feel her shoulder against mine.

'What do you do, Tom?' she said.

'I um, I'm a theatre manager. I run the Willow Tree Theatre, up the road.'

'I know it! I've been! I saw a comedian there last year, Kevin something?'

'Was he good?'

'God no, he was fucking awful. Sorry. It's such a cool theatre though. It looks like a sort of Stalinist prison. Must be an interesting place to work!'

'It is, I—'

Suddenly, there was a member of staff in front of me, and without waiting for her to ask what I wanted, I gabbled out my order in a long, almost incomprehensible string of words. Somehow she understood. Finally, I'd be able to slink off alone. I could taste freedom.

Just then, Kirsten's workmates sidled over, clutching each other around the waist.

'We've found a table over there,' the guy shouted. Then he pointed – to the table next to ours. Of course. Of course it was the one next to ours. She turned to the bar to order a drink and I bravely thought I'd take this opportunity to back away. But as I took a step, without turning from the bar, Kirsten put out her hand and gently held my arm.

'Hang on, I'm coming.'

And so we walked back to the tables together, her slinking effortlessly through the madding crowds, me bumping into everybody, feeling hot and harassed. I couldn't process what I was feeling. I mean, she was obviously beautiful and confident and bored and ... confident. But I was out of practice and out of shape. Whatever was going on, I didn't feel I could offer anything. I felt like I'd been tricked into auditioning for a play that I hadn't read in ten years and couldn't remember the lines or the character, or even what acting actually was. Then we sat down at our tables and she was close to me, and there was that static of expectation between us, I understood that much.

'So, do you have any good shows coming up? It must be exciting. I'm a graphic designer; our office is in the old chapel building in town. Do you know it? I'm designing the packaging for a range of organic fruit teas. They sent us like a whole crate of them to try. Oh my god, it's like drinking very weak Ribena but with bits of twig floating in it. Who buys that shit on purpose?'

I was nodding, pretending to listen and then heard the last part and shook my head vigorously.

'That sounds awful. I . . .'

Just then I spotted Hannah peeking in from the patio area, no doubt checking on her matchmaking handiwork. I made a desperate 'get over here' gesture. She paused, but I think something manic in my eyes communicated that I wasn't joking and that I wanted backup. She sauntered over.

'Ah, Hannah,' I said. 'Sorry Kirsten, this is Hannah, my *daughter*.'

I thought this parental revelation would throw Kirsten off – maybe she'd assume I was too old or, you know, married. If only I still wore my wedding ring. But if anything she looked delighted at the arrival of yet more company.

'Hey,' she yelled, as Hannah sat down. 'Your dad runs a theatre!'

'I know!' said Hannah, in an extremely enthusiastic voice. Then they high-fived. I was out of my depth here.

Our food arrived and while I quietly nursed the molten macaroni cheese, Hannah and Kirsten shared the pizza, chatting happily and occasionally looking over or pointing in my direction, then giggling mischievously. I concentrated on praying for Sally to miraculously arrive and rescue me. It was at least nice to see Hannah unguardedly joking around – even if it was all clearly at my expense.

But then this happened.

'So, what are you going to do when you leave school?' said Kirsten.

If you didn't know Hannah you wouldn't have seen it, but a darkness passed momentarily behind her smile.

'I haven't really thought about it,' she shrugged.

'Oh come on, you must have! When I was your age I wanted to be Madonna or a pilot. What about university? Dad, tell her she has to go to university!'

I said nothing, but shared a glance with Hannah.

'Let me guess what subject you'll study. Art? You look like an artist.'

'I don't know,' said Hannah, quieter now, almost drowned out in the din.

'Huh?' said Kirsten, taking another slice of pizza. 'Oh, not design?!'

'No, I . . .'

'If you become a designer, don't work for a tiny local agency, that's my advice. Go and live in London. Or fucking New York. Oh wow, you have the whole world at your feet. That's so exciting, huh?'

The crowds seemed to be leaning in on us now, a circle of bodies compacting all around, sapping the oxygen. The air was hot and thin, the noise piercing.

'I'm not sure. I find it really difficult to think about the future. Let's change the subject,' Hannah said.

I knew the look on her face; I'd seen it before so many times. The resolution and the fear, swirling against each other, like eddies in the tide. She looked at me and I knew she'd had enough. I knew I was overprotective, I knew Hannah found it ridiculous and frustrating sometimes the way I tried to stage-manage her life, the way I tried to control the cast of characters around her, but *this* was why. People blunder in and they don't know. They don't know how things are.

'Come on,' I said. 'Let's get some air. I'm sorry Kirsten, it was nice meeting you.'

I stood and held out a hand for Hannah, and she grasped at it, hauling herself up.

'I'm sorry,' she said, but I didn't know who to.

'Did I say something stupid?' said Kirsten.

'No, she's just tired.'

'She does look pale. It was nice to meet you too. Can I give you my card?'

She reached into her back pocket, but we'd turned away. I put my arm on Hannah's shoulder to guide her, and she was shaking. We paced toward the door; I was nudging people out of the way, softly at first, but with growing force. When we reached the exit and clattered through it, we were like deep-sea divers surfacing for the first time in hours, gasping at the fresh cool air.

Hannah leaned against the wall, looking up and away from me, rubbing her eyes with the back of her hand and with the sleeves of her trashy blouse. We walked home silently. We both knew there was so much to say, but it was a conversation we'd always avoided; it lurked at the edges of every day. The hospital had always been positive about her prognosis, but they taught us not to take anything for granted. Each time she had a relapse, the unspoken question surfaced: how much time? Really, how much? Her sixteenth birthday was less than two months away. That landmark, that rite of passage. It suddenly felt cruelly distant – one might almost say out of reach.

'Sorry for trying to set you up,' said Hannah, between shivers. 'That was cruel. I kind of knew if you wore that top you'd get attention. It was an evil experiment.'

'To find out what?'

We walked past the theatre, the headlights of passing cars illuminating the concrete edifice so that it resembled a weird Expressionist castle.

'Have you moved on?' she said. 'From Mum?'

'Wow,' I said. 'What made you think about that?'

'I'm always thinking about that,' she said. 'You're so useless. *Someone* has to keep an eye on you.'

I peeled off the sweatshirt and put it around her shoulders so that the BITCH, PLEASE logo was clearly visible on her back.

'Here,' I said. 'You deserve this.'

She laughed and put her arm through mine. I took my daughter home.

Hannah

We're all in my bedroom – my friends Jenna, Daisy and I. Jenna is sitting cross-legged on my office chair, Daisy is sprawled across the end of the bed in a floaty summer dress looking ethereal and distant, like someone out of a perfume advert. We're supposed to be talking about *Jane Eyre*. Instead, I've spent the last half an hour telling them about last night at the Virago café, and how I tried to set my Dad up with a drunk woman. This has caused some hilarity. They are pummelling me for information.

'How did you know she'd be interested?' yells Jenna. 'How did you know she wasn't there with her boyfriend?'

'Hannah has a talent for spotting hopeless lonely souls,' says Daisy. 'She's like that kid in *Sixth Sense*.'

'I see single people,' I reply. 'Walking around like regular people.'

'Is Callum single?' says Daisy. 'You were checking him constantly for, like, the last two weeks of term.'

'I totally wasn't. Get your eyes tested.'

'Methinks the lady doth protest too much.'

I've known Daisy since I started primary school – she has really bad asthma so we bonded over our ultra-intrusive medication.

She is beautiful and blonde and tall, but also friendly and funny, which is completely unfair. Everybody adores and hates her. She loves the Sugababes, American teen dramas and her new camera phone. Daisy is currently between boyfriends, but astonishingly she is not short of offers. Once in a while, she sighs and asks me to manage the production line of creepy flirtatious text messages she gets from the losers in our class. There was this time when a trainee English teacher messaged her and offered to take her to see A *Christmas Carol*. That was literally after having her for one lesson. I mean, he was only twenty-five but still, what a scumbag.

Jenna is a total emo and computer nerd. She wears black jeans, black T-shirts and a giant black hoodie, even when it's 250 degrees outside. She is half-Indian, half-Irish, which she says is a cultural nightmare that involves a lot of parental disapproval. She's in a different form to us, so we only got to know her when we started the drama GCSE last year; we were put in the same group for improvisation class and instantly bonded while pretending to be zoo animals.

Jenna's the best actor in the class by far – I think it's because she spends a lot of time lying to her mum and dad. They won't let her join the drama group, even though she'd love to, because they say it will get in the way of her studies. She seems to be constantly grounded, so practically lives in chat rooms and forums. She was the first person I know to get broadband because she was costing her parents a fortune in dial-up fees and they figured if she was on the internet she wasn't out getting drunk or pregnant. Instead, she's had an array of virtual boyfriends who she hooks up with in the multiplayer video game 'Final Fantasy XI'. We don't really understand what's going on but we try to be supportive when she tells us Olaf The Megalord left her for a wood elf or whatever. But then who am I to judge? I've never had a boyfriend. I'm too lethargic to deal with boys.

Anyways, we've decided to have regular book group meetings

to discuss the English and Drama set texts, because this is the only part of our GCSE preparation that we can face during the summer holidays. When we do finally get around to the text, it is Jenna's turn to speak.

'What I don't understand is, Jane spends the whole book fighting the patriarchy, and then what does she do? She basically marries the patriarchy.'

'Is Rochester the patriarchy?' says Daisy.

'Well, let's see: he is rich and powerful, he owns a mansion, he has servants, he neglects his daughter and he keeps his wife locked up in the attic. So yes, Jenna – yes he is.'

'But Jane only really loves him when he's weak, and she has to step up and save him,' I suggest. 'So she beats the patriarchy and then claims him for her own.'

'Valid point,' concedes Jenna. 'I do love Jane but she's just constantly *thinking*, she must be exhausted.'

'Also all her friends and schoolmates die of tuberculosis,' adds Daisy. 'That's got to be depressing. People were so fragile.'

'I can identify with that part,' I say.

'Oh crap, yeah, I'm sorry.'

'Whatever, it's fine.'

We go back to reading for a second until Jenna starts laughing into her open book.

'Sorry, sorry, I'm just thinking of you collapsing on stage.'

'Oh, thanks!'

'No, I mean it was awful obviously, but . . .'

'God, what a fail. I'm so embarrassed.'

'Don't be! You were ace anyway.'

'How do you feel now?' says Daisy.

'I don't know. I'm fine. I mean, I'm getting tired a lot but whatever, that's nothing new. Don't tell my dad.'

'I'm exhausted all the time,' says Jenna. 'I don't know what it is.'

'I do,' says Daisy. 'You're watching eight episodes of *Buffy* every night, until, like, three in the morning.'

'I'm in love with Spike. Why can't *my* boyfriends be immoral vampire hunks?'

'Don't you mean *immortal*?' I say.

'I know exactly what I mean,' replies Jenna.

'Whatever,' sighs Daisy, picking off her nail varnish. 'You never actually meet them.'

'We should watch a *Jane Eyre* movie,' I say, trying to bring us back on track. 'Then we won't have to read it again. Is it on DVD?'

'I already watched the black-and-white one with whatshisname . . . Orson Welles. It was so shit.'

'That's a classic, you skank.'

'You're a skank. Let's get the Kate Winslet one.'

'Oh my god, Jenna, she wasn't in *Jane Eyre*, she was in *Sense and Sensibility*.'

'Is that on our reading list?'

'No! Jesus, I want out of this reading group!'

'When I leave school I'm done with books,' proclaims Jenna. 'Nobody will be reading these things in ten years, it's bullshit. In ten years' time, I'll be living in a virtual world.'

'So what's new?' says Daisy. 'In ten years' time *I'll* be touring southern Italy in a camper van with Matthew McConaughey. What about you Hannah?' They both look at me. I lean back and chuck my book across the room. It lands with a loud thud.

'What's wrong?' says Daisy.

'Nothing!' I say way too loudly. 'I'm just bored of reading this crap. What can *Jane Eyre* really teach us about anything? And why the hell did Dad put this fucking questionnaire back on my noticeboard?'

I get up, rip the letter off the board and throw it in the bin.

'What are you doing?' says Daisy. 'You've got to hand that in next term!'

'Hannah are you freaking out?' says Jenna.

'No! It doesn't matter, forget it, I'm fine.'

'No, you're not. We're your friends, and we want to know what's going on.'

'Is it about Callum?' giggles Daisy. 'Do you want me to ask him out for you?'

'Oh god, no! It's nothing. I'll get us some drinks. What does everyone want?'

'None of your fucking fruit teas,' says Jenna. 'They taste like weak Ribena mixed with grit. I'll have water. I am trying to stay pure by only drinking clear liquids.'

'Does your dad have any vodka?' asks Daisy.

When I go out of the room, I stop on the landing and hear them talking quietly. Jenna says 'She looks pale' in her ridiculously loud whisper. Daisy agrees. I go downstairs because I don't want to hear any more. Catching your friends bitching about you behind your back is upsetting, but catching them *worrying* about you behind your back is fucking terrifying.

Later, when they're gone, I'm lying on my bed, listening to the summer sounds outside: sparrows tweeting in the gutter above my open window; next door's dog barking; some children in a back garden somewhere, messing about in a paddling pool. All of life just carrying on, but it is so quiet, so distant, I can imagine floating away from it all. I don't know if I've been asleep or just dozing, but suddenly, it's late afternoon and the blue sky is gone, replaced with a dull wash of brooding greys. The clouds look like jagged cliffs. I stand up and my head spins. The colours drain out of the room.

'Oh shit,' I say. I look for my phone but I've left it downstairs. I clatter out onto the landing and make a lunge for the bannister, but somehow I miss. Oh wow, I think, I'm flying. But I'm not. I'm falling. The stairs rush up at me so fast it makes me feel sick.

Bam.

I'm gone. I'm nothing.

A voice says: 'Daddy. Help.'

Tom

I left the theatre in the early evening, the sunlight turning to a rich golden brown as I drove home along the tree-lined roads. A few hundred yards on, there was a small row of local shops that had inexplicably become an official teen hangout. I glanced over in case Hannah was there, but instead I saw her friends Jenna and Daisy sitting on the wall beside the newsagent, deep in an animated discussion. I pressed the horn lightly and the noise startled them both, Jenna screaming dramatically, before seeing me and waving. I pulled over and hit the button to wind down the passenger window.

'Sorry!' I shouted as they bundled over.

'You scared the shit out of me, Mr Rose!' yelled Jenna. 'I mean, you scared the *life* out of me. Sorry.'

'It's fine, Jenna. Is Hannah at home?'

'Yeah,' said Daisy. 'We were studying *Jane Eyre*.'

'Oh, of course you were,' I said. 'How is she?'

'All right, I guess,' said Jenna.

'Well, she seemed a bit washed out,' said Daisy. 'She told us not to say anything, but we're a bit worried about her.'

'I think she's still getting over Friday night,' I said. 'I'm sure she's fine.'

I parked up on the drive and walked into the porch. There were a couple of unopened letters on the mat – a bank statement and something in a brown envelope from the local council, which looked boring. I picked them up and unlocked the front door. I was about to shout hello, but as the door opened, I looked inside and all the breath was sucked out of me.

Hannah was curled up at the base of the staircase, as though she'd somehow fallen awkwardly asleep on her way down. But it was not sleep. Her face was utterly white, her breathing laboured and wheezy, and from her head, a steady trickle of blood was pooling onto the stair below.

'Oh god, Hannah,' I groaned. I dropped to my knees beside her, but didn't know whether to move or even touch her. I could see a gash on the left side of her head, a patch of hair clearly drenched in blood, the wound seeping horribly. She was lifelessly still, dead still. Panic exploded through my body like fuel through an engine. I ran back into the living room and ripped the phone from its holder, punching in 999.

Eight minutes later, an ambulance was outside. One paramedic, a well-built guy, even bigger than Shaun, was past me in an instant and on the stairs, fingers on Hannah's wrist, then her neck, hand on her head, his face low and close to her. He asked for her name and I told him. 'Hannah,' he said, quite loudly. 'Hannah, can you hear me?' Another paramedic appeared, a woman, carrying a stretcher. I backed into the doorway to the living room, feeling useless and desperate. The man had some sort of gauze on Hannah's head, the blood already spotting through.

'Let's get her moved,' he said. Then he turned to me. 'Are you coming?'

'Yes. Yes, I . . . Yes.' I looked around the living room, for what I don't know. I walked out of the house without shutting the front door, mindlessly following.

I found out later that our neighbour had shut the door for us. There was a whole crowd watching the ambulance leave. I didn't notice them.

For Hannah's sixth birthday, I asked her if she wanted to have a little party at the theatre. It made sense because there was plenty of space and the kids could make as much noise as they wanted – which was always a lot. She nodded, but her heart wasn't in it. In the months after her diagnosis, we'd managed to normalise the whole thing. The myriad pills were just another daily routine. But as the one-year mark approached, the reality of it began to creep back in for her. She still didn't quite get what was going on, but she knew it was serious. Desperate, I remembered the year before, how delighted she'd been to see the fairies, and I started to think, if we have a theatre, we should make a play.

I'd always written scripts; through my teenage years I'd devoured every theatre and screenplay writing guide in the local library, and then I took all the practical courses available during my drama degree. Most of my classmates were film nuts who all wanted to be the next Fellini, Paul Schrader or William Goldman, but I was obsessed with Harold Pinter, Jim Cartwright and Caryl Churchill – the way they used the intimate, confrontational nature of the theatre to express their political and emotional fury. When I left university and co-founded the most ineffectual touring theatre company in the history of British drama, it was with the intention of penning and performing original works. This was the mid-eighties, when theatre still really mattered. But it never happened for me. Which is probably just as well.

So Hannah was almost six when we got on the bus to her first annual heart check-up. We took our seat on the bus and she was quiet and anxious, her head resting against the filthy window as we trundled out on the busy road towards Bath. I thought, What can I do? What can I do to make things bearable?

'Do you want a play for your birthday?' I said. 'If we're having a party at the theatre, we ought to have a play.'

For the first time on the journey, she turned her face to me.

'Oh yes!' she said. 'Can we do a fairy tale?!'

The faintest spark of enthusiasm.

'Of course,' I said, desperate to nurture it. 'What else would we do?'

The consultant told us that everything seemed steady, but the medication and annual checks would need to continue. It was hard for her to take in. When we got back, I asked the drama group for help. Most of them said yes, they'd be happy to give up several hours of their precious time to learn, rehearse and perform a ten-minute play that we hadn't actually written yet. That's how it all came about. That's how we hoped we'd bring Hannah back into the world.

Dearest Willow,

I wanted to tell you more about the birthday plays Dad used to create for me at the theatre. You know how superheroes all have origin stories? Well, even though I am not a superhero, this is mine.

The first we put on was The Little Mermaid, *which was for my sixth birthday. I'd seen Disney's movie version of the story, but I remember really hating how they made the Hans Christian Andersen tale all safe and sweet and wishy-washy. I preferred the darker, sadder one in my old storybook. It goes like this: a young mermaid gives her voice to the sea witch in order to become human and marry a handsome prince – but the prince falls for another woman, and according to the witch's spell, the mermaid must die on the morning of their wedding. At the last minute, her sisters win a reprieve from the witch; if she stabs the prince in the chest before he's married, she will transform back into a mermaid and be saved. She had a terrible choice: sacrifice his life, or her own. Even as a six-year-old, this cruel tragedy seemed truer to me than singing lobsters and happy endings.*

Dad wrote out a rough plan for the play, and Sally worked with the actors. They improvised a lot of it. That was part of the magic. On the day of my birthday, Dad took me and my friends to the theatre and the cast all brought their families; Ted and Angela made tea and cakes for everyone – it felt like a little community celebration. I guess it was a strange thing to do, but it felt normal to us. No, not normal, it was wonderful.

I remember only little fragments of the play. I remember there were blue sheets hanging along the back of the stage, and all the lights were fitted with blue and green filters to create this dreamy undersea feel. Kamil built the hull of a wooden ship for the prince to sail on; two of the drama group held a length of organza across the front of the stage, fluttering it to look like waves.

Most importantly, I remember dragging Margaret into the group. She used to come to the theatre every day and just sit in the foyer café drinking tea, but one day Dad asked if she could watch me while he helped unload some deliveries; she chatted to me like another adult. That's how I got to know and like her. I begged her to join the drama group so I'd have her company during rehearsals and she relented, but she stressed that she just wanted to sit in the auditorium and watch. No one minded. I'd crawl up next to her with my books and hope that she'd read them with me, and she did. She read them beautifully, putting on the voices of the characters, filling the pages with life and humour. My dad heard her and encouraged her to audition for a role, but she wouldn't. 'I just want to watch,' she'd say. 'I just want to be here.'

But when we began planning the play, I said to Dad, 'Please tell Margaret to be the sea witch.' He laughed, and said he couldn't possibly – that it perhaps wasn't a flattering thing to put to an older lady. So I asked her myself. 'You would be good because the sea witch is funny and naughty.' She agreed. 'That does sound like me,' she said. When Dad found out he was cross that I'd asked her, but Margaret waved him away.

'It is simply not possible to insult me,' she said. 'If my girl needs a witch, she must have a witch.'

Dad asked if she had acting experience, and she said, 'A little, *but that was a long time ago. I'm not sure if I am still up to learning lines. My memory likes to play tricks on me.'*

Dad told her not to worry, that it was only a short play for friends and family. He said there wouldn't be many lines and that the plan was to make it up as we went along. I remember he said to her, 'If anything goes wrong, we'll all muck in. We always do.'

Margaret wasn't sure if it was okay for a member of the audience to become an actor. I recall Dad's reply very clearly indeed. 'Well, you see, that's the magic of the theatre,' he said. 'Everyone in the room is a performer.'

Margaret told us one of her stories, about how she had attended the London premiere of Hair in 1968. 'At the end we all got onto the stage with the actors. I danced with Zsa Zsa Gabor.' I don't think Dad believed her but he laughed anyway. He said to her, 'Dora is making an amazing sea witch costume for our play. I think it will suit you.' Finally, Margaret said she would give acting a try again.

Willow, she was amazing.

Dora had constructed a kind of monstrous ball gown for the sea witch; it had this voluminous black skirt leading to eight long tentacles made out of foam-filled polyester. Margaret stalked the stage, rasping her lines, terrifying and delighting everyone, including the cast, and especially Rachel as the Little Mermaid. At the end Margaret went over to my dad and she thanked him. 'I never thought I would perform again,' she said. 'This has been a quite wonderful surprise.'

Her return to the theatre would have been the most memorable part of the evening if it hadn't been for what happened later, at the very end of the production. It was something I'd managed to forget about for a long time, something I don't think anyone saw coming.

At the climax of the play, the Little Mermaid has a choice: kill the prince, or allow the marriage to go ahead and perish herself. Well, *we know what is supposed to happen, don't we? The mermaid cannot bring herself to hurt her precious prince; instead she dives into the sea and melts away, her heart broken.*

This was the way our production was supposed to end. But it didn't. Caught in the emotion of the moment, a voice from the audience shouted to the Little Mermaid, 'No, don't die!'

It was my voice, Willow. And before I knew it, I was running onto the stage . . .

Do you want to know what happened next? I'm going to be cruel and leave you with a cliffhanger. You will just have to keep reading my letters to find out.

Hannah

I'm in hospital in Bath. I don't remember how I got here or what happened, but I know that it involved a staircase and now I have six stitches in my head. Dad found me in the hallway covered in blood, like the victim in a slasher movie. I probably resemble Frankenstein's Monster, but I've not looked in a mirror yet.

That all happened yesterday. This morning, after a shitty night's sleep, I was wheeled up to cardiology to get a series of tests, because apparently it's 'not good' to black out twice in a couple of days. When you have issues with your heart, there are two machines you get to know really well: the, echocardiogram and the electrocardiogram. The first is like the ultrasound test they give to pregnant women – except they're not looking for a baby, they're looking for leaky valves in your heart, which is a lot less cute and exciting, and they don't give you a photo to take home. With the electrocardiogram, you lie shivering in a blank white room as a nurse sticks cold sensor pads all over your chest so they can analyse your heart rhythm. You have to wear the hospital gown the wrong way round, which makes you feel exposed and embarrassed. You just get used to that.

Now I am in a bed on the cardiology ward, attached to a Holter monitor, which looks like a Game Boy, but measures heart rhythm instead of playing 'Tetris'. You carry the bloody thing around with you for twenty-four hours so, actually, 'Tetris' would be a cool feature.

I feel numb. It might be the local anaesthetic from the stitches, but I don't think so. I think it's deeper than that. At fifteen, I should be hanging out in town with my friends, or slobbing in front of the TV, or obsessively changing my profile name on MSN. I should not be on a ward, hooked up to a heart monitor. Yet, here I am, watching the clock ticking down until my dad gets back.

I have a cardiomyopathy. I did not learn how to spell it until I was nine. To be even more specific, I have dilated cardiomyopathy. It is a disease that affects the walls of the heart, and it means that the beat is irregular and blood isn't pumped very efficiently. Sometimes people don't know they have it; they may never know. Sometimes people die suddenly. I am somewhere between those two extreme possibilities – though unfortunately I am leaning towards the wrong end. The death end. If my medication works and I have regular check-ups, there's a chance I'll be fine. But there's also a chance something will suddenly go wrong, and boom, cardiac arrest. When you're young, your worst-case scenario should be that the cool girls won't be your friends or your parents won't let you go to that boy band gig on your birthday. My worst-case scenario is that I'll collapse in the middle of PE and never wake up.

Sorry. Hospital always totally bums me out.

Dad went home last night, but turns up again as soon as visiting hours start at 11 a.m., waving from outside the doors at the end of the ward. He has the usual big grin on his face, but he looks creased and tired and his hair is all wonky, like Nikki Six coming out of rehab. When they let him in, he races over and stretches his arms towards me. I grasp at them, trying not to cry from the

71

relief of seeing him. Then he accidentally nudges my head and I draw back in pain.

'Oops, baby, I'm so sorry! How are you?'

I decide not to go full existential angst on him. Instead, I compose myself into alienated teenager mode.

'I'm fine. Bored out of my mind, but fine. They're just waiting for the test results. What have you been doing?'

'Sitting downstairs in the café. I got here at seven, but you were asleep and then having those tests. I read the whole of the *Guardian* from cover to cover. I feel very well informed.'

'You've been downstairs all morning?'

'Yes, of course. You're here. Where else would I go?'

'Dad, you're such a loser.'

Just then, I see Dr Peter Vernon approaching. He's my cardiologist (I like saying this because it sounds like I personally employ him). He works with a lot of much younger children whom he encourages to call him Doctor Pete. I don't do that because it sounds creepy coming from me. Instead, I call him Dr Pete Venkman, or just Venkman, after Bill Murray's character in *Ghostbusters*, and he seems fine with that – I guess he has to be because he is usually giving me incredibly potent drugs or explaining how broken my heart is. It would be churlish of him to object, under the circumstances. Anyway, he's in his forties with blond hair and tanned skin the colour of toffee. He looks like a surfer dude who has somehow stumbled out of the ocean and straight into a medical career. All the girls in the cardiology ward swoon as he passes – although of course they're all lightheaded anyway due to arrhythmia, but whatever.

When he comes over, he pulls up a chair, drops into it softly, and looks at me with his soulful eyes.

'Hey, Hannah,' he says.

'Hey, Venkman,' I reply. 'What's up?'

He is drumming his pen on his clipboard, looking at his notes, then back at me, then at his notes again. Drumming, drumming. This is his stalling tactic. I feel myself involuntarily swallow – a big cartoon gulp of a swallow, an 'oh shit, here we go' swallow.

'So . . . guys,' he says finally. 'I've got some . . . not perfect news.'

'Not perfect?' I reply, and I actually giggle. 'Is this like the time the Apollo 13 had a "not perfect" space flight?'

I feel Dad's hand on the bed, nudging at mine. He takes my little finger in his grip. Time creeps and spreads like thick paint.

'Let me guess,' I say, unable to stop babbling. 'I've failed my SAS medical exam?'

Venkman doesn't even bother faking a smile.

'I've had a look through the Echo and ECG results,' he continues. 'Hannah, we're seeing increased dilation of the heart walls and some quite serious ventricular tachycardia.'

'Right. Can you hit me with that in English?'

'Your heartbeat is particularly fast and irregular – that's why you're having these blackouts. And—'

'So what does all that mean?' says Dad, before Venkman can even get the words out. 'What do we do?'

Venkman pauses and puts on this incredibly earnest expression. You know in gangster films when someone is about to betray an old friend, and they give them a look of profound sorrow – right before shooting them in the face? Yeah, that expression.

'Well, for now we change the meds, see if that helps steady things. I'll be honest, it's a little troubling, but we'll keep a close eye on things.'

Dad tightens his grip. I get a sudden mental slideshow of all these moments through my life so far; these difficult little chats, often in small, stuffy rooms, set aside from bustling wards. The memories are so vivid, I can picture every consultant I've seen, their expressions, the posters on the wall around us, the worn fabric on uncomfortable chairs. When someone is telling you how sick you are, your brain starts recording in DVD high-resolution detail: you remember what you were wearing; you remember the icy cold of the air conditioner; you remember what you were doing with your hands.

'Look, there is no point in speculating right now,' continues Venkman. 'We need to get the meds sorted, do more tests, then see how things go.'

I have a million questions, but I just can't ask them in front of Dad. He mustn't know all the facts about how serious this is. Venkman understands. He'll swing by later and talk to me alone. This is how we operate. When you're this sick, you learn really fast that you have to protect your parents. So for now I let Venkman drift away, up the ward and then through the doors. The clipboard, with all its charts and notes and grim conclusions, is gripped in his hand.

'Well, this is bullshit,' I say.

I look at Dad and he is silent for a while, his eyes flicking between me and the machinery surrounding my bed. His face is blank, his thoughts are, for a moment, utterly inaccessible. When I was a kid, he'd make dumb promises about how we were going to beat this thing, or how everything was going to be fine. It was easier back then; he had a million brilliant ways to make me feel better. We'd go home and make a castle out of bed sheets, then sit eating sweets and reading stories; we'd play I Dare You To Wear; we'd watch a musical; we'd sit in the café pretending to be spies or exiled royals or superheroes; we'd put on birthday plays. Right now, he can't think of anything reassuring to say or do – and that's the saddest thing to happen all week.

Instead, he gets off the chair, sits on the bed and wordlessly wraps his arms around me. I grip on to him, the rough texture of his jacket against my nose. Here we are, the two of us. Another hospital bed, another minor drama. As I burrow into his shoulder, I can hear my heart thudding and I am so fucking furious with it.

I pull away.

'Can you, um, can you go home and get some stuff for me?' I say. 'Some comics to read? Lots of comics. It's so boring here.'

'I don't know. I don't want to leave you by yourself.'

'Dad, you may not have noticed but I am surrounded by medical staff.'

'I think it's best that I stay here anyway.'

'Look, I need some entertainment or I'll go crazy. And you should get some lunch.'

'I'm fine.'

'Dad! Go home or I'll ring the alarm and get you thrown out.'

He doesn't move, so I sit up and thrust my finger toward the alarm button on the wall. 'I'm warning you,' I say. 'Don't make me press this button. The nurses get *really* pissed off if you press it and you're not dying.'

'You win, I'll go! But I think the drama club want to come and see you later. Can you cope with that rabble?'

'Sure, but I can't speak for anyone else in here.'

'At least they won't have to contend with Margaret.'

Margaret has a phobia about hospitals. It's something to do with her husband – apparently he spent the last few days of his life in some vast nightmarish ward somewhere, fading away unnoticed. She once made Dad promise that if she ever became seriously ill he would not let her cork it in a hospital – which, let's face it, was a weird request for him to have to deal with due to the fact that his own daughter is continually on the verge of corking it in a hospital. Typical Margaret. Tactless as ever. God, I want to see her.

'Did she *tell* you she's not coming?' I ask pathetically.

'No, but you know what she's like. You remember The Promise? Anyway, everyone else will be here. They'll cause enough mayhem without her.'

'Shit, I'm going to get thrown out.'

'I'll tell them to rein it in.'

'No, don't.'

A nurse passes and smiles at us. Dad watches her for a second, thinking.

'You know, they're all happy to put something on for your birthday,' he says. 'Just like the old days. Richard has volunteered to do the lights, Dora is ready with her sewing machine. We just need to write something amazing.'

'Uh-huh,' I say. But I'm not really listening, I'm not thinking about my birthday or the revival of our silly tradition. Right now, I'm not assuming anything about where I'll be in a week, let alone a month.

He gets off the bed and looks at me again.

'Are you sure you'll cope?' he says. He sounds a little hurt at my indifference. Or maybe he's thinking the same thing as me: that I'm in a leaky canoe without a paddle, heading straight for shit creek.

'Dad, go.'

'I won't be long. Love you.'

'Love you too. Now get lost.'

He walks towards the exit, but before he leaves, he looks over to me and waves. His eyes are red. He'll go home and he'll see where I fell. He'll have to deal with that by himself. I think back to the night at Virago. I *almost* set him up with someone. It was so close. I promised him I wouldn't do anything like that again, but that was before. Now I'm in hospital and he's at home. The house will be silent. The silence will haunt him until he comes back for me. I can't bear the thought of it. He is not good at being alone.

76

Tom

As a parent, you can't help but map out the lives of your children. As soon as they're placed in your arms, you're asking yourself THE QUESTIONS. What will they look like when they're older? Will they find love? How will they play the Dane? Then you begin to plan for that future, putting money aside for that first car, first house, first uninsured skiing accident in a foreign country. But then sometimes life takes a stomach-churning handbrake turn down an unforeseen avenue, and suddenly, your plans are scattered in the road like litter.

So there I was, driving home from the hospital, the words of the cardiologist on permanent loop in my head. Our response to the initial diagnosis a decade ago had been defiance. Screw you, life, is that the best you can throw at us? Frankly, I've performed in enough Ibsen plays to know that fate mocks us all and you just have to deal with it the best you can. Hannah's script read like a tragedy, but we were determined to play it as life-affirming Hollywood romcom.

I was barely thinking about the road, auto-piloting my way through the quiet midday streets. When I parked up, it took me several seconds to realise that I'd accidentally stopped at the the-atre. I decided I might as well head in, perhaps check the mail, deliver a soliloquy, anything really. Anything to put off going home. I used the main entrance, unlocking the automatic doors and letting them slide open in front of me. The familiar smell of detergent and stale beer flooded my nostrils, and with it, memories of the foyer packed with expectant theatregoers standing in groups in their nice outfits, ordering G&Ts, perusing their programmes. I was about to head upstairs when Sally erupted from the corridor leading to the backstage area, carrying two bulging refuse sacks under her arm. She looked startled to see me.

'Oh god, I thought you were Phil!' she exclaimed, dropping the sacks either side of her.

'Phil? What would he be doing here?'

'Oh, he's off work today, repairing the guttering at home. DIY always puts him in a bad mood so I'm hiding out here, tidying up. How's our Hannah?'

'She had to have six stitches, and she went into cardiology for tests this morning. They say there's been some deterioration.'

'Oh Tom.'

'We've been here before. Each day as it comes and all that.'

'How's she taking it?'

'Oh you know, with cynical detachment. A typical teenager. She's sent me home to collect her comics.'

'Of course.'

'I just want to keep things going.'

'You will. You always do.'

As we stood there in silence, a man in a grey suit emerged from the auditorium doorway and approached us. I looked at him quizzically. He had a sharp, charmless face and the blank eyes of a gutted fish.

'Oh, this is Mr Benton from the insurance company,' she said with a pained smiled. 'He's here to examine the damage.'

'Hello, Mr Rose?' He offered his hand. It was limp and wet.

'Well?' I said. 'Anything I can help with?'

'I'll prepare my report and we'll be in touch.'

'Are there any problems?'

'We'll be in touch.'

He walked off, pulling a mobile phone from his jacket pocket. We watched him talking as he climbed into a Ford Mondeo in the car park. The engine started and he was gone. Sally looked at me, waiting for some sort of reaction.

'We should start planning for Hannah's birthday play!' I said.

Her face took on a quizzical expression.

'Well, are you sure she'll be up to it?'

'Of course!'

'But . . . I mean. Is she maybe getting a bit old for that now? She doesn't want to spend the day with all of us messing about in a theatre, surely?'

'She does! Of course she does! She was desperate to get on that stage last week. This place is in her blood. It'll take our minds off everything.'

Sally looked strained and uncertain.

'I'd better go,' she continued. 'We're all heading up to the hospital later. See you there?'

'Yes, definitely. Thank you, Sal.'

At home, I took the small suitcase out from under my bed and carried it to Hannah's room. I found myself knocking on the door, idiotically, then I slowly pushed it open, worried about infringing on her privacy. Everything was tidy, as it always was; a few articles of clothing on the unmade bed, but mostly serene order. This was always Hannah's room, from a little girl to a teenager. The white walls bore the little Blu-Tack scars of old pictures long since taken down. Now there were big posters of comic books and rock bands, and a noticeboard crammed with school timetables, and photos of friends and family. I reached up and touched a snapshot of Hannah and me, taken at the Edinburgh Festival a few years ago. We were looking freezing but happy outside a theatre. We saw a dozen plays, most of them awful. She wrote reviews for her blog. I remember saying, 'Maybe you'll be a critic when you grow up.' She didn't answer. Even then, she never liked to talk about the future.

I examined her bookcase. The top three shelves were crammed with fairy tale collections: Andrew Lang's fairy books, modern-day translations of the Grimm Brothers and Hans Christian Andersen; Angela Carter's anthologies. The bottom four were all comic books. Hundreds of them. This was her other literary obsession. It started when she was seven and I bought her a copy of something named *Justice League of America* after yet another visit to the hospital. I had no idea what it was, I just saw Wonder Woman on the cover and figured she might be a good role model. Hannah read it so many times it fell apart in her hands. I had to go to a comic shop in Bristol and buy her all the back issues. There is, I realised, a continuity between fairy tales and superhero adventures: they're mythic stories of good versus evil, filled with terrifying monsters and supernatural powers; and in the end, righteousness wins out against the odds. I could see why all this appealed to Hannah. But I couldn't keep up with her. I had no clue what she was reading these days. I grabbed a random selection and hoped for the best.

I was searching for a change of clothes when I found it. Stashed in a drawer beneath piles of mismatched socks, a photo printed out onto a sheet of A4 paper – a photo of me and Elizabeth, a long time ago, before Hannah was born. We were sitting in a pub, our pints raised toward the camera. I can't remember where it was taken, but I'm clearly wearing stage make-up, so it must have been after a performance somewhere. We looked happy. The weird thing was, I had no idea where Hannah would have got it from. I hadn't seen the original photo in years. Not since Elizabeth left. I put it back. Before I left the room, I checked her wastepaper basket. I removed the A Level letter, carefully flattened it out and pinned it back on her board. Then I bounded down the stairs to the door. The house had never felt so empty.

On the drive back to the hospital I passed the theatre and thought of Mr Benton poking around in the boiler room. What exactly was he looking for? It didn't matter; the visit was surely just a formality; there won't have been anything amiss. The insurance company would pay and everything would work out. Everything would definitely work out.

Hannah

An hour after my dad leaves to get my stuff, there's a commotion outside the ward and I know I have visitors. The doors burst open and I hear a shrill voice yelling, 'I haven't been in a hospital since 1994!'

Oh my god, it's Margaret! She came! For the first time in hours I have the will and energy to sit up in bed. She spots me and waves manically.

'I see they are still miserable places,' she shouts, her voice exploding around the restrained, antiseptic environment, like someone gunning a Rolls-Royce past a funeral procession. A couple of the other patients eye her wearily as she swoops past their beds, oblivious. 'I swore I'd never come back unless on a trolley with a tag around my toe. Shows how much I love you, darling.'

She plants a lipsticky kiss on my cheek, and sits down in the armchair next to the bed. She is dressed in a sort of salmon-pink velvet trouser suit, her wild lilac-tinged hair calamitously gathered under a floppy-rimmed red hat – it is a look that's perhaps best described as 'witness-protection-programme chic'. Then the rest of the drama group regulars are swarming around us, hugging me and looking for places to sit. Their warmth is like nectar. Sally and Natasha perch on the bed, upending a plastic bag filled with magazines and chocolate bars onto the starched sheets. Ted pulls up another chair, still in his cycling helmet; Jay shuffles in last, wearing a plaid shirt and boot-cut jeans, staring at his phone screen. He trips on his shoelaces and almost knocks a kidney dish out of the hands of a passing nurse. Sally leans forward and takes my arm, her earnest expression out of place amid this bizarre tableau.

'How are you doing? Do you mind us coming?'

'Not at all,' I say. 'I was bored to death. Sorry, just an expression.'

'I made you a card,' says Jay, launching something into my lap. It is a drawing of a stick figure in a crude depiction of a bed with the words 'Get up, you lazy bastard' scrawled along the top.

'Thanks, I'll treasure it for ever,' I say.

'Ah, there's Tom,' says Sally.

Everyone turns and Ted automatically shoots out of his seat, offering it to my dad, who bumbles in dragging a sports bag.

'Hey, how are you?' he says. 'I've brought clothes and reading material.'

'Chocolate, comics *and* bed,' says Natasha. 'I think I'll go home and throw myself down the stairs.'

'Thanks so much for coming, everyone!' says Dad.

'Nonsense,' says Ted. 'There's nowhere else we would rather be.'

'I can think of many places I'd rather be,' says Margaret. 'They don't even serve alcohol in the café. How are people supposed to get better?'

'Margaret,' says Dad, 'I did not expect to see you here. Thank you.'

'Yes, well, I'm still holding you to your promise,' she replies. 'If I look at all deathly, you're to get me out of here at once.'

'That's fine,' says Dad. 'I mean, it's incredibly inappropriate, but fine.'

Amid the general tumult of affirmation and assurance from everyone else, Dad takes my hand and squeezes it. 'Has the cardiologist been back?' he says.

'Not yet,' I lie. Venkman swung by again just after Dad left and went through everything with me. Apparently, my heart is really struggling; it is a knackered marathon runner. I might need an internal cardiac defibrillator, which Venkman described as a little box that would sit under my collar bone and punch my heart in the face every time it looked like stopping. Venkman is good with metaphors.

But for a few minutes, amid the chaotic chatter, I'm able to forget all that. Natasha tells us about her latest attempts to integrate into country society, getting her boisterous daughter Ashley into the Young Equestrians' club.

'She was sent home for chasing the horses. The other mums won't talk to me. We're outcasts.'

'Why don't you get Ashley to join the children's drama club?' says Sally. 'She liked the play the other night, and—'

'No, drama club is *mine*!' says Natasha in a really loud voice. 'I'm sorry, it's just that I need something of my own, something that makes sense to me, that isn't about the children, and isn't full of bitchy mums in green wellies. Is that too much to ask? Confession time, guys, I was never that into drama. I joined because your meetings were on the one night Seb could look after the kids. It was either this or beekeeping. Don't judge me.'

After that bombshell, Ted updates us on his increasingly desperate attempts to sweep Angela away on holiday ('she turned down a weekend in Weymouth in case her sister had a fall'). His precious motorcycle remains untouched in the garage – or as he puts it, 'rusting in its ignoble tomb'. Jay tells us about how annoyed and sweary his Dad is getting while fixing up the bathroom ('it's like a one-man Tarantino movie in there').

All too soon the ward sister wanders over. 'All right, you lot,' she says. 'We're doing lunch in a minute, so you'll have to think about heading off. Sorry.'

'But we have only just arrived,' says Margaret.

'The visiting hours are clearly stated on door. We're as flexible as we can be, but there are rather a lot of you.'

'Terrible timing,' says Ted.

'Story of your acting career,' shoots back Margaret.

There is a brief but chaotic whirl of hugging and chatter; Dad leans down and kisses my forehead like he has always done, and tells me he loves me, like he has always done. And I nod in the time-honoured fashion. Our hands link and then drift apart. Margaret asks if I need any of her sleeping pills, but I politely decline. Then they are all heading out together, like some sort of middle-aged, middle-class street gang. Before she goes, Sally bends down and kisses me on the cheek.

'You'll be out soon,' she says. 'When you feel up for it, let's go for a coffee and a gossip.'

'That would be nice.'

'Great. I'd better catch up with Jay. I don't want him getting run over by an ambulance again.'

I clear all the comics and magazines and Mars Bars off the bed, keeping busy. With the crowd gone, the ward takes on its unsettling silence and seems somehow darker and smaller. It feels as though it's closing in around me, like the trash-compactor scene in *Star Wars*, except I have no robots to rescue me – although I do have an annoying bleeping box next to the bed doing a twenty-four-hours-a-day impression of R2-D2. As the heart monitor plays out its bleeping rhythm, the screen shows a jumble of fluctuating numbers and jagged animating lines, like a really bad video game. Strange to think these lines literally represent my life. This is existence reduced to its stark basics: the electronic spasms of one fist-sized muscle. Except mine isn't so much a fist as a limp handshake.

On the opposite side of the ward there is a younger boy, asleep or unconscious, his parents sitting cowed and silent beside him, clutching each other's hands, reassuring one another. The woman gets up, checks her purse for change and heads towards the door. She's getting coffee maybe, or some food for them both; the man watches her go. He's smiling at her.

They're a team, they'll get through this together, whatever happens. They have each other.

A few hours later I'm in the car with Dad, heading home, clutching a goody bag full of meds. I've got beta blockers to manage my heart rhythm, a little dash of Enalapril, which is an angiotensin-converting enzyme inhibitor (just google it, for god's sake), and then there's an exciting new diuretic to stop my body retaining fluid. As goodbye presents go, it's pretty disappointing. Side effects include tiredness, dizziness, dodgy kidneys and – my personal favourite – completely batshit insane nightmares that make those Japanese supernatural horror movies look like Pokémon cartoons.

The next day I slope about the house, feeling separate from the world, feeling contaminated – by what, I don't know. Outside my bedroom, the street looks distant and artificial, like a film set. A gust of wind could blow it all over. I summon the energy to meet Sally in a café, a darkened hovel in an old cloth-worker's cottage at the end of the high street, with black slate floors, a wood-burning stove and big trestle tables, the benches lined with patterned cushions. I have come here to ask for Sally's help with something; it's been on my mind for years, but recent events have brought it to the forefront. First, though, I have to navigate the familiar, ultra-earnest questions about my health.

86

'How are you?' sighs Sally, cupping a giant latte. 'What's the latest?'

Well, Sally, I think, it's the same old story; my heart might keep ticking away, or it might get worse, or it might stop. People want reassurance, but there isn't any, and it's agonising to see their faces as this becomes clear. Maybe I could find an FAQ on the internet about explaining your heart disease in a socially acceptable manner. Maybe I could write one.

'I'm not *amazingly* well,' I manage at last. 'But what can I do? On one hand I'm, like, doing my GCSE revision, worrying if I'll remember anything about quadratic equations or oxbow lakes or past participles; on the other hand I'm thinking, I could pop my clogs next week so what does it matter anyway? Oh god, it's so . . . boring. Basically, the machine that pushes blood around my body is defective and always will be – end of story. A nurse once told me that if I could see my heart, it would look like a saggy handbag. She actually drew a picture of it for me.'

'Oh god, what did you do?'

'I took the pencil from her hand and added a Louis Vuitton logo.'

There's a pause. Sally laughs and puts her hand on mine. It is warm from the coffee mug. At least I don't have to protect her quite as much as I do Dad, but there's only so much I can share with her. When I really need to vent about the dark stuff, there's only one person I ever go to.

'So anyway, I need to talk to you about something,' I say in a brighter tone that I hope will shift the mood.

'Go on.'

'How do I put this? You may have noticed something about Dad: he is completely useless. He relies on me a lot. Well, look, um, the way things are going, that may not be good.'

'Oh, Hannah . . .' protests Sally. But I glare at her and she stops in her tracks.

'So yeah,' I continue. 'Sally, he needs to sort himself out. He needs to find someone. But he's just too dumb to see it or do it.'

'Someone?' says Sally, and she seems kind of taken aback. 'You mean, like a girlfriend?'

'Um, yes,' I say. 'Is the idea really that weird?'

I can vaguely remember Dad going out on dates in the past. It was just the odd night here and there – he'd try to sneak away when he thought I was asleep upstairs, quietly recruiting a series of discreet babysitters. But none of these surreptitious relationships ever lasted. I was too young to ask why at the time, but well, I get it now. It was obviously *me*. And it still is. This sounds totally egocentric but clearly I am the sun at the centre of his solar system – so what happens if that sun runs out of nuclear fuel, bloats into a red giant then explodes? (My physics revision is going well at least.) I decide not to explain this to Sally; the whole dying sun metaphor is a bit grim, even for me.

Sally ponders for a few moments.

'I agree,' she says finally. 'Your dad *is* dumb.'

'Thank you,' I say.

'And he definitely needs someone in his life. We all do.'

'Exactly. And, just to be selfish for a second, he does sort of hang around a bit *too* much, you know? It's always, "let's do this crazy thing", "let's play that ridiculous game", "let's go to some weird experimental theatre production in Stokes Croft". Sometimes, I just want to hang around with my friends and do nothing and be bored and cynical like a normal teenager. It's like ... he can't let go of how we were. When I was a kid.'

'So what's your plan? You're not going to enter him into one of those dating shows on TV?'

'No, of course not! Well, not straight away. Not until we're desperate. I was going to start with friends of friends; find out if anyone out there in Somerset is single and available. And then, you know, engineer a date. I don't know. Anyway, this is where you come in.'

'What? How?'

'You know women his age. The only people I know who are that old are my friends' parents and am-dram actors, and those are both banned.'

'That old?' says Sally. 'You do realise *I'm* the same age as your dad?'

'You know what I mean.'

I look at her again, and I feel, not for the first time, that it's a shame she's married. Sally is sort of beautiful. She always has her shoulder-length brown hair in a ponytail, and wears cool jeans and skinny T-shirts, and she has amazing almond-shaped eyes. She could pass for thirty, maybe even younger. She doesn't look like someone with a teenage son. Her husband Phil is one lucky bastard.

'I'll have a think,' she says. 'But I'm not sure he's going to be comfortable with this.'

'Oh, I *know* he won't be,' I say. 'But he's had ten years to sort this out himself and got nowhere, so we're mounting a hostile takeover of his love life.'

'What if there's no one suitable? I mean, as unlikely as that sounds ...'

'Phase two,' I say. 'Internet dating websites. They are a big thing now, they're not just for lonely perverts.'

'You've really thought this through.'

'Well, I've had some down time.'

'That's true.'

'And the problem is, I don't know how much more time I have.'

We let this sink in for a moment. I watch the baristas working purposefully behind the counter, turning dials and jabbing buttons on the great steaming coffee machine, as it chugs rhythmically. An image pops into my head of a heart monitor, towering above a hospital bed. The line is flat, the bleeping has stopped. Someone unplugs it. The machine is rolled silently away.

'Will you help me?' I say to Sally. 'Basically, if anything happens to me, I don't want my dad to be alone because he's a danger to himself and others. That's it. I'm sorry. I'm sorry if that sounds stupid.'

'It doesn't, of course it doesn't. Yes I'll help, of course I will. But you're going to get through this.'

'Whatever,' I sigh. 'The important thing is, I'm going to get Dad on the goddamn dating scene and the first step is telling him.'

Tom

'Dad, Dad, are you listening to me? Dad?'

We were sitting in the foyer of the town's dinky independent cinema. There was a new Disney movie on the big screen, but we'd chosen to see a pretentious French film about a disastrous family holiday in the Dordogne. My daughter had just spent two days in hospital and it felt as though seeing a pretentious French film would be the perfect way to re-acclimatise to real life. I was lost in my thoughts, looking out of the window, watching the evening traffic buzz by.

'Dad!' shouted Hannah.

'Huh, sorry. What were you saying?'

She rolled her eyes extravagantly.

'I said, I've been thinking about dating.'

Here we go, I thought. I've got to handle this correctly.

'Oh yes?' I replied. 'Have you asked someone out? Is it Jay?'

'What? No! Ewww, gross! I'm not talking about me, I'm talking about you!'

'Oh Hannah, this again?'

'Yeah, Dad, this again.'

I couldn't help but shift nervously in my chair, like a foreign spy anticipating a tortuous interrogation.

'I'm fine,' I said. 'I don't need any of that right now.'

'Well, maybe it's not about what *you* need.'

'What do you mean?'

'Oh god, do I have to spell it out? Look, you've had about five dates in the last decade, and I know why. It's not because you're a terrible person – although obviously that's a factor. It's because of me, it's because of all *this*.' She held up her arm with the hospital wrist tag still attached. 'But it's not fair any more, it's not fair to use me as an excuse.'

'Hannah, I'm not. That's not what it's about.'

'You need to have a life beyond me.'

'I do. I've got the—'

'And beyond the bloody theatre.'

'I know, I will, I—'

'But I want to see it, Dad! I want to *know* that you're okay – that you'll be okay . . . if anything happens.'

'I can't . . . I can't think about this. I'm sorry, Hannah.'

A memory comes back to me. University. Second year. I'd just moved into a house with four other drama students. Very quickly, I'd learned a valuable life lesson: do not move into a house with four drama students. Or indeed any number of drama students. Ever. For one week we all loved each other with a glorious passion. It was like some kind of beautiful hippy commune, just with a lot more showing off. Within a month, however, it was a raging maelstrom of drunken arguments, duplicitous shags and low-quality recreational drugs. I spent as little time there as possible for the rest of the year.

Instead, I'd hang out in the library with the real students, pretending to be studying. Elizabeth was a regular. She'd sit at the same desk every day with a vast pile of terrifying-looking economics books, machine-gunning notes onto an A4 sketch pad. She wore thick-rimmed black glasses and sensible clothes, but didn't look dorky or cute; she looked formidable. Coming from a teeny nowhere town in Somerset with a family of degenerate roustabouts and raconteurs, I had never seen anything like her. I'd idle around nearby, trying to look inconspicuous and charming at the same time. One day, I asked if I could sit next to her as the library was very busy. It wasn't. But she said yes anyway; she spoke to me with a brusque efficiency, as though I was a waiter asking to clear her table. That was it. I was in love. Three years later (to cut a long story short) she said yes to me again – only this time I was on one knee holding out a cheap diamond ring and her parents were glaring at us in disbelief. I might come back to this story later.

Anyway, the drama student loser and the business mastermind got married. It was the classic 'opposites attract' story – the perfect romantic comedy. But this is why romantic comedies tend to finish with a marriage rather than start with one. Because the forces that draw two different people together can easily reverse polarity and rip them apart, and then – surprise! – you're a single parent. But on the plus side, I had Hannah so everything was also wonderful. Boy, that was a confusing decade.

Anyway, this memory was clearly a reminder that I met my wife by hanging around near her table in the university library. This is not an option for a forty-something theatre manager. It would be weird. I needed a way out of this conversation and if there's one thing I have learned about teenagers it's that embarrassment is an excellent diversionary tactic. Embarrassment is the smoke grenade of parent–child communications.

'So who's Callum?' I asked.

'What? Who? Who is what now? Why?'

See what I mean?

'When we were in the shopping arcade,' I said. 'Your friend mentioned Callum.'

'She's not my friend.'

'She mentioned his name and you gave her a look that if you were Medusa would have turned her to stone.'

Hannah stabbed a spoon in her hot chocolate and swirled it around with vicious intent.

'He's just a dumb boy in my English class. He sits there and says nothing, and just has this stupid smile on his face like he's judging everyone. And then he wrote an essay on *Jane Eyre* and romantic yearning, and Mr McAlpine read it out in class because ... oh whatever.'

With that, she threw the spoon across the table. I had inadvertently struck diversion gold.

'Was it good?' I ask.

She looked at me, shaking her head incredulously.

'It was fucking beautiful,' she spluttered. 'It was about how, in what is basically an apocalyptic vision of Victorian Britain, this love affair blossoms like a galaxy being born. Anyway, Emilia told everyone I was crying, and I totally wasn't, but you know what it's like: everyone is suddenly all "Oooh, Hannah's in love." Complete bullshit. I'm so not interested in him – or anyone else at that pathetic school.'

'And *you're* the one who's going to be teaching me about dating in the twenty-first century?'

'I didn't say I was going to teach you.'

'You're just going to leave me to it?'

'Not exactly. We'll see how it goes.'

'Hannah?'

'I'm just not sure if you can be trusted.'

'To find love?'

'You don't need love, you need help. You're useless, I need to hand you over to someone else. It's purely selfish.'

'You're mean. You're a mean girl.'

'But you're thinking about it? Dating, I mean.'

'After what happened at Virago? Can either of us face that again?'

'Virago was a practice run. The results were . . . very interesting. Dad, just think about it? Please?'

I looked at her and sighed, then hit on another diversionary tactic: 'Hey, so we really need to be thinking about your big sixteenth birthday play. It's a few weeks away! I'm thinking ice. I've looked into it: a small onstage skating rink is not as expensive as it sounds and . . . Hannah?'

She was looking away, towards the bar, the popcorn machines, the small huddle of middle-class cinema fanatics by the doors to screen two.

'I don't know, Dad.'

'You're right. Ice may be a bit much, especially with Margaret's hips.'

'No, I mean, I don't know about the play. I don't know about anything beyond the next week, the next day . . .'

'Hannah, what do you mean?'

'You know what I mean. Dr Venkman said . . . Look, I just. I can't think about the future. I can't even imagine being there. And Dad, I'm not a kid any more. I can't live in a make-believe world. I've got to be a realist.'

The doors opened, the gaggle of people started to filter into the screening room, chatting animatedly about their days, their lives, about exactly how wrong a holiday in the Dordogne could really go. I turned back to Hannah.

'It's been a rough week,' I said.

'It's been a rough decade,' scoffed Hannah, but as though aware that she'd said something terrible, she seemed to physically jolt herself out of the prevailing mood.

'Are we going to watch this film or not?' she said.

We watched the film. The French family go to the Dordogne because the daughter is about to leave for university and the son has joined the army. It's their last holiday together and it's awful: it rains constantly, their little chateau has a leaky roof and then the electricity generator packs in. So they sit in the dark and start telling each other about their lives and hopes, and they realise they don't know each other at all. Then the boy gets killed during a military exercise in the Middle East. In retrospect, we should have gone for the Disney movie.

Tuesday morning in the theatre office. I'd been twirling around in my chair for barely a minute when I heard the buzzer go on the side door. I thought it was probably Ted or Janice the cleaner, or maybe one of the front-of-house volunteers, but when I strolled down I saw through the glass that it was a man I didn't recognise, carrying a clipboard. By the suit, I guessed Jehovah's Witness. He was looking up and along the building, as though he'd kicked a football onto the roof and was working out how to climb up and get it. This scenario seemed unlikely.

I opened the door with a hefty yanking motion as it tended to warp and swell up in the cold, like everything else in the building.

'Hello,' I said, trying to sound as normal and casual as possible.

'Mr Rose?' he asked. He looked maybe mid-fifties, a neatly trimmed beard and wire-frame glasses, his hair thinning across his scalp.

'Yes, I'm Tom Rose, I'm the manager. Can I help you?'

'I'm from Chapels Surveyors. I'm here to assess the property.'

He said it in a way that suggested I should definitely know what he was talking about. But I didn't. I stood looking at him for a few seconds, unsure if perhaps he was somehow at the wrong theatre, or maybe I was. After everything with Hannah, I couldn't quite collect my thoughts into any kind of sense.

'Um, I . . . are you sure you have the right place? I haven't asked for a surveyor.'

'Oh,' he said. And for a second it seemed as though there had been some ridiculous mistake. 'Well, I'm here for the council. They've asked us to assess the value of the property and surrounding land.'

It suddenly felt as though I had wandered into a bizarre and horrific parallel universe, constructed entirely from nasty surprises. This, I thought, is what it must be like living in *EastEnders*. I opened my mouth to say something but found there was nothing available, not even breath.

'I . . . I . . .'

'It will only take a few minutes, I won't get in your way. I just have to take a quick look around,' he said. His tone had become gentle and placatory – as though he was genuinely worried I was having some sort of turn. What must I have looked like to him? I hadn't showered or shaved, or even looked in a mirror. Did I look infirm? Or terrifying? Either was possible.

'Why?' The word came out in a bizarre strangulated squeak, like a distressed laboratory animal about to be force-fed lipstick. If I looked terrifying, I certainly didn't sound it. 'Why does the council need the building to be assessed?'

There was silence. I don't think either of us could fully process what was going on. We had become a Pinter play.

'Mr Rose, I'm just here to assess the property. I can give you our contact at the council – you'll need to talk to them.'

97

He wrote down a name and number on a piece of paper and tore it from his clipboard.

'Now, if I could get past?' he said.

He tried to squeeze by, but something compelled me to block his way. What was I doing? What was happening?

'No,' I said. 'No, I don't think so.'

'I have authority from the council.'

'I'm sorry, I don't care. I don't know what's going on, but this is not the day for it to be happening.'

'I'm extremely busy. It's not convenient for me to reschedule.'

'How can I put this?' I said, and I literally did not know how to put it because I didn't know what I was about to say. It seemed to be happening without my permission. 'You're not coming in today. Can you please go?'

'Mr Rose . . .'

'I must insist that you go. Immediately. Please?' I could feel this ludicrous adrenaline coursing through my body – like I'd mainlined two hundred cans of Red Bull. I looked down and my hands were balled into fists. Oh god, I thought, am I going to physically assault a council-appointed surveyor? Will I be on the local news?

The man took a step back and quickly glanced at his clipboard again, as though checking his schedule for the part where it said '12.05 p.m.: get threatened by wild-eyed theatre manager'.

'I'll be talking to the council about this,' he said at last, then he turned and briskly walked away.

Later in the afternoon it was the regular meeting of the Willow Tree Theatre executive group. We always had these get-togethers on the stage, to remind us what we were here for, and that it wasn't just any old executive meeting. I arranged our chairs in a circle in the centre of the space, and brought out a little collapsible table for the cake and biscuits, which were mandatory, and duly supplied by Ted, who baked a surprisingly good Victoria sponge. There had been talk of cancelling the meeting considering everything that was going on with Hannah, but I insisted. The show must go on.

Sally led the agenda. There were a few issues with refunds after the weekend's cancelled performances, plus someone had sprained their ankle at the breakdancing class the week before so we had to check the health and safety forms to make sure they couldn't sue us for millions of pounds.

'Anything else on the agenda?' said Sally. 'Tom, have the council been in touch about the insurance at all?'

'Nope, nothing,' I replied, shovelling a ginger biscuit into my mouth. 'Oh apart from a surveyor turning up this morning to look at the theatre. I told him to get lost. All very strange. Are these Waitrose ginger nuts, Ted, they're very good?'

'A *what* turned up at the theatre?' interrupted Ted in a sharp tone that was extremely unusual for him. I immediately understood that I might have fucked up.

'A property surveyor turned up. He said the council had sent him.'

The atmosphere had a tension in it all of a sudden. I decided to keep talking.

'I assumed it was a mistake. I mean, it can't be anything to do with the boiler can it? The council never moves that fast. Do they? Oh bugger. Do you think I should call them?'

'Yes, you should call the bloody council!' yelled Sally.

'There's only one reason they'd send a surveyor round, and it's not to build us a new conservatory,' added Ted.

I took out my phone and the piece of paper the surveyor had given me, artlessly stabbing the number into the keypad. It rang for what felt like several minutes. I put on the speaker so everyone could hear.

'Commercial office,' said a woman's voice on the other end.

'Yeah, this is Tom Rose from the Willow Tree Theatre. Can I speak to Councillor Jenkins?'

'I'm afraid he's not available. Can I take a message?'

'This morning I had a surveyor here who said he'd been sent to assess the value of the building. He said your department hired him.'

There was a pause. I could hear tapping on a keyboard.

'Please hold,' said the voice.

There were a few seconds of crackly silence, then the hold music started – a shaky, badly recorded version of Herb Alpert's 'Spanish Flea'. It sounded as though it was being played by a poorly prepared junior jazz orchestra, trapped in a shipping container full of bees. Abruptly the voice was back on the other end of the line.

'You should have received an official letter,' she said. She sounded frustrated by my mail-receiving incompetence.

'I haven't,' I said. And then I remembered the official-looking letter that arrived the other day – the day of Hannah's accident. Sometimes the council sent theatre mail to my home address thanks to a seemingly irreparable error in the mailing database. I chose not to mention it.

There was something that sounded like a deep sigh on the other end of the phone.

'The commercial department is considering selling a number of properties in the area as a means of generating capital to meet other statutory responsibilities,' she said in a dull monotone – as though she was reading from the letter I didn't receive – or received but didn't open. 'The theatre is one of them.'

'You're selling the theatre?' I said.

'I don't think that decision has been made. I'm not on the board; you'll need to speak to—'

'But I'm the manager. I mean, when were you going to tell me?'

'As I said, you should have received a letter explaining the situation in some detail.'

'I didn't,' I said. But my throat was now dry and bulging and I couldn't get the words out properly. In my head, for a strange couple of milliseconds, I saw Hannah as a little girl, dancing across the stage.

'I'll get a copy sent to you,' she said. 'And I'll ask Councillor Jenkins to call you back. Goodbye.'

The line went dead. I put the phone to my ear, and then shook it, as though this would somehow bring the person back again.

'They want to sell the theatre?' gulped Sally.

'No, of course not,' said Ted. 'They want to sell the *land*. They'll just demolish the theatre.'

We all stared at each other like bumbling bank robbers who'd just set off a silent police alarm.

'Demolish the theatre?' Natasha repeated, as though the words were garbled nonsense. 'But they can't, can they?'

Ted looked at her and shrugged. For a little while we sat in abject silence. Sally put her head in her hands.

'It's weird that they should turn up right after the insurers,' she said. 'Do you think that's a coincidence?'

'No,' said Ted. 'I don't. Perhaps they were looking for an excuse to sell. Perhaps they've just found it.'

'Well, this has certainly been a challenging week,' I said. I felt a duty to keep things light. 'Maybe I ought to open the other packet of biscuits?'

I looked at Ted and he looked back at me. The expression on his face was unmistakable. Fear. Real, wretched fear. The sort even biscuits couldn't curtail. I hadn't seen that in his eyes for a long time. Very quickly, I felt it too.

Dearest Willow,

I'm going to tell you about the play we put on for my eighth birthday, but there is some backstory to understand first. Please bear with me.

I think it's safe to say that the Justice League of America *comic Dad bought for me when I was seven changed my life. It was the beginning of a fresh start for the DC superhero team. A weird, brilliant writer named Grant Morrison decided to re-imagine Superman, Wonder Woman, Batman (booooo) and their allies as a pantheon of modern Greek gods. They were all-powerful deities who fought only the biggest threats to mankind. I didn't understand all that at the time, but the colours, the characters, the sheer explosive force of the stories blew my teeny tiny mind.*

It was also the comic that put Wonder Woman right up there with the big DC heroes and she really kicked ass. Coming up to the second anniversary of my diagnosis, I wanted to be brave and invincible just like her. So the play we put on for my birthday that year had to be The Snow Queen, *Hans Christian Andersen's strange, exciting tale of brave young Gerda and the quest to rescue her friend Kai from the queen's deadly ice castle. I can remember it was our most ambitious production. Dad actually hired a snow machine and a giant fan so that we could make Gerda's journey through Finland to the Arctic Circle even more authentic. For the Snow Queen's castle* where Kai is held prisoner, Kamil constructed an incredible edifice out of mirrored boards and cool white Perspex.

I was so impressed and so excited. I told my dad that I had to be in the play this time, I didn't just want to sit and watch. 'I know who you want to be,' he said. 'The robber girl.'

He was right. On Gerda's journey north she is attacked by a gang of bandits in a forest, but one of them is a really tough girl who takes pity on her, and lets her stay in the robbers' castle for the night. She is completely mad. She has a reindeer called Bay chained up in her bedroom, and hundreds of caged birds. There's a bit where she grabs one of her doves, shakes it until it flaps its wings, then yells 'Kiss it' and thrusts it in Gerda's face. She sleeps with a dagger held next to her chest and constantly threatens Gerda with it. I thought she was amazing. She was fearless and wild, and when she gave Gerda her reindeer, Gerda cried with gratitude and the robber girl told her, 'I don't like your snivelling.' I remember repeating the line to Dad and yelling, 'That has to be in our play.' I was a very demanding collaborator.

I understood this was a story about love and friendship and the way these things often involve a kind of bravery that doesn't need to be spoken. Once again I remember only glimpses of the performance. Rachel played Gerda, wrapped in a fur coat, under frosty blue lights, battling against the billowing snow; Margaret was the Snow Queen, aboard her carriage, dressed in a flowing white dress, a fur scarf around her neck. She looked like Cruella de Ville on a snowboarding holiday.

But the moment I remember most was not in the production but in the technical rehearsal. Ted and Dad were on stage, helping to set the lighting positions. Richard had crafted an ingenious set of revolving multicolour gels and positioned them on two lights pointing at the rear wall of the stage; when he dipped the house lights and switched them on, they produced beautiful swirling beams of colour. The Northern Lights.

Ted looked up, at first in wonder, and then, I don't know, his face just fell. He looked like he'd seen something terrible, some sort of ghost.

He said to Dad, 'This is as close to them as I'll ever get.'

Dad put down his script and walked over to his friend. 'You don't know that,' he said. 'Angela's sister could improve. There's still time.'

Ted shook his head.

'Sometimes you have to accept things. When you get to my age, you realise . . . your dreams fade. You don't notice it at first, but they do. They slip away.'

Dad patted him on the back.

'You'll get there,' said Dad. 'I'm still a dreamer; I have hundreds of them. Don't give up.'

Ted smiled and looked up again at the light show. Dad started to stroll away, checking his to-do list, but Ted turned to him.

'Thank you,' he said.

'What for?'

'For taking in a dull old accountant. For making me a part of this place. I'd always dreamed of working in a theatre.'

'There you go then,' said Dad. 'It came true.' Then he jumped off the stage and smiled at me as he wandered past.

Richard saw Dad leave and he shouted from the back of the auditorium, 'Shall I turn the Northern Lights off now?'

But Ted said, 'No, keep them on. Just for a little while longer.'

He stood and watched the lights swirling, all alone on the stage.

So yes, I learned a lot from The Snow Queen. I learned that the escapism of the theatre means different things to different people. I wanted to be Wonder Woman and Ted wanted to be free.

Tom

The next evening, we met up again in the tiny White Horse pub on the high street, gathering conspiratorially around an ancient oak table. We had the old guard of Ted, Sally and Margaret, then Natasha and Shaun, and a few other members of the drama club. Hannah was staying at home to rest. By this point I'd managed to check the post and discover that the letter from the council was indeed about the surveyor visit; it assured me that no decision had been made, and invited me to call Councillor Jenkins if I had any questions – you know, any questions about demolishing the theatre I'd spent the last fourteen years managing. The pub was empty apart from us, but the wood-panelled room was so small, it felt half full. There used to be Victorian paintings of fox-hunting scenes lining the walls, but the current owner did not want to endorse blood sports, so those were taken down, and replaced with insipid watercolours by local amateur artists, which Margaret said she could cope with if she performed a lot of breathing exercises and didn't look directly at them.

'So we're screwed?' said Sally.

'Well ...' I replied. 'I wouldn't say *screwed*. There's a chance we're in a tiny bit of a predicament that may slightly threaten the future of the theatre.'

'So we're screwed,' repeated Sally.

'At this stage, they're just surveying the building,' said Ted. 'They probably do this all the time, just getting an idea of what they own, and what they can shift if need be. Now, the flood is the big issue. If they can prove the building is going to be too costly to maintain – well, that's a problem.' It was the Ted I knew – businesslike, sensible, rational.

'I don't think they'll demolish the theatre,' said Shaun. Ah, finally, I thought, a note of optimism. 'I mean, the building is almost certainly riddled with asbestos. That's expensive to clear.'

He looked around at the coven of horrified faces.

'It's fine until you start knocking stuff down,' he said. 'Although one speck of that stuff in your lungs and—'

'Thanks for your input, Shaun,' I replied, keen to move the discussion away from carcinogenic chemicals or indeed, knocking stuff down.

'I don't think they'll want to close a theatre unless the fiscal benefits are significant,' said Ted. 'It's not great PR.'

'They tried to close a theatre I worked at in the early seventies,' butted in Margaret, taking a large gulp from her second Dubonnet and lemonade. 'We staged a nude protest outside. The police turned up but they said it was not in their training to deal with thirty naked actors. There were tits and willies everywhere, dear. It was like one of Freddie Mercury's birthday parties. We were on the London evening news.'

Shaun winked at Natasha who batted him on the arm. Sally rolled her eyes.

'Thanks Margaret,' I said. 'We'll bear that in mind.'

'Tom, please don't do a naked protest. Hannah's life is hard enough as it is,' said Natasha.

'Is there any other business?' I said, by now fairly determined to change the subject.

'Well, we have the West Country festival coming up,' said Sally, quickly flipping through the pages of her notebook. 'Shall we move on to that?'

It was a good call – diverting attention to something positive and exciting. The West Country festival, or WestFest, was an annual arts and music festival, taking place just outside Shepton Mallet. Local drama groups were invited to put on scenes and entertainments, but this year things were to be slightly different. In a nod to the exciting new era of the iPod, each group was being asked to produce three scenes from different plays. The scenes are supposed to be drawn from throughout theatre history so Sally had chosen bits from *The Country Wife* (classic *and* fruity, perfect for a festival), *The Seagull* (good old Chekhov) and *Noises Off* (because, considering its portrayal of a disastrous performance, it would work well even if it was an actual disaster).

On the day, we'd all be randomly called onto the stage to perform one of our contributions; then another group would be called, and so on – like a theatrical shuffle mix. The organisers seemed to think this approach would 'appeal to the youth', though actually the youth would of course be in the cider tent, or watching the local bands on the other stage, or – most likely of all – wandering about sullenly trying to find a mobile signal. However, they were offering a fee to participants and given the play cancellations and flood repairs, the money would come in handy.

'So then,' said Sally. 'Rehearsals are going well, we've hired a minibus and the festival has allocated two large tents for us all to sleep in. I need to set some ground rules for the event though, and the first is about alcohol consumption.'

'I'll get the drinks in,' said Ted. 'Though Angela wants me back before ten. She gets anxious if I'm too late. Same again everyone?'

'Angela is always anxious,' said Margaret.

For the rest of the evening, amid the plans for the drama club's festival appearance, the subject of the theatre sale was avoided. But it was there, lurking in the background like a pantomime villain. Just before Ted left, I remembered the other key reason I'd wanted everyone to get together in the first place.

'You know what else is coming up,' I said. 'Our revival of Hannah's birthday play! I have a few ideas that I'm working on – just ordering in some props at the moment. I have an ambitious set design that I'm working on with Kamil.'

It was one of those pub conversation moments when the whole place seems to go silent – like in *American Werewolf in London* when the two boys ask about the star on the wall in the Slaughtered Lamb.

'Of course,' said Ted in a disarmingly placatory manner. 'But let's keep some perspective – we need to find out what's happening with the building before we make any big plans.'

'Nothing's happening with the building,' I said, a little more loudly than I'd planned. 'You said it yourself, they're just keeping their options open. You said it, Ted.'

'I know but . . .'

Maybe it was the oppressive heat of the crowded room, maybe it was the whole business with the phone call, maybe I felt guilty about missing the letter. Whatever it was, I was suddenly and strangely angry.

'But what, Ted? We're running out of time, don't you see? It's got to be good! It's got to be our masterpiece!'

Some slightly startled looks were exchanged around the table. Ted blushed. Shaun looked between us, like a tennis spectator. I was about to speak, but then Natasha's husband Seb burst in with their son wailing in his pushchair. 'I was just passing, trying to get this one to sleep,' he said. 'Thought I'd pop in and say hello and also ruin your evening.'

'That's nice, honey, but where's the other one?'

'The other one?'

'Ashley? Our daughter?'

He looked genuinely shocked for a few desperate seconds.

'Sleepover!' he said at last. 'She's on a sleepover. Jesus, you gave me a heart attack.'

'Are we ... are we the worst parents of all time?'

With the tension of the evening well and truly broken, Natasha gave her husband a hug, grabbed her son and put him on her lap. Everyone started chatting, enjoying each other's company. I looked at Seb and Natasha, cradling their boy, laughing together. It felt like a moment they would remember. I thought back, but I realised I was losing those fleeting memories, I was losing the feel – the very idea – of being with someone. Oh my god, I thought, I'm becoming Philip Larkin.

Outside, when everyone was leaving, Sally stopped me beneath the old Victorian street light just beyond the glow of the illuminated pub sign.

'It's a stressful time,' she said.

'The council won't close the theatre, I'm sure of it now.'

'I don't mean that. I mean Hannah.'

'We're shaken up. I can only guess at how she feels these days. I used to know. I used to really know.'

'That's parenthood,' sighed Sally. 'When they're tiny, they're your best pals. They cling on to you, they do what you tell them;

the next thing you know, they're strangers in expensive clothes who eat all your food and tell you to fuck off. You can't keep hold, no matter how hard you try. Hannah is growing up, Tom.'

'I know.'

'She's not going to want to hang out with us sad amateur actors for much longer.'

'That's exactly why I want to revive our old birthday tradition just one last time. Because afterwards it'll all be boys and parties and moody teenage drama groups. Well, that's what I'll be doing, I don't know about Hannah.'

'You should talk to her though. Just ask her what she wants.'

'I know what she wants.'

'Tom, just . . . listen to her.'

On the walk back from the pub I passed the theatre, dark, still and looming like some terrifying government department or giant sepulchre. It was not difficult to imagine it closed for good, derelict, its ugly exterior goading on the wrecking ball. The thought chilled me to the bone. If the theatre was closed, it would all be over. How could we put on a sixteenth birthday party play for Hannah? There were so many memories tied up in there – our lives, our dreams. If the theatre was taken, how would we keep them alive? Where would we be?

I turned away and shuddered. Clearly, the temperature had dropped. It had dropped so suddenly.

Hannah

I am sitting in the middle of the stalls with Margaret, watching the drama group rehearsing for WestFest. I'm not taking part in this whole project because, you know, revision, course work, life-threatening heart condition, all that stuff. So I get to loaf about here in the cool semi-darkness of the auditorium, trying to read my GCSE English set texts with a torch while fending off text messages from Jenna and Daisy asking dumb questions about Callum, even though Callum is completely *not happening*.

I wonder what he's doing. I wonder where he lives and whether he is sitting somewhere reading the GCSE set texts. I wonder why I am thinking about a boy I don't know and don't care about.

Meanwhile, Dad is sitting with Sally in the front row. They both have piles of play scripts on their laps, but they're also looking at Dad's laptop, chatting and sniggering to each other like kids. Most of the other drama group members are here, including Rachel, our elusive and gorgeous superstar. She's been a member for years but flits in and out, because she's involved with about ten other theatre, dancing and singing groups. She's determined to be famous by any means necessary, and her mum has taken her to all the *Pop Idol* and X *Factor* auditions. She already acts like a complete diva, turning up late to rehearsals, usually with an entourage of friends and relatives. She is so intimidating and brilliant she gets away with it.

Her and Shaun are just getting started on the seduction scene from *The Country Wife* when James, the hot vicar from our seventies farce, comes in. He's wearing a white linen shirt and chinos and he looks totally buff. He spots Margaret and me, and works his way along the row of seats, plonking himself down in the chair next to mine. OMG. I don't know what aftershave he's wearing but it's the nicest I've ever smelled. Christ, how am I supposed to concentrate on *Jane Eyre* now?

'What's going on?' he whispers.

'Shaun and Rachel are doing the seduction scene from *Country Wife*.'

'Ooh, saucy.'

'Whatever you say.'

'Shouldn't you be in a car park somewhere swigging white cider from a plastic bottle?'

I laugh, but it's annoying he sees me as a stupid teenager. He's barely ten years older than me, for god's sake. I wonder if he's got a girlfriend. He never talks about his private life. He's so mysterious. I know he was some sort of web coder, and set up his own company at eighteen because he was already making shitloads of cash. He moved to London, got a flashy apartment, but then there was the big dotcom crash, and he moved back in with his parents. He told me that clients in London used to take him to the National, the Donmar and the Royal Court, he saw Shakespeare at the Globe. So when he came back he joined the drama group. What a comedown. He and Natasha often go on about their time moving and shaking in the big city; every night at a different bar or swanky hotel, cocaine-fuelled parties on Thames cruise ships. He looks a bit lost now.

I go to speak to him, but stop because he is clearly utterly engrossed in what's happening on the stage, which is weird, because they've stopped the action. Rachel is drinking from a bottle of Evian, eyes closed, back arched. Sally has jumped up and is showing Shaun where to stand, her hand on his tattooed arm. James is staring, enraptured. I turn to Margaret and she is watching James too. She smiles to herself.

'What is it?' I whisper to her.

'I know that look of old,' she says, gesturing toward James. 'Our man here is smitten.' And she looks back to the stage.

Goddammit, Rachel.

Before I can think any murderous jealous thoughts, the door at the back of the theatre bursts open. It gives such a loud crack against the wall that everyone on stage stops and turns, as does Dad. It's Sally's husband Philip, standing there in a pair of baggy jogging bottoms and a rugby shirt. His face is all red, no doubt due to the embarrassment of his cacophonous entry. He smiles broadly and waves at the stage, then spots Sally and gestures enthusiastically at her.

'Do you think I could borrow my wife?' he says breezily.

Sally jumps down off the stage and walks briskly up towards the exit. I watch her go and she looks kind of embarrassed or something. I can't tell. I see that Dad is watching her too. She follows Phil out into the foyer, and when she walks back in barely a minute later, she shrugs at Dad blankly. He smiles at her and it's sort of sympathetic but sort of something else. She stuffs her script pages into her bag, and virtually marches along the aisle toward the stage.

'Right everyone,' she shouts. 'I'm afraid I have to go, so we'll finish up here. James and Margaret, I'm sorry, we'll have to work on your Chekhov scene next time.'

And with that, she turns and almost jogs out of the auditorium. Shaun and Rachel watch her go, slightly open-mouthed. They turn quickly to Dad. He shrugs at them and begins to gather up his own papers. As the rest chat on stage, he gets up and climbs back over the rows to get to me.

'Hey,' he says, sitting down in the row in front of me, not looking at me, but at the door behind us.

'Hey.'

We sit in silence for a few seconds, and I wait for him to say something else, but he just sits there with a glum expression on his face. I do not understand the dynamics in here at all. I sigh and go back to my book. What would Jane Eyre do in this situation?

'Well, I'll head off then,' says James. He takes one look at the stage, and I wonder if he's eyeing up Rachel, perhaps considering whether to ask her out for a coffee. The bitch. But then he clambers along the row of seats and out the exit. I would have gone for coffee with you, James.

'So,' says Dad at last. 'This whole dating thing. Would you ... would it be weird for you if I did that?'

I close the book and slam it down on my lap in mock horror.

'Dad, it was *my* idea!'

He carries on without acknowledging me.

'It's been a long time since your mum left and well, maybe I should get back out there, as they say.'

'Dad, this is literally what I told you.'

'It has occurred to me that it's actually not fair of me to rely on you so much.'

Oh my god, he is such a typical man.

'Tell me,' I say. 'What made you think of this right now?'

'I don't know. I'm not getting any younger.'

Silence. I suddenly notice that Margaret is standing in the aisle watching us. Dad looks around and sees her too.

'Goodbye, Margaret,' he says.

She's squinting at us dubiously.

'We should have done *The Tempest*,' she says without stopping. 'Chekhov is such a crushing bore. I dated a Russian once. Beautiful face, lovely manners, but he drank like an ox; smelled like one too. Appearances can be so deceptive, can't they? Especially where men are concerned.' With that, she walks away.

Dad and I look at each other slightly dumbfounded.

'So what's the next step?' I say.

'I don't know; should we get her sectioned?'

'Not Margaret! The next step with your dating!'

'I've no idea. What do people do nowadays? Do I go to a hotel bar and chat someone up?'

'Ew, no! Dad, you are a theatre manager, you are not James Bond. Or a gigantic creep.'

'What then? Where do adults meet other adults in a small market town?'

'Well, I don't know either, to be honest, but we'll figure it out . . . Also, I may have mentioned this to Sally.'

'Hannah!'

'She knows a lot of women!'

'None of the others know, do they? Oh god, you haven't said anything to Margaret?'

'No! Dad! I'm not completely insane!'

'Good, right, I suspected as much, but good to have it confirmed.'

I get up out of the creaky theatre chair and put my hand on his shoulder.

'We can do this,' I say.

And I walk out of the auditorium with a sense of purpose and determination, like Jane Austen's Emma, or better still, Alicia Silverstone in *Clueless*. Something is going to go right, I think to myself. Something has to go right.

Tom

A month after that fateful trip to the GP, the one where our misanthropic doctor first diagnosed Hannah's heart murmur, I sat in a small hospital treatment room with an elderly cardiologist. Via quiet tones and serious expressions, he told me she had cardiomyopathy, and that the thickening of the heart wall might make it difficult for the organ to pump blood around her body. I nodded obediently, my eyes flicking to the door. Hannah was visible in snatched moments through the glass panel, playing with a nurse. He said that people with the disease often had no symptoms and lived in blissful ignorance, but Hannah's condition was a little more serious. I didn't understand what he was trying to tell me; I didn't understand anything until I heard the phrase 'potentially life-limiting'. Even then, his voice was so soft, his words so careful, I did not quite pick up on the meaning. I nodded again.

I didn't ask, 'How long?' The two words that form the basis of every tragic Hollywood prognosis scene did not occur to me in that moment – they came much later. I forgot my lines for a second or two.

Afterwards, I stumbled out into the gentle bustle of the ward, clasping a prescription for beta blockers and a leaflet with a heart symbol on the front. This symbol used to mean love, I thought. When Hannah saw me, she ran up and I lifted her into my arms and held her.

'Can we go?' she said. 'Can we have ice cream now?'

'Yes, whatever you want,' I said.

'Let me down, you're hurting me.'

'Sorry, Hannah,' I said, lowering her to the floor. 'I'm so sorry.'

'You big ploppy. Let's go.' She ran for the double doors.

'Wait for me, you little creep,' I cried, running after her, my arms outstretched.

She laughed, and so did I. I was already lying to her.

I roused with a start when I heard the front door open and then slam shut. I was lying on the sofa in our living room, surrounded by piles of yellowing papers. On the floor were two large boxes stuffed with various files and folders from the theatre. Ted had told me I should start looking for official council documents, anything that laid out how the theatre was owned and operated. I'd spent the whole day going through them, hoping I'd find some crucial binding agreement from the 1970s ensuring the theatre would be supported in perpetuity, regardless of any lucrative property development deals that might present themselves in the next forty years. So far I'd discovered a lot of utility bills; some old programmes; a ten-year contract with a pest control company; all the correspondence from a bitter 1986 dispute with a touring satirical puppet group; a letter from *Blue Peter* congratulating the previous manager on a successful bring and buy sale; and hundreds of old bank statements, now covered in mildew and hopelessly faded. The only correspondence from the council related to annual accounts and a couple of contracts to have refurbishments completed – nothing that said, oh, by the way, we promise we won't knock the building down.

In burst Hannah and Sally. They were carrying a huge takeaway pizza box and two bottles of red wine. I had the strange feeling the course of my night was about to be radically altered.

'Right,' said Sally setting down the pizza on the small dining-room table, 'where's your laptop?'

'Why? What's going on?'

'We've been doing research,' said Hannah, looking around for my computer. 'We have decided on the best dating site and we're going to help you get set up.'

'Why does this sound like a threat?' I asked.

Sally opened one of the bottles and haphazardly glugged wine into three glasses, handing the smallest to Hannah.

'Don't worry,' she said. 'We're professionals.'

Hannah found the laptop on the sideboard and placed it on the table next to the pizza, pulling out a chair for me and lining up another two beside it. Everything was happening at turbo speed, as though they only had five minutes to set up a dating profile or the universe would explode.

'Seriously, what's got into you two?' I said.

'We've been at the café *planning*,' said Hannah. 'We're very motivated and we've got a lot of ideas. So let's get the ball rolling. Sit down here, it won't take long.'

'Oh god,' I said. 'Do we have to do this now? I'm doing important theatre work here.'

'That can wait,' complained Hannah, dragging me off the sofa.

I thought back to the other day, the conversations we'd had. It wouldn't be too much of a chore to play along – and it was unlikely to lead anywhere anyway. Besides, there was clearly no fighting against this tornado of romantic intrusion. I sat down at the table in front of the laptop. Hannah was already typing something into Google. A dating site homepage popped up on screen. It showed a photo of a man and a woman walking along a woodland path holding hands. Ten out of ten for originality.

'Perfect Connection dot com?' I groaned. 'Is this about dating or improving your golf swing?'

'You see?' said Hannah. 'This is exactly why we have to be here to manage your profile.'

'No pathetic dad jokes,' said Sally.

'He *is* a pathetic dad joke,' said Hannah.

They actually high-fived over my head. Oh well, things can't get any worse, I thought. And then Sally went over to the CD player and put on the *Dirty Dancing* soundtrack.

We had to enter my basic details and then upload a variety of photos, 'to show off different aspects of your character'. Hannah wouldn't let me use the photo of me dressed as Widow Twankey from our production of *Aladdin* three years ago, or the shot of me posing with an eight-foot python (star of *The Really Scary Wildlife Show* which we put on in the spring and almost lost a tarantula down a hole on the stage). Instead, she and Sally selected some comparatively normal pictures, including one that Hannah had sneakily taken of me sitting in the Bristol Library café reading *Gravity's Rainbow*, which I thought crossed the line from 'arty intellectual' into 'gigantic pretentious wanker', but she was adamant.

Next were a whole bunch of personal questions. What did I do for fun? Where in the world would I like to visit? What would my ideal date involve? It was a whirlwind of things I hadn't thought about in years. What do I do for fun? Well, I mess about with an amateur dramatics group and do stupid dressing-up stunts with my daughter. Does anyone look for that in a potential partner?

'Just put down that you enjoy visiting theatres, theatrical museums and homes of famous playwrights,' suggested Hannah.

'But won't that make me seem like an unbearable luvvy?' I asked.

'In what way is this inaccurate?' said Sally.

I typed, 'Visiting theatres, galleries and museums. Going to gigs.' I added the last bit to make it clear I was not seventy-five.

'Dad, what was the last gig you went to?'

'Um, well who was that blues tribute act we had at the theatre a couple of weeks ago?'

'Faux Diddley?'

'There you go.'

Hannah let it pass.

'Hmmm, ideal date, ideal date,' repeated Sally. 'Let me guess . . .'

She swivelled in her chair and looked at me for several seconds, her brown-black eyes staring unsettlingly into mine. Some of her hair had come loose from her ponytail, and it cupped her face. Her mouth was screwed into a pout of serious contemplation. For some reason, I wanted her to get this right.

'Don't look,' she said. 'I'll type this in.'

'You're not going to put something ridiculous down, are you?'

'No! Trust me!'

She leaned over me, so close I could smell the soap on her skin, and typed furiously into the text box before hitting return, so that the next page loaded. She smiled at Hannah and then looked back at the screen.

'Come on, what's next?' she said.

Next was a seemingly endless list of personal details. Body type ('knackered' said Hannah), marital status ('knackered' said Sally), best feature ('me,' said Hannah). They were amusing themselves at my expense, but I played along. Then we came to the question about children.

'Put down, "One daughter, brackets, temporary, close brackets",' said Hannah.

'Hannah,' I said.

'What? I'm allowed to make jokes about it.'

The intrusion of this unimaginable reality echoed around the room, silencing us for a moment, pushing everything else out. Hannah finished her wine, and glared at us.

Sally put her hand on my shoulder. 'Come on,' she said. 'We're almost there.'

After another eighty pages of questions, the site finally asked for a personal statement that would go at the top of my profile, something that symbolised me as a potential romantic partner. The suggestions from Hannah and Sally were as follows:

'Surely better than nothing.'

'A poor woman's David Duchovny.'

'A blind woman's David Duchovny.'

'The wacky English teacher you had a crush on at school.'

We decided to skip that one and upload it later. Sally looked at her watch and groaned.

'Phil will be home soon, I'd better get back.'

She took her wine glass out to the kitchen, and Hannah followed. I could hear a murmured conversation that I was clearly not meant to be part of.

Sally emerged from the kitchen, her arms outstretched for a hug.

'Now we play the waiting game,' she said.

'I'm certain the in-box will be crammed by the morning,' I replied. 'I'll have to employ a PA to go through them all. Maybe Ted can do me a spreadsheet?'

'Whatever you say, Romeo.'

After she left, and while Hannah was occupied in the kitchen, I looked back at the profile, scrolling to the section Sally filled in about my perfect date. I paused for a second, unsure if it was somehow an invasion of privacy to read it, until I remembered it was actually about me.

Sally had written, 'A drowsy afternoon in an old country pub, reading newspapers together, sharing the colour supplement, reading out loud from our favourite stories. Then the theatre, followed by coffee and a chat. Talking and laughing and seeing something that makes us think a little.'

Shit, I thought. She nailed it.

Hannah

So this is awkward.

I'm hanging out in our local comic shop, which doubles as a second-hand vinyl record store, making it the most loser-friendly place in town. By 'hanging out', I mean I am lounging in a battered armchair in a corner of the small, cluttered room reading comic books that I can't afford. The owners, Ricky and Dav, never seem to mind. When this place opened three years ago, it was the most exciting new store in town since Superdrug arrived. I knew almost nothing about comics beyond the Marvel and DC stuff Dad was buying for me, so I was totally thrilled. I thought I'd walk in and find *The Simpsons'* Comic Book Guy behind the counter, judging everyone and being gross. But Ricky and Dav aren't like that at all. They say hello to everyone, give good recommendations and don't care if someone walks in and just wants the latest Superman. They fell in love while working at one of the vast comic book megastores in London and decided to get the hell out and set up on their own. Ricky is an old rocker with a love of weird independent comics; Dav is a goth who wears ornate black lace tops and knee-length Dr Marten boots, but weirdly adores shojo manga, the super-cute, bright pink Japanese comics for girls. While her husband was trying to indoctrinate me with Art Spiegelman and Daniel Clowes, she got me reading *Cardcaptor Sakura*, *Sailor Moon* and *Fruits Basket* – all these beautiful magical girls who look sweet and innocent but have tons of drama, power and emotion in their lives. Wow, I wonder why *that* appealed to me. So yeah, Ricky and Dav compete over my comic book education, like I'm their special Padawan or something. I don't know why. Maybe it's because not many girls come in – although I have managed to indoctrinate Jenna now. They don't complain when we sit down and read the whole of V *For Vendetta* or *Hopeless Savages* or Y: *The Last Man* for the seventeenth time before placing each volume carefully back on the shelf five hours later.

Today, Ricky is serving alone, in his Halo Jones T-shirt and battered biker jacket. A few minutes after I arrive, he saunters past with a handful of graphic novels, and high-fives me on the way.

'Hey Hannah. What have you selected from our lending library today?'

I hold the comic up. I am reading back issues of *Black Hole*, the weird Charles Burns series about a sexual disease that turns all the horny teenagers in a small American town into mutants. I think it's metaphorical.

'Huh, good choice,' he says.

'I might even buy it.'

'Urghhh no, the shock! The shock would kill me!'

He clasps at his chest and pretends to collapse. I could be really cruel and tell him that – ha ha – I have a potentially fatal heart condition. But I figure I'll save that one, and just scowl at him instead. He staggers off to put his new books on display, then slopes back behind the counter. In the background, a couple of older guys are perusing the shelves where the new comics are displayed, quietly adding copies to the large piles lodged under their arms. Ricky puts *Scary Monsters* by David Bowie on the sound system and they both nod approvingly. He knows how to make geeky men stay put and spend.

I hear the door opening and closing, and see the shape of a thin figure shuffling in. Ricky shouts 'Hey there' over the noise of 'Ashes to Ashes', but there's no vocal response from the new customer, just a wave of a hand. I think, wow, that's rude, and look up. Oh shit, it's Callum. It's *Callum*. He's wearing a long grey raincoat over a white T-shirt and these gigantic army boots – he looks like he's strolled out of a cyberpunk anime or an eighties movie about rebel teenagers. For some reason my face starts tingling and my stomach suddenly swirls like it's on a spin cycle. The comic book almost drops from my hands, which now seem to be numb and clammy.

No.

Shut up, body.

I do not fancy Callum. He's just that annoying guy in my English class. Shut *up*.

And yet my eyes are disobediently glued to him as he wanders across the shop floor and towards the new comics display. I want to look away, but I can't. Because of course, now I need to know what he's going to browse. If it's *Spider-Man*, he's basically a child, if it's *Daredevil* he's a masochist. I catch myself thinking, go on, pick up *Batman*, that way I can immediately dismiss you as a wanker. But he doesn't. He picks up *Young Avengers*. Ah, you son of a bitch. This series has only been going a couple of months and it already rules. Cool teenagers coming to terms with their abilities, fighting and falling in love. It's genius. He flicks through the pages with mild interest. I try to concentrate on *Black Hole* ... but this only serves to remind me that the cover shows a semi-naked girl being menaced by a giant snake. I am literally ten feet away from this boy and I have a Freudian sex image on my lap. When I glance up again, Callum is standing at the counter handing over *Young Avengers*. He is also looking at me.

Looking right at me.

He smiles – a muted half-smile, a sort of smirk but without any of the implied cruelty. His long fringe flops over his eyes, like a shutter coming down – too soon to see me smiling back.

'Good choice,' says Ricky. 'It's a great run. Allan Heinberg is a brilliant writer.'

'Thanks,' says Callum. He walks away from the counter. I'm not looking; I'm reading my book. I hear him stop and pause. I'm not looking. His footsteps come towards me. I'm not looking. I'm reading.

'Hey,' he says sheepishly. 'You're Hannah, aren't you?'

I look up. His eyes are jade green and he has impossibly long lashes. His face is angular and kind of solemn, but also sweet. His hair is so dark I wonder if he dyes it.

'Um yes, I am. You're Callum.' I say the last part as though I'm helpfully telling him who he is. I don't know why that happened. I don't know what I'm doing. 'Do you come in here often?' I say. Oh for fuck's sake. He smiles.

'Not very often,' he says. 'They deliver, so I just pop by when I want something new. This is supposed to be good, right?'

He holds up *Young Avengers*. I nod, trying not to look impressed. 'It's tolerable.'

'Is *that* good?' he asks, pointing at my lap.

Oh god. I look down. Yep, there it is – girl in bra with snake.

'Yeah, it's kinda strange. I'm sort of getting into independent comics – you know, *Ghost World*, *Love and Rockets*, *Hicksville*. I don't know much but I'm trying to learn. I like manga too. Some manga.'

Why am I telling him this? He looks at his comic and shrugs.

'I guess I'm a bit mainstream,' he says. 'Isn't manga just kids with big eyes doing martial arts?'

I smile at him.

'Isn't Marvel just men with big muscles punching each other?' I ask.

'Touché,' he grins. 'You're not into superheroes then?'

'I totally am! The first comic I ever read was *Justice League*. I loved *X-Men*. *Sensational She-Hulk* was fun, that whole breaking-the-fourth-wall shtick. I like what Greg Rucka is doing with Wonder Woman now. I'm not really into, you know, giant muscly fascists. What about you – apart from *Young Avengers*?'

'Oh, I'm a total *Iron Man* nut.'

I try to hide my disappointment.

'I'm joking,' says Callum. 'He's awful. He's a giant muscly fascist.'

'Tony Stark is such a prick.'

Pause.

'Do you want to look at this?' I ask.

I try to hand him an issue of *Black Hole* and it falls open on a page that shows a boy having sex with a girl who has a tail. He reddens and jerks backwards as though I'm offering him a bin bag full of used nappies.

'I . . . maybe another time. I should go.'

He looks visibly shaken. I have terrified him with my sex comic.

'Of course,' I say, withdrawing the book. 'See you soon.'

'I hope so,' he says.

'I hope so,' I repeat tonelessly, as though I'm some sort of robot parrot. 'I mean, I hope so too. That's what I meant. Another time. I'm going to stay here for a while. I'm reading comics.'

Why can't I just black out now? Seriously. Why can't I just wake up in A&E with no memory of the preceding hour? It would be a merciful release.

He backs away for a few steps nodding at me before turning slowly toward the door. Just before he goes, he does something cool: he rolls the *Young Avengers* comic up and he puts it in his back pocket. That is a good sign, I think, through the veil of shame and embarrassment – it means he's not some prissy collector who cries if his precious booky-wook gets a crease in the cover. He just wants to read the thing. Then he's through the door and down the street. I sit staring after him for several seconds and when I finally come to my senses I realise I am fanning myself with a comic.

You see what I mean. AWKWARD. The whole interaction was a total fail. But the thing that *really* bothers me is why do I even care? I'm too busy for this shit.

I look over at Ricky, who is watching me with a broad grin across his face. He doesn't say anything, but instead makes the okay sign with his thumb and finger, while nodding slowly in mock approval. I jerk the comic back like I'm going to throw it at him and he theatrically ducks behind the counter.

I'm just about to go back to reading – or at least pretending to read – when my phone buzzes. It's a text from Sally.

I think I have a date for your dad x

I immediately get up and punch her number into the keypad, walking quickly towards the door so I don't have to discuss this in the shop. Sally answers as I get outside.

'Tell me you're not joking,' I say.

'I'm not joking.'

'How? Where did you find her? What is wrong with her?'

'Nothing! She's in my book group. Her name is Karen and she split up with her husband last year – it's all very sad. But she's ready to get back out there. I got her a bit tipsy and sold her your dad. Not literally.'

'What's she like?'

'Perfect. Really pretty, funny, clever as fuck. He'll like her.'

'Holy shit. What do we do now?'

'Well, let me talk to him. Sound him out. We've just got to keep it casual. They're both pretty vulnerable. We have to be careful.'

'It's like when they try to get pandas to shag.'

'Yes, Hannah. It's exactly like that.'

'Wow, this is such a weird day.'

'Why, what else has happened?'

I suddenly get a hold of myself: this is Jay's mum I'm talking to. I'm not ready for him to know about this whole Callum thing. Not that there is a thing. But. Whatever.

'Oh nothing,' I say. 'Just stuff. Friend stuff.'

'Right. Well, don't say anything just yet. I'll double-check with Karen. You just act normal. As normal as you can.'

'Thanks, Sal.'

She hangs up and I jam the phone into the back pocket of my jeans. I could go back in the shop and read, but now I feel strangely motivated and energetic – a very weird and unfamiliar sensation these days. I get an image in my head, a momentary snapshot. A boy in a long coat, quiet and cool and aloof. His dark hair falls over his eyes. Those lashes, though. Those lashes. I realise I am smiling. I'm smiling so much my cheeks are starting to ache.

Oh FFS. Nothing can happen with Callum – I don't need the hassle. Maybe I'll call Jenna or Daisy and go somewhere, do something. Maybe I'll call my dad. I need to get Callum out of my head. Seriously. Nothing can happen with Callum.

Tom

And so there I was at our local, *slightly* upmarket Italian restaurant on a Wednesday evening, sitting alone at the small bar, drinking a gin and tonic. Waiting. Somehow, I'd managed to get myself into a date with Sally's friend, and now, I just had to grit my teeth, and see it out. It all seemed like a good idea until I actually arrived – just like that time I went to see a five-hour production of *King Lear* set in a 1960s laundromat.

It wasn't exactly a busy evening at La Casa di Buon Appetito. A group of middle-aged men took up a large table in the centre of the room, laughing boisterously, their chubby faces as red as the wine they were thirstily working their way through. An extremely elderly couple were perched in the corner, saying nothing to each other, quietly scooping food into their quivering mouths. An Italian-looking guy in a vintage suit sat alone near the door to the toilets, reading a newspaper as he plucked at a pizza. I imagined that he was a mafia hitman, waiting for his victim to use the gents so he could follow close behind and garrotte him next to the hand dryer. Then I wondered if I was being mildly racist. I checked my phone to see if there was an apologetic text from Karen to say she couldn't make it; but no, just a message from Hannah: 'Don't be a massive embarrassment. Love, H.'

I thought about playing Snake on my phone so that I could look casual and disinterested rather than desperate, but then the main door opened and a woman walked in alone. She was tall, dark blonde hair, very red lipstick; her white dress was patterned with small red flowers. Oh god, I was expecting jeans and a plaid shirt. I was not expecting intimidatingly glamorous. I was already out of my depth and I was still in the shallow end. She looked around the room, then her eyes fell on me and there was a moment of guarded recognition – I was, after all, the only person in there who could possibly be the other half in a blind date scenario – apart from the hitman, who was eyeing the woman up in a furtive manner. I smiled and waved. At the woman. Not the hitman.

'Are you Tom?' she said in a loud confident voice, swooping past the middle-aged guys, who all watched as she went by.

'Yes! Yes, I'm Tom. You're Karen? Sally's friend?'

'Yes! Phew. I've got the right restaurant and the right man, this is going well.'

My brain was rapidly trying to make deductions. She was clearly attractive, clearly intelligent, confident, maybe early forties, difficult to tell. Her eyes sparkled in the dull light from the weird cheap chandeliers. She referred to me as 'the right man', but it was clearly meant in the context of 'correct man in roomful of strangers' rather than 'the man I want to spend the rest of my life with'. Before I could ask if she wanted a drink, a waiter was upon us, seemingly out of nowhere.

'Are sir and madam ready to be seated?' he asked, grinning at us in an unsettlingly suggestive way. Did he know we were on a blind date? Was it that obvious? He walked us to a table near the window, and handed us menus, maintaining the same slightly crooked smile throughout.

'A drink for madam?' he said in a voice, accent and manner that reminded me of the Count from *Sesame Street*. This was probably racist too and I decided not to share the observation.

'Are we having wine?' she asked.

Uh-oh, the wine conversation. What's the etiquette? Let her choose? Insist on identifying a wine that exactly accompanies our food? What if we don't know what we're eating? What are people drinking these days? Are New World wines still fashionable?

All this time she was perusing the drinks menu.

'We could have wine,' I said brightly. 'I'm easy.' Oh shit. I said I'm easy on a first date.

'Let's have a bottle of the Italian white,' she said, handing the menu back to the waiter. 'It's too warm for red, don't you think?'

'Yes, definitely,' I said.

A moment of silence. I took a tiny sip from the gin and tonic. And then another sip. And then another. Oh no, I looked like a thirsty alcoholic budgerigar.

'So,' she said, at last. 'You run the theatre?'

'Yes,' my voice contained a little too much relief. 'I've been running it for almost a decade. Have you been to any shows?'

'A couple. We tended to go into London for the theatre, make a weekend of it. My husband was a bit of a snob. Sorry, not that there's anything wrong with local theatre, it's just . . . oh god, sorry.'

'No it's fine. I understand. I bet the Royal Court Theatre isn't running a comic tribute to Perry Como next month.' (We were, of course. It was called *Perry Comb-over*.)

'No. More's the pity.'

'So what do you do? Sally didn't say.'

The waiter was suddenly back, pouring our wine and hovering over Karen's shoulder with his notebook out. At least the quick service meant this would all be over very soon.

'Are you ready to order?' he asked, looking at the two untouched menus on the table.

'Not quite,' said Karen smiling conspiratorially at me.

We picked up the glossily laminated cards and studied them. I mustn't automatically go for the pizza, I thought. I must show my class and discretion and have something else, something more mature that reflects my understanding and appreciation of Italian cuisine.

'I always have the pizza,' said Karen. 'I can't help it.'

I smiled at her, feeling suddenly more relaxed, calmer. For the first time I thought this might actually be a bearable experience, rather than a nightmarish social experiment. We both ordered the napoletana. We were practically soulmates. The waiter nodded with satisfaction, then disappeared.

'So yes, you asked what I do. I manage a photography studio – we do family portraits, weddings, that sort of thing. You know those photos you see on people's mantelpieces, the really over-exposed ones with children in fancy dress climbing all over their parents, and everyone is smiling manically against a completely white background? We do those.'

'Ah. Is that fun?'

'Not really, it's not what I had in mind when I went to art school to study photography, but, you know, that's life isn't it?'

'I guess so. I thought I'd be the next Kenneth Branagh.' Uh-oh, nose-diving mood. 'So, what's the book you're reading at the moment? With the book group?'

'Oh,' she says. 'We're reading *Couples* by John Updike. I have no idea why. Miserable book.'

'I've not read it.'

'Don't. Seriously, don't. It's a very nihilistic study of wealthy baby boomers swapping partners and just generally being awful. I wanted to do *Cloud Atlas* but Sophie got her way as usual.'

'I love *Cloud Atlas*! It's the most amazing thing I've read in years.'

'I haven't read it. I want to.'

'I can lend you my copy.'

Was that too forward? The insinuation was that we'd meet again. Maybe she'd read that as too presumptuous, before we'd even been served the main course. I told myself it doesn't matter, it doesn't matter because I didn't want this anyway, did I?

'I'm reading a lot more now that I'm alone,' she said, before absent-mindedly glancing at her phone screen. 'Sorry, just checking the babysitter hasn't texted.'

'Ah, how old are your kids?'

'Just one, Betty. She's six.'

'That's a great name.'

'My husband chose it – after *Betty Blue*. That was probably a bad sign, come to think of it. He was bloody obsessed with Béatrice Dalle. Sorry, I've got to stop mentioning him.'

'No, it's fine, I . . .'

Before I could complete the sentence, a pizza was spun onto the table in front of me, and another at Karen. They were enormous, flapping over the edges of the plates and oozing dollops of cheese onto the tablecloth. We both stared at them in amazement.

'*Buon appetito!*' sang the waiter before rushing away towards the table full of men.

We both gingerly picked up our knives and forks, wondering how to tackle the monstrous discs of molten cheese before us. She looked at her phone again, then clearly annoyed at herself, put it into the bag that she had dropped by her feet when we sat down. The old couple shuffled past us to the door, smiling benignly. The waiter waved them out. I noticed that the mafia hitman had disappeared. It was now just us and the wine-swilling middle managers.

We started to eat, both desperate to ensure we didn't end

up with long ropes of hot, greasy mozzarella hanging from our mouths like cartoon drool. I thought of what to ask: something not too personal, but not boring. I'd forgotten all the acceptable topics that Sally and Hannah had fed me. Should I mention the war in Iraq or steer well clear? Should I do some theatrical anecdotes? I was on my own in the deadly and unfamiliar arena of romance, and now I . . . and now I had pizza down my shirt. I dabbed at it with the napkin and shrugged at Karen, who was looking down at her plate, her face furrowed in concentration.

'This is, um, this is nice,' I said, feeling things starting to unravel. 'I mean, I haven't done it in a while. Dating I mean. Not "it". Although I haven't done "it" for ages either. Oh god.'

I was on a first date with a complete stranger, and I'd accidentally alluded to sex. I took a long swig of my wine, while I thought of something not psychotic to say, but it took longer than I expected and I realised I'd downed the whole glass. Could things get any worse? She looked up at me and I saw that her eyes were hazy. Oh, yes. Yes, they could. She was now crying.

'I'm sorry, I'm so sorry. It's not you, it's me.'

'Shall I get you some water?'

'No, it's fine. It's just . . . oh shit. My husband and I, we came here on our tenth wedding anniversary last year. And . . . Oh I thought I could do this but . . .'

She put her knife and fork down and I watched her uselessly as she dabbed at her eyes with a tissue.

'He left six months ago, completely out of the blue. An affair of course. Of course it was. Some cow at work. I'm sorry, you don't want to hear this.'

'I do, it's fine, I know. I know what it's like.'

And I did. Kind of. In a way.

'Ten years. And he was just gone. He shouted at me. Can you

believe that? When he told me, he was cross with me; cross that it had happened. My mum came and stayed that night. We all slept together, her, Betty and me, in the bed she and Dad had bought us for a wedding present.'

She broke off. I concentrated on cutting a slice out of my pizza, but suddenly she was sobbing loudly and helplessly, her whole body shaking. The waiter had been on his way over to check on us, but now he did a volte-face so sudden he probably left scorch marks on the wooden floor. The businessmen were glancing over and whispering. I stared at her, a dumb, blank look on my face, not knowing what to say or do. I didn't know whether to leap up and hug her, or leave her there, or what?

Very quickly the matter was resolved. She stood, snatched up her bag, appeared to hesitate for a second, but then made her decision.

'I'm sorry, I must go. It's nothing to do ... it's just too soon, I think.'

'It's fine, it's fine, honestly.' I got up too, but for some reason I didn't let go of my pizza slice, and because I hadn't cut it properly, the rest of the pizza followed – it started to fall back onto my plate but I instinctively caught it. She mumbled an apology, spun round and her bag knocked her full wine glass onto the floor with a tinkling crash. Then she was away towards the door and out, launching into the evening. I stood there watching, aware of the fact that I was standing in a pool of wine, with a pizza folded over my arm like a hand towel. There was silence around me; the jocular men were all agog, little smiles edging across their faces – a tale for the office tomorrow. The waiter was there with a cloth almost immediately, kneading it into the polished oak flooring.

'I'm so sorry,' I said. 'I'll pay, obviously ... '

'Shhh,' he said. And he glanced up, a genuine look of sympathy on his face. 'Is fine. No problem. Nothing to pay for.'

I leaned over to offer some assistance – at this point, a handful of the pizza topping slid off onto his head.

It could have been worse, I thought as I left, minutes later, carefully shutting the door behind me and striding out, really rather quickly, into the still warm night. She could have murdered me, or the waiter; or a truck could have crashed in through the wall and killed us all.

On the walk home, my phone buzzed. I wondered if it would be Karen with one final apology, but it was a message from Hannah. 'How's it going? Do I need to rescue you? Remember, no theatrical anecdotes.' Fat chance, I thought.

I felt sorry for Karen, of course I did. I recognised the rawness of her emotion. But what I most felt was relief. Now I could tell Hannah this whole dating idea was a mistake.

I set about constructing a narrative of the evening, something that would emphasise its disastrous nature without making Karen an object of ridicule. I was already thinking of it in dramatic terms. I was already directing the play.

Hannah

'So apparently, Dad's date fled the restaurant crying – this was about ten minutes into the evening. So yeah, everything is going exactly to plan.'

I'm sitting with Margaret in a little café called Crumpets, explaining Dad's spectacular romantic success. It's a place I only come to with her, because it's totally old school and traditional: china cups and saucers, three-tier cake stands, lace doilies, teenage waiting staff dressed up like French maids, that sort of thing. We meet here every other week – I can't remember how or why it started. I guess she always treated me like an adult, and I always wanted to know how many of her theatrical anecdotes from the sixties and seventies were actually true. But it's difficult to get anything out of her about her past, beyond that repertoire of astonishing stories, so we usually end up gossiping about the drama group, about the town, the school, the news, boys, the inevitability of death. I think she likes me because we share the same fatalistic attitude. It's weird, but when we talk about life and more specifically its unavoidable conclusion, we do it as equals – we don't bother to reassure each other. No one else in my life does that – they feel they have to protect me from any mention of death. Or more accurately, protect themselves.

'I can't imagine what your poor father did,' says Margaret, spooning a great dollop of jam onto her scone (we always have the cream tea). 'He's so charming.'

'God, I hope he didn't perform a soliloquy or something, I wouldn't put that past him.'

'What did he say about it?'

'Not much. He told an elaborate story about dropping a pizza on the waiter's head, and then insisted on changing the subject.'

'Will this be the end of your experiment?'

'Are you joking? I'm not giving up that easily.'

We pause to stuff scones into our faces.

'When I met my husband, we were at a dance organised by his church group. I'd gatecrashed it, hoping for booze, and found him instead. I had to do all the chasing. Men are like cattle – essentially stupid, but useful and they have nice eyes.'

'Why don't you ever talk about him?'

'Oh, there isn't much to say, darling. Just another long marriage with highs and lows. Not a thrilling narrative. He was a simple man, happy to stand in the background. He didn't mind me disappearing on tour for weeks. He kept the house and garden tidy and cooked for me. He smelled of cigar smoke and bay rum cologne. Other details are fading, my dear. Everything is fading.'

She looks down at her plate, then out of the window. Something glistens in her eyes. Though they are sunken in their wrinkled sockets, they glow like jewels.

'I'm just extremely old, that's the thing. I wonder how long I will be useful at the theatre. I'm afraid I have started to make mistakes.'

It's true that Sally has begun to find Margaret smaller roles with less line-learning. The cast watch her more carefully. She had fallen badly during a rehearsal of *The Importance of Being Earnest* last summer, and that had spooked some of them. She saw it in their eyes – that fear of mortal weakness; I knew it because I saw it in others too.

'If it comes to it, we'll just put you in a bath chair and wheel you around the stage,' I say.

She lets out a loud cackle. 'I would be excellent at playing a dying patriarch. I have the bearing for it. That's how I'd like to go: on stage, delivering Prospero's final speech from *The Tempest*, then just slipping away.'

'That would be very *you*, Margaret.'

'It would, darling. But I doubt it will play out that way.'

'Let me see what I can do. My dad runs a theatre, you know.'

'I'll remember that.' She pauses for a second. 'But they may not let me back.'

'What do you mean?'

'I have a confession to make. On the afternoon of the play, I was so cold in the theatre, do you remember? Well, I went to the boiler room and it clearly wasn't working. So I just started swirling all the dials and pressing the buttons. That's how I used to get my television set working. Later on, I walked past and heard a terrible banging noise coming from inside; I was too afraid to investigate. I thought it might be exploding. Oh darling, I should have told your father.'

'Margaret, I don't think you caused the flood by twirling a few dials.'

OMG, I think to myself, Margaret caused the flood by twirling a few dials.

'Anyway,' she continues. 'The strange thing is, as I walked away, I heard the boiler room door open and close behind me. I wondered if someone else was in there, and ...'

My phone buzzes into life on the table. The interruption seems to break Margaret's train of thought.

'Oh, I'm just being silly, don't worry. You check your correspondence, I know how important it is for the youngsters to stay in touch.'

'But Margaret . . .'

'It's nothing, honestly. I probably imagined it.'

She levers herself up off the chair. I go to help her, but she waves me away. 'No, no, I can manage,' she says. 'I'll just use the bathroom.'

She shuffles away, and I watch, confused, trying to imagine what on earth she was about to tell me. Perhaps she's regretting her confession; perhaps she's now concocting some kind of bizarre alibi involving a 1960s TV celebrity. Or maybe she really is losing it. Then the phone buzzes again. There are two messages from Daisy:

Where r u? Got news m8

indie night at Duke's on Friday. We hv 2 go. Will be awful. Daze x

Duke's is our only nightclub, situated on the first floor of a Tudor pub on the high street. Usually it is a nightmarish no-go zone of chart dance and two-for-one cocktails called things like 'Shagged To Death', but occasionally they put on a special event. I never go, but Daisy always asks. She likes me to feel included. I'm typing out a standard 'thanks but no thanks' message, when Margaret returns.

'Is it a boy,' she asks, sliding heavily back into her chair.

'Ugh, no. It's Daisy. She's trying to get me to go to a nightclub.'

'And?'

'And I never go. It's too hot and noisy and I don't drink, and . . .'

'You're worried that you may fall ill?'

141

'Maybe. I don't know. It's like, all those people having a good time, they can just forget themselves ... I never feel a part of it.'

'At least your plastic hip wouldn't give out on the dance floor, dear. Count yourself lucky.'

'There is that.'

Her expression changes. It's like she's drifting in and out of the room – or even time itself.

'I've forgotten the old dance moves,' she says, mostly to herself. 'I used to know them all. It feels like a plug has been pulled out, everything is swirling away.'

'Margaret ...'

'Oh it's fine. I'm fine. We're not quite of this world are we, me and you? We can stand back and see it for what it is.'

'Like comic-book superheroes.'

I giggle at this, but she looks at me sternly.

'Hannah, your dad can look after himself. You know that don't you?'

'I hope so.'

She puts her hand over mine.

'Child, you know so much, but you don't believe anything. Life is extraordinary. It carries on.'

'Margaret.'

'Yes dear?'

'Are you going to eat the rest of that scone? Because I'm bloody starving.'

'You're incorrigible.'

'Is that a no?'

'Take it,' she says. 'I must go now anyway. Doctor's appointment. I spend more time there than at home these days. Such a bore. And to think, I used to look forward to handsome young men asking me to lie down and make myself comfortable.'

'Holy shit, Margaret.'

She's up once again, faster this time and smiling now. The waitresses shimmy by her as though she's partially invisible, as though they could pass straight through her. She grips her handbag tightly to her chest; her thin fingers almost skeletal; there are sparkles on the walls from her enormous sapphire engagement ring. I have coveted that thing since I was little. For some reason I think of Callum and what may have passed between us at the comic shop. Was it utter embarrassment or chemistry? Will he be at Duke's? I get a momentary ripple of excitement at the idea. I'm not prepared for a feeling like that.

'Go to the club,' says Margaret, seemingly picking up on my thoughts. 'Fortune sides with she who dares.'

Outside, the sun beats down, the pavements are hot and cracked, the streets buzz with shoppers. I try to imagine what Dad said to that poor woman. I don't think he would have upset her on purpose; he's no Valmont, he's too dumb to be cruel.

How will he survive?

Hannah

The next morning, Dad is furiously packing for WestFest. He's hired a minibus to get the cast to the showground, and it's parked outside the house. He is in a full-on organisational tizzy. I am in my bedroom reading and trying to ignore all the noise, but then he pokes his head in round my door.

'Do you know where my tartan trousers are?' he says. 'They seem to be missing.'

'They're hanging up. In the Oxfam shop in town.'

'What?!'

'Dad, come on, tartan trousers? You looked like a bad Rod Stewart tribute act.'

'Funny story – they were actually given to me by a bad Rod Stewart tribute act.'

'Whatever, they looked ridiculous. You might as well have worn them with a T-shirt that said, "Don't mind me, I'm having a mid-life crisis."'

'You'd have taken that to Oxfam too.'

He hugs me, and then rushes off with a crumpled 'to do' list clasped in his hand. I follow him, keen to see if I can trick any more details of the date out of him while he's distracted.

'So,' I say. 'Are you ready to talk about what happened on Wednesday night?'

'Oh Hannah, I'm really busy,' he says, his head buried in the wardrobe. He is throwing clothes into a battered holdall – it looks like he's fleeing from the mafia. 'We just weren't compatible.'

'There's no chance you could be – oh I don't know – intentionally sabotaging things?'

'That is an outrageous slur,' he says. 'Are you sure you can cope alone for two days? We'll be back Sunday lunchtime. I'll keep my phone on. If you need me I'll be straight home.'

'I'll be fine.'

'Are you completely sure? You look tired.'

To be honest, I still feel a little wiped out after the whole staircase of doom incident. But I don't want him to worry and cancel the whole thing. Living with an overprotective parent means constantly reassuring them that you're taking it easy without making them freak out over how easy you need to take it. It's a constant emotional knife-edge.

'Dad, get out.'

'Jeff and Brenda know you're here alone. They're going to pop over tomorrow to check on you.'

Jeff and Brenda are our sweet old neighbours who Dad has kept on high alert ever since I was diagnosed. If I'm due to be home alone for more than a few hours, he warns them. They don't seem to mind – in fact Jeff did a CPR training course just in case he was ever called into action. He's a bit doddery though, and also profoundly deaf, so I expect I'd be long gone before he realised anything was wrong and roused himself into superhero mode.

'Oh bugger!' I say. 'I was planning a wild cocaine sex party.'

'Well, I'm sure Jeff and Brenda will be up for that. As long as it's finished by midnight and the garden is left tidy.'

He moves on to the bathroom, filling his washbag with way too many toiletries for two nights in a field with a bunch of amateur actors.

'Are you sure you don't want to come? It'll be fun. Ted is bringing his ukulele.'

'Never be a salesman, Dad.'

'Well, do you want me to get some more snacks and DVDs in? You could have a sleepover with your friends? We could decorate the living room with loads of bean bags and blankets and fairy lights!'

'I'm not nine!' I yell. 'I'm just going to lie around and read comics.'

He hugs me for ages.

'Very sensible,' he says. 'That's my girl.'

That's my girl? Right. As soon as he drives away in the bus, I text Daisy, jabbing angrily at the buttons: 'Yes, I'll come to the club.' It's just a night out with my friends. I need to do things like this. I need to rebel.

Tom

It was the morning of the West Somerset Arts and Crafts festival and I was feeling nervous. A tiny bit. Not about the event itself of course – seriously, imagine Glastonbury, but much smaller and with no cool bands, drugs or fashionable young people; a Glastonbury entirely populated by slightly smug middle-class families in Hunter wellies pushing baby buggies through the mud. This was not something to be afraid of.

No, I was feeling nervous about leaving Hannah.

Sure, she'd been on the odd sleepover in the past fifteen years – of course she had. But this was the first time *I'd* been away from *her* – outside of walking distance. So yeah, I may have overcompensated. I may have left a five-page document listing the phone numbers of thirty emergency contacts. I may have alerted all of our neighbours, not just Jeff and Brenda. I may have phoned ahead to the festival organisers to check the likelihood of getting a mobile signal. I may have been awake for most of the night, running through disaster scenarios in my head. I may have tried to call Venkman for advice. At 7 a.m. I may have started to quietly yet forcefully regret ever agreeing to drive everyone to this stupid event.

Two hours after hugging Hannah goodbye, our merry vehicle was in a long queue of traffic snaking along the narrow country road leading to the artists' entrance. I was driving; Sally was next to me clutching her site map and official attendance pack. Behind us we had eight members of the drama group and two of Rachel's friends, all squeezed between dozens of holdalls stuffed with clothes and costumes. Ted and Jay awkwardly shared a seat, the latter spending most of the journey gawping at Rachel and her crew who were all dressed in bikini tops and denim shorts. Natasha had managed to secure a weekend away from the kids and had gone slightly demob happy with a bottle of vodka (someone made the mistake of asking if she'd thought of bringing her lovely daughter along and they got the whole 'drama club is *mine*' speech). James turned up this morning with twenty-two cans of cheap cider, which did not survive long into the ninety-minute drive. Soon everyone was slightly tipsy, especially James and Shaun who spent the whole journey arguing about the best live bands in music history while play-fighting on the back seat. Of course, there had also been a singalong, courtesy of Ted and his ukulele; then, Rachel and her backing vocalists belted out a song identified by Jay as 'Don't Cha' by The Pussycat Dolls. Natasha slid off her seat.

It was one of those perfect summer days; the sky an unsullied wash of azure blue, the sun a ball of shimmering heat. As we pulled onto the site, the dried mud crunched beneath the tyres and the air was thick with the smell of manure and barbecued meat. Jolly people in high-visibility jackets directed us to a parking space amid a sea of camper vans. We gamely grabbed our bags and trudged to a nearby field, where there were dozens of tents already set up for actors and musicians. We had two to share between ten of us, which would be interesting. Also interesting was the fact that we'd be sleeping between a Wurzels tribute band and a theatre group called the Magical Acrobatical Insect Show. When we arrived there were two men dressed as red ants, sitting outside their tent eating burgers and smoking.

'We should probably have a men's tent and a women's tent,' said Ted.

'Spoilsport!' said Rachel.

But it was decided this would be the most sensible arrangement. After unloading the luggage and collecting up our costumes, we made our way out of the campsite and into the festival area, a vast swathe of pastureland, haphazardly dotted with marquees, food tents, beer gardens, fairground rides and wacky merchandise stalls. For anyone in the south-west interested in buying a jester hat, eating an overpriced hot pork baguette then watching a dimly recalled eighties pop group steadfastly belting their way through an optimistically entitled 'greatest hits' set, this was very much the place to be. It was a festival by and for people who had only the vaguest notion of what a festival was, perhaps learned from skim-reading a *Guardian* article.

The 'Shuffle Theatre' was a large grubby white marquee at the far edge of the site, next to the WI tea tent and something called the Tipsy Pig cider barn. We'd been told to arrive by 10 a.m. for a briefing, and when we lifted the entrance flap and strolled in twenty minutes early, there was already a sizeable crowd of amateur actors milling about. Apparently around twenty local drama groups were taking part, and many of them seemed to have blown their annual costume budget on the occasion. Imagine the Mos Eisley cantina scene in *Star Wars*, but many times more camp. There were gaudy Elizabethan dresses, there were Victorian military outfits, there were togas and for some reason there were Vikings. When two men walked past wearing black suits and white shirts, Shaun whispered 'Pinter' to James and they nodded conspiratorially.

A woman in a festival T-shirt jumped onto the stage at the rear of the tent and bellowed 'Hello' into a microphone, the vicious feedback slicing through the convivial atmosphere like an axe through melted butter. Everyone who still had their hearing turned to face her.

'Welcome to the Shuffle Theatre!' she yelled unnecessarily as a bespectacled man awkwardly joined her. 'Thank you so much for taking part in this fun and innovative event. My name's Ann, and I'm the arts coordinator. This is Derek, our technician.'

There was a small ripple of applause. Derek nodded. He was wearing a gigantic walkie-talkie in some sort of holster attached to his utility belt.

As you know,' she continued, 'every group will be performing three scenes throughout the day – but none of us know when and in what order. Each scene has been given a number, and when that number appears on the screen over there, you'll have five minutes to get in costume and get on stage. Is that clear?'

'Yes,' cried the entire audience.

'Derek has programmed a random number generator for the occasion, haven't you, Derek?'

'Well, Ann, as I have explained, random number generators are rarely actually random and very few pass the statistical test for randomness. But I have written a program that will suffice.'

'That's . . . that's great, thank you, Derek.'

She clapped him, which set off everyone else, so we now had a tent full of actors clapping a semi-random number generator. I took the opportunity to check my phone. One bar of signal. No messages.

'She's fine,' whispered Sally.

'So the show begins at eleven o'clock and ends at nine this evening,' yelled Ann. 'There is free tea and coffee for all participants in the WI tent next door. To the right of the stage are male and female changing areas – it's just a few sheets strung up on a line so do try to be discreet. Have fun, everyone!'

There was another a ripple of applause.

'Oh I almost forgot, the Tipsy Pig cider company next door is offering a reduced fee of one pound a pint to actors. You just need to show your artist pass!'

This time, there was enthusiastic cheering and an almost immediate mass exodus from the tent.

'Is that a good idea?' said Ted. 'A long, hot day, excitable actors, cheap booze? It seems like . . . ' But Shaun, James, Rachel and her friends were already sidling away to join the queue at the cider tent. 'Never mind,' sighed Ted to himself.

Half an hour later, the show began. A handful of curious festival-goers had wandered in, the entrance to the tent now wide open, the interior offering shade, giant bean bags to sit on and – who knows – maybe even entertainment. Most of the actors were in the audience too, sipping their cider and chatting merrily. First on stage was a boisterous scene from *The Way of the World*, well acted by a theatre group from Cornwall, who had a magnificent collection of glossy period costumes that they were clearly keen to show off as they had many more actors on stage than the script called for. The audience enjoyed the bawdy horseplay and gave a generous ripple of applause. However, this was followed somewhat inappropriately by a sequence from Ibsen's *Ghosts* in which Oswald tells his mother he has syphilis and is going insane. Why Weston-Super-Mare's Seashore Players decided this scene was suitable for a summer festival was anyone's guess, but the actors – dressed in black polo necks – carried it off with grim determination.

I slipped out during a scene from *History Boys* (performed by a girls' school) to try and call Hannah. The phone took an age to connect, and when it did I could barely hear her.

'HELLO? HANNAH?'

'He ... Dad! ... Not ... [interminable noise] ... The cast?'

'WHAT?'

' ... [weird static] ... on the television ... But ... Just left it, it's fine.'

It's fine? What's fine? What happened?

'HANNAH, I CAN BARELY HEAR YOU. IS EVERYTHING OKAY?'

' ... Fell ... Nothing ...'

'WHAT? YOU FELL?'

'NO! EVERYTHING IS FINE! GET BACK TO YOUR [...] FESTIVAL, YOU COMPLETE ... [angry wasp-like static].'

At that point the line went dead. I stared at the screen, considered phoning again, but then sent a text instead. I could hear laughter and more clapping and there was now a regular stream of costumed actors moving between the theatre and the cider tent – like boozy worker ants. I spotted Rachel and her friends trudging past with two pints each, laughing raucously. The heat made everything shimmer. I could feel the sweat down my back. I wondered what I was doing standing in this field many miles from home.

It was almost two hours before our first performance. The not-so-random random number generator selected the scene from *Noises Off* – the one Sally had picked to cunningly disguise the drama club's own potential incompetence. When it came down to it, however, they weren't incompetent at all. James was great as the struggling director, Sally excelled as frustrated middle-aged actress Dotty Otley, and Rachel did brilliantly as confused young starlet Brooke Ashton, even though she was swaying slightly throughout.

Most of the lines were swallowed in the increasingly noisy tent, but there was applause and even one or two cheers at the end.

Hey, maybe this is going to work out, I thought. Maybe everything won't unravel.

At that precise moment, everything started to unravel.

The next performance – the seduction scene from *Richard III* – had to be abandoned because someone in the audience kept shouting 'He's behind you' to Lady Anne. Richard III then clambered down off the stage and started to punch the culprit until he was restrained by two members of the Totnes Drama Collective, who grabbed him by his false hump. Someone staggered into the sheets shielding the changing area, bringing them all down and exposing three members of the chorus from *Oedipus the King*. A scuffle broke out between two Bristol drama clubs over a talent-poaching incident that had clearly led to weeks of simmering resentment.

Sally headed over, squeezing between rowdy actors in increasingly torn and dishevelled costumes. Members of the public were beginning to flee the scene.

'It's madness in here,' she said. 'I'll just phone Jay – he went to watch a band. I've got to warn him not to come back. There are grown men fighting. Some of them are in togas. It's like the Young Conservatives debating society all over again.'

James and Shaun bounded over and collapsed next to us, red-faced and excited, bringing with them a fug of cider fumes. Festival security personnel were at the tent entrance, trying to help people leave. An elderly woman in full Victorian dress passed us, muttering about the disgrace of it all.

'Turns out the cider is nine per cent proof,' said James. 'No wonder everyone's shit-faced.'

'Have you seen the random number display screen?' yelled Shaun.

We all looked. Instead of displaying a number it now had a flashing message reading BLAIR IS A TWAT. Ann had taken to the stage with a megaphone but couldn't make herself heard. Derek grabbed it from her.

'Who has tampered with my random number generator?' he yelled.

Someone from the audience shouted, 'There's no such thing as a random number generator.'

Ann wrestled the megaphone back. 'We're going to take a short break,' she shouted. An elaborately styled wig flew through the air and hit her on the shoulder. 'I think some members of the various drama groups are suffering from sunstroke.'

'Well,' said Ted. 'I'm sure they'll get everything back on track.'

He got up and so did the rest. I struggled to my feet as well. I had been feeling irritated by the whole thing, but gradually, the farcical power of the scene was beginning to win through. If Hannah had been here, she would have found it hilarious. And thinking of her again, I suddenly felt a weird responsibility to enjoy the anarchy on her behalf, to drink it in, as she certainly would have – if only so that I could tell her about it later. A swell of giddy glee welled up inside me as I surveyed the tent. Two men in dishevelled Shakespearean garb were now kissing on stage while the Pinter actors remonstrated with a security guard, waving their plastic guns. The elderly woman we saw leaving earlier was now back, holding a pint and accompanied by two very young men in torn soldier outfits. She was wearing a Viking helmet. It looked like a scene from a Derek Jarman film. We noticed that behind the stage, two tent support beams were starting to lean dangerously over, dragging the roof down with them. 'We've quite literally brought the house down!' someone yelled, to raucous laughter. Within seconds panicked technicians were hastily removing lighting equipment. Ann bounded back onto the stage, her face a mask of panic.

'Please make your way to the exit flaps,' she yelled. 'I'm afraid the Shuffle Theatre has been cancelled.'

As we joined the throng of stumbling thespians heading for the outside world, Ted put his arm across my back.

'Well, I guess that's that,' I said.

'It sure is,' he replied.

'We're not going to get paid are we?'

'Good heavens, no.'

'We could have done with that money.'

'Yes. Yes we could.'

'Shall we retreat?'

'I think that would be a good idea.'

We left the Shuffle Theatre, our ragtag group stomping unsteadily over the long grass, trying to work out what to do next, half expecting the tent to collapse in flames behind us. The Rachel gang split off to head back for more cider, dragging Natasha with them. Shaun and James wanted to check out the cabaret tent together. Ted, Sally, Jay and I decided to look for something to eat and found a fast food van next to the Magical Acrobatical Insect Show. We bought giant cheeseburgers and sat down amongst a small audience of young families to watch. The two red ant men from earlier were standing either side of a trapeze frame as a woman dressed in an elaborate praying mantis outfit stepped gracefully along the high wire. On the grass in front of them, several people dressed as beetles performed front rolls, somersaults and cartwheels. The Disney song 'Ugly Bug Ball' played over a scratchy speaker system. It was both incredibly weird and utterly captivating.

'Well, that was an experience,' said Sally. 'I was convinced the

Shuffle Theatre riot would be the weirdest thing I saw today, but it just goes to show.'

'I can't believe I missed it,' said Jay. 'I was watching some god-awful local band doing Nirvana covers. I thought Hannah would be here.'

'She's still not one hundred per cent,' I said. 'She needs to rest.'

Jay nodded but didn't say anything. Ted disappeared for several minutes then came back holding three ice-cold bottles of local beer.

'Well, everyone else is drunk,' he said.

And we sat in the sunshine, sipping from our bottles, watching the bizarre show. Festival-goers wandered around us – dads in cargo shorts and rugby tops, mums in sundresses and floppy hats carrying tussle-haired toddlers. The pace slowed, the mix of alcohol and sunshine working its magic. I looked over at Sally and smiled.

'What?' she said selfconsciously.

'I don't know,' I said. 'We just ... we do get up to some crazy bullshit.'

'We do indeed.'

'I wonder if the Shuffle Theatre is on fire yet.'

'I'm expecting a SWAT team to rappel down from a helicopter.'

'Poor Derek and his random number generator.'

'He's the real victim in all this.'

Jay turned to us, wiping his mouth on the back of his hand.

'Did you know that computers can't actually generate random numbers?' he said.

Sally and I looked at each other with wry expressions. Jay took a huge bite out of his burger.

When the show ended, there was some polite applause, and now slightly tipsy, I put my fingers in my mouth and whistled. The praying mantis looked over to us and smiled, taking a deep bow, the front of her papier-mâché head almost touching the grass.

Sally, Jay and I walked to the fairground where we were almost sick on the waltzer. I texted a photo of Jay and me with huge bags of candyfloss. Hannah texted back, You idiots. Have fun xx. And I *was* having fun.

A few of us got back to the tents for about 11 p.m., the sky now dark and full of stars; the temperature falling. Someone had made a campfire. We sat about, silently. It was difficult to work out who was there in the darkness – people kept creeping off to sleep or drink some more. My phone buzzed in my pocket and when I looked at it, I felt a sudden surge of concern. It was Hannah's number on the screen. Why was she calling so late? What had happened?

'Hello?' I said. 'Hannah? Hannah? Are you there?'

I could hear voices, but they sounded distant and slightly muffled. 'Hello?!' I shouted.

Panicking now, I texted her then stared at the display willing her to reply. Nothing.

I was ready to call the neighbours, when a message came through. 'Sorry Dad, sat on phone while watching TV. Hannahx'.

I finally breathed. She was probably watching some god-awful teen movie with Jenna. I texted her a silly message and relaxed again, allowing myself to be calmed by the warmth of the flames.

I was about to call it a night when someone sat beside me and held out a beer. Surprised, I took it without looking up, thinking it was probably Ted, coming back for a nightcap.

'Can I sit over here?' said a voice I didn't recognise. 'It's just that the giant ants are getting really rowdy. It's that bloody cider.'

I looked up in shock. It was a woman in her early thirties with red hair that gathered in thick curls around her shoulders. She was wearing a baggy grey sweatshirt and blue jeans. Her feet were bare.

'I'm Grace,' she said. 'The praying mantis. You were at the show earlier?'

'Yes of course. It was excellent. Thanks for the beer.'

Without the strange costume, she looked much less terrifying.

'Sorry if I startled you.'

'Oh no it's fine, I thought you were Ted.'

'Ted?'

'My accountant. Well, the theatre's accountant. I manage the theatre. Can I start that again? Hi, I'm Tom.'

'Hi Tom, I'm Grace. Like in *Will & Grace*. Do you ever watch that?'

'I do, I love it! And you have ... '

'The same hair as Grace. Yes.'

'And no one has pointed that out before, of course?'

'No, that has definitely never happened.'

We stared at the fire for a while. Little flecks of burning ash buzzed about us like fireflies.

'So you're actors, then?' she said at last.

'Yes, we were supposed to be performing at the Shuffle Theatre, but, oh god, everyone got drunk on that cider. It was astonishing.'

'They had to get the police in, didn't they?' she laughed. 'We missed all the excitement, being in the family field. So unfair. Still, Greg and Andy are doing their best to catch up.'

She glanced over towards her tent, where the two giant ants were lying on their segmented backs, passing a joint from one to the other, like some weird stoner version of Franz Kafka's *Metamorphosis*.

'Did you have a good day?' I said.

'It was fun, but the costumes weigh a ton and it's like a furnace in that mask. Plus you've got kids coming up and prodding you all day and asking if you're a real giant insect. I do sometimes wonder how I got myself into this.'

'How did you get yourself into this?'

'Oh you know, the old story: girl studies dance, girl goes for twenty million auditions while working in a Wetherspoon's; ten years later, girl gets desperate and joins insect acrobatics troupe.'

'We've all been there.'

'So now, every summer, I tour the country with this lot in a Transit van, doing festivals and fetes and corporate events.'

'You're good on the trapeze.'

'Ah yes, that was three months spent at circus school. You should have seen my dad's face when I asked him to pay for *that*.'

'I was in a touring group for a while. We did pretentious takes on modern classics. This was just after my degree. Eight of us – and a Transit van of course.'

'Of course.'

'It was fun. So much fun. Learning lines in motorway service stations, sleeping in cheap hotels, four to a room; once in a while making teenagers actually watch and believe in some old Terence Rattigan play. No worries, no responsibilities, no clue about the future.'

'Then?'

'Ah, well. I got married, had a beautiful daughter . . .'

'The classic story.'

'Almost. My wife left. My daughter was . . . quite ill. My touring days were over. Now I run this little theatre an hour away from here. These guys are the local drama group.'

I wafted my arm in the general direction of our two tents, but then, as it completed its slightly drunken arc, my hand somehow landed behind Grace. Oh god, I thought, I've just done a 'yawn, stretch and arm over shoulder' move, like a teenager in a cinema – but by accident. To my astonishment, she shuffled in closer to me.

'Are you based nearby?' I said.

'No, we're up in Stockport,' she said. 'We're heading back to the frozen North tomorrow morning. That's why I have to make the most of this warmth while I can.'

I saw shapes moving in the darkness, away from the glow of the fire; other campers searching for the toilet block, or coming back from the all-night dance tent. Which shut at one.

'Should we have a guitar?' said Grace. 'Should we be singing Bob Dylan songs?'

'Well, Ted does have a ukulele.'

'Then again, why ruin a perfectly nice evening?' she replied.

The moon hung above us, bright and crescent-shaped, a glowing apostrophe in the sky. The air felt dense and heavy, and I was incredibly aware of Grace's body near mine.

'The wife that left,' she said. 'Is she still around?'

'No. Well, I mean she's still alive. But no. We don't see her.'

'And your daughter is . . .'

'It's hard. She has this thing wrong with her heart. We don't know how serious. I mean, we know it's serious. We just don't . . .'

'I know,' she said quietly. 'I know what it's like.'

She didn't elaborate but I looked right at her, and her eyes were telling me something. I should have been able to read it, but I couldn't.

'The show must go on,' she laughed, and she slapped her hand down onto my leg. It stayed there. 'The show surely must go on.'

'Hey,' I said. 'We're off stage. This isn't a show.'

Suddenly, I felt completely intoxicated – even though I'd only had two or three beers all day. I was drunk on *something*. There was that feeling in the air, the crackle of possibility, invisible but nonetheless palpable. Was there something happening between us? My intuition was a little rusty. She took a big swig of her beer, finishing the bottle in a couple of glugs. The light from the flickering fire cast shapes across us; the shadows covered parts of our faces like dark stage paint. Her hair reflected the orange of the flames, taking in their warmth. She was smiling.

'There's something about camp fires, isn't there?' she said dreamily.

I was out of practice, but it seemed the comment was leading somewhere. I leaned in until our faces were very close. She didn't move. I closed my eyes and moved closer still.

'Um, I'd better go,' she said, and before I could respond she bounced lithely to her feet. Oh my god, I'd completely misread it. I'd misread the whole thing. I had made a monstrous error. I think the horror was scrawled across my face like graffiti.

'It's just that we're heading off very early,' she said in a placatory tone. 'Got another event in Cheshire tomorrow.'

'I'm so sorry, I got the wrong ...'

'No, it's fine, I just didn't ... I wasn't ... Good luck with your theatre.'

'I really am completely sorry.'

'It's fine, honestly.'

I couldn't think of what to say or how to extricate myself from the situation with dignity. I considered simply walking into the campfire as a sacrificial offering to the gods of romance, who were clearly furious at me. Instead I opted for being really polite and then running away.

'Well, it was nice to meet you, Grace,' I said.

'It was nice to meet you, Toby.'

In that dreadful moment, I relearned a valuable lesson about life. Every moment is open to interpretation, there is no such thing as objective reality. I thought I was experiencing the magical possibilities of two strangers connecting at a campfire; but she was just talking to some guy called Toby in the next tent while finishing her beer. As an actor I should have understood this. I turned away and took out my phone. It was a message from Hannah: 'I miss you Dad.' Oh Hannah, I thought, your dad is an idiot and he is still not ready for this.

I crept to our tent and wriggled awkwardly into my sleeping bag beside Shaun and James, sighing heavily as I settled down on the hard ground.

'Is everything all right?' whispered Shaun.

'I just had an embarrassing encounter,' I said. 'I am not good at reading signals apparently.'

'I know that feeling,' he said.

But we were too drunk and tired to compare experiences.

Hannah

Jenna's parents think she's at my house for a sleepover. This is not completely a lie. Jenna really *is* at my house, and she really is sleeping over. But we're not staying in and watching *Buffy* like we said. We're going out. We're going to an indie disco at a semi-rural pub, which will probably be full of old goths and punks and teenagers who shouldn't be allowed in. It's the social event of the decade.

But right now, we're in my room, getting into the correct grungy mood by blasting out Elastica on my CD player. Dad has spent the last ten years indoctrinating me with his nineties music collection and now it's finally paying off. Jenna is sitting on the bed stealing all my mascara and drinking supermarket own-brand vodka mixed with tropical fruit juice. I've had a couple of sips but it's gross. We're clothed entirely in black, her in jeans and a clas-sic Nirvana smiley T-shirt, me in a vest top, tight skirt, laddered tights, army boots. She has given her nails a fresh coating of the horrible black varnish she buys at the market, and she's done mine too. We look like trouble. The anticipation of the evening, the thudding music and the smell of alcohol all make us feel slightly crazed. For a few minutes I'm not thinking about how ill I am or how ill I'm going to be or *anything* serious or boring. It is so liberating.

'My dad is really freaking out about the A-level questionnaire,' says Jenna.

Oh, well, it was fun while it lasted.

'God, Jenna, what a buzzkill. Do we have to talk about this *now*?'

'He wants me to make a spreadsheet of my options so I can cross-reference it with my strongest GCSE results later,' she continues, regardless. 'I mean, we've not even done our mock GCSEs yet! The bit where it asks, "where do you want to be in five years" – I'm just writing, "as far away from here as physically possible". Jesus, school sucks. Parents suck. What did your dad say? Does he know you threw the letter away?'

'Yeah, he got it out of the bin and pinned it up again.'

'Ha ha, busted.'

'Not really. I chucked it back in.'

'What? Why?'

I turn the dial up on the speaker, and the sound of 'Stutter' pulverises our eardrums.

'Because fuck the future!' I yell.

And then we're moshing around the room, pushing each other over. Jenna puts on My Chemical Romance and we totally lose it, singing along with the lyrics to 'I'm Not Okay'. I check my phone to see if Dad has texted. He tried to call earlier, but I was sitting in the park reading and could hardly hear him, and then I was attacked by an angry wasp and instinctively threw my phone at it; I've had a couple of texts since – something about a drunken orgy in the theatre tent. Sounds like they're having a ball. He deserves to have a nice time.

*

An hour later we meet Daisy in the high street outside the pub. She is wearing a short flowery dress, matched with sky-blue tights and green nail varnish.

'What the hell are you wearing?' asks Jenna as we approach.

'What? This is grunge, isn't it?' says Daisy.

'You look like Courtney Love's drunken grandmother,' Jenna offers.

'Well, that's close enough for me. Anyway, guys, this is Dave,' says Daisy, gesturing vaguely towards the doorman. He has a buzz cut and is roughly six feet wide. 'He's letting us in.'

'Don't get shitfaced, ladies,' says Dave. 'More than my job's worth.'

'Right,' says Daisy, heading in and gesturing for us to follow. Dave holds the door open and I feel his eyes locked on us as we pass. He is nodding and grinning; we are being checked out. I wonder if men understand that we *always* know when they're doing this? While old guys are nursing their pints of ale in the main bar, we can already hear the pounding music coming from the club upstairs. As we climb the stairs, the music gets louder, and the bass is already vibrating my insides. There are a few older teenagers hanging about in the corridor talking and checking their phones. A couple I don't recognise are sitting on the top step snogging, getting in everyone's way. Daisy high-fives some guy in a Green Day T-shirt. She seems to know everyone – she's definitely the cool, collected one in our little trio. When she swings open the door, the noise blasts out of the darkness, along with an array of flashing disco lights. There's already a small group of guys on the tiny dance floor, knocking each other around to some speed punk track I don't recognise. Little groups of twenty- and thirty-somethings sit around the few tables that haven't been cleared away, drinking lager from plastic pint glasses and yelling in each other's ears.

Almost everyone is in jeans and plaid shirts. There are some older women at one table, mouthing along to the song and laughing, clearly recalling it from the first time around. The whitewashed walls, ancient oak floors and blackened beams criss-crossing the ceiling make for a weird backdrop to this grunge-a-thon.

Daisy is immediately darting to the bar at the back, hailing someone she recognises; Jenna and I hold back, acclimatising to the noise, searching for familiar faces. Beneath everything I feel my heart beating. Thud . . . thud . . . thud.

'Shall we get a drink?' I yell at Jenna.

'Will they serve us?' she shouts back.

'Let's find out.'

When I ask for two Heinekens (the first thing I think of), the man behind the bar gives me a long, unconvinced examination, but serves me anyway. Jenna looks at her drink with amazement, as though she's just been handed the Turin Shroud in a pint glass.

'If my Dad could see me now he'd shit himself,' she shouts, right into my ear.

I turn around, take a sip, grimace and survey the room.

Almost straight away, I spot him.

He's sitting at a table near the centre with two older guys and an extremely pretty woman. Callum is wearing a thin navy-blue cardigan over a tight stripy T-shirt, matched with brown cords and Converse trainers. He hasn't gone grunge at all, which makes me immediately conscious of looking the same as everyone else in the room apart from him. The DJ starts playing 'Jesus Christ Pose' by Sound Garden. Callum picks up a bottle of beer, leans back in his chair and takes a long, luxurious swig. I feel like I'm going to melt through the floorboards.

'Who are you looking at?' yells Jenna. 'Have you spotted some-one we kn . . . oh, I see.'

She nudges me in the side with her elbow.

'What?!' I say.

Jenna shakes her head, smiling. I spend the rest of the song pretending not to stare at Callum, while Jenna and Daisy shout in each other's faces. I feel like I should join in their conversation instead of totally not ogling a boy, but before I can say anything, the unmistakable bass line of 'Lithium' by Nirvana kicks off, and Daisy is at us, dragging us towards the dance floor, taking a huge puff on her inhaler. Sometimes I forget she's broken like me. While I'm hiding in the theatre or reading comics, she's out drinking and shagging. She's so much better at being chronically ill than I am. The tiny dance space is suddenly a swarming mass of people in band T-shirts and jeans, leaping up and down and into each other as every chorus hits its defiant crescendo. We stay on the floor for the next few tracks, a pulverising combo of Blur's 'Song 2', Green Day's 'Basket Case' and Metallica's 'Battery'. Some of the much older guys are on the dance floor, too, lumbering at the edges, swirling their balding heads, oblivious to everything and everyone else – transported back to the days when they had actual hair. We're somehow in a core group in the middle, squashed and buffeted against dancers we don't know, steam coming off us, clothes drenched with sweat, the smell of BO and deodorant permeating everything. At first, it's an amazing release, a rush of euphoria as the beer meets the music. But by Green Day, my legs are giving, and even through the mass of bodies I can feel my chest burning, and my heart pulling its own stuttering rim shots. I try to tell Jenna but she's in full dance ecstasy mode, eyes closed, head down. Instead, I start to push through the bodies alone, my legs struggling for traction amid the stomping mass, the effort of it making my body ache even more. The first inkling of panic.

I seem to lose it for a few beats. One second I'm at the edge of the dance floor, the next, I'm at the bar, taking deep breaths, trying to stay calm, trying to get myself back together. My first instinct is to call my dad, but what can he do? He's in a field in Somerset somewhere, hours away. If I call him and then faint, he'll be totally distraught. I've got to just relax. I should get some fresh air, that's it. The DJ breaks with the retro theme and puts on 'In The End' by Linkin Park. The place explodes. I go to walk forward, but my legs feel like they're many miles beneath me and completely unconnected. There's a familiar swirling pressure at the edges of my sight. I'm just about to turn back to the bar and ask for water, when I see someone's hand in front of me, offering me a glass. It is Callum. I grab it and thank him, taking small sips while trying to act cool while also not fainting.

'You don't look well, how can I help you?' he asks. But instead of shouting it in my ear, he mouths it clearly and calmly.

'I've got to get out,' I yell.

He puts the glass on the bar, then takes my hand and tries to pull me towards the door that leads to the landing, but I know that's going to be crammed with people. I find the energy to pull back and point at the emergency exit on the other side of the room. Before he can say anything I'm already dragging him there. We wind through a group of really old goths, one in a top hat and undertaker suit, another dude with weird black contact lenses, dressed in some sort of leather gimp outfit. I start to think I'm hallucinating. When we get to the door, Callum pushes the long metal 'emergency release' bar, but then turns to me.

'It won't budge, it's locked,' he yells. 'I think we should go the other way.'

I shake my head. Feeling increasingly desperate, I pull him away, lean back and with all the vision and strength I still have at my disposal, I stride forward and kick the bar. I expect the door to just vibrate silently in the frame, but to my surprise and relief, it blasts open, expelling me onto the iron walkway. Without thinking, I start to pinball down the narrow stairs, the cooler night air flooding my senses. When I reach the bottom, I swirl away and flatten myself against a van, breathing heavily. My hands are on my knees, my head is down. Straight away, Callum is there, his hand on my back.

I just keep breathing.

'Feeling any better?' he says at last. Only this time, I can actually hear him. He is concerned but calm. I'm still fighting the dizziness.

'Yes,' I manage. 'My heart is … it's fucked, basically.'

'I know. I mean, I heard at school. Do you want me to call an ambulance?'

'No. I just need a moment.'

My eyes are closed. I can faintly smell Callum. It's kind of beer mixed with candyfloss. It's definitely not Lynx, thank fuck. I hear cars swooshing by on the road nearby, and there's a couple having an argument somewhere else in the car park, but I can't make out what they're saying.

When I finally open my eyes, the swirling blackness is gone from my peripheral vision. I'm coming back.

I slowly straighten up. Callum moves his arm and steps away slightly. We stay like that for a while. Together and silent.

'That's better,' I say. 'Phew. Shit. That's better.'

'Shall I get your friends?'

'No! I mean, not yet. It's fine. I'll be all right. Can you just stay here for a second?'

'Yeah, of course,' he says.

The arguing couple stagger past us, now arm in arm – and they walk straight into the road. A car slams to a halt and beeps them. Callum and I watch them shouting at the driver, and then everything is quiet. Oh god, what do we talk about?

'You really showed that door who's boss,' says Callum. 'The next time I lock myself out of the house I'll give you a call.'

He smiles and then I'm smiling too.

'I just got a bit desperate,' I say. 'You can go back now if you want.'

'Oh please, no. I'm not into nineties music at all.'

'So why . . . ?'

'I'm with my older sister and her boyfriend. They're into all that stuff. She got me in because she knows the DJ. How did you get in?'

'I'm with Daisy. She just has this way of getting in places.'

'Ah yes, of course. I like her, she's funny.'

'Oh, *everyone* likes Daisy.'

'I didn't mean like that.'

'No, it's fine. I know what you meant. Everyone has one incredibly popular friend, right?'

'Not me.'

I fumble with the silver bangles Jenna made me wear and they jangle noisily. He looks briefly up towards the fire door. I wonder if he's thinking of a way to escape.

'Can I ask you a really serious question?' he says. And he's looking at me with this concerned expression, his forehead all wrinkled. My stomach sinks, because I just think, I know what comes next. What exactly *is* wrong with my heart? When did I find out? Is it fatal? Am I scared of dying? When I first started at my school, I had to do a little talk about cardiomyopathy in front of the whole class. A few of the boys decided it was their job to protect me, which was fun for a while, but then some girls got jealous – like, literally jealous of someone with a life-threatening heart condition. They bullied me for a bit and one of them flushed my phone sim down the toilet. I didn't talk about it again.

'Here goes,' he says. 'And honestly, you don't have to answer if you don't want to.'

I ready myself.

'Right . . .' He clears his throat. 'What's your number one favourite comic book of all time?'

Involuntarily, I burst out laughing; it's so loud he physically jumps. 'Oh my god!' I say.

'I know, I know, it's too personal. We barely know each other.'

'You're an idiot.'

'Just answer the question.'

'Oh man, this is so sad. All right, so the *Fables* series is up there because I have this thing about fairy tales. I won't bore you with that right now. But I gotta say *Ghost World*, that's definitely it. I love the characters, the art, the whole funny sad vibe of it. The way Enid and Rebecca just drift around cafés and shops being bored and lonely and bitchy because there are just no places for them to, like, exist in their shitty little town. I don't know how Daniel Clowes understands what it's like to be a teenage girl, but he does. What about you?'

'Oh I don't understand anything about being a teenage girl.'

'No! I mean, your favourite comics!'

He takes a big dramatic breath, and then in one long stream: 'Right now I'm into *Daredevil*, specifically the Brian Bendis stuff, *Preacher*, *Swamp Thing*, *The Ultimates* . . .'

'Oh riiiiight.' I nod knowingly. 'You have a thing for tortured guys. Got it.'

I immediately regret being so judgemental, but he laughs. He has this habit of looking away when he laughs. This is something I know about him now.

'I've started sort of drawing my own comics. They're not very good.'

'Wow, can I see them?'

171

He shakes his head and in a flash somehow the mood has changed. 'I don't think so. I shouldn't have mentioned it. Actually, I ought go back in. My sister will worry that I've run away again.'

'Again?'

'It's a long story.'

'Are you trouble, Callum?'

'I'm not interesting enough to be trouble.'

'Let me be the judge of that.'

I decide to launch myself off the van when I say this, to emphasise how cool and unflappable I am, but when I go to stand up properly, my legs give a little bit. Callum darts in, his arm behind me, gripping around my waist. My spine actually tingles.

'You go back in,' I say. 'I'm just gonna head home. I think I've had enough indie music for one night. Could you let Jenna or Daisy know I've gone?'

'Sure. Of course.'

But he's still standing with his arm around my waist, his face close to mine and he's not going, and I'm not making him. The air feels so hot and close, like a physical presence between us. We're looking at each other. That's when I hear my dad's voice.

'Hannah? Hannah? Are you there?'

At first I think I'm having some sort of guilt-induced hallucination. But then it finally hits me.

'Oh shit, my phone!' I drag it out of my pocket. 'Oh no, my butt phoned my dad!' I hit the call cancel button. 'Oh shit, I wonder if he heard us, he'll be so pissed off.'

'With your taste in comics?'

'No, it's not funny! I'm not supposed to be out, I'm supposed to be having a sleepover with Jenna!'

'Just tell him you sat on your phone while you were watching the TV really loud.'

'Oh yes, my dad *is* that dumb.'

'Sorry.'

'No, I mean, he actually is.'

I type in exactly what Callum said then stare nervously at the phone, preparing myself for it to ring. What am I going to say? Instead, a text comes back. Relieved, I show the message to Callum. 'Get to bed, you two!'

He grins at me suggestively.

'He means me and Jenna,' I say.

His grin becomes a leer.

'Oh for god's sake! Look, I'm going home. Thank you again.'

'I didn't do much, but you're welcome.'

We nod at each other, but don't say goodbye. He walks towards the pub entrance, looking cool. I head up the road, but almost trip on a loose paving stone. I'm shivering and I feel nervous, and my stomach is all in knots – I mean, it's obviously because I thought Dad was about to catch me out, but the prospect of pissing him off doesn't usually affect me like this.

'Oh, Hannah,' Callum shouts. I spin around to face him. 'Do you want to, I don't know, meet sometime? Soon? Or something?'

'Um, sure,' I say.

'Ah good. That's great. I'll text you!'

'Great! Bring your artwork!'

I'm five minutes up the road before I'm capable of forming any coherent thoughts. I'm ten minutes up the road before I realise he doesn't have my number.

Tom

Ted and I sat in our swivel chairs looking at the letter, glumly dipping digestive biscuits into lukewarm mugs of tea. A week had passed since the calamitous arts festival – and my disastrous tryst with the praying mantis. I didn't tell anyone about that, because I didn't want everyone to know that my most meaningful romantic experience in several years was being rejected by a gigantic insect. The theatre was quiet; there wasn't a lot to do apart from fret over the two shocking revelations we'd been hit with in the preceding days. First, the insurance company got in touch to tell us that, unfortunately (this was their wording), they were unlikely to pay out on this occasion. Ted called the weaselly inspector who had snuck around the theatre; he claimed the flood was the result of accidental damage or human error rather than a technical fault, which meant the insurance was forfeited. It was utterly ridiculous. Sally had gone in and wrestled with the archaic beast a couple of times, but not that night, surely? And if she had, she would have said something.

Whatever the case, we were facing a considerable repair bill, and no amount of Culture Club tribute acts or Hollywood musical nights were going to pay it off.

The second disaster was a letter from the council planning department, asking me to attend an 'exploratory meeting' about the future of the theatre. The Executive Buildings and Planning Group would listen to my pleas then make their recommendations to the council itself. Afterwards, there would be another big meeting and a vote. It felt like we were being entered into a nightmarish version of *Pop Idol*, but one where the losing contestants would be demolished with a wrecking ball.

'This isn't good is it?' I said to Ted at the exact moment half of my digestive broke off and sank into my tea. 'Fate is conspiring against us.'

'You can probably fish it out with a teaspoon,' he replied.

'No Ted, I meant the insurance and the council letter.'

I tried to fish the digestive out with a teaspoon, but it had already become too mushy and the sloppy remains disappeared below the surface. It was clearly an ill omen. Do the gods speak to us through biscuits? I wouldn't put it past them.

'If we were in a Gene Kelly musical, I would spring to my feet and yell, "Let's put on a show and save the theatre!"' I said.

'I think my tap-dancing days are over.' Ted shrugged. 'Besides, we don't have a budget. Or, currently, a functional theatre.'

We drifted into silence and I was happy to see out the day quietly, partly because I didn't want to think about the repercussions of the leak and partly because, somehow, I had another date night to contend with. When I got home from the festival I discovered a message on the dating site, sent by a woman named Vanessa, who suggested a 'casual meet-up'. Her photo seemed to have been taken in some bustling Indian city; she was wearing a khaki shirt and sunglasses, and resembled one of those adventurous women from the 1930s who climbed mountains and flew aeroplanes looking stern and imposing. I was being asked out by Amelia Earhart. She provided some ground rules: no talking about work or politics. This led me to believe she might be a spy, which was an intriguing enough proposition for me to send a reply, even *without* Hannah standing over me brandishing a blunt instrument. I didn't expect a response because she was clearly beautiful and serious. I got one within an hour. We had a date. There was either a real drought of eligible men in the southeast Somerset area or I was more of a catch than I thought I was.

'Uh-oh, she wants to go to the cinema to see *Mr. & Mrs. Smith*,' I said to Hannah.

'Oh, that's supposed to be good! And you don't have to talk much, which reduces the chance of you saying something stupid. It's a win-win situation.'

'Yes, but won't a romantic movie starring two of Hollywood's most desirable actors just set up impossible standards for our own date? I mean, Brad Pitt for god's sake? I'm more William Pitt.'

'Who?'

'Christ, do they even teach history at school these days?'

So after I left the theatre, having directed Ted to start getting repair quotes, I stopped off in town to buy a serious shirt. While there, I spotted James sitting alone and forlorn outside a café, aimlessly tapping at his mobile phone. I sidled up to him, weaving through the shoppers sitting about enjoying the chance to be all European by having their coffee out of doors.

'Hello, James,' I said, loudly enough to make him drop his phone onto the metal table with a loud clang.

'Oh hi,' he said. 'I was just trying to message someone. I think whoever invented predictive text was just really good at interrupting other people's conversations.'

Awkward silence.

'I've bought a shirt,' I said. 'For a date. I'm going on a date.'

'Oh, well done,' he said with genuine enthusiasm.

'Waiting for someone?' I asked with a sort of conspiratorial wink, which was meant to suggest an affinity between two lusty men engaged in romantic entanglements, but probably just looked very creepy.

'No. God no. I'm just sitting around, reading and thinking.'

'Oh. Poor you,' I said, feeling genuinely envious.

'I mean, there's someone I like. I've liked them for ages but it's not ... it's not going to lead anywhere. So I guess I'm in the same boat as you.'

'Ah, unrequited love. As an actor, you need to remember this sweet misery. The next time you have a romantic role, it's material.'

'Thanks Tom, that really helps.'

I detected a note of irony in his voice. This wasn't the pep talk he was hoping for. I made a mental note to work on my laddish small talk.

I drove to the cinema an hour early, just in case there were no parking spaces and I had to try to negotiate the terrifying multi-storey car park next door. This 1970s edifice was seemingly designed by a frustrated video game developer who filled it with impossibly narrow passages and swirling interconnected rampways. Every bare concrete barrier was lined with the scratched paint of a thousand cars. I carefully manoeuvred in and parked between two massive pillars, which meant that I had to crawl into the back seat to get out. Then I stood in a vast oily puddle, sending blackened water up my entire trouser leg.

After spending several unsuccessful minutes in the cinema bathroom trying to wash the stains out, I went through to the café area with suspicious wet patches all over my clothes. Here, I nursed five pounds' worth of latte and waited.

It was a typical multiplex – a huge open auditorium, reeking of popcorn and populated entirely by overexcited teenagers filling buckets with pick-n-mix sweets that had a higher per-gram price than gold. When she walked in five minutes earlier than we agreed, Vanessa couldn't have been more at odds with the environment. She was wearing an expensive-looking light blue woollen dress, with oversized black buttons, and her short black hair was perfectly and completely styled into an Audrey Hepburn crop. She looked like she'd just walked out of one of the many Hollywood posters lining the walls. My breath caught in my throat.

'Tom?' she said, approaching the tiny table I was perching on. I detected a hint of disappointment.

'Vanessa?' I said, sounding more disbelieving than I had intended. 'I parked in the multi-storey over the road and then fell in a puddle.'

She looked around the foyer with quiet detachment, noting the huddles of people forming at the ticket counter.

'Did you book our tickets?' she said.

Oh bugger. Oh bugger it. I'd already messed up.

'Um, oh. No, I'll go and buy them now.'

'That may be a good idea, it's getting quite busy.'

She said it like a primary school teacher patiently informing a child that they should perhaps not be doing a handstand on their desk.

Once we'd fought our way through the pick-n-mix teens we made a lunge for the counter, where an entirely disinterested teenager told us that *Mr. & Mrs. Smith* had sold out. I turned to Vanessa trying not to look pathetically apologetic, but I suspect failing.

'We could try that courtroom drama they reviewed in the *Guardian*?'

'Also sold out,' said the boy, who was much more interested in the group of girls being served by his co-worker.

'Look, what *do* you have?' said Vanessa.

He sighed and stabbed at his touchscreen computer terminal.

'*We Don't Live Here Anymore* is not full,' he said. 'It's a drama about the breakdown of two marriages.'

Vanessa looked at him blankly.

'Well, that sounds like a perfect date movie,' I said.

There was now a growing queue of people behind us, tutting and checking their watches. I looked at Vanessa for some guidance, but she was still staring at our server with a look of utter disbelief on her immaculate face.

'We'll take two tickets.'

We strolled down the long corridor leading to the numerous screens, both silently glancing at the fortunate couples who'd booked ahead for the Brad Pitt and Angelina Jolie movie.

'So,' said Vanessa. 'What sort of films do you usually enjoy?'

My mind was immediately a blank. I didn't want to say that I usually go to the theatre, because we weren't supposed to be talking about our jobs. The last thing I saw was *Madagascar* with Hannah and Daisy. We ate so much candyfloss we were effectively hallucinating through the entire thing.

'Oh you know, comedies, thrillers, romance, adventure . . . '

'You mean every sort of movie there is?'

'Um, yes, it seems so. And you?'

'I am also a big fan of comedy romance adventure thrillers,' she said. 'You see, we already have so much in common.'

She smiled at me, and her face was filled with such unexpectedly genuine warmth that I felt a giant wave of optimism and excitement. It passed as soon as the film began.

We Don't Live Here Anymore was a revoltingly worthy

relationship drama where everyone has joyless affairs. Once or twice during the ninety-minute torture session, I glanced across at Vanessa and was actually relieved to see her on her phone, possibly texting someone for help. 'Do you want to go?' I asked at one point. 'I would,' she whispered, 'but I'm worried someone I recognise will see me and think that I chose to see this.'

So we sat it out, right to the very end, and as the credits finally rolled, I wished there was a button on the arm of my chair that would eject me into the sun.

'That was quite an experience,' I said.

'It reminded me of my own marriage,' she replied. 'Filled with simmering resentment and slightly too long.'

'Shall we get out of here and never come back?'

'Yes, I think that would be for the best.'

Still shell-shocked, we walked out into the balmy summer evening, surprised to find that it was still light.

'We could get something to eat?' said Vanessa.

I hesitated momentarily, not because I didn't want to, but because I was astonished that she'd asked. I thought that as soon as we got outside she would vanish into the distance, like the Road Runner.

'Um, we could try one of these places?'

This being an out of town multiplex, the cinema was surrounded by a series of garish theme restaurants, gamely and inaccurately offering an array of international dining experiences. There was Chinese, Thai, Italian; there was a Mexican place called Mucho Mexicano, where everyone was given a plastic sombrero when they went in. That got my vote, but Vanessa demurred.

In the end, we selected Sal's New York Steak House, designed to resemble a Manhattan tenement, complete with fake fire escape. Inside, there were rows of wooden booths with bright red polyester seat cushions, and every wall was covered in New York-themed paraphernalia: taxi signs, theatre posters, fire hydrants and giant prints of the Empire State Building. Waiters in white shirts and red bow ties were rushing about carrying huge trays, serving excitable families with platefuls of floppy French fries and blackened burgers. A jukebox was playing Frank Sinatra. It was an astonishing scene.

'Wow,' said Vanessa. 'I thought this was a restaurant, but we appear to have walked straight through the gates of hell.'

'Well, those burgers have certainly been burning here for all eternity.'

'I'm not convinced about the authenticity.'

'Oh come on,' I protested. 'Look, they have the front of a Cadillac sticking out of the wall over there. You literally can't get more authentic.'

We were still deciding what to do when a waitress dressed as Marilyn Monroe in the *Seven Year Itch* shot over and yanked us towards an empty booth. We sat down obediently, opening the menus with the sort of immense trepidation usually reserved for post-Christmas bank statements. I looked at Vanessa as she studied the sticky laminated card with glassy detachment. She was maybe mid-thirties, but her smart, stylish clothes made her look older – or at least more mature. She seemed serious, but with an ironic undertone. She looked like she was used to dealing with unpredictable situations. She looked capable. She looked confident. Oh shit, she looked up and caught me staring at her.

'So,' she said, keen to break either the ice or my stare. 'You have a daughter?'

'Yeah, Hannah, she's fifteen. Very smart. Smarter than me, obviously. She's great. And you?'

'I have a son who is eleven so he only talks about computer games. My daughter is thirteen and doesn't really talk to me at all.'

She mimes tapping away on a mobile phone.

Marilyn Monroe was suddenly at our table with her pad and pencil ready.

'I'll have the New York strip steak, medium rare,' said Vanessa without looking up.

'Do you want that with regular or scorching chilli fries?' asked Marilyn.

'Who would want scorching chilli fries?'

'Some like it hot,' I said, winking at Marilyn.

She just stared at me waiting for my order.

'I'll go with the Momma's Macaroni Cheese,' I said.

Marilyn smiled a desperate smile, then she was gone.

'Do you think this is going to be better or worse than the movie?' I said.

'Unless our food is delivered by a husband and wife going through a painful divorce, it can't be worse, can it?'

'I'm sorry. I should have booked the tickets.'

'It's fine. I'll have something to talk about with my mother – I think she went to see it last week. On purpose. We don't have much in common so it's a godsend really.'

'Well, I'm glad the evening hasn't been a total bust for you.'

We smiled at each other, then looked around, trying to come to terms with the fact that we were in this restaurant. Even though everything was going sort of wrong, I felt oddly relaxed.

'I used to work in a place like this,' I said. 'Just after I left university – I was in that weird "I don't know what to do with my life" period. Did you have one of those?'

'Oh definitely,' she said. 'I went travelling for three years. Australia, Thailand, Vietnam, China, then across to South America. I go a bit crazy if I don't bugger off somewhere new every few months. I love exploring. I was obsessed with *Raiders of the*

Lost Ark when I was a kid and I guess I just want to be Indiana Jones. But then don't we all?'

'I wanted to be Derek Jacobi,' I said.

'Right. So anyway, I took the kids to Mumbai for the Easter holidays. My daughter ran up a £250 bill texting her friends and my son fell off an elephant, sprained his ankle and spent the last three days in the hotel room playing on his laptop. They couldn't wait to get back. Kids, eh? So how come it's just you and Hannah? If you don't mind me asking?'

'I . . . well, we were very different, my wife and me. We got together and had a baby quite young. It was hard. We were always pulling in different directions. I sort of potter through life, she was very driven, very committed. How about you?'

'My partner – ex-partner – Daniel, he's what they call a serial entrepreneur. Very driven, very committed. He's in San Francisco now, working on some technology that's apparently going to change all our lives. I don't know. Maybe we should introduce Daniel and your wife, they seem like the perfect power couple.'

'But *you* seem . . . I mean you are . . . You're very . . . smart.'

'You know those mad professors in films – the ones with crazy hair and weird clothes, but inside they're steely and focused and indomitable? I'm the exact opposite. I go through the motions, I do the work, but really I just want to be outside wandering the Mendips with a nature guide and a flask of coffee. I know my happiest memory is supposed to be my wedding, but it isn't. It's the time I went snorkelling on the Great Barrier Reef, and I was surrounded by these beautiful little fish and they swam up and around me, like I was in a Disney movie. I cried for two hours. I like to see and feel new things. I'm very driven and committed about that – also, regional food. It has to be right or I lose it, I'm afraid.'

'Uh-oh,' I said, looking around at everyone else's plates. 'So, you didn't think about moving to San Francisco with your husband?'

She shook her head.

'When the opportunity came up Daniel wanted to take the whole family – he assumed that would be fine; that I'd want to go.'

'But it wasn't fine?'

'No. No, it wasn't. The children are settled here. They come first. And I knew he wouldn't be around. We'd have to fend for ourselves. So here we are. I'm desperately trying to get the kids more interested in seeing the world, though. I put this big map on the kitchen wall and we stick pins in where we want to go. The kids have put in a couple each. I've put in eighty-two. I'll get there one day, but for now . . . well, you compromise don't you? For love. Daniel could never see that.'

'I honestly think some people just don't function as part of a unit – whether it's a family or an office, or whatever. They just can't understand or relate to other people. They don't mean to be cruel, they just . . . it's just the way they see the world.'

'Oh Daniel *was* cruel. Now I have to be civil when we see each other. For the kids, you know? We have to pretend to be grown-ups, when really I just want to kick him in the balls.'

'Ugh, I hate pretending to be a grown-up.'

'You are a grown-up though. You're comfortable with yourself, you're looking after your daughter.'

'I don't know. I need people around me all the time. I need a big support network.'

She smiled at me.

'That's being a grown-up,' she said.

Marilyn arrived with the food. My macaroni cheese looked and smelled exactly like reheated vomit. Vanessa's steak looked like it had been caught in a nuclear explosion.

'What's this?' she asked.

There was a slight change in her tone. It wasn't aggressive, it was businesslike. It felt like she was beginning a transaction that absolutely would end in her favour.

'It's a New York strip steak, medium rare,' said Marilyn, checking her notes.

'No it isn't,' said Vanessa. 'I've been to New York, where incidentally they never call it a *New York* strip steak – just strip steak. This is the wrong cut of meat and it's really overcooked.'

Marilyn did not seem entirely surprised by this.

'I'm so sorry,' she said. 'The chef is being a total shit today. He thinks he's so much better than this place, but the food is bollocks, isn't it? I really am sorry.'

Vanessa looked at her for a second.

'Honestly, this is not your fault,' she said. 'You've been brilliant. But could you do me a favour? Could you take this back to the kitchen and tell the chef that his strip steak resembles a meteor that's just blasted through the ceiling of the restaurant and landed on my plate?'

'Yes ma'am,' said Marilyn. She took the plate away, a defiant smile on her face.

I looked at Vanessa. She sat back in the booth and took a sip from her wine. Before I could say anything, the door to the kitchen area burst open and I heard a loud, gruff voice yell, 'Right, who said it?' Vanessa and I looked over and saw a giant red-faced man in a stained white apron furiously surveying the room, Vanessa's plate gripped in his hand. It was the chef and he was coming to murder us.

'Oh my god,' said Vanessa. 'It's Gordon Ramsay on steroids.'

'I can't look. Is he carrying a meat cleaver?' I said.

'It's worse than that – he's got my steak.'

185

A kerfuffle started. The chef clearly wanted to interrogate everyone in the restaurant, which was reasonably busy with startled families. I thought this would provide the cover we needed, but as soon as he spotted us, he immediately seemed to know we were the source of the complaint.

'It was her, wasn't it?' shouted the chef.

'Uh-oh,' said Vanessa.

He started to make his way over, but Marilyn grabbed him and held him back, helped by two kitchen workers and a woman in a smarter suit who looked to be the manager.

'Maybe we ought to leave,' I suggested.

Without another word, we got up, slung enough money at the table to cover the bill and walked with accelerating pace towards the exit.

'That's right,' yelled the chef, struggling to free himself. 'Fuck off!'

I got to the door first and opened it wide – just as the chef picked the steak off the plate and threw it at us. Vanessa ducked with expert timing and it hit the window next to me, where it stuck fast.

'After you,' I said, making a long sweeping arm gesture towards freedom.

'Very kind, I'm sure,' said Vanessa. Then she turned back toward the chef and made an obscene hand gesture.

We bundled outside, holding hands and giggling. The sun had dropped and the night was coming. We stood for a second, trying to take in everything that had happened, perhaps wondering what else could go wrong. She still had her hand on my back.

'We'd better go,' I said. 'Before he comes out and kills us.'

'What now?' she said. 'I could take you back to my place and show you my photographs of South East Asia?'

Bathed in the trashy neon glow of the restaurant signs, she

looked transcendentally cool. Her smile was sweet and her eyes were on me. But as I looked into them I suddenly recalled the campfire.

'I think you'll agree this evening has been an enormous success,' I said.

'I can't fault it.'

'It was so good, perhaps we should go our separate ways and forget it immediately, so that we don't live the rest of our lives worrying that it could never be bettered.'

She looked at me and stepped away.

'Oh,' she replied. 'I suppose maybe you're right.'

Phew, I thought, this time I read the signals correctly. There was nothing going on this evening apart from fear and calamity. We didn't air-kiss or exchange numbers. We just parted. I walked back to my car and clambered in through the boot, tearing a great jagged hole in my trouser leg in the process.

As I was driving home, there was an image I couldn't get out of my head. Vanessa, outside the restaurant, nothing but the shimmering breeze between us. We held hands and we laughed – the way couples do when they have had an adventure. I hadn't felt that way since ... oh goodness, since Elizabeth.

How odd. As soon as I thought of her, I felt guilty. The marriage was over long ago, she was thousands of miles away, but she was still there in my head.

Amid this bewildering vortex of emotions and recollections, one theme finally emerged. I kept thinking of the things that had gone wrong this evening, and I couldn't stop smiling.

Hannah

The day after the nightclub incident, I'm on my laptop and I see that Callum has added me on MSN; he must have grabbed my email address from someone at school. Sneaky boy. As soon as I'm online, my message window pings. It's him.

How are you feeling? he types.

Much better! Sorry about almost fainting and everything.

It's fine. Just glad yr ok. Do you still wanna meet?

I think about it for a few seconds. I mean, do I? Do I really need to bother with all this?

I notice that Jenna is online too, so open a chat window with her.

Wtf happened to you last night? she types. Callum said you went home. I texted. U ok?

Felt faint, Callum helped me out.

> Ooh Prince Charming!

> Shut up. We're chatting now, he wants to meet up. Should I?

> Do you want to?

> I don't know!

Jenna sends me the heart emoticon.

I jab furiously at the keyboard: I DON'T FANCY HIM.

Jenna sends the smile emoticon followed by Just meet him. What have u got to loose?

> OK fine. But whatever happens is your fault. Also, u can't spell.

I go back to Callum.

> Yes, let's meet.

He says he'll be in town tomorrow morning, on the bench at the end of the car park; the one near the river where everyone hangs out. So romantic.

The next day, an unfamiliar set of anxieties hit me. What do I wear? Do I go super casual and pretend I don't care, or do I put in actual effort? Wow, these are the things normal people worry about all the time. Approaching the mirror on the back of my bedroom door with some caution, I immediately notice that I am very pale, there are dark circles around my eyes and my hair looks like I accidentally slept on a Van de Graaff generator.

'Good morning,' I say. 'Pleased to meet you, I am the bride of Frankenstein. Yes, my husband is well, thank you. I'll pass on your good wishes.'

I'm excited and not excited. I'm looking forward to it and I'm dreading it. I have forgotten what Callum looks and sounds like, but he's all I can think about. When I hear the letterbox clang and something dropping onto the carpet, I have this goofy fantasy that it's a formal invitation. 'Mr Callum Roberts requests the company of Miss Hannah Rose on the occasion of hanging out in the car park behind the shopping arcade.' But it isn't that. As I race down the stairs I see the envelope is plain brown and official-looking, with a little address window. It has my name on it. I take a deep breath and rip it open.

The letter is from the hospital – it's the date for my next set of tests.

Incredible timing. My handbag heart sinks like a stone. Now I don't really want to go out somewhere with this boy I barely know. Now I want to go back to bed, or run to the theatre and find my dad, or call Daisy and get her to come round and make popcorn and watch TV. It feels like a cruel little life lesson: don't make plans, don't look forward to things. You'd think I'd have learned by now.

But somehow I manage to convince myself that if I'm going to mope around, I may as well do it somewhere nice. Like a car park. The whole thing will be a disaster and I can just tick it off and go back to my familiar life of fear and loathing.

When I arrive, Callum is sitting with a bunch of kids from our school; some on the benches, some on the wooden fence that runs along the steep bank leading down to the river, some on the grass verge. Everyone in T-shirts and shorts and tiny skirts. The sun is glaring down so hard it's making the asphalt melt, releasing a tarry scent into the air that mixes with the exhaust fumes from passing cars. The boys are loud, lounging across the seats, jabbing at each other, trading catchphrases from *The Catherine Tate Show*, an echoing chorus of 'Am I bovvered?' I see Emilia and Georgia lying on the grass side by side, sharing earphones, listening to the same iPod. I see Jay talking to some guy from school, and he smiles and waves at me. Callum is on the end of one bench, constantly jostled by the boy next to him, but paying more attention to his phone screen. He's wearing a pink Lacoste polo shirt, light-blue skinny jeans and scuffed white Converse boots. There is a pair of Ray-Ban-style sunglasses hanging from the neck of his top. Something in my head is throbbing. I think about turning around and walking away. I'm pleading with myself to do that.

'Hey, Hannah,' a girl shouts. I don't know who it is. Callum looks up and smiles. He puts his phone away, hauls himself up and walks towards me.

'Hey,' he says.

'Hey.'

'So I was just texting you. A group of us are gonna get some drinks and head up to Westway field.'

'Uh-huh.'

'And hang there for a bit. Then Ben's family are having this big barbecue thing and ... Are you listening?'

'Yes.'

'Are you sure?'

'Yes.'

This is *not* what I want to do. I am regretting everything. My heart is thudding.

'So yeah, Ben lives at this huge, like, mansion just outside of town, some of us are staying over, I thought it would be cool if ... If ...'

Ba-bump, ba-bump, ba-bump. Deep breath. I don't want to

get stranded in the middle of nowhere. I don't want to end up in a room with drunk boys. I don't want Callum to put me in this position.

'You go,' I say in an assertive tone. 'It's fine. I don't think I will.'

'Hannah?'

'It's fine, it's fine. Please don't worry.'

There's a sense of decisive movement behind us. The lads are up and chasing each other around the car park, squirming in and out between the vehicles. I look over for Jay, half hoping my old pal will come and rescue me, but when I spot him he's just staring at me and Callum with this really cold expression. Then he wanders off too. He doesn't even wave goodbye.

'You guys coming?' someone shouts to us. 'Cazza's got a coolbox full of booze and an eighth of blow. It's gonna be sick.'

I feel a lot of emotion welling up. Callum is staring at me and I don't want him to. Something is going to happen.

Then one of his friends is right next to us. He's breathless from running around and he smells of deodorant and lager.

'You coming, mate?' he says.

'Just go,' I say to Callum.

I want to be out of this situation. It was a mistake. Something is pricking at my eyes. I have to move out of the way because a car is trying to park where we're standing. I see the driver through the windscreen, scowling and gesturing at us, insensitive to the little psychodrama that's playing out here – mostly in my head. I know that Callum will go. It's a beautiful day and they will spend the evening drinking and laughing and listening to music on a tiny beatbox as the sun drops beneath the tree line. Then people will pair up and disappear. Callum will go and that will be the end of it.

'No mate,' he says. 'We've got plans.'

'What?' says his friend.

'Me and Hannah have got plans, sorry. I'll text you later, bud.'

His friend backs away, looking at us, smiling, shaking his head. 'Typical Callum,' he says. 'Always disappearing.' Then he's off, running across the concrete, tugging at another pal's shorts. Callum watches him go.

'We've got plans?' I say.

'Yeah. Well. I've got plans. Well one plan.'

'What's that?'

'To do what you want. Whatever that is. That's my plan.'

'That's a good plan, you've obviously thought it through.'

'It took me all morning.'

'I'm sorry about the … field and stuff.'

'Oh, you know. I can go there any time. It stinks of hot cow shit anyway.'

'What did your friend mean? About you disappearing?'

'Oh nothing. He's just being a dick. How are you feeling?'

'Not brilliant. But I don't want to talk about it if that's all right?'

'Sure. I can relate to that. So anyway, I've told you my plan. Now, you have to tell me yours.'

'My plan for this afternoon?'

'Yeah, what else would I mean?'

He chose me.

The sun is hot on our faces. In the distance, at the edges of the car park, the light is shimmering. There is a golden hue to everything. It would possibly be more beautiful if we were at a beach or on a hillside looking out over swooping countryside, rather than amid an expanse of Volvos looking at an Argos superstore. But it is beautiful anyway. It makes me feel good.

'I have a plan,' I say.

And I take the sunglasses hanging from his shirt and I put them on.

He chose me – but then, who wouldn't?

'Let's go.'

Approximately twenty-five minutes later, we're in the comic shop. Callum is browsing the shelves, but I'm sitting down, getting my breath back. The small coffee table in front of me is littered with new things we haven't read, and old things that we love. Dav is behind the counter wearing a purple velvet dress and huge platform boots that lace up to her knees. Her talon-like nails are painted glossy purple too. I love Dav because she's who she wants to be and she looks how she wants to look. I totally admire her for that. When Callum is out of earshot, she scoots over and nudges me.

'Are you and him . . . ?' She makes a frantic gesture between me and Callum.

'Are we what?'

'You know!'

'I really don't.'

'*Together*?'

I just look at her.

'He's *buff*,' she whispers.

I decide not to reply, but I find myself nodding. I have been betrayed by my own head movements.

Callum comes and sits opposite me and we're just together, reading and geeking out. He tells me about how he grew up reading 2000 AD and how he never knew his dad so he got all the male guidance in his life from Judge Dredd, Rogue Trooper and Strontium Dog, which doesn't sound ideal. I tell him my comic book mothers were Wonder Woman, Black Widow and Storm from *Uncanny X-Men* ('they taught me it was important to be strong, independent and to have really giant hair'). He won't say much more about his home life, apart from the fact that his mum has had a succession of useless boyfriends, although the latest one seems just about okay. I tell him about my childhood in theatre, how I spent most of my time watching play rehearsals, how I idolised Oscar Wilde instead of Justin Timberlake. I even tell him about the birthday plays.

'So let me get this straight,' he says. 'Every year, the whole drama club put on plays just for you and your friends?'

'Yes.'

'Plays that you wrote?'

'Kind of. They were all based on fairy tales – which I was also completely obsessed with, did I mention that? And we never really wrote scripts. Me and Dad planned them out and the actors improvised them.'

'Wow, so you basically had your own real-life toy theatre to play with? I wish I could have seen that.'

'I guess there are probably photos somewhere. It's sad that we never wrote the plays down, but Dad and I are a bit chaotic. It must all sound pretty weird.'

'No! Well, yes,' he says. 'But it's really nice that your Dad did that for you. And it's cool that you're into comics *and* the theatre. That's kind of a random combination.'

'Ah, well, have you read *Sequential Art* by Will Eisner?' I am aware I have transformed into a nerdy lecturer, but this is my favourite subject and I can't stop. 'He writes about how comics and theatre frame the action in a similar way. They both, like, reduce every scene to the most important elements, and you have to sort of fill in the gaps with your imagination. They use lots of the same techniques, the way they create space and light, and ... sorry, I guess I've thought about this a lot.'

'Don't apologise,' he says. 'Don't say sorry for being smart.'

'I'm not smart. That essay you wrote on *Jane Eyre*, that was smart.'

He shrugs, and looks away from me. 'Hannah, look. I ... I should tell you something.'

Here we go, I think. He has a girlfriend. Or a boyfriend. Or he's moving to Scotland. Or all three at once.

'I have a sort of problem. A medical problem. Kind of. I mean, it's not as bad as yours, but ... I have depression. I'm on medication for it, and I go to therapy every fortnight. But yeah, that's me right now.'

'Shit,' I say. 'I'm sorry.'

'It's just – it can be bad sometimes. Sometimes it's fine, but a lot of times it isn't. Sometimes I ... well, I just have to be alone. I can't face people. I wanted you to know. Just in case. I don't know. Fuck, whatever. Some of my friends know, but just don't tell everyone at school.'

'I wouldn't.'

'I know.'

'Is that what your mate meant, when he said about you disappearing?'

Callum nods. 'So I'll understand if ...'

'What?'

'If you don't want to hang out.'

'Why wouldn't I want to hang out?'

'It's a lot to deal with.'

'So is heart disease.'

'Right. What a pair. Do you want to talk about it?'

'What, heart disease?'

'Yeah, tell me a fact. A heart disease fact.'

'Um ... I take ten tablets twice a day and one of them is a diuretic so I have to wee a *lot*. Is that the sort of fact you were after?'

'Yes, this is exactly what I wanted to know, thank you.'

I could have told him anything. I could have told him about

196

cardiopulmonary exercise tests, or abdominal ultrasounds, or literally anything else about cardiomyopathy. Instead, I went straight for peeing. Why, god, *why*?

Anyway, that's that. That's our deep conversation done for the day. We go back to reading, but I am secretly wondering about what depression feels like and what it means exactly. Is he just sad a lot? Is he suicidal? And a small terrible selfish part of me thinks, do I need this? What am I doing here with this guy? I've just sort of accidentally drifted into this whole thing and now it turns out that it's going to be complicated. But then Dav puts Nick Cave on the stereo, and I think, well I'm sitting here reading comics and he's nice, and everything is actually bearable. The shop door opens and Ricky blunders in, and I guess Dav must have texted him or something, because he strolls over to me carrying two cans of Coke and a bag of doughnuts.

'For our guests,' he says. And he puts them on the table for us.

I could have cried at the kindness of it.

So when it gets to six o'clock and the shop is closing, it's a wrench to leave. The other geeks shuffle out clutching their plastic bags filled with stories. Callum and I put all the books we can't afford back onto the shelves. Dav hugs me goodbye; Ricky makes a Spock salute.

Then we're outside again, looking around, uncertain about everything.

'Thank you,' I say to Callum.

'For what?'

'For your excellent plan.'

'Well, it was mostly your work.'

'Thank you for not making me go with your friends. Thank you for asking me what *I* wanted to do.'

'You're totally welcome.' Then he said, 'Hannah?'

'Yes?'

'Do you ever have those moments when you're thinking, like, whatever happens, I have this day. Like, I *own* this, no one can take it away. All the crap that might happen to me, it won't happen today. Today is mine and I can just enjoy it, and all the memories will be safe. Does that make any sense?'

'Yeah, it does. It totally does.'

'Well, this was one of those days. For me, I mean.'

'For me too.'

'Really?'

'Really.'

'Hannah, can I give you this? It's really fucking stupid, but . . . I just want you to look at it.'

He takes something out of his backpack – it's a large exercise book. I go to flick through it, but he stops me.

'No, not yet, wait until I've gone. I'm . . . it's embarrassing.'

'What? Why? Oh you haven't written me a sonnet have you?'

'No.'

'Have you drawn me like one of your French girls?'

'What?!'

'Oh, you know – it's that scene in *Titanic* where Kate Winslet gets her boobs out and . . . '

'No! Just take it home and have a look later. And, well, let me know what you think.'

'I definitely will.'

Now I have mentioned Kate Winslet's boobs. I really am a pro at this.

'There's a comic convention in Bristol in a few weeks,' he says. 'They have this thing where you can take in art and have it assessed by publishers and editors.'

'Oh cool. Are you going?'

'I don't know. I doubt it. Shit. No, I don't think so.'

'Why not?'

'I told you why.'

I look at him but he won't meet my eye and I don't want to push it and ruin the whole afternoon.

'I'd better go,' I say. 'Dad's expecting me.'

'Goodbye Hannah Rose.'

He gets really close, and the feeling is familiar. It's like that moment this afternoon, the heat shimmering in the distance; the light becoming golden. He kisses me on the cheek, then once again really close to my mouth. We pause for a second, my fingers trace up his arm. He has goose bumps.

Every year, when I was a kid, my Dad put on a play for my birthday. He did it to help me cope with my annual heart check-up, and also the fear and uncertainty that I felt pretty much every day. He called them the Days of Wonder, because he said wonder beat everything. He made those days strange and incredible. He'd hire musicians to play outside the theatre when my friends and I were arriving. There would be cakes and sweets and fizzy drinks in the foyer, served by costumed characters. It felt that all the good in the world emanated from that theatre, like the Cosmic Cube in the *Captain America* comics. The ultimate source of light and power.

But today, god, today was up there too. There was no performance, no stage, no theatrical magic. Just me and this boy and the way we made each other feel. This is going to sound really dumb but when I touched his arm, what I felt was . . . wonder.

So whatever is coming, it won't get me today. Not today.

Today.

Is.

Mine.

Tom

As August wore on it became increasingly clear that summer was actually happening, and that it wasn't going away. This being Britain, people loved it for a few days; the beaches were crammed, kids frolicked in park fountains, the air smelled of barbecues – but then everyone got food poisoning and the trains broke down and it was anarchy. I headed into the theatre most days wearing my new uniform of cargo shorts, white linen shirt and Panama hat. I let my beard grow. Hannah said I looked like a wine-loving serial killer hitchhiking through Provence.

I visited the dating site a couple of times to see if there were, by some bizarre miracle, any messages from Vanessa – but there were not. Hannah caught me browsing through the page and made me check for new matches, which she then forced me to accept. This is how I ended up going on three dates in three nights – the romantic equivalent of binge drinking. There was Jocasta, an environmentalist who insisted we ate in an expensive organic vegetarian bistro called the Physic Garden. It was in the middle of nowhere and full of strange earthy people in hand-woven clothes. I was worried they'd realise I was a closet meat-eater then drag me outside so that I could be sacrificially burned in a giant wicker aubergine. Then there was Oregon, who had once modelled in shopping catalogues but now ran an agency arranging childcare for the swathes of upper-middle-class families moving into town. She mostly fed me gossip about her celebrity clients. Apparently one of the cast members of a long-running hospital drama was having an affair with an actual doctor and claiming their hotel bills on expenses because she said that it was effectively research. Finally, there was Eva who explained in her message that she was very much into experimental music, which I thought sounded interesting. However, our date was a concert in Bristol where a man slowly disassembled a grand piano over the course of two buttock-numbing hours. We were supposed to go for a drink afterwards to discuss it, but instead I told her that I needed time alone to contemplate what I had seen and heard, and then sped away in my car with Oasis blaring on the stereo.

When I got home that night, Hannah was out with Daisy. I found a bottle of port in the back of the understairs cupboard. I poured myself a glass and I took the photo of me and Elizabeth from the mantelpiece. I sat on the sofa – the sofa that Lizzie and I had bought together and then dragged through a succession of crappy rented flats to our first house. There was a red wine stain on one of the cushions from that night we'd got drunk watching the *Eurovision Song Contest*. We sang along to every number. All I could hear now was the central heating humming, and the quiet swish of passing cars. I held the photograph and traced the line of Elizabeth's smile with my finger. The memory of the humiliating campfire non-kiss popped into my head, taunting me, like Banquo's ghost. Perhaps this port is out of date, I thought.

Hannah was sneaking off every morning to meet Callum at (oh the glamour of young love) the car park. I'd always wondered how

I would feel when this happened. I was determined not to be one of those crazed protective fathers who threaten their daughters' boyfriends with physical violence. To be honest, I would not be entirely convincing in that role, as I have all the aggressive menace of a *Carry On* movie. I resolved to be kind and welcoming and not too strange. But there was a wrench in my heart because I knew some of the adventures in her life would now take place with him as a co-star. I would need to make room. In the afternoons, she was still seeing Jenna and Daisy for their reading coven, but I felt sorry for Jay; their once close friendship was hanging by a thread. He came to the theatre a few times looking for her and leaving with a glum and despondent expression on his face. I asked him how he was and he mumbled about things being 'weird' at home, but that was clearly a cover story because things never seemed weird for Sally. She was the most sorted person in my life.

Anyway, I was thinking that Hannah seemed pretty together, but then, this morning I went into her room to put the A Level questionnaire back onto her noticeboard and I saw the latest cardiology appointment letter pinned there, with an unhappy face scrawled on it. She had not told me it had arrived. She always told me about appointments. I wondered if, deep down, she was feeling pushed out by my own dating regime.

I felt like we needed some quality time together and I remembered about a new restaurant opening in town. Obviously this would be the perfect opportunity for a game of I Dare You To Wear. I texted her and asked if she'd meet me on the stage at midday. Then I spent an hour raiding the costume room, pulling together a selection of three ridiculous outfits for her to choose from. I hung them on a rail and hid it behind the curtains at the rear of the stage – it would be an amusing reveal.

She arrived at 12.15 looking hot and harried, tapping away

on her phone as she walked down towards the stage. I'd set up a table and two chairs so it looked a little like the set of a kitchen sink drama.

'Hello, Casanova,' she said as she climbed the side steps and walked into the light. 'How was the date last night?'

'On a catastrophe scale from one to ten?'

'Of course. How else would we measure them?'

'I think maybe a three.'

'That's positive. How was the music?'

'It was smashing.'

She took the seat opposite mine and peered at me.

'It's not working out is it?' she said.

'What, dating? I'm having the time of my life, darling!'

'Dad. Tell me the truth.'

'Will you tell me something first?'

'Sure.'

'Why didn't you let me know about the new hospital appointment?'

She looked down, her face lost beneath a tumult of curls.

'I was going to. It's just that a lot of other stuff has been happening.'

'Do you want me to stop all this dating nonsense?' I asked.

'No!' she said, suddenly looking right at me. 'That's the opposite of what I want!'

'But it's not working. They're just not like . . .'

'What?'

'Nothing.'

'They're not like Elizabeth. That's what you were going to say, isn't it? Dad, she's been gone for ten years!'

'I know.'

'You've got to move on!'

She slammed her hands down on the table and the noise echoed around the empty auditorium. It seemed obvious she was avoiding the real issue, which was her appointment.

'Hannah, it's not that simple. It's like ... your mum is part of me, she's part of my life. The times we had together, the way I felt about her, it doesn't just go away. And every time I end up sitting opposite a stranger at some café, or pub or bistro or concert, feeling awkward, desperately trying to carve out a conversation, I think of her and how it wasn't awkward, and it wasn't desperate. And I miss her. I really, really miss her.'

This wasn't the direction I wanted this to go in. I had departed from the script and was improvising wildly.

'You've just got to keep trying,' she said. She took my hand. 'You need someone. There will be a date that goes well, that's fun, that works.'

I shook my head.

'I just can't see it.'

'Dad, don't be dramatic! You've had, what, five dates? That's nothing! Come on, I promise you, something will click. You'll keep going and eventually, you'll meet someone and it'll be like, of course! Of course. This is it!'

Vanessa.

'I won't.'

Outside the restaurant, the neon, the stars.

'You don't know that! There will be one, there will be someone, there will be *one* chance. It will happen!'

'It won't, Hannah, because I think it already did happen and I blew it.'

Walking away, hand in hand, the way couples do.

'What? What do you mean? Dad?'

'Vanessa. You know, the one I went to the cinema with.'

And for the first time, I told her the whole story. I told her about the terrible movie, and the restaurant, and Marilyn Monroe, and the steak, and when I got to the part about running away from the chef she was laughing.

'You're joking? You got chased out? You had to flee your own date?'

'Yes, and we got outside and . . . you know, it was a lovely night, and so peaceful, and I don't know. We went our separate ways. The end.'

I watched as Hannah's smile slowly drifted into a frown.

'That feels like it should be the start of a story,' she said. 'Not the end.'

'It's fine! Hannah, it's just one of those things. Anyway we've got enough on at the moment. I think we should put this whole sorry episode behind us, and I have the perfect solution.'

'Dad, I . . . '

'You know, that new restaurant opening up in town this evening?'

'The thing is . . . '

'Well, I have reserved a table for Mr and Miss I Dare You To Wear!'

This was always the way, she would pretend not to be interested and then she would grudgingly concede, because that was our rule, and we'd go out and have fun and forget everything. Together. It was our rule. I sprang out of my seat, ready to reveal her outfit selections.

'I'm sorry, I can't,' she said, almost in a whisper. I stopped dead. 'I'm going to see *Batman* with Callum.'

'But . . . but you don't even like action movies. And you *hate* Batman.'

'I know, but . . . we're just going to laugh at it and throw popcorn at the screen.'

'You call him the Caped Creep.'

'I know.'

'The Dark Shite.'

'I *know*. But Callum wants to see it. Is that all right? Do you mind?'

I sat down again. 'No, of course not. That will be nice.'

'Are you sure?'

'Absolutely.'

'I'm worried about you.'

'Don't be silly. You go and have fun.'

Her phone buzzed and she whipped it out of her pocket.

'It's Callum,' she said making a pained expression. 'I'm so sorry, I sort of promised to meet him.'

'I understand,' I replied.

'Can I . . . go?'

'Yes. Yes, sorry, of course.'

I reminded myself of my new policy: kind and welcoming and not too strange. Then I let her go.

Hannah

I did something I probably shouldn't have done. If Dad finds out he'll probably kill me. Or he'll die of embarrassment. Or he'll kill me and *then* die of embarrassment. I contacted Vanessa. I went into Dad's dating profile and I emailed her. I wrote a message explaining that I was his daughter and wanted to meet her, and hey, here was my email address and phone number. Honestly, I was just messing about and had no intention of sending it. But then I just kind of pretended to hit the send button, and pretended a bit too hard, and sent it.

That was bad enough, but then forty-three minutes later, she only bloody texted me back. 'Happy to meet,' went the message. 'Where is good for you?'

'Oh shit.' That's what I'm now saying to myself, over and over again. 'Oh shit, oh shit, oh shit.' That's what I say under my breath as I desperately try to think of where it would be safe to meet her – somewhere Dad would never go. I text her suggesting my third home and preferred awkward-meeting venue: the comic store. She replies, 'Yeah, sure, 1 p.m. tomorrow?'

'Oh shit!'

Is this the weirdest, stupidest thing I've ever done? It must be up there. It's not like I've ever got shitfaced on Smirnoff Ice then thrown up in my friend's hair or accidentally dated my second cousin (both Daisy). I tend to be reasonably careful about stuff. I think things through. I mull them over. I do not make secret contact with my dad's prospective girlfriends. Though to be fair, I haven't had the opportunity before. Jesus, who knows what I'm capable of?

The next day, I decide on a longer route into town so I don't pass the theatre and don't accidentally bump into Dad. It means that I walk past Callum's house. He hasn't, like, officially invited me round or anything yet, but he made the mistake of telling me where he lives, and I figure that while I'm living life on the edge, I may as well just sidle up to the door and say 'Hi'. I have an excuse anyway, because I need to return his sketchbook. I finally summoned the courage to look at it last night. It's always a bit nerve-racking when a friend shares something creative with you – like that time Jenna made me read her *Lost* fan fiction. But the drawings are amazing. They're mostly of a young girl with wild black hair and clenched fists, looking ferocious and accompanied by some kind of giant black wolf. In one she's standing over a body in a smoke-filled alley, in another she's in a library, and all the books are flying out of the shelves around her. It's all super heavy shadows, anger and violence, like *Sin City* or *Walking Dead*. I'm seriously impressed.

Callum lives in a bit of a rundown estate next to a great big food-processing factory. The houses look like Lego buildings with their bright red bricks and dark, empty windows. Most of the gardens are overgrown and filled with weeds and broken bikes and toys. When I get to his place, I have to squeeze past a jeep up on bricks in the driveway. I try to ring the doorbell but all the wires are hanging out so I knock instead. The bright mood I was in starts to fade a bit. I knock again and this time, the sound of manic barking comes from within. I take a few steps back.

Seconds later, a middle-aged woman comes to the door, holding a book and looking harassed and cross. Her face is prematurely old, but not ugly. She has her long frizzy hair pulled back into a ponytail and she's wearing jeans with a light pink Juicy Couture hoodie. Oh god, I think I'm meeting his mum.

'Yeah?' she says.

'Is Callum home?' I ask, trying to sound polite but also considerably less like a BBC Radio presenter than I think I usually do.

'He's in bed, love.'

'Oh,' I say, and without thinking I check my phone screen for the time.

'Will he … will he be up soon?'

'I doubt it. He's having one of his bad days.'

'I just wanted to say hi. We're friends. Well sort of friends. No, we actually are friends.'

She gives me the merest inkling of a sympathetic look.

'When he feels like this, it don't matter who you are, love, he won't see you. What's your name? I'll tell him you came by.'

'I'm Hannah.'

Her face suddenly brightens.

'Oh *the* Hannah? God, darling, I've heard all about you,' she says.

'Really?'

'Yeah, he's been going on about nothing else. He'll kill me if he knows I told you.'

I can feel my face basically igniting, like a giant firework display of embarrassment.

'Well, I'm glad you did,' I stutter.

'I'm Kerry, his mum.'

'Hello, Kerry,' I say. Oh god, this is so weird.

The dog runs up behind her and barks at me from behind her legs, snapping me out of my humiliating boy trance.

'SHUT IT, SWAMP THING!' she yells.

'Let me guess,' I say. 'Callum named him?'

'He always was a daft kid. I'd invite you in for a cuppa but the place is a right state, and I don't think we'll see him today. He gets very down sometimes.'

'I know, he told me.'

She looks surprised, but then smiles.

'He doesn't talk to many people about it. Keeps it all inside. Typical bloke.'

A guy comes down the hall behind Callum's mum, and I guess it's the current boyfriend Callum mentioned in the comic store. He has really short, cropped black hair, and looks craggy and aggressive. But then, without saying anything, he kisses her warmly on the cheek and smiles at me. 'All right,' he says, and shuffles past us to get to the car. She watches him flip open a toolbox and disappear under the hood. Then looks back at me expectantly, clearly waiting for me to go. Swamp Thing starts barking again so she bashes it lightly on the head with her book. I notice it's *Of Mice and Men*, the worst of our English set texts. The dog whimpers and walks back into the house. I know how it feels.

'So um, can you tell Callum I came to see him?' I say. 'And tell him I liked his art.'

'I will, love.'

'I hope he feels better soon.'

She shakes her head. 'He gives me a lot of worry that boy.'

'Goodbye,' I say. But the door is already closing.

I walk down the pathway and then look back at the house. In the smaller of the two upstairs windows, the curtains are drawn, but I'm sure I see them move a little.

At the comic store, Ricky is reordering his 'Recommended' section, creating a Batman display to celebrate the release of the *Batman Begins* movie. I stand in the doorway scowling at him.

'You sell-out,' I say.

Ricky looks up at me guiltily. 'I was dreading this moment.'

I choose not to tell him that I saw the stupid film. It was a total fail. Christian Bale putting on a ridiculous gruff voice, doing the whole 'white guy discovers martial arts' thing and whinging for two hours. Callum and I giggled through most of it.

'So which Bat Fascist masterworks are you endorsing?' I say.

'Oh, you know, the usual.'

'*Dark Knight Returns, Killing Joke, The Long Halloween* … haven't all your geek boys bought those already?'

'Hannah, I . . .'

I'm just about to launch into another blistering attack on the Caped Psycho, when I hear the door opening behind me and turn to see a woman in her thirties wearing a gorgeous Hobbes dress. She has a kind of boyish Audrey Hepburn beauty and her hair and make-up are perfectly styled. Somehow, I immediately know that she is not a regular.

'Vanessa?' I say.

'Hannah?'

'Yes.'

We stand and look at each other awkwardly. Ricky senses a chance to escape, scuttling away to the counter.

'I'm sorry, this is a bit strange, isn't it?' I offer.

'Well, yes,' she replies. 'But then, to be honest with you, Hannah,

I'm at a point in my life where I like to do strange things. Monday was Pilates, yesterday I joined a choir, today I'm meeting a teenager in a comic shop about a date with her father. So let's go for it.'

I gesture towards the two knackered armchairs in the corner, as though I'm showing her to my office. We walk over in silence and she takes the seat that Callum sat in on our first 'date'. It is a weird re-creation of that moment, only now I'm here with *Dad's* date, which makes me feel like I'm in a soap opera or Greek tragedy. It's only when we're both sitting and looking at each other again that I realise I have no plan. I have no idea what I'm actually doing. I feel suddenly really fatigued.

'This place is wonderful,' says Vanessa. 'Why don't I come in here? I used to love comics when I was a girl. I read every *Tintin* book. I used to mark off all the places he'd been on a big map of the world on my bedroom wall. I had a crush on Captain Haddock until I was about fifteen. I was a weird child. Anyway, hi, what can I do for you?'

I like her immediately. I mean holy shit, she's beautiful, she's sophisticated and she seems really comfortable in herself. I start to worry that maybe she isn't interested in Dad at all. I decide to broach the subject as subtly as possible.

'Well, I just . . . I think Dad was . . . I mean after the date . . . Oh god, look, do you like him?'

She bursts out laughing, and it's such a loud, unselfconscious sound that I start too. A guy perusing the manga section looks at us with suspicion.

'You don't mess around,' she says.

'Life's too short,' I reply. And I wonder if Dad said anything to her about me because her mouth instantly straightens. It takes her a while to answer.

'Yes,' she says. 'I did like him. I mean, the date was a giant nuclear disaster, but it was the fun sort of nuclear disaster.'

'There's a fun sort of nuclear disaster?'

'A few months ago, I wouldn't have thought it was possible, but this is my new life now, a life where I date men and do Pilates.'

'He told me a little bit about it.'

'Did he tell you about the chef who threw the steak at us?'

'I thought he was making that bit up.'

She shakes her head with enthusiasm. 'No, it's all true. I think if we hadn't escaped, we would have ended up on the menu.'

'He likes you,' I say.

'The chef?'

'No, my dad!'

'Really? He didn't take my number, or email me or anything.'

'I think he was embarrassed, you know – by the fact that everything went completely wrong. And also, he has a ton of difficult things going on. Work. Me . . .'

'You?' she says.

So I sort of explain everything because maybe Dad didn't. I tell her about Mum leaving and my diagnosis and what an absolute fucking drag that's been recently. I make it very clear that I'm not emotionally blackmailing her into seeing him again, but I guess I am. He's going to *kill me*. I don't say anything about the theatre because Dad's been funny about discussing his job with dates. I think he wants to be the one to tell them – in person – that he spends his life booking brass bands, blue comedians and educational puppet shows. Which is totally understandable. In return she tells me a bit about herself, and her divorce and the fact that she's always busy in a boring office job and everything is so serious all the time and she just wants to escape to Africa or Ecuador or Japan. It's weird, I feel like an adult, having an adult conversation in a coffee bar or something. She is funny and really clever and frustrated and passionate.

'You know what I miss?' she says. 'Just hanging around in places like this. When you grow up, you take on all these burdens – family, work, ambitions – and you think it's adding to your life, and it is, obviously, but it's also taking away. It's so easy to lose sight of yourself amid all the demands and responsibilities. You lose a sense of who you are and what you like. I mean, why am I going home and reading reports every night? Why aren't I reading ...' She looks around the store for inspiration. 'Why aren't I reading *Batman*?'

'Oh, of all the things you could have gone for,' I groan.

'Bad choice?'

'Don't get her started,' yells Ricky from the counter.

'Maybe I should get some recommendations?' she replies.

'*Persepolis*,' I say immediately. 'You are totally a *Persepolis* fan. It's about a young girl growing up in Iran in the seventies and rebelling against the expectations of society.'

'Does she have super powers?'

'No. It's not that type of comic.'

She nods, looks quickly at her mobile phone, then back at me. 'So what do we do now?' she says.

'I don't know. Do you want to see him again?'

'Yes. But ... maybe something casual. Where there's no pressure. And no chance of us being chased out of a restaurant by a maniacal chef.'

'Hmmm, that's tricky. And he can't know we've spoken. He would think that was weird.'

'To be fair he'd have a point. Oh wait, there is one thing coming up ... No it's too silly.'

'Believe me, nothing is too silly for my dad.'

'Well, the music teacher at the local school runs these sessions every Thursday evening at the community hall – basically music lessons for adults. You just go along, have a glass of wine, choose an instrument and do a class. My neighbour has convinced me to go with her. Do you think I should invite him? He can bring people too. That way, it's not a *date* date.'

'Oh my god, honestly, this is totally him. And he definitely knows people who'll come.'

'Well, this looks like a plan. I mean, it's a stupid plan, but god help me, that's where I am right now.'

She gets up and so do I. Then she puts her hand out and I shake it. We appear to have just done a business deal. She goes to leave but then stops.

'Do they sell that *Persepolis* book here?' she says across the store.

'Yes we do,' shouts Ricky.

'Well then, what the hell, I'll take a copy.'

Wow, I should get a job here, bringing in Dad's prospective dates and selling them comics on commission. When she's gone I decide to take a leisurely look through the 'just in' section and see they have the first issue of a new *Daredevil* run in stock. I take it to the counter, groping in my pocket for some change.

'What? Another sale?' says Ricky. 'I'd ask you to come in more often but I'm not sure that's technically possible.'

'Just sell me the damn comic,' I say. 'Oh, and can I borrow a pen?'

I go back via Callum's road again. When I get to his house, the curtains in the upstairs bedroom are still drawn. I take the comic out and look at it briefly. In the corner of the cover I've scrawled I DARE you to get out of bed. Hannah xxxxx. I post it through the letterbox.

About fifty yards from his house I start to regret writing that. He's got actual depression – what if he thinks I'm trivialising it by telling him to get up? Also, why did I have to put FIVE kisses?

But, not for the first time, the thought underlining absolutely everything else is, why am I even doing this?

Tom

There were two surprises about the text message. The first was that Vanessa had contacted me again, completely out of the blue, and the second was that she wanted to take me to a school music lesson for adults. Naturally, the idea appealed to me. Also, she was bringing her neighbour so it was not technically going to be a date – unless I'd massively misunderstood the situation. It didn't take me long to round up my own chaperones. James said he was just about lonely enough to consider it (I told him it was a notorious pick-up place) and Natasha told me she was – as usual – looking for any excuse to leave the kids and if that meant playing the bongos in a community centre, that's what she would do. I texted Vanessa and told her I had formed a band and would see her there. A second date. A sequel. Date II – this time it's personal. And unlike most sequels, surely it could only be better than the original?

James, Natasha and I met up outside the theatre to walk over together, but Natasha was delayed because she had to express some breast milk. 'The little bastard won't touch formula,' she explained breathlessly. 'Just my luck to produce delicious milk. I caught Seb putting it in his coffee the other night. I mean, what the fuck?

Thank you so much for getting me out of there. I'm not sure I'm a natural parent. What do you guys think?'

We don't answer.

The community centre was a converted Victorian church building, which doubled as a drill hall for the local sea cadets (we are about forty miles away from the sea so god knows what they get up to). We followed a rabble of assorted hippies and arty types into the small hall, which radiated threadbare community chic: seventies checkerboard wooden tiles, horrible orangey-yellow patterned curtains over large single-glazed windows; a giant steel tea urn on a trestle table in the corner, and next to that, another table loaded with bottles of cheap white wine and plastic cups.

We all plodded over, poured glasses ('Just the one,' said Natasha, 'it'll add some pizzazz to the milk') and looked around at the other attendees, awkwardly glugging back the supermarket own-brand alcohol. There were a lot of baggy jumpers, dungarees, dreadlocks and flat caps in various combinations. But there were also groups of men and women in jeans and shirts, sipping and chatting as though at a corporate social event. The nicest thing about living in a small town in Somerset was that everyone had to make their own fun. If someone put an event on, whether it was ballroom dancing for kids with ADHD or gangsta rap knitting circles, people would just come. Sometimes we struggled to fill the auditorium at the theatre, but we always had an audience.

The teacher, a ruddy-faced woman in her fifties with crazed blonde and black hair like the singer out of Berlin, started pulling musical instruments from a big box and putting them on a table in the centre of the room. I was watching this process when Vanessa walked in. She was dressed more casually than last time – a short denim skirt and a cami top embroidered with sparkly gold flowers along the neck and waist, and dark red boots. Her short hair was gelled and glistening. She looked younger but still breathtakingly stylish. Her friend was in a floral dress and trainers – she was maybe about the same age as James and from the way she barged in, immediately seemed confident and fun. Had the matchmaking gods smiled upon us?

'Vanessa,' I called over from the wine table.

She looked and smiled. It was radiant. I felt my knees wobble slightly and put it down to the high alcohol content in the wine. We did the introductions. Her friend was called March, because her wacky parents had decided that, no matter what, they would name their baby after the month she was born. She made silver jewellery and sold it through an online store. She was more outgoing than Vanessa, seemingly taking the lead role in their friendship.

'I can't believe none of you have been to this before,' she yelled over the increasingly loud conversational noise. 'It's such fun!'

She was just about to explain everything when the teacher clapped her hands loudly.

'Right!' she said. 'Some of your children may know me as Ms Baker, but you may call me Gwen. Welcome to our music class. I hope you have all helped yourself to wine.' (I looked around – everyone really had.) 'Good! Now as usual, we shall get into small groups of four or five, then I will ask you all to come to the table and select an instrument. You will then work together to compose a short piece based around a theme. Does everyone understand?'

We are all suddenly twelve again, nodding obediently.

'Right we have to be quick,' whispered March. 'The best stuff goes fast, so don't hold back. The bongos are the favourites – if you want them, you need to be ruthless. The glockenspiel is also popular.'

She was still explaining the musical hierarchy when Gwen clapped her hands again and suddenly everyone was converging on the music table like ravenous zombies. Natasha pushed past us all, darting for the aforementioned bongos and grabbing them victoriously. James tried for the maracas, but settled for sleigh bells. March got a tambourine. I got stuck behind a large woman in a leather jacket, but took advantage of her crippling indecision to grab the first thing I could get my hands on – a ribbed wooden object with a separate stick. I looked at it with incomprehension. 'That's a güiro,' shouted Gwen, noticing my confusion. 'You rub the stick along the grooves. Did you not do music at school?'

It was a ridiculous escapade, a giant boozy jostle, but when I caught Vanessa's eye she looked at me with a mixture of joy and triumph. She had a large triangle. We emerged bruised from the scrum and went back to our corner, sitting down cross-legged in a circle, comparing our spoils. There was a lot of noise and laughter, punctured by the odd parp from a bike horn, or the beat of a snare drum.

'Right, does everyone have an instrument?' shouted Gwen.

This time we all shouted 'Yes!'

'Excellent, then the theme of your composition is: the sounds of the city. Don't think about trying to write a song, think about creating the atmosphere and experience of the urban environment. You have twenty minutes!'

There was an immediate buzz of activity as people gathered closer in their little groups. I took the opportunity to shuffle nearer to Vanessa.

'So, thanks for inviting me to this . . . thing,' I said.

'You're welcome. To be honest it's not *my* thing, but March is a gigantic bully. She told me I needed to get out of the house. It was either this or a singalong showing of *The Little Mermaid* at the cinema.'

'How are you doing?'

'I'm bored of work, I'm bored of being alone. I'm having the world's most restrained and respectable mid-life crisis. Is this too much information? Why did I go for the triangle?'

'Sometimes I have these moments where I think, how much are we really in control of in our own lives? How much is actually just blind luck?'

She nodded seriously. 'I should have gone for the glockenspiel,' she said.

'I'm trying to make a serious observation about the fallacy of self-determination.'

'I'm sorry. So what do you do in those moments of existential angst?'

'I get a mug of hot chocolate and listen to the radio.'

'So you're not one for confronting things then – for grabbing the bull by the horns?'

'Oh lord, no. Where did that ever get anyone?'

She laughed, but the sound pulled us back into the group. Suddenly they all wanted to know what we thought of their plan.

'We're going to be a bus,' said March. 'Natasha, James and I are the engine. Tom, you are the doors. Vanessa, you're the bell. It makes perfect sense.'

'Nothing about this makes perfect sense,' she said.

March poured us all some more wine, and seemed to move herself closer to James. Hmmm, interesting. Natasha was busy just belting away at the bongos with increasing speed and ferocity.

'This is extremely therapeutic,' she said. 'I'm going to buy some.'

Over the next ten minutes we worked out a reasonable bus composition: March, James and Natasha would play together, building up speed then slowing down to a stop; I would give a rasp on the güiro to signify the doors opening, then another for them to shut; then Vanessa gave two tings on the triangle and the engine started again.

'This is an experimental masterpiece,' exclaimed Natasha.

'Eat your heart out, Brian Eno,' I said, and was pleased that Vanessa clearly got the reference, or was polite enough to smile anyway.

When the twenty minutes were up, we all had to sit and listen to every group's composition. There were street sounds using bicycle horns and castanets, there were department store sounds (great use of the glockenspiel for the lift music). It was ridiculously enjoyable and the room was filled with happy, proud faces. Adults rarely give themselves the opportunity to be creative, but when they do they reconnect with something in themselves that was once natural and plentiful. It was sort of magical.

While the others went on for another drink, Vanessa had to get home to relieve her teenage babysitter so I walked with her. We strolled along, up the cobbled lanes of the old part of town, past a row of old Victorian shops converted into houses. We talked about music and children and living in small towns. We talked about our marriages and tried to explain to each other (and also ourselves) where things had gone wrong.

'I look back on it now and I'm not sure what was real and what wasn't,' I said. 'When were we happy? Was she always dissatisfied? I don't know which memories mean anything any more.'

'Here's what I think,' said Vanessa. 'When you're in a relationship with someone, you have these nice defining moments early on and you just keep reminiscing about them until your stories don't bear any relation to what really happened. You actually start to manufacture a history. That's what a relationship is: it's a factory of memories – and when one person leaves, the machine breaks down, and all the truth leaks out like fuel.'

She stopped walking and seemed momentarily annoyed at herself for her scepticism. 'But you know, not all factories are ugly.

I went to Rio in my early twenties and when you drive out of the city towards the airport you pass all these old abandoned industrial buildings, hundreds of them, they seem to go on for miles. And it's weird but, to me, it was the most beautiful thing I'd seen in Brazil. I don't know why. Buildings are memories, aren't they? Anyway, sorry, this is me.'

She pointed to a large house at the end of a row, with giant windows and pristine plastered walls in some tasteful Farrow & Ball shade of green.

'You're pretty wise,' I said.

'I am. It's all the travelling I've done mixed with the experience of marrying a complete dickhead.'

She smiled brightly; she had the most expressive eyes I'd ever seen. I felt like scholars would need to study them for years to translate the complex and beautiful language they communicated in.

'Well, that was a pleasant night,' I said. 'I wasn't sure I'd hear from you again.'

'I wasn't sure either, to be honest. But someone told me I should give you a chance.'

'Please thank them from me,' I said. It was a bit awkward then, and I was getting ready to walk away.

'Tom,' she said. 'We should have kissed. When we got out of the restaurant that night. We were in each other's arms; the sky was full of stars, we'd escaped a meat-wielding chef. If it had been an Indiana Jones movie, we'd have kissed.'

'Can we perhaps try again?' I asked.

'Hmmm,' she pondered. 'Not now, not here. But I am certain we'll get another chance – there will be a perfect moment, like the one before. This time, you need to take it.'

She turned and walked towards her house. I already wanted to see her again. I wanted to build our own factory of memories.

Hannah

Here is an unexpected turn of events. I'm supposed to be meeting Margaret for tea, but then she phones and tells me she's not feeling well, so can I go to her house instead of the café? I've never been there before – I don't think anyone has, so I say yes, definitely, because it's bound to give me intriguing clues about her life story. Then, just before I head out, I get a text from Callum.

I'm feeling better, it says. Can I see ya?

I mull it over for about two milliseconds.

Sure, I type back. I'm on my way to my friend's house. Do you want to come?

Yes.

One thing though – she's 81.

There is a slight pause.

ROFL, he replies. I think u made a mistake, u wrote 81!!

That wasn't a mistake.

Slightly longer pause.

Whatever, I'm in.

I'll pick ya up on way.

When I get to his house I see that the bedroom curtains are still

223

closed. I knock on the door and there's no answer. I knock again. Nothing. Not even that crazy dog yelping at me. I think maybe he's had second thoughts; maybe in his vulnerable state, the idea of having tea and cake with some old biddy is a bit much. I can't actually blame him.

I turn away and walk back down the path trying not to feel too disappointed while simultaneously feeling really disappointed, and also wondering *why* I feel disappointed. I'm about ten yards up the road when I hear a door burst open behind me, and I turn to witness Callum tumbling out at great speed, pulling on a sweatshirt. I see a brief glimpse of his torso. He is very tanned and lithe.

'Wait,' he yells, and he runs up the path towards me. Then he's right there, breathing hard, bent over, hands on his knees, smelling of boy.

'Oh shit,' he says. 'Sorry, I've been in bed for, like, three days. Depression is fucking exhausting.'

'I totally understand. I'm always tired.'

'Thank you for the comic you brought round.'

'It's nothing.'

'Mum says you're pretty by the way.'

'Your mum is clearly mental. Sorry I didn't mean ...'

'No, it's fine. You met her boyfriend Joe too, right?'

'Kind of. He seemed nice?'

'Was he lying under a car with his arse hanging out?'

'No.'

'Wow, a rare event. He runs a garage that sells car parts to those sad blokes who modify Ford Escorts until they look like spaceships. He's completely obsessed. He keeps trying to teach me how to repair engines and fit wide body kits, whatever the fuck they are.'

'It sounds like he wants to help you.'

'I wish he'd just leave me alone. I don't need another loser drifting in and fucking everything up again.'

'What do you mean?'

'Nothing, it's fine. Anyway, tell me about this friend of yours.'

So as we stroll along in the afternoon sun, I explain about Margaret and how she tells us all these wild tales, and I try to explain how we struck up our crazy friendship.

'Does she really know all those TV stars?' he asks.

'We don't know! That's why I'm so excited about seeing her house. There might be clues!'

It's not exactly a long walk but I get a bit out of breath anyway, so we detour into the park and sit on the swings for a while.

'Mum said you liked my drawings,' he says. 'Is that true?'

'Yeah. I love all the black. It's very Charles Burns.'

'I kinda like all those really inky *2000 AD* artists. Frazer Irving, Ashley Wood . . . Sorry, I don't usually get the chance to talk about this stuff.'

'It's fine! Neither do I. Nobody at school likes comics. Or the theatre. It's so lonely. That's why they invented web forums. Suddenly all these people who like the same things are just, like, *there*. You can talk to them.'

'Without leaving your bedroom.'

'*Exactly*. So what is your comic about?'

'You promise you won't laugh?'

'I can't promise that, Callum. I have a really cruel sense of humour.'

'Do you promise not to laugh for longer than five minutes?'

'I'll do my best.'

'All right. So I have this idea for a superhero comic. Except it's not really a superhero. The lead character is a girl who kind of falls into this terrible depression – and it's, like, all-consuming; it's this blanket of complete and utter darkness. But then she discovers she has the ability to conjure her feelings into real life, into a sort of force … it looks like this kind of giant hound monster thing. And she sets it on bad guys. The comic is called A *Darkness*. You know, after the, um, Bonnie Prince Billy song. Which is also about depression. That's sort of it. It's bullshit right?'

'You're writing a superhero comic about depression?'

I must sound really dismissive because he looks at me like a wounded puppy. I feel like scooping him off the swing and into my arms, but I'd collapse.

'I guess,' he shrugs.

'That's so cool,' I say.

His face lights up into this great toothy grin. Ah, it's so amazing to make someone feel good. He pulls himself back on the swing then lifts his legs up and lets himself go. Soon he's whooshing backwards and forwards unselfconsciously.

'You really like it?' he says as he swishes past.

'Yeah, I really like it. You've got to make it!'

'Will you help me?'

'What? How?!'

'I need a writer. A better writer than me. I can't … When I try to write about how I feel, it all dissolves.'

'Oh god, I don't know. That's a lot of responsibility. I'm not sure it's me.'

'But you love comics, you love theatre, you must have thought about being a writer when you leave school?'

The sound of the swings' rusting chains creaking is like the whine from a cardiac machine. I don't answer.

'How *does* it feel?' I say. 'Depression, I mean.'

He jumps off the swing and wanders around the frame for a few seconds.

'It's like everything in the world is grey. Like there are no highs or lows or bright colours. There's no point to anything, there's nothing good or fun or interesting. People think it's like being really sad, but it's not. I just feel blank and lifeless. Sometimes it feels like I'm being erased.'

'Shit. I'm sorry.'

'That's kind of why I started drawing – it helped me make sense of it. My therapist said it was a good idea. But when I try to make a story, it just . . . it's hard. I feel like I need someone else to unscramble it all. So would you help me?'

I don't know what to say to him. I get off the swing and take his arm.

'You're not the only one who feels like they're being erased,' I say.

He turns to me. 'Are you scared?' he says.

His eyes are wide like planets. The wind jostles at the swings behind us.

'Pft, whatever,' I laugh. 'It's only life. Fuck it.'

Then I drag him away.

I am completely unsurprised to discover that Margaret's house is a grand old wreck, hidden behind several gnarled apple trees and this mega overgrown hedge with a sign on the gate that says BEWARE THE DOG. The vast bay windows are cracked and dirty, and ivy crawls over the ruined brickwork like alien tentacles. We stare up to the crumbling roof and notice the two weird turrets. It completely looks like something out of a horror movie.

For a few seconds we both just stand on the pathway and drink it in.

'Your friend lives *here*?' asks Callum.

'Yeah.'

'Hannah, she's not a skeleton sitting in a rocking chair wearing a dress is she?'

'Not the last time I saw her. Come on.'

I fight my way through the nettles spilling onto the path, towards the huge wooden front door. There's no bell, so I lift the iron knocker, thudding it several times against the suspiciously soft wooden surface.

Nothing. I knock again.

'Does anyone actually answer their doors any more?' I say.

'I think she's out,' says Callum. 'Let's go somewhere less scary. Like a Native American graveyard.'

I'm about to suggest coming back later, when we hear a latch creaking on the other side of the door and – slowly, unwillingly – it opens. There in the semi-darkness, lit by one ancient lamp on a wooden cabinet in the background, is Margaret. She looks frailer than I've seen her before, her hair in disarray, her eyes and cheeks sunken, as though being sucked back into her head. She is wearing some sort of long flowery housecoat, and smoking a brown-coloured cigarette.

'Ah, come in,' she says. 'I'm afraid I haven't dressed.'

Callum looks at me and I glare back, then Margaret shuffles into the shadow seemingly expecting us to follow. I enter first, sheepishly followed by Callum – and for the first time, I'm worried that he's going to embarrass me. We tail Margaret through the hall, the chipped mosaic tiles crumbling beneath our feet, and into the living room. I don't know what I was expecting – a mad collection of theatrical crap? A wall covered in photos of Margaret posing with famous people? A Tony award maybe? But instead it is a boring old person's room, with a worn old sofa, an armchair with a threadbare floral pattern and an ancient wooden television. There are a couple of framed photos of Margaret and her husband on the mantelpiece alongside a totally kitsch ornamental clock, but nothing weird or flamboyant. I can't help it, and I feel awful, but I'm disappointed.

'Come in,' she says. 'Sit down, I'll make some tea in a minute.'

She takes the armchair, lowering herself carefully into it. I rush over to help, but she waves me away, sending fag ash flying.

'No thank you, dear girl,' she says, pointing towards the sofa.

Callum and I both sit down awkwardly, like we've been sent to the headmistress for making out in class. He stares down at his feet – I've never seen him look so awkward, so much like just another teenage boy, desperate to be out of a crappy family get-together. The only sound is the ticking from the clock, which reverberates around the room. I nudge him in the ribs, desperate for him to say something.

'So, you are Callum?' says Margaret, eyeing him up and down.

'Yes,' he replies, before looking away selfconsciously.

'I think you meant to say "Yes, *ma'am*",' scolds Margaret, and her voice is all shrill and strict. Callum looks horrified, but she slips me this secret little smile. What a bitch. I love her.

'Sorry, ma'am,' he says.

Margaret and I burst out laughing.

'What?' he moans.

'Ma'am!' I repeat, shoving him, playfully. 'She's joking, you jerk.'

'Oh, don't let's be cruel, Hannah,' says Margaret, flicking her cigarette vaguely towards a chunky glass ashtray on the arm of her chair. She winks at Callum and his face is immediately and explosively red. Suddenly, I am very much enjoying this. With the tension broken, we start to talk. Margaret asks about school, she complains about her health and the drugs she's on that make her drowsy; Callum and I both sympathise. We're like a bunch of old cronies.

'So how do youngsters court these days?' Margaret asks.

'Oh god, don't look at me, I'm totally clueless,' I say, realising almost instantly that Callum now knows I've never had a proper boyfriend before.

229

'We're both into comics,' he says. 'That's how we hooked up.'

Margaret tuts and shakes her head. 'Whenever my father caught me with a comic, he would roll it up and spank me with it,' she says.

'Same here,' I reply.

Margaret laughs; Callum looks shocked.

'My mum never minded,' he offers. 'She just seemed happy I was actually reading something. She loves reading; she says it kept her sane, through ... well, through everything. People think she's dumb 'cause she left school at fifteen with no GCSEs or anything, but she's not. She's a teaching assistant now.'

'You have brothers and sisters?' says Margaret.

'Two sisters,' I say for him. 'And his dad left when he was little. He grew up in a matriarchy!'

'Ah,' says Margaret in the tone of a television detective who has just worked out who the murderer is. '*That's* why he's so polite.'

'So anyway,' says Callum, his face an explosion of scarlet once again. 'Every year she'd buy me a Penguin Classic for Christmas – usually Dickens or Austen or whatever. I was into mountain bikes and messing about with my mates, so I never looked at them, I just filed them all on my bookshelf. But Mum kept buying them. And then when we started doing English Literature, I opened one up, you know, just to find out what sort of boring bullshit I was in for. That's when I found out. Every single one of them was ... what's the word? Annotated. She'd written all these notes and underlined the important bits for me in different colours. She'd obviously spent hours on them – and I'd just shoved them on a shelf. I've actually started reading them now. Mum's notes are bloody helpful.'

'So that *Jane Eyre* essay you read out in class?' I say.

'Yeah, I wouldn't have known half of that stuff without my mum. She basically wrote it.'

There is a moment of quiet.

'Tea anyone?' says Margaret. She gestures towards Callum to help her, and slides her arm through his as they walk to the kitchen.

'Margaret, can I have a look around? I'm dying to see your house,' I say.

'Be my guest,' she says. 'Though there isn't much of interest. I don't like the past hanging around, gloating at me. Now Callum, tell me more about your life . . .'

I leave them chatting, because I'm itching to explore. Across the hall is a dining room, empty and cold, apart from a shiny wooden table and two chairs, one at either side. The bare walls are cracked and yellowing. Upstairs, there is a large bathroom with big black and white tiles and a huge freestanding tub; behind that, a wooden shelving unit is crammed with expensive-looking toiletries. It's the coolest room in the whole house and I'm incredibly jealous. Then I slowly push open the door to Margaret's bedroom – half expecting this to be where the treasure is hidden. But no, just a cast-iron bed, an old dressing table and a wooden wardrobe. Everything smells of lavender bags. I don't know what I'm looking for, but whatever it is, it's not here. It feels in a weird way like Margaret herself is barely here, like her presence is sort of ghostly. I try the door at the end of the hallway but it is locked. I try to peek in through the keyhole, but can only see a couple of old suitcases and some boxes.

When I get downstairs again, Callum is bringing a selection of cakes through to the living room on a dainty three-tiered stand. Obviously, I snatch my phone out and take a photo of him. 'Blackmail material,' I say. Then he brings through a teapot in a pink cosy and I could die happy.

We sit and scoff Battenberg slices and French fancies, drinking our tea out of china cups. Callum asks about Margaret's past and she tells him some familiar stories involving long-dead London theatres and little-known TV shows; I know these tales off by heart, and hate myself, because I start to listen out for inconsistencies. He looks impressed at the name-drops and laughs at the dirty anecdotes. I move closer to him on the sofa.

'So Callum,' says Margaret with an air of finality. 'What do you plan to do with your life?'

He is so taken aback by the sudden formality of the question he almost chokes on his Mr Kipling Country Slice.

'He's an artist,' I say as he recovers. 'He draws these amazing characters and stories but he's too shy to show anyone. There's a big comic convention in Bristol soon where they let people show off their work – I'm trying to get him to go, but he won't.'

'Whyever not?' says Margaret.

'It's expensive.' Callum shrugs. 'The entrance fee, train fares and everything. I haven't really gone to a city by myself before. Well, there was one time but . . . anyway, I'm a mega coward. Let's leave it at that.'

'Hannah will go with you, won't you, Hannah?'

He looks at me and back at Margaret.

'I don't think Dad will let me,' I say. 'I mean, it's . . . I'm not supposed to be going anywhere busy or stressful right now.'

Margaret shakes her head and puts her withered hand up in a gesture of defiance.

'Well darling, my motto is, "Don't ask permission, simply apologise later." We regret the things we don't do more than the things we do. I have to admit, this philosophy has got me into a lot of trouble, especially that time I yelled "Thatcher Out" during the encore at the Finchley Playhouse production of *Mother Goose* in 1987. But Hannah, life is full of risk and it's full of people who kill themselves trying to minimise it.'

Her eyes are watery, and she looks worn out by her outburst. She is visibly fading. I can't bear to tell her that things have changed for me, that they are worse now. We've always been close, Margaret and I. I can't tell her that now we're probably closer than ever.

'Anyway,' says Callum. 'It's too expensive, so . . .'

The clock ticks. Shadows crawl across the room.

'When I first moved to London in the 1950s, I lived in a bedsit in Dulwich,' says Margaret. 'In the flat above mine lived this very suave gentleman; I can't even remember his name. He was very courteous, always had a smile on his face. We stepped out a few times, but it never went anywhere. He was a little older than me, and I was this silly thing from the Midlands trying to make it as an actress. Anyway, he confessed to me that he was a pickpocket, and an incredibly successful one at that. He used to get the bus into Soho every morning and make a fortune from tourists. He even taught me a few of his tricks – how to create diversions, how to read the movements of others; he said it might be useful for my career. Then one day, I came home and he was walking up the path with a suitcase; he was leaving, just like that. Perhaps he'd made enough money, or perhaps he'd robbed the wrong person, I don't know. But before he left, he kissed me and said, "Don't wait for what you want, just take it. Steal the future." After he'd gone I discovered that he'd slipped five ten-bob notes into my coat pocket.'

'So,' says Callum. 'You're telling us to rob enough money to go to the comic convention?'

'No,' laughs Margaret. 'I'm telling you to take what you can, when the chance comes – accept good fortune, grab the future with both hands. It's yours. But it won't be for ever.'

We finish our drinks and take the cups and plates back through to the kitchen.

'Well, it's time for my nap,' says Margaret. 'It's been lovely to see you both. Take care of each other.'

I go to hug her and am terrified by the feel of her tiny, bony body, so frail and exhausted. She hugs Callum too and he accepts her embrace, which lingers a little longer than he was perhaps totally comfortable with.

We stroll back along the path, the sun sending shafts of light through the apple tree branches. When we're past the gate, I take his hand.

'You were good today,' I say.

'Does that mean you're going to write a comic with me?'

'Don't start! What did you think of her? She can be a bit much.'

'She's awesome,' he says. 'Those stories! She should write her memoirs.'

'I guess.' I shrug. 'I used to believe them all, but I'm not sure now. I looked round the house and it's all so . . . boring. The rooms are empty.'

'Were you expecting her to have Ian McKellen locked in the bedroom?'

'No! Gross! I just thought there would be some proof. Something to show that her life happened.'

'Does it make a difference?'

'It does to me. I want to believe it. My life must look pretty weird to you.'

'No, it's cool she's your friend. It's cool you have the theatre. It's like a big messed up family. Your life is a *Little Britain* sketch, only funny.'

'I suppose it is,' I say. 'Dad's parents died when I was young, and I never met my mum's family. So I guess, Margaret is sort of like my nan. Ted is sort of grandpa, and Sally is sort of like my mum, or maybe my older sister. I have so many "sort of like" relationships.'

He looks at me for a second. 'Am I sort of like your boyfriend?'

'Oh, honey,' I say. 'You're *nothing* like my boyfriend.'

He suddenly stops walking and looks at me with a shocked expression on his face.

'I was *joking*,' I say, slapping him on the shoulder.

'No, it's not that,' he says. I hadn't noticed but while we'd been walking, he'd put his hand into the back pocket of his jeans. When he pulls it out there is something closed in his fist. He looks at me and opens his hand. There are three crisply folded £50 notes on his palm.

'What? Where did that come from?'

'That hug ... she must have ... I'm going back,' he says.

'No wait.'

'Hannah, I can't take this, it's too much.'

'I know her, Callum. If you take it back she'll be well pissed off. Oh my god, I can't believe she reverse-pickpocketed you!'

He looks behind us towards the house, then at me, clearly torn and bewildered.

'You know what this means?' I say.

'At least one of her stories is true?' he replies.

'No, dummy. You're going to the comic festival!'

He thinks for a second and smiles at me. 'This time I'll make *you* a deal,' he says. 'I'll go to the festival and show my art if you think about writing my comic.'

'Oh god, whatever.'

'You'll really think about it and take it seriously?'

'Cross my heart.' I cross my fingers behind my back.

'One last thing,' he says.

'What?'

'You're coming too. We can make a weekend of it. We'll stay at my sister Zoe's, hit the convention for a couple of days, then hang out in Bristol on the Monday. Separate rooms obviously.'

'You're crazy. My dad will never let me.'

'We'll give him Zoe's phone number and address. You can call him literally every two hours.'

'I don't know.'

'Hannah?'

'I don't *know*!'

He takes out the fifty-pound notes and wafts them at me. 'We have spending money. Think of all those new comics . . .'

'I really want to! I just have to think of a way to get permission.'

I don't tell him I have a hospital appointment on the Monday. I don't want to think about it, and I don't want his sympathy. I want to breathe in the possibility of adventure. He leans towards me, and I lean in too. He looks like he's about to say something, but instead we kiss slowly on the lips. I feel electricity buzzing around me.

'Just out of interest,' I say. 'Our day at the comic store – why *did* you choose not to go with your friends? Why did you stay with me?'

'Jeez, Hannah,' he laughs. 'Have you ever actually hung out with you? Seriously. Have you ever talked to you? Have you ever listened to the things you say, and the jokes you make? Have you gone home and thought about them all day and all night? I have.'

'You're dumb. Shut up.'

'I'm serious.'

'You're seriously dumb.'

On my way home, I ponder this whole strange week. I think about my meeting with Vanessa and her loud unselfconscious laughter. I think about Margaret in her empty house. But mostly I think about Callum and his depression and his drawings and his tanned torso. And I feel on my lips, for the rest of the day, the kiss that he put there.

236

Tom

'I'm thinking of leaving Angela.'

I was in the car with Ted, driving to the council head office for our meeting about the theatre when he dropped this megaton marital bomb on me. I almost swerved off the road into a hedge. As if I didn't already have enough to deal with.

'What? Why? I mean, I know why, but, what?!'

'It's just, this horrible rut we're in – I can't see any way out of it. Every night, we eat in silence, we sit and watch television in silence, we go to bed in silence. I can feel the walls closing in. The tension in the air is unbearable, it's crushing us.'

'Have you talked to her about this?'

'Tom, are you asking me if I have talked to her about the fact that we find it impossible to talk to each other?'

'I get that. But I mean, what do you want to happen?'

'Anything! We've been together for forty years, but I don't want to just accept this . . . this slow creep towards oblivion.'

'Ted. This is the worst pep talk ever.'

'I'm serious!'

'I know. I'm sorry. Look, you've got to give her a chance at least. Just tell her how you feel.'

'I'm a man in my sixties, I don't just tell people how I feel. This isn't *Celebrity Big Brother*.'

'You're an actor though – act it! You've got nothing to lose. If things are so bad you want to leave, then what's the point in not telling her? Or just surprise her! Just fix that damn bike, book a hotel, and ride her to, I don't know, Pontefract. The point is, you do have the power to change it, you just have to be decisive. Sometimes people have to be shocked into change – and the shock of seeing you standing there in your motorcycle leathers could well be the push Angela needs.'

Silence. Then he turned to me.

'Pontefract?'

'It was the first place that came into my head.'

'Not Paris, or Rome, or the Northern Lights . . .'

'I've got a lot on my mind, Ted.'

We turned off the dual carriageway onto a narrow B road, the sun glinting through the windscreen, blasting us with heat.

'Anyway,' said Ted. 'We've been through this. We can't go away, because Angela needs to be available for her sister. She has no one else; if she has a fall . . . As for the bike, who am I kidding? It's a rusted, immovable hulk. Life just gets harder when you're my age. Your options calcify.'

'Ted, there are always options. Right until the end.'

This was a conversation we'd been through many times. I wanted to be sympathetic, I wanted to co-pilot Ted through his frustrations and anxieties, but a voice in my head was saying, 'Will Hannah ever get to tell people that being old sucks?' I dispelled this ghoulish thought immediately. I was clearly stressing about the theatre.

'Look, I'm sorry, it doesn't matter,' said Ted, brightly, as though reading my thoughts. 'We have serious business to attend to. Now listen. This meeting is about sizing us up. They want to know if they can just quietly pull the building down or if we'll fight. For our part, we've got to illustrate to them why the Willow Tree is an important asset.'

'We'll make theatregoers of them all,' I said. 'This time next week, they'll be queuing up to see ... what's meant to be on next week?'

'The Brass Trap,' replied Ted. 'It's an all-female brass band that does sexy funk covers.'

'Of course. Of course it is.'

'Brass Trap, you see. Bra. Strap.'

'Yes, I get it Ted. I booked them.'

The council building was a monstrous modern office block in the centre of a spectacularly ugly new town. It looked to have been constructed entirely out of giant Lego blocks the colour of semolina pudding. Behind the windows, bored-looking council workers sat staring at computer screens, no doubt making very important decisions about refuse collection. We parked in the expensive pay and display next door and I marched determinedly into reception, with Ted scuttling behind carrying his briefcase and notebook.

'Hello,' I bellowed at the receptionist. 'I have come to save my theatre.'

I hoped this would strike a suitably confident and assertive tone.

'Name please,' she said.

'The Willow Tree Theatre,' I replied.

'No, *your* name.'

Once it had been established who I was and why I was there, the receptionist chaperoned us into a small conference room with a long white table surrounded by cheap office chairs. 'Wait here,' she said, and then disappeared. Ted and I looked around.

'Do you think we're being watched?' I asked. 'I feel like we're being watched.'

The room was as bright and soulless as the reception area, and it instantly brought back memories of all the hospital waiting rooms that Hannah and I had been herded into over the years. Except here, the walls were lined not with flowery watercolours or Disney posters, but with framed photos of various Somerset towns – a half-hearted gesture at civic pride. We took seats at the head of the table so as to assert our dominance. Then we sat looking at the door for several minutes.

'They're playing mindgames with us,' I whispered. 'It's psychological warfare.'

'Tom, this is the district council, not the KGB.'

'That's exactly what they want you to think.'

At that moment, a stout middle-aged man wearing thick tortoiseshell glasses and a striped shirt walked in, followed by a ridiculously tall, completely bald colleague in a charcoal suit that was at least a size too small. They looked like a 1970s television comedy duo.

'I'm councillor Bob Jenkins, this is councillor Vernon Spenser,' said the short one. 'We're just waiting for Ms Bale, our planning consultant, then we can begin.'

They took seats at the other end of the table and shuffled some papers. Outside the room I could hear a woman seemingly talking into a mobile phone. I couldn't pick up on the conversation, but her voice sounded weirdly familiar. As she got closer, I was just beginning to place it. The door swung open.

'Ah here she is,' said Bob. He stood up. Vernon stood up. Ted and I stood up. 'This is Ted and Tom from the Willow Tree Theatre. And this is Vanessa Bale, an urban planning specialist assisting us on this project.'

Vanessa walked in and went to greet us, but when she saw me, and I saw her, we both paused, arms outstretched, frozen in a pre-handshake rictus. Our mouths dropped like demolished buildings. For a few milliseconds I pondered the astonishing cruelty of the universe.

'Hi,' she said.

'Hi,' I said.

'Oh,' said Bob, somehow picking up on the raging tsunami of awkwardness that had engulfed the room. 'Do you know each other?'

'Yes,' she said.

'No,' I said, at exactly the same time.

'Well, no,' she said.

'Well, sort of,' I said.

Vanessa looked more severe amid the merciless halogen-lit indifference of the council office. She was wearing a skirt and jacket so stiff and formal that she could conceivably have walked out of them and they'd still be standing there, suspended in time and space. She seemed harried and uncomfortable, but then of course, this third date we were having was hardly ideal. Now I understood why she'd put work talk off the agenda. I wondered how many dates she'd been on where she was inundated with questions about potholes in the high street or why a neighbour was given planning consent for an ugly conservatory. There are certain jobs – doctors, teachers, politicians, therapists – where you're probably never really off duty. At every dinner party you go to, you're only ever one prawn vol-au-vent away from 'Look, I know you're not at work, but . . .'

We all sat down at our opposite ends of the table, as though the awkward exchange had not happened. Vanessa sat between Bob and Vernon who now resembled evil henchmen. It was Bob who spoke.

'As you know,' he said, 'we are currently assessing the viability of the Willow Tree Theatre. We appreciate that it is a community asset; however, it is expensive to run, and now with the flood damage, which according to the insurance investigator was caused by misuse, it is going to be expensive to repair. There is extremely high demand for residential property in the town, and at this time we must prioritise planning decisions that will facilitate the provision of housing.'

He stopped and looked at Vernon, who took up the lecture in the same robotic monotone. 'It is the opinion of the Commercial Buildings and Planning department that the Willow Tree is not meeting its obligations as an entertainment venue. There is a meeting of the council in one month. We will advise that the building should be condemned and demolished to make way for a sizeable residential development.'

'What? When?' I gasped.

'We will look to close the building within two months,' said Bob. 'Until then, all events must be cancelled pending the council vote.'

Of course, this was the worst-case scenario that Ted and I had pretended we were expecting – but to have it confirmed, so starkly, so unambiguously, was a shock that stunned us into slack-jawed silence. This was it. This was actually happening.

'Do we get any say?' Ted asked, his voice crackly and faint as though being broadcast over a short-wave radio in the next room.

'You will be asked to put forward your case at the council meeting,' said Bob. His tone was controlled and entirely lacking in empathy. 'There is a chance the council will vote to maintain the theatre. However, if the vote goes with the planning department . . . '

He stopped talking. I saw the wrecking ball swing through the air.

'This is preposterous,' said Ted.

'I'm very sorry,' said Vernon. But he did not look sorry; he looked as though he was mentally preparing for his next appointment.

'This is why you have to come to the meeting,' said Vanessa. 'If you make a good case . . . you never know.'

Bob and Vernon eyed her with something approaching surprise.

'But, we're getting people in,' I said, sounding like a whiny child. 'The numbers are adequate.'

'They're not enough for an asset of this size,' said Bob. 'If you compare the attendance figures to the local multiplex cinema—'

'Stop calling it an asset,' I said. 'It's a bloody theatre.'

'Mr Rose, please.'

'Come on, Tom,' said Ted.

'No, this is crazy,' I said. 'You can't compare the theatre with a multiplex! The theatre is a symbol, not just for the people who come in, but for people who walk by and see it every day. It means we live in a civilised, artistic society. Multiplex cinemas are just vast warehouses where people watch movies – they're the entertainment equivalent of shopping malls. But the theatre is something else, it's ancient. Obviously the Willow Tree itself is not ancient, but you understand what I mean. Even if we're not pulling in the box office numbers, its symbolic value is immeasurable, surely?'

'The council does not have the budget to support a symbol, Mr Rose,' said Vernon. 'Especially not when someone has flooded it, invalidating the insurance.'

'Is that it?' I said. 'Are we being punished for an accident?'

'No one is punishing anyone,' said Vanessa. 'It's just, we have to think about what's most important to the people the council represents. And right now, that's housing. We have a growing community, and . . . '

'What's a community without a heart?' I said. 'But then, what would you people know about that?'

I stood up, my chair falling backwards in the process. Before I'd really had a chance to think I was striding to the door. Obediently, Ted gathered his unused notes back into his shabby case and followed. Vanessa got up too.

'Come to the meeting,' she said, getting up as well. 'Put forward your case.'

'You bet we will.'

'Tom.' She put her hand on my arm. 'Be charming and funny, you're good at that.'

She had said too much, and we both knew it; I wanted to be furious but I was completely disarmed by her reckless sympathy. My head felt like an auditorium filled with a vast baying audience of conflicting emotions. Ted had to drag me away. I trudged down the corridor, looking back towards the meeting room. Vanessa emerged, and we stared at each other communicating a silent crossfire of bewilderment. She turned away, back towards her colleagues who would no doubt have questions of their own.

Ted and I were in the car again before we really spoke.

'Well,' he sighed. 'We know where we stand now.'

'Yes, we do know that.'

'You've met Vanessa, then?'

'Yes. We dated. Only twice, but . . .'

'You liked her?'

'Yes.'

'And you didn't know she worked for the council?'

I shook my head.

'How very awkward.'

We headed out of town, towards the dual carriageway. Ted put Radio 4 on, then switched it off again.

'I liked her,' I said. 'I mean, our first date was a giant disaster. But I liked her. We just had fun, you know? Life really does love playing little games with us, doesn't it? Now it looks like our fourth date is going to be a council meeting where I have to stop her destroying the theatre.'

'Look on the bright side,' said Ted. 'This is practically a relationship.'

We drove on. The sky was covered in a wash of orange light that was so vivid it was almost unnatural. The beauty and brightness of it made my eyes water.

When I got home, Hannah was curled up on the sofa reading, with Malvolio asleep on her lap. It was a very welcome picture of domestic bliss. I made us hot chocolates, sat beside them and told her all about the shocking events of the evening, including the climactic revelation about Vanessa. I may have enacted some parts for dramatic effect. Afterwards, Hannah mulled it all over.

'So, I mean, what happens if they *do* close the theatre?' she asked.

'They won't! It won't happen. We'll blow them away at the council meeting. It will be our finest performance. There won't be a dry eye in the house.'

'Dad, it's a council meeting, it's not the end of *Flash Dance*.'

'We'll see about that.'

'For god's sake, don't wear a leotard.'

'I won't make promises I can't keep.'

Keen for something else to think about, I asked about her and Callum; she told me all about the date at Margaret's and about his depression. She was worried about how to deal with it all.

'Well, it's early days,' I said. 'It's not like you're getting married. You're not getting married, are you?'

245

'Dad! I'm being serious! He's maybe a bit fragile, and I don't know whether I'm the right person to deal with that.'

'Maybe you're exactly the right person.'

'Anyway, let's get back to *your* dating life.'

'What, with Vanessa?'

I took a long deep breath. I needed Hannah to understand that today's meeting was the last straw. I was completely done with romance. It was just going to be me and my daughter for the fore-seeable future.

'Look, today made me see things in a new light. Vanessa is funny and beautiful and sophisticated and interesting, but she is also helping the council to destroy the theatre. That, to me, is a major barrier.'

I felt this was a clear and unambiguous message. Dating was over. Vanessa was over.

Hannah

Dad has admitted he's serious about Vanessa. Sure, he said that the whole situation with the theatre had made things a little bit complicated – specifically, the part about the council threatening to blow it up – but it's obvious he's totally into her and he needs to figure out how to make things work. I mean, he was crap at explaining all that because he's an idiot, but the message was clear and unambiguous. Vanessa is totally on.

The next morning I'm heading to the Willow Tree to meet Callum, because during an 11 p.m. MSN chat last night, I typed You've got to come and see my home – I mean my real home. He then admitted to me that he doesn't 'get' the theatre. I sat silently glaring at the screen for about forty-six minutes, while he typed Sorry over and over again. Finally, I replied, Right, I'm taking you for a tour TOMORROW, 10 a.m. Be there. I ended with a frowny emoticon, then I logged off.

And I'm strolling along the main road in the sunshine, when Dad and Vanessa pop into my head and I get this very strong feeling that I can't quite place. It's not quite excitement, it's not nervousness – though there's plenty to be nervous about when it comes to Dad and relationships. Finally, it occurs to me: the weird, unfamiliar emotion I am experiencing is hope.

I turn up the music on my iPod – its Blur singing 'The Universal'. This is one of those moments of synchronicity that can happen when your music player is on shuffle because this is a song about understanding the eternity of the cosmos and just letting go and falling into it. This could be a complete downer, but as the chorus swells, I see a figure waiting outside the theatre and my feelings just gush over like a shaken-up Coke can. I recognise him by the way he stands. Head down, fringe over his eyes, hands stuffed in low-slung pockets, feet slightly pointing towards each other. He's wearing layered T-shirts in soft pastel colours. I know before I get to him that he smells good. Why don't more boys understand how important that is?

I take the earphones out and straighten up my expression. 'What do you mean you don't *get* the theatre?' I say to him, hands on hips.

'Hi to you too,' he says. He's grinning up at me.

I continue to glare at him.

'I'm sorry,' he says finally, his stance crumbling. 'Come on, show me around, I'm sure it'll be . . . fun.'

Then I hit him with it. My double whammy.

'My dad's around too,' I say. 'We'll go and say hi.' I'm not asking him, I'm telling him.

'So I'm meeting the theatre *and* your dad?' he says. 'You do realise I'm in a fragile mental state?'

I hold out my hand to him. 'Come on, I'll get you through this. And if he's in a good mood maybe we can ask him about Bristol.'

The auditorium is cool and dark. I switch on the house lights at the wall, illuminating the rows of seats swooping down towards the stage, which is empty apart from a table and three chairs – Dad has obviously had one of his meetings. Millions of dust particles hang in the air like stars. Whenever I come here, I get a flood of memories, like Keanu Reeves jacking into the Matrix. I see snapshots of my life whizzing past.

'This isle is full of noises that give delight and hurt not,' I say. Callum looks at me like I'm mad. 'So yeah, anyway, this is the theatre,' I continue, with a broad sweeping gesture. 'That's the stage area down there; that's where the actors and the scenery go, up there are the rows of stage lights – that's how you see what's happening . . .'

'Are you patronising me?' he says.

'No, I'm just not clear on what part you don't get?'

He takes a deep breath. 'Look, I mean, it's just a room, right? When you watch a movie or read a comic, they can show you anything and take you anywhere, and the artist or the director or whatever, they can make you see things in a certain way. But look at that table – that's only ever going to be a table in an empty space. It doesn't tell you anything.'

I stare at him, my mouth open in horror.

'I'm in a lot of trouble aren't I?' he says.

'Come with me,' I growl.

I grab his hand and drag him along the rear of the auditorium and into the lighting box. It's a small space with a mass of black cables churning along the floors and walls, and a big lighting desk underneath the window looking out over the stage.

'This is a Strand MX 24,' I say. 'It's our lighting engineer Richard's pride and joy. Dad and Richard brought me up here when I was little and showed me how it worked. By the time I was six, I was basically Richard's lighting assistant. I know what every button does; I know which lights are controlled by which sliders, I know how to set up a basic rig, I know how to program cues and effects. So I'm gonna show you how to make this space tell the audience things.'

I power up the desk, listening out for the electric hum, then I drop the house lights so the place is pitch dark apart from the little lamp above the controls, and quickly position a few sliders.

'First, I'll use that big light, right over the stage; it's got a warm amber filter on it. Around that I'll bring up some smaller lights with a cooler colour. Now, nudge that main slider.'

I feel like I'm in the flow, like a cool DJ. Callum just looks dumbly at the desk. I take his hand and put it over the controls; he has the slider switch in his fingers and I slowly bring it up. The stage is suddenly bathed in a warm glowing yellow light, edged with blue.

'Where are we?' I say.

'Wow, it's like . . .'

'Yes?'

'It's like we're outside. Like, in a sunny field?'

'Exactly!'

'How did you do that?'

'I told you, a big spot, downstage, slightly angled, with a warm filter. That's the sun. The colder colours are blues; they create the sky. It's pretty basic. So it looks like a nice sunny picnic. That's pretty unmistakable, right?'

'Yeah, I suppose.'

'Now watch this.'

I flick the main slider back down and we're in darkness again. Then I set up a different range of lights and nod to him. He knows to go for the main slider.

'Bring it up slowly,' I say. 'And only halfway.'

The lights come up, but this time it's a single Fresnel in the left downstage corner, handily fitted with a cold filter. As the fader rises, the table and chairs project monstrous black shadows across the stage and onto the walls; the criss-crossing shapes look like prison bars; the space is icy cold.

'Is that the same space?' I say.

He shakes his head.

'What does it look like now?'

'Somewhere like a dungeon?'

'Right,' I say. 'Shadows on a stage are like the inking in comic books – they add all the depth, the feeling. It's exactly the same concept. And lighting makes the space change too. You can bring up all the sidelights, so the stage feels like it goes on for ever, or set a profile light directly above the stage and close the shutters and it projects a square of light onto the floor so it feels like everything is in a tiny space.'

I set up a profile and pull all the other lights down, so the stage is just a chair and a table and nothingness all around. I'm enjoying showing him stuff, teaching him. When I look across at Callum, through the darkness of the tiny cabin, I see a glimmer of something cross his face. It looks like recognition, but it's not good, it's not positive.

'Callum?' I say.

He points at the stage. 'That place. I sort of recognise it. That's like ... That is exactly what it feels like sometimes. When I'm ... I ...'

Oh shit.

He's upset. I've upset him with a lighting effect.

I drop the profile light and bring up a row of the filtered Fresnels so that there's a little more colour on the stage.

'Callum, I'm sorry.'

'No it's fine.' He does this big comedy shake-out, wobbling his limbs like he's warming up for a marathon. 'It's cool, everything is cool. Wow, I guess you showed me, huh?'

'Well, I did warn you,' I say.

He laughs a little and so do I. There is so much we still can't talk about.

'Right,' I say. 'I think you know enough about lighting to do a test.'

'A test?'

'Yes, a test. I'm gonna go out to the foyer to get us two Cokes and I want you to play around with the sliders a little, experiment, have fun, go crazy. Then I want you to create a lighting scene that illustrates an emotion of my choosing.'

'Okaaaaay,' he says slowly. 'What do you want me to make?'

I pretend to think about this for a few seconds; I pretend I haven't been leading up to this for the last ten minutes.

'I want you to make a lighting scene that shows how you feel about me.'

He stares at me, a cautious smile spreading across his face. 'Right,' he says. 'This feels like a trap.'

'Let's just see,' I say. 'Come and get me when you're ready.'

'Aye aye, boss,' he says.

I let myself out of the booth, and walk along towards the exit. Before I reach the doors, I look back and see him puzzling over the board. He glances towards me and makes a shooing action with one hand.

Out in the foyer, I go behind the bar and grab two bottles of Coke from the fridge. Janice the cleaner is pottering about, dragging a vacuum cleaner behind her.

'Enjoying the holidays?' she asks.

'Yeah,' I say.

'Keeping yourself busy?'

'You could say that.'

'My lot are sitting at home on the bloody PlayStation,' she says. 'Six weeks off school, lovely and sunny outside. What are they doing? Bloody video games. They should be out experiencing life, not blowing shit up.'

For a second, this reminds me of Jay and I feel a bit bad because I'm not really seeing him or answering his texts at the moment. When I use MSN, I set it so he doesn't know I'm online. He's got a bit weird and needy, always asking where I am and what's going on. I am just about to reply to Janice when Callum's head pokes out between the double doors.

'I'm ready,' he says.

'That didn't take long,' I reply. We walk back towards the booth and I'm thinking, oh, this is going to be disappointing. What if he hasn't even bothered? What if he's just made some sort of joke? It's weird but suddenly this feels really important, even though I still don't know why I'm even bothering with this boy in the first place. When we get into the little booth, I see he's put a piece of paper over the controls so I can't see how they're set – I can only see the master slider. Very sneaky.

'Let's do this,' I say, switching the house lights off and plunging us into darkness once again.

'*You* have to push the slider,' he says.

I stand very close to him in the gloom. 'How fast and how high?' I say in my best sultry movie star voice.

'Really fast,' he says, playing along. 'And all the way.'

I put a finger beneath the switch, but keep my eyes locked on him.

'So this is how you feel about me?' I ask.

'Yeah,' he says.

I pout a little and let him sweat for a bit, then I flick the switch straight to the top.

The effect is instant.

A wave of white. A blinding flash, like coming out of a long tunnel into hot sunshine. He has put every light in the house up to max. Everything. The Fresnels, the profiles, the floods, even the house lights; all up as high as they will go. Not just that – he's even managed to find the mirror ball controller, so overlaying the wall of light, there are sparkling dots spinning across every surface like shooting stars.

'Oh my god,' I say feigning blindness, putting my arms up over my face. 'It's all the light in the universe!'

Pause.

'Exactly,' he says. He's looking right at me. The shapes and lights are in his eyes. '*Exactly.*'

Before I can think, I step forwards and take his face in my hands, and then my lips are on his and our mouths are open and our eyes are closed. It feels like we're the only humans alive; it feels like we're in a capsule, floating past a supernova – floating past the end of time. It feels like—

'Hey, no snogging in the lighting room,' says a voice to the side of us. 'This is the number one rule of the theatre!'

Oh fuck. I pull away ever so slowly from Callum. Our lips are stuck together for a second, and then they part. Slowly, I think. If I go slowly, it's possible I have totally imagined the voice, or that it'll just go away. If I'm slow, there's a chance that this isn't Dad, and that he hasn't caught me snogging in the lighting room. But I turn around, gradually, carefully, and there he is. Smiling at us in the doorway.

Instinctively, Callum hits the main slider and all the lights go down.

'It's maybe a little late for that,' says Dad. 'I'm Tom, by the way, Hannah's father. Could you perhaps put the house lights on so I can see you?'

I switch on the lights. Dad has the biggest grin on his face. He is relishing this. He is in dad heaven. He is going to let this scene play out for as long as possible. I'm desperately thinking of something clever to say, something that will diffuse the horrible mix of tension and farce.

'This is Callum,' I say.

'I should hope it is,' says Dad.

Callum is completely still and silent. He looks like a life-size cardboard cut-out of Callum. If I wasn't so mortified I'd find it funny too. I look at Dad imploringly, but he is enjoying this moment too much. Like any shameless old thesp he's going to wring everything he can out of it. I am clearly the much-needed comic relief after the shock of the council meeting. I am the drunken porter in his *Macbeth*.

'Well,' he says at last, clapping his hands together. But before he can finish his sentence, the auditorium doors slam open and Shaun leans into the room.

'Tom, can I have a word?'

'Is it important?' he says. 'It's just that I'm quite busy embarrassing my daughter and her gentleman friend.'

'It's about the flood.'

'In that case I'd better come. Callum, it was lovely to meet you. As soon as I'm finished with the boiler, we can continue our discussion about lighting box rules.'

We stand in silence watching Dad and Shaun head purposefully out through the auditorium doors.

'I think that is our cue to get the hell out of here,' I say.

'You don't think we should wait for your dad?'

'God no, he's going to be insufferable. We've got to escape while we have the chance.'

'What shall we do then?'

'To be honest, I think I'm just going to head home and crash out for a few hours. I feel sort of dizzy. It must be all the excitement. The lighting, the kiss . . .'

'Was it that good?'

'It was pretty good.'

I smile. He smiles. We're all smiling again.

'I might pop in to Margaret's house on the way,' I say. 'Just to thank her for the money she planted on you.'

'Are you sure you don't want me to come?'

'No, it's fine. I just need to take it easy sometimes. Go and see your friends. Hang out in the car park. Play video games. I'll catch ya later.'

'All right,' he says, but he sounds gutted, and this is very pleasing. 'Thank you for inviting me to the theatre. And for teaching me about lighting design.'

'You're welcome,' I say. 'I liked your whole "blinding the entire audience" concept. I may use that one day.'

And we kiss *again*, and his lips are still soft, and my head is still swirling.

Tom

A few minutes later we were down in the back room with another plumber friend of Shaun's called Benji. The three of us were standing in a line examining the boiler like police officers at a crime scene – an analogy that would turn out to be more accurate than I could have imagined. Benji, it appeared, wasn't just any old plumber; he was something of a forensic expert. He was the CSI of plumbing. And when Shaun brought him down to survey the damage just one last time before estimating the cost of repairs, he'd noticed something.

'Look,' he said, pointing to one of the main pipes leading into the gigantic old boiler. 'You see – there's a fracture here, but it's all dented.'

We dutifully examined the pipe for a few moments. The plumbing whisperer was waiting for us respond.

'So what does this mean?' I said.

'It means the damage wasn't caused by someone fiddling with the controls. It was caused by someone hitting the pipe with something heavy.'

I looked at him, trying not to look too incredulous. 'Someone . . . tried to murder our boiler?'

257

'Mate, I'm only telling you what the evidence says. But yeah, in my professional opinion, someone belted it one.'

'I don't understand,' I said. 'Why would anyone want to damage the theatre? We were putting on a 1970s farce, we weren't performing *Saddam Hussein: The Musical*. I mean ... could it have been the council?'

'Tom,' said Shaun firmly. 'I don't think Somerset council has an industrial sabotage department.'

Benji shook his head. 'Whatever the case, it wasn't accidental damage and it wasn't misuse. It was vandalism,' he said. 'Open and shut case, mate.'

'I don't believe it. I can't.' I just stood shaking my head, trying to make sense of everything. Shaun put his hand on my shoulder.

'I know this is hard to take in, but listen – if we report it to the police as vandalism, the insurer may still pay out. I mean, it might not save the theatre, but it'll help?'

We spent an unproductive few minutes exchanging theories and then decided to look for clues. I took off my jacket and rolled up my sleeves, getting into the role of the hardened detective. There were a few more dents on the side of the boiler, but no one could remember if they'd always been there or not. Benji found a scaffolding pole discarded in a darkened corner and grimly identified it as the possible murder weapon. Otherwise, the room contained little else but two industrial shelving units crammed with old lighting equipment, cables and tools. Nothing seemed to have been stolen.

I couldn't make any sense of it. I just couldn't. I headed back up to the theatre, but Hannah and Callum had bolted. I wanted to send her a text, apologising for my behaviour and telling her that Callum seemed nice, but I realised I'd left my phone in my jacket in the back room. Unwilling to return to the scene of the crime so soon, I instead headed up to the office where Ted and I brooded all afternoon. 'Who would want to vandalise the theatre?' we wondered to each other as we gorged on chocolate digestives. I was just pulling the last crumbled biscuit from the packet when Sally burst in.

'Tom, have you not been checking your phone?'

'I left it downstairs. Sally, you won't believe—'

'No listen, we've got to go. We've got to go right now. We've got to get to the hospital.'

She grabs at my sleeve and pulls me towards the door, but I wrench her to a halt.

'Sally, please! Is it Hannah? Is it Hannah?'

Within five minutes we were in my car, swaying fast along the narrow roads leading out of town. While I drove, Sally was on her phone, methodically dialling everyone in the drama group, telling anyone who answered, get to the hospital, something has happened. There was a feeling of unreality. The smell of cut grass flowed in through the air vents.

By the time we had reached the hospital, parked and barrelled through the double doors of the A&E department, James was already there, chatting animatedly to the receptionists.

'Hey, what's going on?' I said.

'I just got here,' said James. 'I'm working nearby so ...' His explanation tailed off. 'It's terrible.'

'Can we go and see her?' said Sally.

'They're just trying to find out where she is.'

Around us in the waiting room, the standard dramas were playing out. A little boy crying and clutching his arm; a woozy-looking workman in a hi-vis jacket holding a bloody rag to his head; an old guy coughing god knows what into a tartan handkerchief.

The receptionist came back to us. A woman in her late forties, her hair in a bun, whole strands coming loose and tumbling; her make-up stale and dry. She looked confused.

'Can you confirm who you are here to see?' she said.

'Margaret Wright,' said Sally. 'She's had a stroke, she was brought in earlier.'

'We don't have a Margaret Wright, but we have a Margaret Chevalier. Suffered a subarachnoid haemorrhage this morning. Is that her?'

We looked at each other gormlessly. Margaret Chevalier?

'Are any of you Tom Rose?' continued the receptionist, becoming quietly desperate to move us on. I raised my hand. 'She has you down as her next of kin.'

'That's it then. That's our Margaret. How is she?'

'She's been taken up to the medical assessment ward for a scan,' she said after a long breath. 'She's with the young girl who found her.'

Hannah. Oh god, what would she be making of all this?

Just then, Shaun arrived, with Jay and Ted in tow. Sally turned towards them, puzzled.

'I thought Dad was bringing you?' she said.

Jay shrugged. 'He said he had other stuff to do.'

'I picked him up, it's no problem,' said Shaun.

'What's happening?' said Ted.

'They might not let you all in the ward, it's very busy,' continued the receptionist. 'But you need to go through that corridor and up in the lift. Just follow the signs.'

We were already off, our ragtag group, beyond the bustle of A&E, crashing through multiple sets of doors, James and Shaun at the front; Sally quietly taking Jay's arm. In the long corridor we passed porters pushing huge trolleys of bed linen, chatting and laughing amongst themselves as though everything were normal;

I supposed it was to them. One, a wiry young man with tired, friendly eyes got into the lift with us.

'Where you going?' he asked in a thick Eastern European accent.

'The assessment ward?' replied James.

'I'll take you,' he said.

Then we were out into an identical corridor, the same green walls, the same shiny floor. The assessment ward was past a series of doors leading to departments with unfamiliar medical names. We struggled to keep up with our guide. We weren't talking.

'Here,' he said, hitting a buzzer beside the doors. He waved us goodbye.

Inside there was instant noise; nurses rushed between steel-framed beds, pushing strange equipment; someone was moaning in pain from behind a curtained-off area; as we stood uselessly in the doorway two nurses yelled for us to move, pushing a trolley housing an unconscious young woman, her skin tinged with yellow. I headed towards what looked like a reception area, but a nurse with cropped blonde hair cut us off.

'Can I help?' she took a moment to scan us all, already trying to assess what to do with this weird clan cluttering her workplace.

'I'm Tom Rose,' I said. 'This is my drama group.' I couldn't gather my thoughts. 'We're here to see Margaret.'

The nurse grabbed a clipboard from the reception counter.

The seconds ticked by. There were no windows, the air smelled of ethanol. Along the ceiling, huge lighting panels bathed the room in stark pitiless white. I was trying to look over the nurse's shoulder, along the row of beds, the row of quiet, haggard faces.

A young man in a bright pink shirt was rushing by, but the nurse turned and grabbed him by the elbow.

'Dr Fitzpatrick, these people are here for Mrs Chevalier. Dr Fitzpatrick is the junior doctor. He can help.'

'We've got that paracetamol overdose coming in,' he said, ignoring us.

'There are no beds,' replied the nurse in a slow, practised monotone. 'There won't be until we clear bed four.'

'Right,' said the doctor. 'Let me know.' He turned to us. 'Are you family?'

'Yes,' I said. 'Kind of.'

'We're fellow actors,' offered Shaun, then he changed tack. 'We're her friends.'

James put a hand on Shaun's shoulder.

'This is where we are: I'm afraid Margaret has had a very serious bleed on her brain. If she was younger, we'd operate to repair the blood vessels, but . . . I don't think she would survive the procedure, at her age, in her condition. It's only a matter of time before we see a second bleed, and that is likely to be fatal. I'm sorry, but the best we can do is make her comfortable.'

'She's . . . she's dying?' said Ted.

'I'm afraid so. Let me take you over, she's in the bed at the end. She has a young girl with her. Hannah? She's a bit shaken up.'

We followed the doctor along the line of beds, dodging by nurses, our ears now fine tuned to the fragments of urgent conversation. Then I saw Hannah, sitting beside the last bed on the left-hand row. She was holding one of Margaret's hands; it looked as frail and veined as an autumn leaf. Above the starched white covers, Margaret's face was barely visible, shrouded in wild grey hair. As we approached, more tentatively now, Hannah looked up, her eyes watery, mascara running in blackened lines down her cheeks.

'Dad!' she cried. 'I went to her house to say thank you for the money. I saw her through the window. Oh, Dad.'

I sat in the empty chair next to my daughter and I held her in my arms. 'It's okay,' I said. A part of me wanted to ask 'What money?' but now really wasn't the time.

'I called the ambulance, I didn't know what to do.'

'You did the right thing. Exactly the right thing.'

Momentarily, Hannah let go of Margaret's hand and it dropped to the bed, a lifeless weight.

'God help us, here comes the cavalry,' said Margaret suddenly stirring, her voice crackly but still as loud as ever. She surveyed us without moving. 'I hope you have come to break me out of this depressing place.'

'Margaret,' I started. 'Have they told you . . .'

'That I'm for it? Yes, darling, of course they have. It took a while but I badgered it out of them.' She took a wheezing couple of breaths, her eyes momentarily sinking back into her skull. 'I may be old, but I still know how to get what I want from a man. Which reminds me,' and she lifted her hand and pointed a bony finger. 'You made me a promise, Tom.'

'I know,' I said.

'I am not to die in here. It's unacceptable.'

'I know.'

At first the nurse was not having it.

'Mr Rose, she's in no condition to leave.'

'No, you see, well, we promised her. We promised if anything like this ever happened, we wouldn't let her die in hospital.'

'But she's on heavy pain medication, and she could pass away at any moment. It's just not practical for her to be taken home. I'm sorry.'

Just then Dr Fitzpatrick bustled up to us.

'The OD is on hold downstairs,' he said. 'Any chance of making some room?'

'We've got an industrial accident coming in now,' said the

nurse. 'Two males, multiple fractures ... I can't magic space out of nowhere.'

There was a brief pause before, in a moment of almost comic choreography, they both slowly turned back towards Margaret.

'If we could clear bed twelve?' he said.

Five minutes later, we were sprinting out of the ward accompanied by a young porter pushing Margaret in a wheelchair. She had been swiftly discharged into our care, and someone had managed to secure an ambulance to take her away. Once we'd all squeezed into the lift we had a chance to take stock of the situation.

'Right,' I said. 'We've got to get Margaret back to her house. Hannah, what's her address?'

'No!' cried Hannah. We all looked at her in surprise. 'There's something she wants to do first. She told me about it. I made her a promise too.'

'But Hannah, she's *dying*,' whispered Sally.

'I can hear you,' said Margaret.

'Can we try?' begged Hannah. 'Please, Dad?'

Hannah was looking at me. Ted and Sally were looking at me. The porter was looking at me.

'Fine,' I said. 'Where are we going?'

Hannah told us, and really, I should have known.

When the lift doors opened, we bowled out into reception, almost colliding with Natasha who was heading in the opposite direction.

'Oh god, everyone, I'm so sorry I'm late,' she said. 'I had to get the bus.'

Her face was glazed with sweat, her eyes hidden behind smudged sunglasses; she was pushing an elaborate and expensive pram.

'How is Margaret?'

'Not good,' said Sally. 'We're taking her to the theatre.'

'The operating theatre?'

'No, the Willow Tree. She doesn't have long. I'll explain on the way.'

'Oh god. Poor Margaret.'

'Don't "poor Margaret" me,' said Margaret. She was sitting in the wheelchair with an almost regal air, her bag on her lap. Her face was almost translucent, her crazed hair white under the harsh hospital lights.

'This is like the time my husband bailed me out of jail,' Margaret said as we ran at the main entrance. 'It was 1969, I was smoking pot in a club in Chelsea with two members of Pink Floyd. There was a police raid and before I knew it I was being arrested. I looked around and Pink Floyd had buggered off – climbed out through the bathroom window.'

Parked outside was what looked like a white minibus with a ramp leading up to an entrance at the rear. The porter screeched to a halt beside it and a paramedic strolled round to meet us.

'Are we taking her home then?' he said.

'Kind of,' I replied, wondering if this was technically becoming a kidnap. The paramedic seemed unconcerned.

'Sally, you and I can go in the ambulance—'

'No, I want to be with Margaret,' said Hannah. 'Please, Dad.'

'I'll take Hannah with me,' said Sally.

'Shaun, can you take the rest of us in your car?'

'Are you kidding? It's a Triumph Stag. I can get four at a push – and there's no room for a pram.'

'Ah, it's not a pram, it's a *travel system* – this part is actually a completely removable car seat,' said Natasha, frantically demonstrating. 'It got an excellent review in *Modern Parenting* magazine for ease of use and . . . This doesn't matter right now.'

'Right,' I said. 'Hannah and Sally in the ambulance. Ted, James, Jay and Shaun in the car, me Natasha and the baby will grab a taxi.'

Everyone nodded with militaristic intent. Sally put her arm around Hannah and led her towards the ambulance as Margaret was being pushed aboard.

'Once more unto the breach, dear friends,' she shouted, and then slumped over again, as the doors were closed behind her.

The others rushed to the car park, while Natasha and I headed to the taxi rank. I waved over a cab and Natasha wrenched the seat free from her elaborate buggy and threw the chassis in the boot.

'Where to, guv?' the driver asked as we got in. Natasha set up the car seat in the back and I watched as the ambulance pulled away and headed towards the main road. Seconds later we saw Shaun driving his ridiculous vintage Triumph out of the car park with Ted and Jay crushed in the back, the two vehicles forming a strange convoy.

'Follow that car following the ambulance,' I said.

The driver turned towards me, his rugged face twisted into a look of utter incredulity.

'Are you having a laugh?' he enquired.

'Absolutely not,' I said. 'And step on it.'

To his credit, that's exactly what he did.

By the time our taxi pulled up at the theatre, everyone else was parked. Ted and Jay were desperately trying to wrench themselves from the back of Shaun's car, while the paramedics were lowering the ambulance ramp to make their fragile delivery. Then one of them gently rolled Margaret out in her chair; she was slumped and still, the colour all gone from her now, her body almost non-existent beneath the blankets piled across her. Following her from the vehicle came Sally and Hannah, their arms around each other.

'The theatre,' said Margaret. 'You've brought me to the theatre'.

Hannah knelt beside her.

'Do you remember what you told me that time in the café?' she said.

'My dear girl, yes. Yes, I do.'

'Do you think you can manage it?'

'Darling, I've never missed the chance to perform.'

'AHEM' grumbled the male paramedic in charge of the chair. 'Where to?'

'Through the glass doors, to the right,' I said.

'Can I remind you that I am a human being and not a parcel delivery,' said Margaret, without opening her eyes. 'Now let's get a move on, I refuse to die in a car park.'

So we all burst in. Through the doors, past the box office, where a few volunteers were busy tidying up and unrolling new posters. Sally quietly explained to them what was happening, and they put their things down and joined us – as did the cleaners hoovering the bar area. Our bizarre procession made its way along the passage to the theatre, and then into the blackened auditorium. It took four of us to lift the wheelchair up the steps and onto the stage.

'Shaun,' I said, when we had set it down. 'Can you go up into the lighting box and switch a spot on?'

'I'll come too,' said James.

Margaret watched them go and nodded to herself.

'Hannah,' she said. 'Be a dear and push me to the centre.'

Slowly, Hannah pushed the chair out across the stage, while the rest of us stood around at the front of the theatre, unsure of what to do next. For a few moments there was silence.

'What's she actually going to do?' asked Natasha, as she gently rolled the pram backwards and forwards.

'I don't know,' I said. 'Hannah hasn't really explained. I think she maybe just wants to be on stage, just for a bit.'

'Maybe we should all leave?' said Jay. 'Maybe she just wants to be alone?'

'Jay, darling, this is Margaret,' said Sally. 'That's the last thing she wants. I think we should all sit down?'

We took seats along the front row, the actors, the volunteers, the cleaners and perhaps most strangely of all, the two paramedics. On stage, amid the darkness, I could just make out Hannah kneeling beside the wheelchair, talking quietly with Margaret. The old woman leaned forward towards my daughter, put out her hand, as white as bone, and touched Hannah's face.

Then she reached into her bag and pulled out an envelope, which she gave to Hannah. 'Open it later,' she said.

Hannah walked away, down the steps towards us. The spotlight came on and found Margaret, alone, hunched, seemingly barely with us. Her head nodded once, and then nothing. The air was thick with silence.

'Is she dead?' said Janice. Another angrily shushed her.

My arm was across Hannah's shoulder and she turned and put her head onto my chest. Sally turned to me.

'I wonder if we should . . .'

But just then, Margaret cleared her throat, the sound ricocheting around the room like a rifle shot.

'I never played Prospero,' she said. Her voice was clear and pure. 'It's my one regret. Women have played him, but not many. Prospero was Shakespeare's great old fogey. Don't talk to me about King Lear, that mad old shit, railing against the injustices of the world. Typical man. Prospero had grace and warmth and guile. He understood that the world is filled with magic; he created his own court of beasts and spirits. When it was time for him to go, he accepted his death gracefully.

'That is the best way. We are surrounded by wondrous things, all our lives, however long or short they may be. As I always told my husband, it's not the length, it's what you do with it.'

There were a few giggles from the auditorium.

'*The Tempest* was Shakespeare's last play. It ends with a speech by Prospero delivered directly to the audience. Some say it was Shakespeare's own epitaph. He was asking for one final ovation. As am I, my darlings.

> Now my charms are all o'erthrown,
> And what strength I have's mine own,
> Which is most faint. Now, 'tis true,
> I must be here confined by you,
> Or sent to Naples. Let me not,
> Since I have my dukedom got
> And pardoned the deceiver, dwell
> In this bare island by your spell,
> But release me from my bands
> With the help of your good hands.
> Gentle breath of yours my sails
> Must fill, or else my project fails,
> Which was to please. Now I want
> Spirits to enforce, art to enchant,
> And my ending is despair,
> Unless I be relieved by prayer,
> Which pierces so that it assaults
> Mercy itself and frees all faults.
> As you from crimes would pardoned be,
> Let your indulgence set me free.'

Ted and I were the first to clap – I expect we knew this speech the best – but the others joined in. It was a modest ripple, produced by just the small group of us, but it echoed out around the chasm, collecting volume – an acoustic trick that had flattered every cast we'd ever welcomed. Then, still clapping, Hannah stood up, teary-eyed, and I joined her, followed by Ted and Sally, and very quickly, all of us. Margaret lifted her hand in a limp royal wave.

'Thank you,' she said. 'Please, you are too kind. My performance is over. When my husband died I thought I would be alone. But I wasn't. I was here with you all. How wonderful it's been. Perhaps now it is time to see Arthur again. Take care of each other, take care of this place. All theatres have souls. This one will have mine.'

She was quiet again. The spotlight stayed on her while the rest of us began to shuffle in the darkness, not sure how her surreal goodbye was supposed to end.

Eventually, Shaun cleared his throat. 'Do you think she's . . .' he started.

But then Margaret animated herself like some grim fairground fortune-telling machine. 'And you,' she said, pointing to James. 'You are quite clearly in love with Shaun. For heaven's sake, tell him.'

An astonished silence. All eyes were suddenly on James. He looked like he was about to say something, then he stopped, and thought, and started again.

'You're right,' he stammered. 'I don't know how the hell you know, but you're right.'

Shaun looked at him. 'Why didn't you say anything?'

'Because . . . I didn't want to . . . I couldn't . . . I mean, you're straight.'

The two men stared at each other in the semi-darkness of the auditorium.

'Am I?' said Shaun. 'Mate, I'm really not so sure.'

The little audience was silent around them.

'Honestly,' said Margaret. 'What are you all going to do without me? Actually, I feel rather well now. I wonder if there has been a misdiagnosis? Please get me off this stage and take me home. I am absolutely and completely fine.'

Hannah

Margaret died twenty-three minutes later. We got her to the ambulance, but she lost consciousness on her way home, and that was it. Gone. Her last words were, 'Don't bump my wheelchair, you oaf, I once dined with the Queen Mother.' It's probably how she would have wanted to go – a bit of tragedy, a bit of farce. Everyone saw the funny side. Everyone except me. I feel completely empty and sore, like someone had used a mechanical digger to scoop out my emotions.

A week later, we're getting ready for the funeral. Turns out it's faster to organise these things when there's almost no one to invite. At least the theatre group are all here, gathering outside the crematorium, which looks like an ugly bungalow dropped into the middle of a cemetery. No one else is coming. No family, no other friends, no surprise last-minute appearances from 1970s television actors. Just us lot, waiting for our allotted time. Apparently, we get twenty minutes to say goodbye. A whole lifetime summed up in less time than an episode of *EastEnders*.

All week Dad has been on the phone, making the arrangements. From my bedroom I've heard him answering the same questions over and over again: no, there's no husband, no siblings, no children. Then, grim-faced funeral directors sit with you looking all solemn and sorry as they explain how much it costs for a standard cremation package, like they're selling double glazing.

Callum came round. Dad let him sit with me in my room. Callum said, 'You don't have to talk, I'm here. I'm just here with you.' We sat side by side on my bed for a really long time. I put my hand out and our fingers touched.

'I really want to go to Bristol,' I said.

Now I'm standing outside this ugly modern building and nothing is real. Faces swim around me, coming in and out of focus. Ted in his old office suit, Angela beside him in a cardigan looking disapproving. Sally's arm is on my shoulder for a few moments. Someone says 'Good turnout', but it isn't. Dad is busy herding people about. He keeps asking, 'How are you holding up?' and I keep nodding. How is anyone holding up?

The service before ours ends, and when the door opens, a bunch of grieving relatives start to file out; they are smartly dressed in black and white, holding on to each other like survivors. There are a lot of them – young men and women, children, old people, whole families. A group of spotty lads are the last to leave, poking at each other and laughing. One of them leers at me as he passes. Then it's our turn.

'Here we go,' says James. I see that he has his hand on Shaun's back.

A hearse, jet black and shiny, pulls up beside us. I recognise the undertakers. My dad greets them. The boot opens and they pull the coffin out like a suitcase. When I see it, I feel a horrible swooping in my chest, a sudden fall, like a roller-coaster. This box contains my friend. We'll never talk about anything again.

They lift the coffin and we all skulk into the crematorium

building. The air is still and thick. There are wilting flowers in brass vases on the windowsills. Jay says, 'Can I do anything for you?' and I shake my head. He's sent me a bunch of texts, but I just haven't felt like responding. I follow my dad to the front row of chairs. He takes my hand. I don't want to be touched.

The vicar is short and podgy and his shiny face radiates concern, but as with the pall-bearers it is well rehearsed and stale. He called my dad a couple of days ago and asked, 'Are there any stories from her past that I could bring into the service?' 'None that would be suitable for a consecrated building, father,' said Dad. I know he will tell everyone this at the reception after the funeral.

The piped organ music starts. I hear someone get up, then the rear door opens and shuts – they've clearly had enough of this sombre crap already. Dad helps to lift me up. The hymn is 'Abide With Me', and the group sing it really loudly. I can pick out their voices: Ted's faltering baritone, Sally's sweet alto. This is the part that they get right, determined to put on a good show for Margaret. I glance at the coffin, which is now on a wooden plinth at the front of the room. A week ago, the person in the coffin had ideas and stories and feelings. How can all of that just go?

When the music stops, the vicar says, 'Now, Tom Rose will say a few words', and Tom Rose gets up, steps forward and turns to face us all.

'Margaret was a true one-off,' he begins, his voice loud and sharp, echoing around the dull room. 'People often say that about their loved ones, but Margaret was the real deal. She could be amazingly warm and also terrifying and offensive all at the same time. She told brilliant but incredibly rude stories that no one else would get away with. She grasped life and shook it until everything fell out.'

People are murmuring and nodding. Dad looks at me, his face is a mash-up of sympathy, concern and fear – as though he has just realised something terrible. He visibly breaks himself out of the spell.

'We had unforgettable times with her, didn't we? Nobody will ever play the wicked stepmother in *Cinderella* the way she did. She snuck so many dirty jokes into our 2001 production that we received three official police complaints.'

There is laughter now. My head is spinning and my throat aches. I try to swallow but I can't.

'Now though, Margaret has exited stage right. She has gone to the great green room in the sky.'

More laughs. I frown at the noise and Dad looks my way again.

'In the language of us actors, she is resting. She is between roles. Soon, I suspect, she will join heaven's repertory theatre, where she'll no doubt . . .'

I am suddenly standing. I don't know why or how, but something has yanked me from the chair like a puppet. 'Oh for god's sake, Dad, just say it!' I yell.

My dad stops and there are a few whispers around me. I waver slightly and grab the back of the chair for support. Sally's hand shoots up to my elbow but I swat her away. I look at Dad.

'She's dead. You can say it. You can say the bloody words. She died, Dad. She died.' And my voice is a damaged instrument, all busted and broken.

I am running now. From nothing to running, bolting along the aisle, ignoring the shuffling noises behind me, ignoring the voice saying 'Hannah, Hannah'; slamming into the door, like I did that night at the club, and once again, it gives and I'm through, spat out into the world. I keep running, ducking between the weeping willows and along the line of chipped, slimy-green gravestones, ancient and uncared for. My foot slips on the sodden grass, but I stay up. I don't know where I'm going.

And then I see her.

Sitting on a bench beside the stream that meanders through the cemetery. It's Angela, all alone. I slow to a walk, and approach her from behind. My heart is pounding, my breath is all wheezy and pathetic. But she doesn't turn to greet me. I sit beside her. And we're there in silence for a few seconds.

'Is it over?' she says at last. 'I'm sorry I left early.'

'I left early too.'

'It's just ... my sister—'

'Is she—?'

'No. But, soon I think. Very soon.'

There is a rumble of thunder, very distant, very low. The stream has been parched to a trickle; I guess it is soon going to be filled.

'Julia,' she says. 'My sister's name is Julia. She is seven years older than me, but we've always been very close. When we were girls, she had all these beautiful dolls. We'd spend hours combing their hair, dressing them. Our nanna knitted the outfits; she'd send them to us in brown paper parcels. And then all through school, and boyfriends and exams, all of that, she was always there to watch over me. She was so funny, so *bright*. I adored her. She was the first one in our family to go to university. When I visited her she took me for afternoon tea and bought me books and make-up. As you get older, you see each other less, you know; you have work, a home to manage, children if you're lucky, all of that. But, we were always close.

'Three years ago, just after her husband died, she started getting confused, forgetting things – important things. It got very serious. We had to find her a residential home – we chose a nice place, not far away. The staff are lovely, but she can be difficult. Shouting, throwing things, swearing.'

She stops talking and I feel her whole body shaking. I put my hand on hers.

'She's my big sister, Hannah. She gave me driving lessons in her Reliant Robin. She came with me to choose my wedding dress. When our oldest son had whooping cough, she stayed with us for two weeks. She did all the cleaning and cooking. She said, "You're my little sis. This is my job." Now everything we were is slipping away, and I can't let go. Ted has that bloody motorbike falling apart in the garage; I know he's angry with me that we can't just ride off on it, but what can I do? She looked after me. I'm sorry. I'm so sorry. This is the last thing you need.'

'No,' I say. 'You're wrong. This is exactly what I need. Everybody in there is treating this like … like something funny. Good old Margaret – did her bit on stage and corked it in the ambulance. What a great show.'

'But she was your friend?'

'Yes. But that's not it. Not all of it anyway.'

'What do you mean?'

'I couldn't stand it in there. Everyone laughing and chatting and singing, and looking forward to the reception. They'll tell a few stories about her, they'll raise their glasses in her honour, but that'll be it. I just want someone to say, Margaret is dead, and we're really sad, and we're going to remember her. I want her death to mean something more than just the chance to reel off some anecdotes and get shitfaced. What if no one remembers what she was really like?'

'You'll remember,' says Angela.

Without thinking, I do this weird snorting noise, which is supposed to be a derisive laugh, but it makes my eyes water and there is a lot of snot. Angela hands me a tissue and I blow about ten gallons of runny green goo into it. Maybe I'm allergic to graveyards. There are the gentlest drops of rain on our faces; a soft wind arches through the willow leaves.

'Anyway,' I say. 'Forget it. Everything is fine.'

'Hannah, you ...'

'Whatever, I'd better get back.'

'Hannah ...'

'Angela, do you want to know what I think is the best thing you and Ted can do for your sister? I mean, you probably don't because I'm, like, fifteen.'

'No, I do. Go on.'

'Just ... be happy. Take care of each other. Have a life. That's the thing. The sister who played dolls with you and took you to university and taught you to drive. I think that's what *she'd* want.'

Angela looks at me for a second, and I wonder if she's angry. Who wants to get life advice from someone who isn't old enough to drink, drive or join the armed forces? But her face softens into a smile.

'Out of the mouths of babes,' she says.

And then we're walking back to the crematorium, arm in arm. I am trying not to look at the gravestones. Instead, I am thinking of having tea with my friend and gossiping and laughing. She was clever and alive but now she's gone – like ashes on the breeze.

Tom

Naturally, we decided that if we were going to have a get-together after Margaret's funeral it should be at the theatre. It was her life. It was her obsession. It was cheap and convenient. When I stepped out from the crematorium, I saw Hannah and Angela walking along the narrow path towards the colourful groups of mourners. I smiled weakly, uncertain of what had happened between us. I couldn't remember a time she'd ever run away from me. I was usually the one she ran *to*. But grief makes people do funny things – just look at Juliet, or Oedipus, or . . . I should stop drawing life lessons from tragic plays.

'Hey,' she said, not looking me quite in the eye, fidgeting with her sleeve. 'I'm sorry, I just totally freaked out.'

'It was a poor speech, I should have done better.'

'It was fine, I just needed to get out. Come on, let's get to the theatre before those greedy bastards eat all the sausage rolls.'

She didn't want to talk on the way to the theatre. I put my arm around her shoulder, but she drifted away from it. The rain became more insistent, the light spray building towards a downpour until we were running for the theatre doors. Inside, Sally was laying out snacks on the bar and James and Shaun were talking together behind a group of box-office volunteers whose paper plates were already piled high with sandwiches and crisps. Someone had put a Billie Holiday CD on the sound system. There was a convivial air to the occasion. People were saying, 'Margaret would have loved this', and nodding in agreement. Dora came over to speak to me, and just as she did, I saw Jay emerge from the crowd and gingerly approach Hannah.

'Lovely do,' said Dora, picking up a Scotch egg from her plate and examining it with zeal.

'Yes, it's nice to be together at a time like this,' I said. But I was rather distracted by the conversation going on at my side.

'Hey,' said Jay.

'Hey,' replied Hannah.

'How are you doing?'

'You know, not great.'

'I haven't seen you much. You haven't been around.'

'I know, I'm sorry, it's just . . .'

'Have you got my texts?'

'Yeah.'

'It's just . . . you haven't replied.'

'I'm really sorry, Jay.'

'We used to be best mates.'

'We're still mates Jay. Honestly.'

'I wasn't going to say anything, but seeing you . . . I miss you.'

'Jay, please. I really am sorry. I've just got a lot on. Oh sorry, hang on, I'll be back.'

With that, she darted off towards the door. I watched her scurry through the small crowd, her expression – her whole demeanour – gradually changing from a sort of pained indifference to something approaching delight. It was such a dramatic transformation that I guessed who had arrived before I saw him. And when she finally reached Callum, she threw her arms around him. I looked to my side and saw that Jay was watching too. His expression was more grey and overcast than the sky outside. I decided it was my duty and responsibility to lighten the mood – this was, after all, a funeral.

'It's just the exciting new thing,' I said, nudging him on the shoulder, and looking over at the couple on the other side of the room. 'You know what it's like. Someone fresh and different and charming comes along and suddenly that person is all you think about. It's human nature.' An image of Vanessa cruelly popped into my head. 'I mean, look,' I continued, 'Jenna and Daisy are just coming in now; they're her best friends too but I bet she'll hardly acknowledge . . .'

Immediately, Hannah hugged them both warmly, then dragged them towards Callum looking the happiest she'd looked since that morning in the lighting box. Was this the big moment, the big official introduction? At a funeral? Typical teenagers – so self-absorbed. The emotional attention span of gnats. Anyway, the whole scene literally could not have gone any worse for my pep talk. I looked back to Jay and was not completely surprised to discover him ever so slightly more despondent.

'Do you like him?' said Jay, his tone mournful but measured.

'Well, he seems nice – we've only met briefly, though. He could be terrible. In which case, I'll have him killed like all the others.'

I smiled at him conspiratorially, but his expression didn't change.

'But you don't mind that she's going to the comics festival in Bristol with him this weekend?'

A twinge of concern. Just a twinge. Because obviously there had been some kind of huge mistake.

'Going where to what?' I said.

'She's going with Callum to Bristol; I know his mate Ed and he was talking about it on MSN. They're staying at Callum's sister's house. Shit, sorry, I thought you knew.'

'I ... Oh yes, I remember now. Yes. They're going to Bristol. They're going to Bristol alone and staying overnight. That's definitely something we discussed. Excuse me please.'

The room felt very strange, like one of those movie scenes where they try to simulate the effects of taking hallucinogenic drugs. Everything became dull and muddied, the voices lowered into a mumbling dirge. I was walking towards Hannah, but it also seemed as though she was getting further away. I realised to my astonishment that I was extremely angry.

Hannah saw me approaching and turned, smiling. She was about to say something but I interrupted. It felt like we were on stage and a furious scene was about to play out.

'Hannah, what's this about Bristol?'

Immediately, the smile dropped from her face. A whole cavalcade of emotions seemed to flit across her eyes, as though she were fast-forwarding through some internal videotape. Teenagers experience something akin to the grieving process when caught out by their parents: denial, anger, bargaining, depression, acceptance and, finally, being grounded. But until now, this had only ever been something I'd observed at a distance. Now I had a front-row seat.

'I ... I was going to talk to you about it,' she spluttered. 'But—'

'But you knew I'd say no.'

'Dad, I—'

'You knew I'd say no because I barely know this boy, and because you have a hospital appointment on Monday.'

'We can change the appointment, Dad, it's just—'

'No, we cannot!' my voice was louder than I'd meant. Good projection – the actor's curse. A hush descended on the room. I was dimly aware of bodies shifting to face us – to get a better look at the performance. 'This is serious, Hannah.'

She muttered something low, under her breath, looking downwards.

'I beg your pardon?' I said, sounding more and more like a cross between Laurence from *Abigail's Party* and Captain Mainwaring.

'I said I know it's fucking serious!' She spat it back at me with shocking force. 'It always is!'

Callum cleared his throat. 'Tom, if I could just—'

'No you cannot!' I shouted. 'I think you've done enough and I'd really like it if you left my theatre, right now.'

'Dad!'

'Tom,' came another voice from behind me. It was Sally. 'Tom, should we all go somewhere and talk this through?'

I swung around towards her and, to my surprise and horror, she flinched. I felt a spasm of guilt, but my anger won out.

'Did *you* know about this? Your son certainly did.'

'No, I did not,' said Sally. 'I'm finding out as it's happening – just like everyone else *at Margaret's wake*.'

I looked back to Hannah, who had fixed Jay with a stare of such unadulterated aggression I feared he might spontaneously explode.

'Let me make this clear,' I said to her. 'You are not going to Bristol with Callum or anyone else, and you are certainly not staying over. I don't know him, I don't trust him, and you cannot miss a hospital appointment! We also have your birthday play to plan out, which was—'

'Oh for god's sake, screw the stupid play!' screamed Hannah. 'I don't want to do it, I never wanted to do it, I just didn't want to upset you! I'm fifteen, Dad! It's embarrassing. You're embarrassing! Come on, Callum.'

She grabbed him by the arm and turned towards the doors. A small huddle of people quickly parted, reluctant to get in her way. But Callum wasn't moving. He looked at me. His expression wasn't angry or guilty, it was . . . bereft. He looked bereft.

'Please, Callum,' said Hannah. Her tone had changed from fury to desperation. This was a key moment, I could tell – a key stand-off, a key test of his will and loyalty. He seemed terrified by the weight of her expectations, the proverbial rabbit in the headlights. I did not think he could possibly move.

And then he did.

Without turning from me, he accepted the pressure from Hannah and followed her towards the door. In one smooth motion, they were through and out. I breathed in deeply, and jerked forward, determined to follow, but I felt a strong hand on my elbow, dragging me backwards.

'Don't,' said Shaun. 'She's angry and so are you. Nothing good will come from you chasing her out. Believe me.'

I tried to move forwards again, and this time I was restrained by James as well. It was a weird feeling, a kind of red-tinged euphoria. A tiny part of my brain was observing the whole thing as an absurd one-act play – and it was very impressed by my emotional commitment to the role of angry, spurned father.

'The show is over, everyone,' I grinned. 'Just a minor disagreement. Margaret would have approved, I'm sure. I expect she's looking down and enjoying it all, sherry in hand!'

There was a smattering of laughter and people turned away. James asked if I needed a drink and I shook my head. I saw that Sally was with Jay; they were talking quietly – a stark contrast to the raging tableau that I had just concocted.

In the 1930s, the famed German dramatist Bertolt Brecht introduced a performing arts technique he referred to as

Verfremdungseffekt, which can be loosely translated as 'the alienation effect'. He asked actors to distance themselves from the words and emotions they were conveying in order that audiences could think dispassionately about the political themes of his plays. But I don't think he realised that the detachment of his players was a much more accurate depiction of human emotion than all those wailing naturalists and method actors 'feeling' every sentiment. I think Brecht had stumbled on a universal truth: you actually never know what you're feeling – it gets buried beneath layers of habit and subterfuge. You have to stand back and really examine yourself to find the truth. Because the truth is often horrifying.

And often it is also quite simple. I was scared of her growing up. I was scared of being alone. This was what I realised while standing in the foyer of the Willow Tree Theatre, surrounded by whispering mourners, watching my daughter storming away through the car park, and then along the pavement and then completely out of sight.

Hannah

The windows are really dirty, so I can barely see the fields whizzing by outside. Callum and I are crammed together in the crowded train, sharing our seat with a mother and her small daughter who keeps kicking my leg. We're not really saying much because there is too much to say. This sweltering carriage, jam-packed with noisy families, is not the place. So we sit and look out and pretend we can see the scenery through the dust and grime.

We're doing it. We're running away. Well, we're going to a small comic book festival in Bristol and then we're coming back in two days. But it's not the coming back that's important right now – it's the fact that we stuck to the plan we concocted as we marched away from the theatre. In a way, Jay made it happen. Chances are, if I'd have actually got round to asking Dad and he'd said no, that would have been the end of it. But because everything exploded the way it did, I was fucking determined to go. I went home, crammed a backpack with clothes, left a really short note for Dad (can't remember what I wrote), then stayed at Daisy's for the night. Callum met me at the train station at 8 a.m. this morning. Then we were gone. I have about forty missed calls from Dad, and I know that he phoned Daisy's mum to make sure I was alive, but he didn't demand to speak to me and he didn't say I had to go home – he just told her he was there if I needed him. I have to admit I felt bad for him and started questioning the whole plan. But then I remembered the way he'd shouted at Callum and that wasn't right. We'd planned to ask him if we could go; we were going to introduce Dad to Callum's sister and reassure him we'd be staying in separate rooms (we definitely are). I was prepared to compromise and come home on Sunday night rather than Monday, so we'd be in time for the hospital appointment. But I didn't get the chance because Jay fucked all that up. And for some reason, I did not want to go to the hospital anyway – not this time. I've always been a good patient: I've done everything they told me to do, taking all the pills and precautions, doing the exercises – all my life. I want to rebel, just this once.

The train suddenly swings around a curve and the wheels stutter from their hypnotic rhythm. The noise is really jarring. Callum's hand moves onto mine and I hold it.

The festival is in a big hotel not far from the station. In his rucksack, Callum has a sketchbook stuffed with the best examples of his work. I mean, I think it's all amazing, but apparently last night he spent hours going through it all and slowly rejecting beautiful pieces. Today he keeps switching between excitement and crazy anxiety. It's hard to keep up, so I just let him gabble on as we walk through the warm, unfamiliar streets.

'This is a bad idea, isn't it?' he keeps saying. 'I bet there are hundreds of artists coming. Who's going to look at my crappy stuff? Shit. Sorry. God, this building is huge. Did you see that Gareth Ellis is going to be at the festival? Fucking hell. Fucking HELL. How are you doing? Do you want to go home?'

'Callum, shut up.'

When we arrive, he does shut up, because he is stunned into silence. The festival takes up a huge conference hall on the ground floor of a giant modern hotel. In the main area there is a long row of dealers, their tables overloaded with boxes of comics, toys and action figures; there are stands with small presses and individual comic makers, showing off their cheaply photocopied works all stapled by hand. Swarming between them there are hundreds of people – mostly thirty-something men in jeans and T-shirts, balding and bulging – flitting around, barging each other out of the way. I feel like an exotic alien.

We're given a slim programme as we walk in and Callum checks the timetable. The portfolio session is at 2 p.m. A bunch of editors from DC, *2000 AD* and loads of other places will sit down, meet new artists and look at their work. We decide to spend a couple of hours just browsing and getting our bearings. I'm having trouble taking everything in. I've never seen so many comics in my life. I'm in a different world. We find a dealer specialising in independent American comics and spend ages elbowing between stern-looking collectors, flicking through the latest stuff from places like Avatar and Oni Publishing.

We split up, and I discover a tiny little room dedicated to manga, quarantined away from the serious comics – but at least it's here. The vibe couldn't be more different; the walls are lined with bright, colourful *Dragon Ball*, *Naruto* and – yes! – *Sailor Moon* posters and there's a small stereo playing insanely fast-paced J-pop music; there are women at the stalls, and even a couple of teenage girls browsing and chatting. One is wearing an astonishingly ornate pink dress, with a huge billowy skirt and giant white bow, like she's walked out of an anime video. I just stand dumbfounded in the doorway. I have never seen other manga fans in real life before. I sit down to catch my breath and get talking to an artist who makes actual manga-style comics. We talk about *Blue Monday* and *Scott Pilgrim*. She asks me if I'm okay and I tell her about my heart and she says there's a manga named Millennium Snow about a girl with heart disease who falls in love with a vampire. We swap MSN details. Callum has to come in and drag me way. I feel like Alice in Wonderland.

'It's time,' he gulps.

When we turn up at the portfolio session, there's already a lengthy queue snaking along the wall outside the room and down the corridor. We take our place at the end of the line and notice that some people are carrying huge leather art folders. Callum looks down at his battered sketchbook selfconsciously, then shoves it into his rucksack. He looks pale and gloomy.

After about an hour, we're nearing the front of the queue, looking into this chaotic room filled with artists proudly pulling out big, bright pages of their work. Along the far side are the fabled editors, joking and chatting. Callum looks like he's going to pass out. The room is stuffy, crowded and noisy enough to make me uncomfortable too. It's the first time the old concerns start creeping back in. Even beneath the chatter of excitable comic book nerds I hear the quickening noise. *Baddum. Baddum. Baddum.* It'll be so embarrassing if we *both* pass out. Still, it might get him noticed.

Eventually we're shoved towards the next free desk. An older guy in thick-rimmed glasses and a plaid shirt unbuttoned over a T-shirt with a big *Flash* logo stares us up and down. His name badge says that he's a senior editor at DC. Fuck. He's probably met Alan Moore.

'So, what ya got for me?' he says in a gruff Californian drawl.

Callum seems utterly stunned. I'm suddenly full of adrenaline. I nudge my boyfriend, which startles him into action. He puts his backpack down on the desk, almost knocking the editor's beer can over, then pulls out his sketchbook. When he hands it over, he has this really guilty expression, like all he's drawn is a stick figure with massive boobs or something.

The editor starts flicking through.

'This is just something I'm working on,' says Callum, his voice quiet and brittle. 'It's a sort of superhero story called *A Darkness*. It's this character here. She has depression, but she gains the ability to draw other people into, like, her world. She has this giant hound that attacks them. It's . . . sort of a metaphor for . . .'

'Man, that sounds like a bummer,' says the editor.

'Yeah, I mean, it's quite dark, but . . .'

'The art is good, dude, but I'm not sure the world is ready for depression as a superhero.'

He's already looking behind Callum, almost pushing the sketchbook away. I can see this ending right here. It's not fair. I glance at Callum, but he's got nothing. He's reaching for the book. Someone has to act.

'So *Batman* isn't about depression?' I say.

Oh shit. What am I doing?

'Pardon?' says the editor.

'Hannah,' whispers Callum.

'The Dark Knight,' I continue. 'The lonely gazillionaire who lives in a cave and fights all these crazed bad guys who are probably figments of his imagination – that's not about depression?'

'Well, I . . . ' says the editor.

'Hannah, stop,' pleads Callum.

I am not stopping.

'*Green Lantern: Rebirth* isn't an allegory about depression? Hal Jordan falls apart and has to literally face fear itself. *Alias* isn't about depression? Jessica Jones retreats from her life as a superhero, denies she has any powers, and drinks and fucks her life away. The way Michael Gaydos draws her so she is *always* in shadow, in every single frame. That's not depression?'

Callum is now trying to drag me away.

'A *Darkness* is about a girl whose depression is so fucking huge it enters the world as a deadly force. But she's special. She's so strong, she learns how to control and direct it. I mean, that's basically every emo kid's fantasy scenario. It's goddamn exciting. Forget about men in Lycra bodysuits. The world is dark and shitty. Everyone is retreating onto the internet or their mobile phones. You know what? *The Flash* doesn't really have much to say to us right now. But a girl who uses depression as a super-power to get revenge on her enemies? It's basically *Hulk* meets *Carrie*. Who wouldn't read that?'

The guy stares at me, his face a complete blank. I wonder if we're about to get thrown out. Callum won't look in my direction.

'Are you the writer?' the guy asks.

'No,' I say.

He slides the sketchbook back to Callum.

'Come back next year and bring a story – get your pal here to write it. These sketches are pretty cool but they aren't saying a tenth of what she just yelled at me.'

Callum's sister lives in a suburb about twenty minutes outside the city centre. We have to get two buses, and by the time we arrive at her battered little terrace, my legs are knackered. The tiny front garden has been cemented over and is a mess of weeds and empty wine bottles. The curtains are drawn in every window. Callum goes to ring the bell, but of course it's busted, so he knocks instead. A few seconds later there is a loud shoving noise and a muffled voice shouting, 'This fucking thing is stuck again.'

'Step aside, I think this is my speciality,' I say, trying to lighten Callum's mood.

But before I can do anything, the door bursts open, and there is a student girl standing in front of us with shoulder-length hair that's been dyed bright red. She's wearing a T-shirt and leggings under a long fluffy blue dressing gown. She looks sort of insane.

'Not today thank you!' she yells, then pretends to shut the door, then smashes it open again, then finally bear-hugs Callum, who looks irritated by the whole charade. 'Is this Heather?'

'Hannah,' I say.

'Argh, sorry, Hannah! I'm Zoe, but everyone calls me, um, Zoe.'

She hugs me too, squeezing what's left of the breath out of my lungs.

'Come in! Everyone else is away for the weekend so we have the place to ourselves. I'm stuck here writing an essay on Plato. Boring Greek bastard.'

The inside of the house is an eye-bursting collage of patterned wallpaper and carpet. There are stripes, there are flowers, there are salmon pinks and avocado greens. It's like every bad interior decorating idea from the 1970s and 80s has come here to die – or, more accurately, explode. Zoe guides us down the narrow hall into the living room, which is a mass of cheap mismatched furniture, fairy lights and candles. There is an enormous banner pinned to the wall above the sofa, with BLAIR AND BUSH ARE WAR CRIMINALS written on it in large, surprisingly neat letters. A giant boombox in the (presumably unused) fireplace is playing Goldfrapp.

'Can I get you two a drink?' she asks. 'Callum, you look so tired!'

'I think I'll just crash, Zoe. It's been a long day.'

'You can't just turn up here and go to bed! I have booze! We can do underage boozing! I thought that's why you were coming!'

'I'm fine.'

292

There is a brief glance between them, and it feels like a lot is being communicated that I'm not getting.

'No problem, little brother,' Zoe says at last. 'You're sleeping in Will's room, first on the left up the stairs. There's a huge *Donnie Darko* poster on the wall. Can't miss it. Here, let me get you a glass of water.'

She disappears into the kitchen.

'I'm sorry,' he says.

'For what?'

'For dragging you to this thing and wasting your time.'

'What are you talking about? I needed to get away! And the festival was awesome. We'll go back tomorrow and we'll queue up and we'll get some bigwig at Marvel to give you a job.'

Callum shrugs. That is clearly his default response to *everything* when he's in this mood.

'Marvel aren't here,' he says. 'I'll see you in the morning.' And he wanders out into the hall, his coat still on, his backpack still slung over one shoulder. So now I am standing in a stranger's front room, alone, not sure what to do. This is so not what I was expecting. I imagined that we'd get back here, have a cider or three, then sneak off to some darkened room and . . . I don't know. But I was looking forward to figuring it out. I haven't been in a lot of situations like this – my life has been kind of sheltered, I may have mentioned that. But I was expecting physical contact. Just a bit. Maybe more. I don't know. Oh god, this is all so weird.

Zoe shimmies back into the room holding two glasses and a bottle of white wine and catches me staring vacantly at the banner.

'It's from the anti-war protests in March,' she says, handing a glass over to me. 'A whole load of us took a bus down to London. Amazing atmosphere. Did you know that Tony Blair's son is at my university? The little shit.'

I don't want to tell her the whole Iraq thing feels kind of distant and irrelevant from our teeny Somerset town. I mean, there was a peace camp in the local park for a while, until the police arrested everyone for smoking pot on the climbing frame. Earlier in the summer, Jenna got quite politically motivated and started wearing a CND T-shirt, but then *Harry Potter and the Half-Blood Prince* was published. After queuing for two hours outside our local bookshop to grab her copy, she lost interest in any conflict that didn't involve wizards.

I can't think of anything to say, so give myself some time by yawning loudly.

'Oh I get it,' says Zoe. 'Is this the whole "we're knackered so we're going to bed" ploy? You know, the one where you both disappear upstairs and then ten minutes later I hear the bedsprings creaking? Because I explained this to Callum, that's not going to happen. Not while I'm on horny teen duty.'

'No!' I say, sounding a bit more horrified than I'd meant. 'I'm not a . . . horny teen.'

She bursts out laughing.

'I believe you. And Callum is clearly not in a good place, am I right?'

'He took some of his art to the portfolio viewing, but they were sort of not interested. Then I accidentally insulted *The Flash*.'

'Ah,' she says. She sits on the sofa and clears a huge pile of papers and books out of the way. 'Come on, sit down. Tell me all about it.'

So I do that. I tell this stranger with flaming red hair about how the idea of going to the convention came up, and how I persuaded him to go. I tell her about Margaret reverse-pickpocketing him, and then we get on to the argument with my dad, and the way we stormed off like dumb juvenile delinquents in a John Hughes movie.

'Ha!' she exclaims. 'I like the way you thought "I'll show my dad – by running away to Bristol, a small comparatively safe city twenty miles away from where I live".'

'It's the furthest I've ever been without him,' I say.

'You guys are close?'

'My mum left when I was three, so yeah. And I have this heart problem, so he's always been totally overprotective. It's boring, you don't need to know about all that.'

'Callum told me about your heart. I'm sorry.'

'Whatever. Anyway, it's just us. Just me and Dad. Oh and the massive idiotic group of amateur actors that he seems to have adopted.'

'Right. I mean, that sounds like a pretty standard family.'

'It's been fun, but . . . sometimes it would be good for things to be normal.'

'Well, Callum thinks you're amazing.'

I almost spit my wine all over the Ikea coffee table and Zoe's course notes.

'What?! Why?! No! What?'

She pours us more wine.

'Has he told you about our family?' she says.

I shake my head.

'It's complicated so . . . deep breath. Do you wanna know his superhero back story?'

'Of course.'

'My parents had me and my older sister, Polly, when they were really young. Four years later, they went through a rough patch, Mum had a bit of a fling, and then – pow – it was 'Oh hello Callum, oh goodbye Dad'. So yeah, Callum has internalised a lot of guilt, let's put it like that. Then, when he was thirteen these dickheads at his old school started picking on him. You know those happy-slapping videos? Yeah, well, he was happy-slapped. And they emailed everyone at school with it. A few months later he ran away. Well, he tried. He meant to go to London but got on the wrong train and ended up in Cardiff. Mum drove over and picked him up. He was in a right state. He missed weeks of school and had all this treatment for depression, but reacted really badly to the drugs. It's been tough for him. And then there's me and his other sister. Polly is a genius – she's doing an MSc in physics, for fuck's sake. And I'm here studying Philosophy and Politics. We're an impossible act to follow, basically.'

'Shit,' is all I can muster.

'Shit indeed,' she says. 'Do you want some more wine? Just don't tell your dad I got you smashed.'

Later, slightly tipsy and unsure on my feet, I clamber up the stairs to the other spare room. I put on a T-shirt and stripy pyjama bottoms and brush my teeth in the horribly damp, mouldy bathroom. I am just about to tiptoe back to my room, when I stop and think. With utmost stealth I creep to Callum's room, push the door and look in.

He is lying bunched up on the very edge of the bed, facing out towards the door, still awake, looking miserable. Wrapped around him is a My Little Pony duvet.

'Go to sleep,' I say.

'I can't. Too much going on in my head.'

'We'll go back tomorrow and we'll totally kill it.'

'Hannah, I don't want to go back. I want to go home.'

'Why?'

'I'm scared.'

'What do you mean?'

'I don't want to find out that I'm not good enough. I can't

deal with that right now. And there is no way you're missing that appointment.'

'Oh fuck the appointment! I'm not going. All my life I've done everything that bloody hospital has told me to do, so I'm having a day off. Screw them.'

'Hannah, I don't want you to get ill because of me.'

I look at him, this stupid boy, curled up in bed like a child. We barely knew each other a month ago, and now here we are, passing our fears back and forth between us.

'Callum, I am already ill. I'm always going to be ill.'

'You must think I'm pretty pathetic.'

'I don't! I think you're cool. I mean, not at the minute because, Jesus, have you seen the duvet they gave you?'

He looks at it. The smallest trace of a smile passes across his lips.

'This is mine,' he says. 'I brought it with me.'

'I think our relationship might be over.'

'It was nice while it lasted. It's just me and my ponies now.'

'Maybe not,' I say, looking down the stairs towards the living room. 'Is there room in the stable for one more – just for a few minutes?'

He doesn't answer, but I creep into the room anyway, then onto the bed, then under the duvet, shuffling in behind him. We're not quite touching. I put my arm over him and he holds it in his hands. I can hear him breathing, and I can feel the mattress rise and fall. Oh shit, I'm in bed with a boy – Jenna will flip her lid. This is so weird. Where am I supposed to put my other arm?

I feel his heartbeat.

The rhythm is fast but steady. Really, really steady.

I move closer so I'm pressing against his back. I can hear the beat from the music downstairs.

'Callum, are you asleep?'

He doesn't reply and his breathing is really heavy. Should I be insulted? Relieved? I think about our day, and the moments of excitement, exploring the show floor, finding crazy new comics, waiting in line to see actual DC editors – and then, holy shit, arguing with DC editors! I realise it was one of the best days I've had – away from home, away from my dad. And now I don't really want to go back. I feel like I've broken free, like maybe the future that I was facing doesn't have to happen in the same way. Maybe I can escape. But after every song drifting up from Zoe's CD player, we're plunged into silence, and I hear my own heart, stumbling, tripping over itself. It reminds me. It whispers to me exactly what I've been trying to hide from myself. Things are getting worse. I am constantly exhausted. Just sheer leaden exhaustion. For hours. For days. For months. For ever. I know what it means. It means I shouldn't be making plans with this boy, or anyone. Those plans will not amount to anything.

'Are you asleep?' I say again.

No answer.

'Callum?'

No answer.

'Callum, I think I'm dying.'

There is no answer.

Tom

I walked very quietly away, past the finger buffet and along the bar where several mourners were surreptitiously ordering drinks despite the drama playing out in the foyer. There were whispers and concerned glances, but I ignored them and snuck up the stairs towards my office.

The desks, the floor and the bookcases were all piled high with cardboard boxes and weird objects that had been delivered over the last two days. I'll admit, I had spent some time recently on eBay, and on the websites of various theatrical stockists, buying and renting possible props for the birthday play. It was presumptuous of me, but I had succumbed to creative enthusiasm and it provided some light relief from organising the funeral. Of course, even while booking this stuff in I knew there was a slim chance I would not need ten adult-sized fairy costumes, a deluxe wolf outfit, a smoke machine, a huge net of twinkling lights, twenty tins of silver paint, several crowns and a throne. But I just wanted to show Hannah that I was taking this play seriously – that it was going to be big. Now here they were, towering in vast piles all around the room, threatening to fall and crush me in the most ironic fatal accident of all time.

What was I thinking?

I heard footsteps coming up the stairs and then Ted popped his head around the door.

'Tom, I just wanted to ... oh my good god, what the heck is all this stuff?'

His eyes scanned the office, then settled on me, then did another lap of the room in disbelief.

'I may have ordered some props. For the birthday play.'

'Oh Tom.'

'I know.'

'We did try to tell you.'

'I know.'

'She's going to be sixteen. Sixteen-year-olds don't want to write fairy-tale plays with their dads. They want to be hanging out with their friends, eating pizza, going to ... Take That concerts?'

I shook my head.

'Spice Girls? Girls Aloud? That's it. I'm all out of pop groups.'

I sighed heavily, and he sat down in the chair next to mine, levelling me with a sympathetic gaze.

'Was I wrong to be angry?' I said.

Ted stared out over the boxes of sparkling stage accessories.

'It's hard, isn't it – when they grow up and want their own lives,' he said. 'You spend years managing everything they do, everything they eat, where they go, who they see ... and then almost overnight you're just supposed to step away? It's hard enough going through this when you can share it with someone else, but, doing it alone? That's tough, Tom. That's very tough. But you've done everything you could do for Hannah and more besides. You're always going to be there for her. All I can say is, when they're this age, sometimes it's not about finding the right way to protect them. It's about finding the right way to let them go. I'm sorry, I may have picked that line up from one of Angela's movies.'

'I can't,' I said quietly. 'I can't.'

'Tom, listen to me. She's going to make it.'

'It's just . . .'

'Tom?'

'Yes?'

'Tom, *ten* fairy costumes? *Ten?*'

I smiled, despite myself. 'They were on special offer.'

'Look, she should have told you about the comic thing. She knows that. Nothing makes a teenager more angry than knowing they're wrong. They can't stand it.'

'I suppose I only have myself to blame for her sense of the dramatic. You know I hate to quote the bard, but when he wrote, "All the world's a stage, and all the men and women merely players", in her case that isn't a metaphor, that's literally her childhood. Oh god, that reminds me. We have the big council meeting on Monday night, right after Hannah's hospital appointment.'

'We do indeed.'

'Can I tell you a secret, Ted?'

'Of course.'

'I'm really worried. I'm worried about losing this building. It's not just a building, is it? We've sat here in this room, year after year, booking in an *army* of, well, often quite terrible acts. The young touring companies on their way up, the end-of-the-pier comedians on their way down, the variety acts that never were and never would be, even the occasional misunderstood genius. We've had them all. It's been more like a home really – they were our guests. I wouldn't change a moment of it. Ted, what if . . .'

But I didn't finish the sentence. I looked at him and my eyes were blurred.

'Come here,' he said.

And he hugged me.

I'd almost forgotten about the funeral gathering. When I went downstairs and saw all the mourners, I shivered to my very core.

Saturday passed in a seemingly never-ending fug of stress, solitude and self-recrimination – like being trapped alone in an experimental Edinburgh fringe production. I sat in the living room, texting Hannah, checking to see if she had replied to my texts, reading and analysing her note, knowing that it was no doubt loaded with hidden meaning and intent.

Dad. I've gone to Bristol. I know you don't want me to, so we're going to have to deal with that. I wish you hadn't shouted at Callum, he was on your side. I'll text you. Please, just leave me alone for a couple of days. Trust me not to do anything stupid. May need to reschedule the hospital appointment. Don't go mad, it's the first time ever. Once won't kill me.

Hannah.

P.S. Don't waste the weekend being cross. Prepare for your big day in court!

In fact, I'd already prepared our argument for not demolishing the theatre. During the week, Ted and I (mostly Ted) had looked up the council's budget and realised the building was relatively good value compared to some of the other strains on its finances. Also, Sally had gone through bundles of old programmes and discovered that one of the cast of the *Harry Potter* movies had once performed in a Willow Tree production of *Pygmalion*, so we figured the building had historic interest. It wasn't much, but it was something.

On Sunday, I got a text message. From Callum. Tom, you probably don't want to hear from me, but I am trying to persuade Hannah to go to the hospital appointment tomorrow. I started typing a reply but did not send it.

By Monday morning there was still no word from Hannah. I tried to call but the phone rang and rang. I felt like I was in an odd sort of daze, like I was caught in a rip tide and being dragged away from everything I knew. I was on the bus to the hospital and I didn't remember getting on it. I had my notes for the council meeting in my hand, but they were falling onto the floor.

The appointment was supposed to be at 10 a.m., but when I arrived ten minutes early, there was no sign of Hannah. The ward receptionist said she hadn't seen her; she put out a call for Venkman. I sat in the waiting room and I waited. I didn't know how long to stay before I gave up. I wondered what I should do if Hannah wasn't home when I got back, or what I should do if she was. An hour later, I had seen nurses come in and out, ignoring me or smiling politely, offering no information. A mum had passed through with a toddler who spent a few minutes playing with the dirty Duplo bricks spilled across the floor, but they were called away by a doctor I didn't recognise. I stared at my phone willing a text notification to appear, but it didn't. I paced and sat down. Finally, I got up to leave. I thought about what I would say to Hannah – how I would communicate how this felt, but as I went to open the waiting room door there was a boy standing there, blocking my exit, looking at me. His expression was strange and empty.

'We're in here,' the boy said. 'You have to come.'

It took several seconds of dumbly staring at him before I realised who it was.

'Callum!' I said at last. 'I've been waiting here like a lemon, why didn't you tell me you were already here, I could have—'

'Mr Rose, I'm so sorry,' he said. And I stopped talking. I stopped because he was crying. 'I'm so sorry. I think it's really serious.'

'Callum, calm down,' I said softly. 'Take me to her.'

I followed him out of the room and along the long white corridor. The lights were so bright. A porter passed us pushing a large trolley filled with bed linen. I was slowly beginning to get some sense back.

'Where is she?' I said.

He stopped and looked at me.

'Down here. I'm sorry. I had no idea, I . . . '

'Come on,' I said and I walked ahead of him. Faster now.

'She's in there,' he said.

I looked into a small treatment room and saw Venkman clearly trying to console someone.

'Dad.'

Hannah.

She was sitting on a plastic chair beside the desk, looking gut-wrenchingly pale. White-pale. She was wearing an over-sized black hoodie that I did not recognise. It may have been Callum's. The sleeves were clutched in her fists. She couldn't look at me; guilt was etched into her whole being. Somehow, in that moment of confusion and impending horror, I knew it wasn't about the argument, or about running away. She felt guilty about what was coming next.

I could hear my pulse thudding in my ears.

'Mr Rose,' said Venkman. He was on his feet now, patting me on the shoulder. I tried to focus on him. 'You should sit down.'

I sat down. Fear makes you compliant in a hospital. Callum lurked at the edge of the room, and then slunk away, the door closing quietly behind him. I was already thinking, what drama is about to play out in this little room? What cruel act is coming?

'So, Hannah's heart is in trouble,' says Venkman. 'There has been a significant decline in function. It has happened quickly, and because of that, I think things are only going to get worse.'

For some reason, I noticed he had a red splodge on his shirt, just left of his thin blue tie. Ketchup, no doubt, from a hurried breakfast. Maybe a bacon bap from the hospital café. I used to treat Hannah to one every time we came here.

'We'll need to refer her to one of the major UK cardiac centres, probably Great Ormond Street, but I'm certain they will agree with me about what must happen next.'

'What's that?' I say.

'Hannah needs to be put on the waiting list for a heart transplant.'

I stared at him, nodding slowly. I looked at Hannah for a reaction, but she was hunched and looking down towards her feet. A girl outside the headmaster's office.

'As a precaution?' I asked.

He shook his head.

'She needs a transplant, Tom.'

'When . . . when will that be?'

'I can't say. She needs to have some tests; Great Ormond Street will have her there for a few days. They have a whole team dedicated to this – surgeons, specialist nurses, psychologists . . . Then of course we have to wait for a suitable donor organ to become available. It can be months, it can be . . . significantly longer. But the operation has a very high success rate. She'll be on her feet and causing trouble again in no time.'

He smiled briefly, but it passed across his face like a shadow. 'Hannah,' he said gently. 'Do you have any questions?'

She didn't say anything; she didn't even glance up. She shook her head. I took her hand in mine, and it was cold. She looked younger, she looked tiny. She looked too small to cope with what was happening. I felt light-headed, as though I wasn't quite there. I couldn't align my thoughts into a response that made any sense. Venkman obviously decided that, in the absence of any kind of response, he should continue quietly imparting information.

'Great Ormond Street has an excellent cardiac team,' he said. 'They'll take great care of Hannah through the whole process. I know it's very frightening, I know that. But we're all—'

'What if I don't?' said Hannah.

Venkman stopped talking and looked at her. There was a sheen of sweat on his forehead.

'I'm sorry?' he said.

'What if I say I don't want a transplant?'

Her voice was almost inaudible, an SOS from some stricken ship miles out to sea. Venkman seemed to consider her words for a few seconds before slowly leaning forwards, towards my daughter.

'Hannah, listen to me,' he said. 'That's not an option for us now.'

We trudged out to the car park, engulfed in shock and silence, the unreality of ordinary life suddenly glaring and obnoxious – the kids running around the hospital reception area; the patients lurking just outside the doors, smoking; people complaining about the bus service into town. I walked with my arm around Hannah, while Callum stayed behind us, clearly uncomfortable and uncertain, but I didn't have the strength to reassure him. Instead, I told him that I would give him a lift home and I said no more. When we pulled up outside his house, he sat for a second, perhaps searching for something to say.

'I'm sorry,' was all he could manage. She didn't acknowledge it and neither did I. Instead, I gripped the steering wheel and looked ahead as though I was still driving. I heard him get out and close the door, then he was gone, and we were alone. I tried to think of something uplifting to say, something to puncture the mood, the perfect one-liner, the perfect anecdote. This is what I had always managed, every time, no matter what. But I had nothing. Nothing. Instead, I started the engine and drove away, and the deadening silence followed us.

At home, Hannah mumbled about needing sleep and as I fetched her rucksack from the boot of the car, she let herself into the house and padded straight up the stairs. I stood in the hallway, not knowing whether I should give her time and space, or whether I should follow her and hug her and reassure her, over and over again, as many times as it took to make us both believe it. But deep down, I was worried that I would not be able to say those words. Because I didn't feel them. Instead, I felt useless and frightened.

I thought I could make us hot chocolate. I could make it and take it up to her and maybe she'd be asleep and I could leave it beside her. But when I got to the kitchen and pulled the jar from the cupboard, I saw that it was empty. I looked at it for a few seconds, and then somehow I threw it against the wall where it shattered into glass shards and clouds of cocoa dust. I stood looking at the mess and to my great shock the phone began to ring in the living room. I ignored it and the answer machine kicked in.

'Good day, this is the residence of Tom and Hannah Rose. We are currently indisposed. Please leave a succinct message ... '

'Tom, Tom, are you there?' It was Ted's voice and I knew instantly where he was and why he was phoning. I walked robotically through the house to the handset.

'Ted,' I said.

'Ah there you are! Councillor Jenkins called. He said you didn't turn up to the meeting?'

'Ted . . .'

'What happened, for god's sake? I think we're really buggered this time.'

'Ted, it's Hannah. It's Hannah.'

'Oh no. What is it?'

'It's Hannah.'

I pressed the 'end call' button on the handset and let it fall to the floor. In a horrible sort of daze, I walked back to the kitchen and leaned heavily against the work surface. On the door of the fridge, held in place by a magnet shaped like a miniature bunch of bananas, there was a photo of Hannah and me, both of us beaming. Jay took it with his Polaroid camera on the first day of rehearsals for the 1970s farce. She had a pink and blue striped bobble hat on; I'd bought it for her as a joke, but she liked it and wore it constantly for days, even though the weather was warming up. It was there in the pocket of her rucksack on the kitchen table. I walked over and pulled it out, and looked at it. I felt it in my hands.

'My favourite hat,' said Hannah.

I looked up and she was standing in the doorway, still wearing the big hoodie, still deathly pale, apart from the black circles around her eyes.

'Dad,' she said. 'I'm really scared.'

'I know. I'm scared too.'

'I just don't . . . what did I do wrong?'

'Nothing, honey. You did nothing wrong.'

'Then why is this happening?'

'It's just bad luck, Hannah. It's the worst luck, that's all.'

Her eyes were glazing, I could see it. For the first time in ages, in so long I couldn't even remember. She looked down and these great tears fell. My own heart broke in that moment. I knew I would never forget it.

'I'm sorry I ran away,' she said, her voice thick and liquidy, her shoulders hunched.

'It's fine, don't think about it. It's in the past. I probably won't even ground you.'

'And the theatre ... the meeting ...'

'It doesn't matter, Hannah. It doesn't matter now.'

She was walking towards me, slowly, shakily. I remembered her at two, taking her first steps. She used to grip the sofa and haul herself up, then just let go and casually stride toward Elizabeth or me like she'd been walking for years. Then she'd collapse in a heap. Sometimes we'd catch her before she fell, and she'd laugh. She'd really laugh about that.

I caught her this time too.

'I'm sorry, Dad. Oh my Daddy, I'm so sorry.'

Her legs gave and I had the whole weight of her in my arms as she sobbed. I was terrified that I might let go, that I couldn't keep her safely held, that we would both fall. I felt in those seconds that everything in the world depended on me holding fast – like the final embrace at the end of a tragic scene.

Because in the end, actors must always hold their positions. As the lights fall and the stage is gradually immersed into blackness, they must hold. If they don't, the illusion is shattered.

Hannah

They say bad news comes in threes. It turns out they miscalculated. Margaret, the theatre, the transplant – that should have been the end of it.

It wasn't.

Two days after my appointment, after word of my health situation had spread to everyone in town (and everyone on MSN), I got a text, a fucking *text*, from Callum. He said he was sorry, he said my situation was 'a lot' to deal with, but what he meant was 'too much'. He was saying goodbye. So yeah. It's over.

I'm so hurt and furious, even though part of me knows I can't blame him. He's troubled enough as it is without having to cope with a girlfriend on the heart transplant waiting list. But still – a text. The few steps we'd made together meant nothing now. As Jenna always puts it, boys are all shitheads or cowards. I don't call him though. I don't shout 'How could you?' I don't have the energy. I just let it go, like a balloon on a string, released into the blank blue sky.

The days crawl by; they slip unnoticed from light to dark and back again. Dad is trying to help but he's a wreck. He stalks around the house, his eyes red and livid, his beard rough and unkempt, like some sort of mad shipwrecked sailor; I keep telling him to go to the theatre, to make some sort of plan, but he won't. Sally has been by and I've heard them talk downstairs, but there are long silences. He is frightened and he is making me frightened too.

I lie on my bed, the curtains half-drawn and I think and I sleep. Tiredness pushes me down into the mattress like a dead weight. Sometimes I'm not sure if I'm awake or dreaming, but there doesn't seem to be much of a difference between the two. I wonder if this is how Callum feels when he's really low, but then I get angry at myself for thinking about him.

Malvolio won't leave me alone. He sits at the end of the bed purring, and nudging me in the face with his head. Dad has to bring his food up because he won't go downstairs. Stupid cat – I thought they weren't supposed to care about people. Maybe he's broken like me.

School is starting again soon, and this may sound completely crazy, but the worst thing about the whole week so far was Dad telling me I didn't have to go. I cried for so long my head was pounding. Everyone else getting back into the old routine, putting on their crappy grey uniforms and bitching about how boring it all is – everyone except me. I don't want to be the misfit, the weirdo, the oddball, the madwoman locked in the attic. I want to be in the class, in the common room, sitting on the bench by the sports centre, hearing about important stuff, like how Britney Parsons got drunk on eight vodka Red Bulls at Stammo's party or how Ryan Benton fingered Jane Clough behind the recycling bins at Tesco. I want to get back to normal, but I know normal will never be the same again.

And then I wake up one morning, and it is my birthday. I told Dad – I begged him – no fuss, no surprises. He brings me breakfast on a tray with a pile of cards and a few presents. I don't open them. While I'm still lying there worrying about falling behind on school gossip, I hear the doorbell ring. I barely register it until I recognise a voice downstairs, and I know that Dad has disobeyed my direct order: no visitors. The next thing, there are feet pummelling up the stairs, and onto the landing, and then fists banging at my door.

'Hannah?' says Daisy. 'I hope you're decent, we're coming in.'

The door opens and the light from the window in the hallway is blinding. I put my arm across my eyes and groan like some sort of sickly vampire.

'Happy birthday,' says Daisy. 'Oh good grief, it smells like the boys' changing room in here. Let me open the window, you stinky bitch.'

She makes her way across my rubbish-strewn floor and throws open the curtains, and then the window. A breeze blows in immediately, as though it had been waiting outside for days. The air fills with the flowery smells of hairspray and birthday-best perfume. My friends have made an effort for their visit.

'Look, I really appreciate you coming,' I drawl, turning and squinting into my pillow. 'But I don't want to see anyone.'

'Shut up,' says Jenna. 'This is an intervention. First, we're gonna get you up, then we're gonna knock your dad out and shave his beard off.'

'I'm sorry,' I say. 'I'm not ready for jokes.'

'She's not joking,' says Daisy. 'She's been listening to System of a Down for days and it's made her very aggressive.'

'It's your shitty dance rap pop that makes me aggressive.'

'Please,' I murmur. 'I know what you're trying to do, but please ... please just go.'

They are quiet for a moment, and even through the fog of my sadness and fear, I know they are staring at each other, willing each other on. They're coming up with a new plan through the teen language of glares, eye-rolls and frantic flapping gestures. I am aware that a small part of me, hidden somewhere far away, doesn't want them to give up.

Then someone sits down on the bed, and there is a hand on my arm, warm and soft. I know it's Daisy, because Jenna would never be this gentle. I keep my back to them, but it is clear they have arrived at a change of tactic.

'Hannah,' she says. 'Remember when I was ten and I had that terrible asthma attack? You know, the one where I almost died? They rushed me to hospital and put me on a ventilator and I was shitting it. The next morning you came in to see me with your dad. I was completely minging and didn't really know what was going on, but you sat for ages and gabbled away, then I heard you put down a plastic bag on the table by the bed. Do you remember what was in it, Hannah?'

I don't move or say anything.

'Ooh, I know this one,' yells Jenna. 'It was a Sherbet Fountain and a Simpsons comic!'

'Thank you, Jenna, this is not a fucking classroom. Anyway, the point is, I can remember thinking to myself, I just need to get through another day, another day of feeling like this, and then I am going to read that comic and I am going to stuff my face with sherbet. It was just this little thing to look forward to. The next day, the doctors were telling me how serious my asthma was and about all the crazy drugs I needed, but when they left I sat up in bed and I read my damn comic and ate my damn sherbet and I felt good. I think that's how things get better. In, like, little steps. With little treats. I never tasted a nicer Sherbet Fountain in my whole life.'

'And she's eaten a lot of them, let's be honest here,' said Jenna.

'Jesus, stop ruining my fucking Oscar speech!'

'Look,' said Jenna, now flopping down onto the bed as well. 'I have no idea of what you're going through. I can't even imagine. I also have no idea what Daisy's sherbet story was about. But we're your friends and we're here for you. That's how things work, right? You're never going to be alone, whether you like it or not.'

'Thank you, I—'

'Although we do actually have to go because your dad said we could only have five minutes and my mum is waiting in the car outside. I've got to go to a fucking careers fair. My dad's new idea is that I should be a systems analyst.'

'We didn't think we'd be allowed up, to be honest,' says Daisy, stroking my back. 'We should have thought this through.'

Jenna sighs at her. 'We shouldn't have wasted three minutes on that sherbet story you mean.'

'Anyway, see you tomorrow. We're just gonna keep coming back.'

'Like herpes.'

There are splodgy kisses on my cheek and forehead, and then they are gone, trailing the scent of sweet flowers and hair products behind them. The room suddenly feels static and cold and overbearing. I turn onto my back and look up. Above me, all over the ceiling, are dozens of glow-in-the-dark stars, which my dad stuck there for me when I was five because I liked to pretend I was sleeping in a woodland glade with a troupe of singing fairies. That was when I believed in magic. That was when anything seemed possible. Now I *know* anything is possible, but in a different and incredibly crappy way. I know that, at any point, everything you thought you knew can be pulled away from you. If I had the strength and energy, I would stand up on the bed and rip the stars down.

*

Later, I lift my head and feebly glance around the room trying to reorientate myself. I see that on my desk, my friends have left me something. A Sherbet Fountain and a copy of *Spider Woman*. I almost smile. But then my gaze falls on the envelope from Margaret, which I've left on the desk, propped up against a pile of school books. I take hold of it and run it between my fingers, feeling the hard object inside. In one quick motion, I tear it open.

The object is a key. A big chunky old key. It is attached to a cardboard luggage tag on which Margaret has written 'The green room'. In my messed-up mental state it takes me a long time to work out what it means. At first I think she's somehow stolen the key to the green room at the theatre, but that makes no sense because it's a totally different sort of lock and why the hell would she do that? Then I think maybe it's a green room in another theatre, but then that would be equally crazy because what was I supposed to do, spend the rest of my life visiting every playhouse in the country asking if I could try my key in their door?

I lie there thinking about the last time I'd really spoken to her. It was that afternoon at her house with Callum. The afternoon I explored her home. The afternoon I went upstairs and looked in every room. Except the room at the end. The room with the locked door. And I now remember, later perhaps than I should have – that the locked door was painted green.

Tom

We stood outside the theatre, Hannah and I. Silent and still, we looked in through the glass frontage, to the little box office, now closed and locked up. It probably wouldn't open again. The weather was turning away from summer, towards the first crisp chill of autumn; brown leaves drifted across the car park in big clumps, like tumbleweed.

After several days locked in her room, it was the key that drew Hannah out at last. I don't think I ever realised how much Margaret had meant to her – and how important their meetings had been. Now this final connection between the two of them had given my daughter the strength to get out.

'What time is Sally picking you up?' I said.

'Any minute now.'

'Are you sure you're up to this?'

'No, but I have to do it. What about you?'

I'd come in to clear up some things, to speak to volunteers, to begin the process of shutting the theatre.

'They're busy ringing building contractors,' I said. 'When they build houses here, I suspect they'll call it the

Willow Tree Development – a little faux acknowledgement of the past.'

Hannah grimaced.

'Theatre Street,' she said.

'Drama Crescent.'

'Tragedy Close . . .'

That one was, perhaps, a little too meaningful at the moment.

'I'm sorry,' she said. 'I'm sorry you didn't make it to that meeting.'

'There were much more important things to worry about. I phoned the next day and explained the circumstances, but they weren't interested.'

Hannah shivered against the wind. I thought, what do I say about all this? How do I make it go away? There, there, the theatre is closing and you're having a teeny heart transplant, but otherwise we're fine – chin up!

Incapable of comforting each other, we drifted into silence once again. We were so lost in our thoughts that when a car pulled off the road and into the theatre car park, we both jumped. It wasn't Sally's car and I immediately knew it couldn't belong to one of our staff because it looked new and shiny, and wasn't held together with duct tape and rust.

As soon as the door opened, I recognised the driver.

'Hello Tom,' she said. 'Hello Hannah.'

'Hello Vanessa,' I replied. She looked beautiful and Parisian in a long grey coat and thick woollen hat and scarf. I noticed she was carrying an A4 brown envelope. 'Is the council hand-delivering eviction notices now? That's a nice touch. Very personal.'

'How is everything?' she asked, ignoring my snide tone.

'We're as well as can be expected.'

'I can't imagine how difficult this is.'

'No, you can't.'

'Tom, I'm sorry.'

'Why couldn't you have moved the meeting? It wasn't much to ask under the circumstances.'

'It's not that easy to move a council meeting. We had dozens of building disputes to get through. However—'

'But this isn't just some building, Vanessa.'

'It is when there are budgets to balance, deadlines to meet . . . everything moves so fast, we didn't have the luxury of time. But I—'

'There should have been someone to speak up for this place!'

'There was! That's what I'm trying to tell you.'

'Who?'

'Me, Tom. I did it. I thought about what you said – about this being more than a building, about it being a symbol for something bigger. I put that to the council. I stood up in that big bloody chamber and I said the town needed a cultural hub. I said that we would be poorer if we lost it. That's why I'm here. It's not much, but I've bought you some time. This letter is from the head of the planning and building group. If you can prove the theatre has ongoing value to the local community, if you can raise the money to repair the flood damage, the council may reconsider its redevelopment plans.'

I looked at Vanessa and wondered if she'd angered her colleagues, speaking out for us when it would have suited everyone to let it go. She looked back at me wearing the same expression of slightly detached but defiant amusement that I recalled from our first date. I liked it. I really liked that look. Then I read the letter.

'They want a report, with detailed evidence of the theatre's sustained community value, and they want assurances that the building will pass a health and safety inspection. But they want it in two weeks.'

'It's the best I could do,' said Vanessa.

'It's not enough time,' I replied.

'There's never enough time,' she said. 'That's life.'

'And how are we supposed to raise money if we can't even use the theatre building?'

'I don't know. Do you have a mailing list? Is there a Friends of the Willow Tree group? Can you get some kind of event together somewhere else? You know, some sort of "save our theatre" thing?'

'Vanessa, you know why I missed the meeting don't you?'

'Yes,' she said, and she turned to Hannah. 'I'm sorry. How are you doing?'

Hannah shrugged and dug her hands into her coat pockets.

'So no, I can't get an event together,' I said.

Vanessa moved forward and put her hand on my shoulder, just briefly, but there was warmth in the touch.

'You have good people around you,' she said. 'Let them help.'

I nodded with very little conviction.

'I'd better go,' she said.

She was walking back towards her car, but then stopped and turned to me.

'I studied urban planning at university,' she said. 'I guess I wanted to change the world – one roundabout at a time. I liked the idea of making cities function better, about making people happier where they lived. Instead I've ended up helping to demolish things. It turns out I am good with broken and vulnerable assets.'

'Ah, so *that's* why you liked me.'

'No, I liked you because you were honest and funny and genuine.'

'So were you.'

She pulled her car keys from her coat and pressed a button, unlocking the doors.

'I'd do it again,' she said. 'I mean, I'd go out with you again. If that was ever on the cards.'

'I don't think so.'

'That's a shame,' she said. She opened the car door, but stood still for a second as though waiting for something. 'Tom. Remember what I said to you, outside my house, the night of the music lesson?'

I nodded.

'I still believe we'll get that moment. I hope we take it.'

She got into the car and started the engine. Before she could reverse out of the space, Hannah ran to her window and knocked on it. The window opened.

'Did you read it?' Hannah said. '*Persepolis*. Did you read it?'

I had no idea what she was talking about but it seemed that Vanessa did. She turned to Hannah, the wind blowing her jet-black hair across her face.

'Yes,' she said. 'What a brave girl. Her whole world collapsed, but she rebuilt it. What a survivor. I admire her.'

Then Vanessa took one last long look at the theatre, seeming to drink in every element of the façade, every pane of glass, every cracked concrete slab. 'Don't give up,' she said to me. '"This above all: to thine own self be true." I'm not sure that's entirely relevant, but it's the only Shakespeare I know. I don't even know which play it's from.'

And then the car pulled away. I waved after her as she headed out of the car park and onto the road.

'*Hamlet*,' I whispered to myself. 'Act one, scene three.'

I turned back to Hannah, ready to ask what that was all about, but I noticed that she was looking at me and, almost imperceptibly, she was shaking her head.

Hannah

It seems like a hundred days since I last left the house and every step I take feels wonky and uncertain. My ankles are weak, my lungs burn, my saggy handbag of a heart drums weakly against my ribs. There is a bit of a scene at the theatre when Vanessa shows up offering some hopeless last chance to save the building. Dad can't deal with this at all. I'm relieved when Sally arrives, but as I approach the car, I'm shocked to see her looking in the rear-view mirror, hurriedly wiping away mascara. It is obvious she's been crying. When I open the passenger door and climb in, she turns and smiles brightly, but she can't hide it. Sadness is like a cold – it's catching.

'Sally, what's wrong?' I say.

'I'm fine, nothing's wrong. Are you ready to raid Margaret's house for treasure?'

'Please – there's still mascara on your cheek. What's happened?'

She looks away, down the road, towards nothing in particular.

'Do you want me to fetch Dad?'

'No! No, honestly. Thank you.'

She runs her hands through her hair and puts it up into a

321

ponytail. When she holds the steering wheel again, she grips it as though we're about to start a race.

'What's going on?' I say.

'We're having some problems, Phil and I. We've been having them a long time, but I ... Oh look you don't need to hear this.'

'I do. I really do.'

'I don't know how to explain,' she says, and she's looking up as though asking for divine intervention. 'He's a bully, Hannah. He's always been a bully. This summer he's just got worse – there's a lot of pressure at work, I don't know. He demands to know where I am and what I'm doing all the time, criticising the state of the house, the garden; if I cook dinner it's not what he wants or it's just shit, if I don't he goes mad ...'

'Phil?!' I say it almost incredulously – and I feel immediately guilty for that.

'Oh, he's very good at putting on a show, being the nice guy, the life and soul of the party, but at home he's very different. He's very ... he has to be in control of everything all the time. The house, our money, our holidays, Jay, me. If he's not in control he gets angry. He gets really angry.'

'Oh god, has he ever ...?'

'No. Not that. He's been close – he's thrown things, he's smashed up the room, but not me. This morning, he asked me where I was going and when I told him it was none of his business, he lobbed his coffee cup at the wall. That's why I'm late. He wants me to give up the drama club, he hates the fact I go there and meet people he doesn't know. He thought that with the theatre in trouble I'd be at home more, but that hasn't happened and he's furious. You know the WestFest show? I had told him I was taking Jay to my mother's for the weekend. I knew there'd be a big argument otherwise. But then he came into the theatre that day and caught me running the damn rehearsals. I took Jay to the show anyway, but that's made it so much worse now. And Jay, my poor boy. He's been stuck in the middle of everything. I don't know if he understands what's going on. I try to talk to him but he just shrugs it away. Shit, shit, shit.'

'Oh, Sally.'

I lean over to hug her and she hugs me back gently, but she's not quite there. 'This is all so trivial compared to what you're going through.'

'No, it isn't! But I mean, I just don't understand. Why are you still with him?'

She almost scoffs, despite herself, and I see her eyes are tearing up.

'Oh god, I don't know. Habit? Fear? When we got together, things were so different – I was different. Then we had Jay and . . . the years just slip by, Hannah. If you let them, they slip by. What I feel now is humiliated; I'm embarrassed I didn't stand up to him. I'm embarrassed people will find out how I failed; how useless I am. I feel so pathetic and stupid.'

'You're not, Sally. You're amazing.'

'Ha! I'm so amazing, I'm still here feeling guilty, still trapped.'

'Then leave. Take Jay and go.'

'It's not that easy.'

'Why not?'

'You don't understand, you're just a . . . '

'Child?'

'Yes. I shouldn't even be telling you all this.'

'Do you know what my cardiologist once said to me? "Hannah, you have the heart of an eighty-five-year-old." He meant because it's so bloody knackered, but it's not just that. I've grown up thinking I could drop dead at any second; I've had to watch my dad cope with that, I've had to warn my friends; I've had to fucking warn and prepare everyone I've ever met for it. I've been on drugs my whole life; I've had more medical tests than I can even begin to remember. This piece of shit thing in my chest reminds me how pathetic it is sixty times a minute. Sometimes I feel like I've lived every single one of those eight-five years. I'm *not* a child.'

When I've calmed down, Sally takes my hand.

'I mean, let's face it,' I say, quieter now. 'My best friend was a pensioner. While everyone else at school was out drinking and shagging, I was in the tea shop eating Battenberg slices.'

There is a moment of silence, then we both burst out laughing. It is raucous uncontrollable laughter. We're laughing so helplessly, we can barely breathe. Sally grips my arm. 'You win,' she says, gathering the ability to string a sentence together. 'I'm sorry, but you are more pathetic than me.' And that starts us off again.

When Sally finally manages to compose herself she sits upright in her seat, wipes her eyes, then looks at me.

'Do you have the key?' she asks. I get it out of my pocket and show it to her. 'Then what are we waiting for?'

'I'm scared,' I say.

'Don't be,' she replies, wiping her eyes. 'We're superheroes now. We're indestructible.'

I want to say you were always my hero, Sally, but I don't.

Dearest Willow,

By the time I was eleven, I started thinking about the birthday plays in a different way. Dad had bought me a book on the history of theatre design and I became really interested in the workings of the stage; the scenery, the use of fly towers and lighting rigs; all the tricks and techniques. This was the magic that interested me now.

I'd also come to a life-changing realisation. Many of the fairy tales I'd been brought up with depicted girls as victims or prizes; they were locked in towers or poisoned by witches or expected to weave straw into gold for nights on end. They were possessions to be traded between fathers and princes, they were to be married or sacrificed. This was in contrast to the comics I'd been reading. Wonder Woman would never marry a prince just because he'd danced with her at a ball. I think I was having a feminist awakening. Have you had one yet? They're fun.

So in September 2000, I told Dad I wanted to put on Sleeping Beauty for my birthday. But there was a catch. The beauty had to be a man, and he was to be saved by a princess. Most of the younger male members of the drama club were sort of hesitant about the idea, but Shaun – tougher and cooler than the rest – said he was born to play the role of a handsome guy waiting to be rescued. Rachel volunteered to be the princess. We had our lead players. I sat with Sally night after night and she showed me how to build sets, how to use flats, how to employ materials like plaster, wood and muslin; we had beautiful plans for the ending of the play, when the prince falls asleep and the giant hedges grow up around the castle; we would rig pulleys to pull our cloth brambles and thorns upwards around the sleeping monarch.

But as the day loomed there were two major problems. Shaun was put on a week of nightshifts and had to drop out. And then, a tiny bit more seriously, I came down with a bad chest infection, which became pneumonia – and that put me in hospital. A day before my birthday. I was utterly bereft. I was inconsolable. There have been a lot of times in my life when I've felt anger and frustration at my condition, but this was the darkest, the most all-consuming.

But Sally wouldn't be beaten. She reached out to the matron in charge of my ward, she talked through a crazy plan with her. They could put the play on in the family room just down the corridor from my bed – all the children would be welcome to watch. Somehow she got permission.

That's how, on my eleventh birthday, Dad ended up carrying me down the ward to the makeshift theatre. The stage was a bed, strung with fairy lights and surrounded by painted cardboard turrets to resemble a castle. When the king and queen welcomed their daughter into the world, it was actually a resuscitation doll. A heart monitor doubled as the spinning wheel. It was Jay who stepped in at the last minute as the prince. He told his mum he wanted to help his friend (me!). At least he got a kiss from Rachel, who played the hero, fighting her way to the slumbering monarch through crêpe paper brambles strung across the corridor.

Also in the little audience, crowded into the bright, white medical room, were friends and family – the usual bunch. I saw that Phil wasn't there and Dad asked why. 'Oh he's not well,' said Sally and she changed the subject as quickly as she could. It was years later that

I discovered he had actually refused to come. He'd taken exception to Jay playing the Sleeping Beauty, yelling about his son being a laughing stock. But his son stood up to him and so did his wife. I wonder if that was the moment Sally started to question everything about him.

I'll never forget that play. It's where I learned that the whole idea of theatre is sort of malleable; it does not need to be confined to a certain place. There were dozens of us packed into that room, illuminated by fairy lights and the green hue of an exit sign. Bright shafts of light crept in from the ward outside and shadows played across the scene whenever a doctor or nurse walked past. I was so weak and tired, it felt dreamlike. Part of me still wonders if it actually happened or did I dream it? Have I constructed the whole play from my sickly hallucinations?

I read later that some historians believe fairy tales were first told by old women to young girls; they were coded warnings about men and society. All I knew at the time was that I'd fallen out of love with the magic of fairy stories, but that night – through the bravery of my dad's best friend – they claimed me back again.

Hannah

We are standing at the end of the path that leads to Margaret's house. The key is clutched in my hand. I have made it this far.

So yeah, let's do this.

I'm feeling mega heroic, right until the moment I push the creaky black gate open and a couple of sparrows fly out of the hedge, scaring the shit out of me. Ahead, the apple trees seem to have taken on sinister new shapes, their branches twisted and gnarled like a cursed forest in a fairy-tale book.

'Do you want me to come in too?' says Sally from the pavement.

'Do you mind?' I say.

She smiles and we creep along the path together, avoiding the nettles and the rotten fallen fruit, buzzing with wasps. At the front door, I look in through the glass panel and see that everything is as it was when I was last here, only now the little table in the hall has a pile of unopened post and local newspapers. When we stopped off to collect the front door key from Margaret's solicitor, he told us he had been in to tidy up a little, but he had no key for the green door. 'I'm intrigued to know what you find,' he said. 'I can't imagine it will be much. She was very fastidious, and despised clutter.'

But I need to know.

When I open the door, the smell of furniture polish hits me, and for a second, it takes me right back to that day with Callum. He'd made it out of his sickbed to come along – I thought that was so cool of him. But I need to keep him out of my head right now – I can only deal with one massive, crushing disappointment at a time.

Sally follows me in and she spends a few seconds staring at Margaret's decor, admiring the mosaic floors. The air is still and deathly quiet. I wonder if her ghost is here now. The thought of it makes me shiver. Sally puts her hand on my back.

'The room is upstairs,' I say.

We clatter slowly up the wooden staircase, me gripping the handrail and Sally beside me, her right arm hovering beside my elbow, as though I'm some sort of invalid. Which I sort of am, I suppose. The steps creak as we climb. A small window above us lets in a shaft of golden light; it is filled with shining dust particles, which immediately reminds me of the day when I showed Callum the theatre lights. Jeez, I've got to get him out of my brain. We look down the corridor, past the bathroom, past the bedrooms, towards the door at the end. The green door.

'You know, if there's nothing in there, it doesn't matter,' says Sally. 'She's still our Margaret.'

I nod, but considering everything else going on, I don't agree. It does matter. I don't want her life to have been a dumb fantasy, I don't want it to be a big book of tall tales. I don't want it to be a lie. I feel like I need something to hold on to, something that isn't a story. And for a few seconds, the sheer weight of this realisation freezes me to the spot. I can't move. I can barely breathe.

'Come on,' says Sally. 'Let's get this over with.'

She takes my hand and starts forward, and almost in a trance,

I follow. We pass Margaret's bedroom; we pass the guest room. I look down at the long, ornately patterned hallway rug beneath our feet, and I wonder how many times Margaret walked down it. Then we are at the door. The key is hot and sweaty in my palm. I lift it slowly towards the lock and slide it in. When I turn it, I expect resistance, but the mechanism is really smooth and I hear it click open. I clutch the round brass handle and turn it.

What do we ever really know about the people we love? I mean, when you stop to think about it – how much of it is made up in our own heads? There are people in our lives that play certain roles; the rebellious friend, the moody lover, the eccentric aunt – who are these people? What do they want? The times you had together – were they really that fun? Sometimes when you fall out with a friend, you discover things about them that you just never saw. Sometimes the most painful part of losing someone is realising you were wrong about them all along. What if you were wrong all along?

Oh god, what am I doing?

'Last chance,' says Sally. 'We can just lock the door again, go home and let the solicitor come and do it.'

'Margaret wanted it to be me,' I say. 'She wanted me to see this.'

'But she was getting a bit absent-minded by the end. Maybe she *thought* there was something in here you should see; maybe she imagined it? I'm just worried because she was always a bit of a fantasist wasn't she? You're not in the best shape right now – I don't think you need to be dealing with that.'

'No,' I say. 'Maybe not.'

And slowly, without saying anything else, I close the door again. Sally puts her hand on my shoulder and we walk away. We walk away from whatever is in there and whatever it means or doesn't mean. It doesn't really matter, in the grand scheme of things. Considering what I'm facing and what I'm going to have to get through, it doesn't . . .

Margaret would open the door.

The thought hits me so hard I can feel it in my bones. If the world was reversed, if it was my house, my lock, my door, Margaret would burst in without a second thought. Because you regret the things you don't do more than the things you do.

And I'm turning around. It's happening in slow motion. It's happening in comic book frames. I'm turning around and I shake Sally's hand loose from me. Then I'm striding towards the door, almost sprinting, the thin rug rucking up beneath my feet, and the corridor seems to be getting longer, like some weird surrealist sequence in a *Dr Strange* story. The truth is coming anyway, I think – I may as well face it. The truth will get us in the end. And I grab the handle, pause for a millisecond, then throw the door open.

The air is dense and musty – that's what hits me first. It's not unpleasant, it's like dad's office, or the school library – any place with a lot of old papers. In that instant, I know. I don't have to look around, I don't have to investigate. I know about Margaret.

I step back towards the doorway and I look at Sally.

Her eyes are on me, expectantly, hopefully. But they are sad too because she has seen things go wrong before. Her hands are ready to catch me if I fall.

But this time I won't fall.

'It's all true,' I say. 'Everything she said is true.'

The walls are covered in framed photos, black and white images of plays, dozens of them, all showing the same beautiful young actress. There are posters, some hung, others just leaning against walls. They are from theatrical productions, and judging by the design, all from the 1950s to the 1970s. Most are from plays I haven't heard of at places like the Bush Theatre, the Oval House, the Orange Tree. There is a wooden bookcase, containing piles of theatre programmes. Greedily, Sally and I grab handfuls of them and flick to the cast pages, where the same name keeps coming up. It is Margaret Chevalier. Her maiden name. Her stage name. On another shelf, more framed black and white photos with faces I faintly recognise from nostalgic TV shows and old movies, most of them signed, all to her. *To Margaret, for an unforgettable production. For Margaret, the naughtiest Lady Bracknell I ever met. To Margaret, with love, Brian Blessed.*

We throw open a battered old suitcase and find a collection of lavish evening gowns, folded and stored in tissue paper. Each has a handwritten note pinned to it: the Evening Standard Theatre Awards 1965; the Royal Variety Performance 1968; the Sun Television Awards 1973.

It is too much. It is everything.

'Look,' says Sally. She takes a large paper folder from the writing desk below the sash window, opposite the door. There is a single word written on the front:

Hannah

I take it from her cautiously, as though handling something delicate or dangerous. And I guess it's sort of both, because this is what Margaret wanted me to find and to open. This is why I'm here.

I open the flap.

The first thing that comes tumbling out is a small object that rolls along the desk and then falls into my hands, the circle of large blue gems twinkling in the light. It is Margaret's sapphire engagement ring.

I need to sit down. I pull out the chair from the desk and slump into it. Next there is a wad of papers, at the front of which is a note dated June 2005, written in Margaret's swooping, beautiful hand.

Dear Hannah

If you are reading this, I have popped my clogs. I feel as though it has been coming for several months. I hope you are not too upset. What is it the young people say? 'Shit happens'? It certainly does. I've had a long and eventful life, as you can now see. Why did I hide all this away? Because I found it difficult to look at. I prefer the past to live in stories rather than relics. Seeing these old programmes and posters tells me that these things happened long ago, but my mind tells me they were yesterday. I prefer the latter. The things we do and experience, the times we have, they stay with us, don't they? They are only ever a thought away. I gave up acting to move here with Arthur many years ago; it was what we both wanted, and I did not want to be haunted by the past; I wanted it to live on in my mind. Loss is always hard, Hannah, but we can make it easier on ourselves by understanding that memories are real and alive.

Having said that, this folder contains something I want you to have, because it seems like you and your father have lost it, you hopeless things. I think you should use it again somehow. There is also something of mine, which is now yours. I saw you admiring it. It will look beautiful on you, and perhaps one day you will pass it on.

Stay strong my young friend – you are the strongest person I ever met. I saw you grow up; I have treasured knowing you and watching you become a brilliant young woman. My dear, I never knew anyone in the way I know you. I understand that things have been hard, and that they may even get harder. Remember that life isn't measured in years, it is measured in moments. There are over thirty million seconds in a year, did you know that? Hannah, grasp as many of those seconds as you can, they're yours. I will be

333

smiling down on you. Let us go on meeting for tea and cake every fortnight. Let us always catch up.

Your friend for all time,

Margaret

I touch the words with my fingertips. I trace the sloping lines.

'I wish she was still here,' I say. 'I really wish that. She was the only person I could talk to about ...'

Sally stands beside me and puts her arm around my shoulder.

'About what?' she asks.

I don't want to answer but I do anyway. 'Dying.' I say. 'How fucking ironic is that?'

And for a little while I can't say anything else.

Finally, there is the wedge of well-thumbed papers, crumpled and torn at the edges. I flick through them and it takes me a few seconds to work out what they are. I can hardly believe it when I do.

'Oh my god, Sally.'

They are transcripts of my birthday plays. All of them. Every scene, every word. She kept Dad's hastily written production notes, but added all the dialogue, all the stage directions. I look through, catching little snippets that make the memories spark into life; half-recalled lines reconstruct themselves in my head. For the first time in days, I smile. I actually smile.

'Are those what I think they are?' says Sally.

'The birthday plays,' I say, my voice busted up with emotion. 'Margaret kept all of them. Me and Dad couldn't manage it. But she did.'

Among all these treasures of an amazing career, she kept my scripts, my life. It meant something to her. I hold the papers to my chest and I cry. I really, really cry.

*

334

When I get home, Dad is in his little study area, staring into space.

'Dad, you won't believe what I found at Margaret's,' I yell.

He turns in his chair.

'Is Sally with you? I need to speak to her.'

The weirdness of his tone stops me in my tracks. I wonder if something has happened with Phil or the theatre. I can't read the look in his eyes, but I know now is not the time for nostalgia. Instead I go up to my bedroom and spread the scripts out on my desk.

Even though I'm knackered and frightened and sad, and Sally's whole marriage is crumbling to pieces, we were both lifted by this epic discovery. It's weird how little things can do that – the smallest of pleasures, the weakest shafts of light, the faintest of fair winds. Sometimes that's all you need to draw you away from the big drama in your life, if only for a little while.

Margaret saved the plays. The plays were about the magic of the theatre. Our theatre.

I get the inkling of an idea; a potentially unworkable idea. I wonder if it might be the medication, the exhaustion – perhaps I am hallucinating. I think about telling Sally, but it's too dumb, and too late.

Or is it?

Just as I'm thinking this, I hear Sally yell goodbye from down-stairs then the front door opens and closes. I really do not have the energy to run after her, so I send a text instead.

'I think we should save the theatre.'

The handset starts to ring almost instantly.

'Hannah,' says Sally. 'Haven't you had enough excitement for one day?'

I tell her my ideas; they pour out of me. Half an hour later, I've managed to convince her I'm not crazy. It's as though the spirit of Margaret is working through me, like a cross between Maggie Smith and Yoda.

'If we're going to do this, we need everyone else on board,' says Sally. 'And we can't tell your dad. He's got enough on his plate without more theatre worries.'

'What do you mean?'

'Oh ... oh nothing. It's fine, just ... boring stuff. Anyway, we need to arrange a meeting for everyone – but not at the theatre, somewhere else. Somewhere less obvious.'

'I know just the place.'

Tom

Hannah had been out with Sally for over an hour when the phone started ringing. My first thought was, oh god, what's happened? Life had taken on the quality of a melodrama – I expected every knock at the door, every letter, every phone call, to be delivering catastrophic news.

So when a voice I didn't immediately recognise said, 'Tom, is that you?' I felt a frisson of relief. This wasn't Sally calling to tell me that Hannah had collapsed; it probably wasn't the council letting me know that they'd launched a successful missile strike on the theatre.

Then I realised who it was.

The voice was faint and crackly; it was coming to me from thousands of miles and another lifetime away.

'Hello Elizabeth,' I said.

I used to call her Lizzie. It was over a year before I found out she detested it – that a girl at school used to walk along behind her chanting 'Busy Lizzie, Busy Lizzie' while yanking her hair back. This carried on for weeks until, one day, Busy Lizzie turned round and punched her in the face, knocking a tooth out. No one else ever called her Lizzie again – until I stumbled along. For some reason, she didn't stop me, she didn't seem to mind; it felt like something intimate between us. That was gone now.

'I just got your messages,' she said. 'I'm so sorry, I've been away on business in Abu Dhabi. How is she?'

'She's coping, but I don't think it's really sunk in yet – for either of us.'

'Oh god, my poor darling,' she replied, as though referring to a pet hamster undergoing a minor surgical procedure. Her calm was almost surreal, it brought out all my fear.

'I'm scared for her,' I said. 'I don't know what she's going through. I don't know any more.'

'She's strong, she's a realist – she'll take it in her stride. So what's next? Are the doctors going to keep us up to date?'

I paused while trying to digest her use of the word 'us'; it stuck in my windpipe like a chunk of gristle. There was no 'us'.

'She has to go to Great Ormond Street for three days of tests,' I said, my voice somewhat strangulated. 'Then we'll know more.'

'I have a friend in London, a prominent cardiologist. When I arrive on Saturday I'll call him immediately.'

The world went silent, I felt like my ears had popped; the phone felt weightless in my hand.

'Are you still there?' yelled Elizabeth.

'I . . . what do you mean, when you arrive?'

'I'm flying back. My PA booked it all yesterday. I'll email you the details. Bloody Gatwick Airport of all places.'

'But—'

'Oh don't worry, Tom, I'm not just going to turn up on your doorstep, I'll arrange somewhere to stay. I appreciate this isn't going to be easy, but I need to see her. My god, she's had a tough time.'

338

'I'm sorry, but what do you know about it? Elizabeth, Jesus, you haven't seen her or spoken to her for ten years.'

It was her turn to pause. There was no reply to me but static. For the first time, it felt like I'd punctured through a layer of her well-structured defences.

'No,' she said quietly. 'No, of course not. I'm sorry. You must think ... I'm sorry.'

My mind was blank, the script completely forgotten. It felt like I was on stage and the shoddy boards beneath me, always wonky and precarious, had now begun to splinter; the beautifully painted sets were warping, the wood too thin to hold. Oh dear. I knew things were *really* bad when I started to think entirely in apocalyptic theatrical metaphors.

'So I'll email the details over,' she said, bright and businesslike again. 'I'd appreciate it if you met me? At the airport? We could catch up then.'

Some part of me somewhere wanted to demand: 'Why now? Why come back now? Why not years ago?' but I couldn't form the words, or even the thoughts behind the words.

'All right,' was all I managed. All right? We had spoken for approximately a minute and she'd already brute-forced her way back into our lives. Was that the best I could do? Yes, apparently it was.

'I know she might not want to see me,' said Elizabeth, sounding blithe and pragmatic. 'I'm prepared for that.'

'That's good.'

'Until Saturday then.'

'Yes,' I said. 'Until Saturday.'

The line went dead. Elizabeth was coming back. How was I going to explain this to Hannah?

*

When Hannah and Sally arrived home from Margaret's I could barely look my daughter in the eye – I had no idea how to tell her what was happening. Instead, I waited until she'd gone upstairs and explained the whole story to Sally.

'What should I do?' I asked her.

'You should go to Gatwick and meet your ex-wife.'

'But what if she wants to come here and see her daughter?'

'Of course she does.'

'So what do I tell Hannah?'

Sally put her face in her hands then looked at me with sheer exasperation.

'Oh god, Tom, I don't know! Jesus! I'm sorry but there's so much going on right now! And you're not the only one with a . . .'

'With a what?'

'It doesn't matter. It's nothing. It's just something I'm having to deal with. Look, I've got to go, but if you want my advice, go up and tell Hannah now. You've got to take some decisive action in your life. Don't be a gigantic coward.'

I didn't go up and tell her – because of everything going on and also because I am a gigantic coward. I put it off until the day before Elizabeth's scheduled arrival. To be fair, I'd also been holding back in the forlorn hope that Elizabeth would change her mind and text me with some terrible excuse about a last-minute engagement in Qatar – but that didn't happen. Instead I received a curt message explaining that she was boarding her plane on time and would expect to see me at Gatwick later in the day.

Hannah was dozing on the living-room sofa, Malvolio stretched out by her side. Her face, buried amid great swooping curls of hair, was ghostly pale and childlike; she looked like a Pre-Raphaelite painting come almost to life. I did not want to disturb her; it felt like everything happening to us at the moment was filled with dread and consequence – like living in an Ibsen play. I thought perhaps I should make a drink – that way I could say, 'Here is a nice mug of hot chocolate with whipped cream, and also I'm just off to meet your estranged mother at the airport – you know, the one who left when you were three? Yes that's the one. Anyway see you later.' No, that probably wouldn't be right.

'Dad, why are you silently looming over me like a psycho?'

Hannah shifted into an upright position on the sofa, groggily grabbing Malvolio and planting him on her lap. 'What time is it?'

'It's nine o'clock. In the morning. How long have you been lying here?'

'I don't know. My chest hurts.'

'Let me get you some water. Do you need your pills?'

'Uh-huh.'

I went out to the kitchen and filled the glass very slowly to put off the inevitable conversation for just a few more seconds. When I returned to the living room, Hannah was holding Malvolio out in front of her.

'Why won't you leave me alone, you dumb cat?' she said.

'Your mum was furious when I bought him,' I began, setting the glass down on the little table by the sofa. 'She said cats are riddled with fleas and parasites and it was irresponsible to have one in the house with a baby.'

'Well, Malvolio may be flea-ridden, but at least he stayed, didn't you, you fat idiot?'

'On that subject,' I said, smoothly, 'Hannah, your mum phoned me a few days ago. I'm just going to come straight out with this. She's flying to Britain. She wants to see you.'

Hannah let Malvolio drop back onto her lap.

'Her plane gets in tomorrow afternoon,' I continued. 'I have to go and meet her at the airport. I'm sorry, Hannah, I should have let you know sooner. It's just . . . I didn't know how to tell you.'

'Dad! Is she coming to stay here?'

'No, of course not. She's staying with her parents in Bagshot, I've no idea for how long. But she does want to come up.'

'Wow.'

'I know.'

'*Wow*.'

'I *know*.'

'She never told me . . . I mean, she never warned you that she was thinking of coming?'

'No. I called her about the transplant, but only got her answer machine. The next thing I know she has plane tickets.'

'Fuck. Sorry, Dad. But I mean, what does she think is going to happen? We'll have a nice mother–daughter reunion and go shopping?'

'I doubt she's thought that far ahead. You don't have to see her. I told her you might not.'

Hannah buried her head in her hands, but more out of astonishment and incredulity, I think, than trauma. Then she looked up suddenly. 'What about you, Dad?'

'I'm fine. I have no idea how I'll feel when I see her, or what we'll say to each other, but honestly, compared to everything else . . .'

Hannah took a sip of water. 'Do you still love her?' she said.

I felt the colour drain from my face. This wasn't a question I'd expected. It wasn't a question Hannah had ever asked before. Had she thought about it? Was this why she had stopped bugging me about that dating site – because she thought I was still in love with Elizabeth? Very quickly I realised I had no answer prepared. For some reason, I looked around the room, scanning it for clues. There were books and pictures and pieces of furniture that we'd chosen and bought together – all loaded with memories. There were artefacts of our marriage everywhere. Did these little fragments fit together into something solid?

'I don't know. I don't think so. I mean, I'm still very angry at her, I still feel deserted. Is that love? Maybe. I'm very confused.'

'I know,' she said. 'I know what Mum's like.'

And that was sweet of her, because really, how could she know? She hadn't spoken to her mum for years.

Hannah

'I know just the place,' I'd said to Sally. And I did.

Daisy's mum drives us to the comic store. Usually, Daisy claims the passenger seat for herself, but this time, without even saying anything, she opens the door and bundles me in, before clambering into the back with Jenna. Heart conditions can sometimes bring small and unexpected benefits. Here's another example: yesterday, I texted Ricky and Dav and asked if we could hold a meeting at their shop – and they got back straight away and said yes. I was just expecting them to cram us in somewhere, but when we arrive, I see they've pushed all the chairs into a circle around a small table, overloaded with chocolate biscuits. I'm sure I've cost these poor old goths more than they've ever made from me in comic sales. Sally is already here, sitting in the armchair, holding a clipboard, so it's clear she means business. Ted, James and Shaun are here too, and Natasha has brought her whole family. As they spot me I pretend not to notice the looks of shock and concern on their faces. I know, guys. I know. I am pale as fuck, and I'm losing weight. Look, it's not as bad as it could be. Sometimes people in my condition start

344

to retain water and blow up like the Michelin Man – but not me. I'm fading like a sick Victorian. I'm going out like a Brontë. Jenna and Daisy are flanking me like bodyguards – these days everyone is permanently poised ready to catch me when I fall. I feel like a dying empress being wheeled out to see her courtiers one last time.

'Come and sit down,' says Ted, and everyone stands up to offer their chairs. I take the one next to Sally's throne, and lower myself onto it slowly, trying to conceal what a relief it is to be sitting. The others gather around, some taking up chairs, a few sit on the floor. This is all happening while customers leaf through comics in the background, pretending not to stare – it's such a surreal scene. Maybe they think this is some new store initiative: story time with Sally and Hannah.

'Greetings everyone,' says Sally. 'Thank you for turning up. Obviously, I emotionally blackmailed you all into being here, but we get to do that sort of thing now, right, Hannah? So here's the situation . . .'

Just then, the shop door wheezes open and a guilty-looking teenage boy stands head down in the entrance, eyes locked to the floor in front of him. The whole crowd turns and stares at him.

'Are you here for the meeting or for comics?' I demand.

'The meeting, if you'll have me.'

It's not Callum, it's Jay. I haven't spoken to him since he dropped me in it with Dad. Seeing him ashamed and hesitant in the doorway, knowing what is going on at his home, I feel a pang of remorse for our friendship.

'He's having a rough time, with his dad and me and everything,' whispers Sally. 'He is really sorry for what he did.' She's used to making excuses for the men in her life.

'Come in and sit down,' I growl. 'I'll deal with you later.'

He tiptoes in and sits cross-legged on the floor, leaning up against Sally's chair.

'Anyway,' she continues. 'I think most of you know by now, the theatre is in trouble. Big trouble. The council wants to pull it down and build executive houses, and they've given Tom two weeks to save it. But Tom is struggling, we can all see that, right? He can't sort this out alone. Which is where we come in. For all of us, that theatre has been a refuge, a sanctuary, a place to escape and to perform. For Hannah, it's been a sort of home – she grew up there. So did Jay, I suppose. I think we've all found out things about ourselves in there.' With that she glances at Shaun and James.

'But for Dad, the theatre is even more than that,' I say, even though I was planning to let Sally do the talking. 'It's his life. I have to help him.'

There are nods around this small band of friends, colleagues and amateur actors, but no one is speaking. I have a sudden fear that they're not actually that bothered; that this isn't really important to them. There are other theatres nearby, other drama groups, other audiences. The show must go on and all that bollocks.

But Sally is clearly in no mood for self-doubt.

'This is Hannah's plan,' she says, slamming the clipboard down on her lap so loudly everyone in the shop turns to listen. 'In two weeks we want to put on a production at the theatre. We'll invite the whole town, we'll have tea and cakes, we'll do tours of the building, and at the end we'll put on a play. A special play that Hannah is writing, but that some of you may recognise. We're going to start a petition to save the theatre, and we're setting up a proper membership scheme. We're going to show the council that this isn't some commercial asset to be demolished and replaced, it's the heart of the damn town.'

'But the council has said we can't put on a play,' says Ted. 'They've revoked our entertainment licence. We'd technically be breaking the law.'

'But if we didn't charge people,' says Sally. 'If we just ask for donations ... it's technically a private party.'

'But what does Tom—'

'We're not telling Dad,' I say. 'He'd be worried about me if he knew I was doing this, and I don't want him to feel like there's hope for the theatre when there might not be. Also, if we all get arrested, we'll need him to bail us out.'

Suddenly, Sally leans forward in the chair, raising her voice. 'I'll be honest,' she says. 'It's going to take a lot of bloody hard work to organise this and we might not make it. Even if we do pull something together, even if we get some donations and signatures, the council probably won't give a shit. But we've got to try. Margaret once told us she took part in a naked protest to save a theatre. We're not going to be doing that, because it's cold and because we're not mental, but we have to show some of her determination.

'I know you all lead busy lives, you've got other responsibilities, but if any of you could help, even if it's just to gather petitions, or bake a cake, or be a fairy, then please just put your hand up. I'll start.'

Sally's hand is in the air and I follow immediately. There is a split second's delay – a moment of uncertainty; once again, I worry we've overestimated how much everyone ...

Ted's hand is up before I can finish the thought, so is Shaun's, and he drags James's up too. Jenna and Daisy, Jay, Natasha, Natasha's husband, and Ashley. Daisy's mum. Everyone in the group. A small sea of hands. It doesn't stop there. I look around and realise that Ricky and Dav have their hands raised, and not only them but several of their confused-looking customers; a middle-aged rocker in a Saxon T-shirt lifts his tattooed arm; a smartly dressed guy in chinos holds up his copy of *Captain America*. I feel like we're in a Hollywood underdog movie; I feel like there should be a swelling orchestral soundtrack, or the *Rocky* theme tune. Instead, Dav puts Sisters of Mercy back on, which is fair enough – it's her shop.

'Well,' says Sally, a note of emotion cracking her voice. 'We should assign some jobs and get this thing moving.'

Everyone starts to stand up.

'Oh, one last thing!' she shouts.

Everyone sits down again.

'We sort of need a young girl for one of the roles. It's the start of a new school term and there's a vicious stomach bug going around, so a lot of the young drama group are unavailable. If anyone has an enthusiastic relative we can borrow? Maybe a daughter? Who's very keen to try acting?'

Sally looks at Natasha.

'Please, mummy?' pleads Ashley.

Now *everyone* is looking at Natasha.

'Oh for god's sake, have my daughter,' she groans. 'But Ashley, this is where I draw the line. You are not joining my wine tasting club.'

While Sally starts gathering the names and details of the unwitting volunteers, Jay edges over to me and sits in his mum's chair.

'I'm sorry,' he says. 'I'm sorry for telling your dad about you and Callum. It was a shitty thing to do.'

'You're right, it really was shitty. Why did you do it? Dad said it was an accident, but it wasn't, was it?'

He shook his head slowly. 'I was jealous. I'd always thought that me and you ...'

'What?'

'I don't know. Forget it. Can we still be mates?'

'I want to be, but just because we've been friends for ever, it doesn't mean I owe you anything else. Do you understand? You

348

don't have dibs on me. If that's what you think, I can't be friends with you any more.'

'I know.'

He looks completely crestfallen.

'And if we *are* friends,' I say, 'it means you have to tell me when things are wrong. You have to talk to me. Do you understand? I'm ill, but I'm still here, I'm still me.'

Over the course of the next hour, we sort out jobs for everyone. Sally is director, I am her deputy; Ted will administrate; James is making some posters; Daisy and Jenna are on press and publicity, mainly because Daisy can charm anyone into doing anything and Jenna knows better than anyone else how to spread information through message boards and forums. In fact, she gives us a fascinating eight-minute lecture on MySpace and 'going viral', which confuses the hell out of almost everyone, but feels convincing. It turns out the heavy metal guy is an artist (this makes me think of Callum and I get a twinge of sadness that he's not here, and not with me) and says he can make us a sign. By now I'm starting to feel exhausted, which Sally picks up on, ending the meeting.

'You are all now members of the Save the Willow Tree Committee,' she yells as everyone is filing out. When the usual order of the shop has returned, she comes back to sit next to me.

'Are you sure you're up to this?' she says.

'Are you?'

'Well, my marriage is buggered, your heart is . . .'

'Also buggered.'

'This is idiotic and irresponsible, and will probably fail. Your dad will kill me when he finds out.'

'So we're agreed – we're going ahead with it.'

'I've never been more sure of anything in my life.'

Tom

Airports are the strangest places – they look austere and aloof, like cold modern office blocks, but they seethe with drama and emotion. In airports, there are really only two plots – goodbye and welcome home – but there are a million variations; not all good, not all welcome.

It took three hours to drive here; I set out at 7 a.m., winding through the sleepy local roads, then onto the A303 with its rolling fields and commuter towns. I thought of Hannah, of what she had to face and what it would mean. But also, despite myself, I thought of Elizabeth and what it would be like to see her, and how that would feel. I couldn't imagine it not being a terrible, wrenching disaster. On a dual carriageway, in the early morning, it is difficult not to linger on worst-case scenarios – they come at you like traffic. Even Radio 2 didn't help.

Something really struck me about our phone conversation the other night. She hadn't been in our lives for years, but when I told her that I was afraid for Hannah, that I didn't know what she was feeling any more, Lizzie said, 'She's strong, she's a realist.' And that is so true. Hannah loves stories but she's not a hopeless dreamer like her dad.

It made me think, even over this great distance – and even after all that has happened – that there must still be some intractable bond between mother and child. And when Elizabeth found out about the transplant her immediate response was to arrange a flight. No thought, no wrangling, just 'I'm flying back.' She seemed . . . prepared.

The Gatwick arrivals area was packed with expectant people; whole families waiting for loved ones, nervous men and women standing alone, tapping away on phone buttons, the thickset guys in suits, holding up boards with names scrawled on them. I was so busy scanning the crowds, wondering about the reunions about to take place, that I didn't notice the gabble of weary travellers exiting from the customs area; I didn't see the woman with the refined face and glossy, shoulder-length hair, the woman in designer casual wear, looking fresher and more alert than anyone else. I didn't see her until she was a few steps away, looking right at me.

'Hi Tom,' she said.

She looked crisp and elegant, even after a six-hour flight. There were a few strands of silver among the curls, but that was the only concession to age. Her mouth flickered into something like a smile. I saw Hannah in her face straight away.

'Hi Lizzie,' I said.

We both knew we had to cement this meeting with some sort of physical contact, but unsure of etiquette or each other, we settled on an air kiss that left so much air between us we were in two different time zones. It was the most metaphorical air kiss of all time.

'How are you?' she asked.

'Not great. A lot has happened.'

'I know.'

'Do you? How could you know?'

'Not right now, Tom. Not here.'

Around us, families embraced, couples kissed, dogs jumped and licked returning owners. The traditional airport dialogues played out: how was the flight? Did you get any sleep? Have you eaten? The kids are so excited to see you. But all I wanted to say was, how could you go? How could you come back?

'Will she see me?' said Elizabeth, straight to the point as ever. Her tone was clipped but faltering.

'She isn't sure. It's a lot to take in. I'll text her, let her know you're here. Then it's up to her.'

Elizabeth nodded, distractedly. We had agreed that I would come and meet her, that we would go for a coffee, talk, discuss what would happen next – like sensible adults. That's as far as the plan went. I got the feeling she was used to mobilising at short notice; she was slick and prepared.

'So,' she said. 'Shall we get a drink?'

'There's a coffee place over at the far end of the concourse. It doesn't look great, but—'

'It'll be fine. It can't be worse than Big Billy's.'

Big Billy's was the café we used to go to when we first lived together in Bristol. It was a dirty little hovel three doors down from our tiny terraced house, selling bacon baps and mugs of tea to local car mechanics and night workers. We'd go every Saturday morning, nursing hangovers; Elizabeth, who had this amazing job in aerospace, would bring huge folders of work, while I scoured *The Stage* for jobs and auditions. The chairs were broken, the tablecloths were stained, the clientele were terrifying, but it was our place. I was momentarily touched that she'd remembered.

We ordered two Americanos and found a small table beside a noisy family who were evidently seeing a teenage boy off on a gap year excursion. I filled Elizabeth in on the last month – the drama of the funeral and Hannah's escape to the comic book event, then the shock of the hospital visit. The news Venkman gave us so carefully, with no jokes. Elizabeth nodded her way through it, as though receiving a briefing on some business project.

'I spoke to that friend of mine, the cardiologist,' she said. 'There is a very high success rate with heart transplants nowadays; immune suppressant drugs are improving all the time. He said a donor heart can last for many years, if—'

'We're taking it one step at a time,' I said, cutting in quickly. I was aware that my hands were manically flicking through the menu on the table.

'But Tom, I think we should . . .'

'One step at a time. She's not even on the transplant list yet. There are tests to go through, and then once she's on the list, there are no guarantees. This isn't something we can just reason our way through.'

I didn't mean it as a dig. But at the same time, I absolutely meant it as a dig. For some reason I was feeling cornered. The family next to us had all stood up to begin a scrum-like mass hugging session; the skinny teenager at the centre of it looked barely sixteen years old. I noticed he had a moth-eaten old teddy bear sticking out of the back compartment on his new rucksack. He was going off on an adventure – there would probably be many more. Would he remember this moment? Would he tell his children about it? The pages of the menu were crumpled in my fingers. I could not identify the emotions surging through me. I did not know what they were or where they were going.

'So what do we do now?' said Elizabeth.

'We?' I said.

Elizabeth stared at me. 'She's my daughter.'

I snorted. An actual snort. An ugly, brutal noise.

'You left us,' I said. 'You made your choice.'

'Let's not do this again. We've been through it all a thousand times. I left because I just ... I'm not a parent. I tried. It's not who I am.'

'Oh, I know why you left. What I can't understand is why you're back now.'

'Because Hannah is sick! I'm worried, I need to see her!'

'Hannah has been sick for years. Where were you when she was diagnosed? Where were you when she spent two weeks in hospital with an infection? Where were you last month when she fainted at the top of the stairs and spent two days in Casualty?'

'Tom, please! I'm no good at this. You know. You know I can't do it. I never could. Oh god, I never should have ...'

'What?'

'Nothing.'

'Never should have married me? Never should have had Hannah?'

Silence.

'I don't regret marrying you.'

I sat back, incredulous, flabbergasted. 'So you do regret Hannah?!'

The look of shock and hurt that crossed her face was genuine. 'Tom, we're both exhausted and emotional, we shouldn't be discussing this now. This isn't the time or the place.'

'There hasn't been a time or a place for ten years. You came back a handful of times! You missed her growing up. She's our girl. She's our girl, Lizzie!'

'I couldn't face you both!' she shouts, loudly enough for the family next to us to pause their goodbye rituals and stare across at us. 'I was ashamed! I was ashamed that I left, that I wasn't there! Do you really not understand? From the bottom of my heart, I know that leaving was the right decision – not just for me, for all of us, but Tom, I will never forgive myself for making it.'

In a single moment, the studied composure was gone. I caught a

354

glimpse of the Elizabeth I saw in the week before she left – tearful, haunted, broken.

But just not broken enough to stay.

And we sat in silence, a long impenetrable silence that rolled in like a thick fog. The airport faded around us; the people became ghosts. It felt like we were lost somewhere unfathomable. My instinct, suddenly and surprisingly, was to find a way out.

'Do you remember that time we took your mum and dad to Big Billy's?' I said.

Clearly despite herself, Elizabeth broke into a broad smile. 'Oh god,' she groaned. 'The drugs bust.'

A few weeks after we moved into our terrible house in Bristol, Elizabeth's stately upper-middle-class parents had driven over from Bagshot to bring some of her stuff and, of course, to check out the nightmarish urban wasteland I'd dragged their daughter to. For some reason we decided we should take them to Billy's for brunch, and while we were making desperate small talk, a police van drew up outside. They were raiding the house three doors down from us. Elizabeth's parents were sitting with their backs to the window, but Lizzie and I watched in barely disguised horror as a succession of heavily armoured officers clambered out.

'Oh Tom, you just kept going on about the Old Vic and how Peter Ustinov was directing an interesting season at the Theatre Royal – and there was this cop outside with a battering ram.'

'Everyone else in the café was just carrying on, eating their bacon butties – even when they dragged that man out of the house and flung him on the road.'

'"This is an up and coming area, Daddy. Please just ignore the screaming." Happy days.'

'It was a more innocent time.'

We watched as the family next to us moved off, the younger kids now bored and tired, the parents unwilling to let go just yet. Are you sure you have your passport? Make sure you buy a bottle of water for the flight. Ring us when you get there. Be safe. Be safe.

'I'm staying with them for at least a week,' said Elizabeth.

'Huh?'

'My parents – it's not far to you and Hannah from there. I could get the train, or borrow Dad's car. I could be with you in a couple of hours.'

'I'll talk to Hannah when I get home. Please, Elizabeth, don't just turn up on the doorstep. Wait to be invited.'

'Like a vampire?'

I nodded, still lost in the memories of our early years, our origin story. Elizabeth, calmer now, chatted on.

'I've bought her some of those Japanese comics she's always going on about. I don't know if they're the right ones, it's hard to keep up. The last time we chatted, she ...'

She stopped and looked at me. Snapped out of the reverie, I looked back. It took a moment to register.

'The last time you chatted?'

'Tom.'

Oh.

'Tom.'

'When were you chatting? How? How long have you been ... I mean, I always told her she could phone you or write letters.'

'I know.'

'But she said she didn't want to. That's what she said.'

'It started two years ago, maybe. She added me on MSN. I was as surprised as you, honestly. They were short exchanges at first, weeks apart. She'd log on, ask me something, then log off. But then, we started to chat. It just went from there.'

'She didn't tell me.'

'Tom, don't be cross with her.'

'I don't understand.'

'She was worried. She was worried about hurting you.'

'But she ... but I said ... What do you talk about?'

'Oh, I don't know. Stuff? She asks a lot about my job and what I do, and where I live. She tells me about school, her friends, what she's doing. She tells me about the theatre.'

'Does she tell you about her health? Her heart?'

'Tom, yes.'

I felt the world drop away; like a trap door opening beneath me. I felt wrong and stupid. A thought flashed across my consciousness – I'd always believed we were coping, that I was doing a good job. But it wasn't enough. Oh god, of course it wasn't.

The shock, the confusion, must have been painted all over my face, because Elizabeth reached forward and put her hands on mine.

'Tom, mostly, what she talks about is you. You and her. The daft things you two get up to. She told me about her birthdays; the plays you put on for her. She idolises you.'

My eyes were bleary. The early drive, the hassle of the car park, this fraught meeting in a crappy café at the far end of the arrivals hall. All too much.

'I don't know what's happening any more,' I said. 'They're closing the theatre; Hannah is so ill, Lizzie. I don't know if I can get us through.'

'You can, Tom. You can and you will. I know it. Whatever happens, I know it. I always believed in you. Always.'

With that, she gripped tighter and as I glanced at our interlocking hands I noticed something utterly unexpected – one final revelation. She followed my gaze down, then looked back at me sheepishly.

'You see,' she said. 'I never really let go.'

She was still wearing our wedding ring.

Hannah

Operation Willow has begun. This is the codename for our theatrical rescue mission – it is not very imaginative, but look we're up against it here, and we're saving our mental resources for more important things. I've collected everyone's mobile phone numbers and their email addresses, and Jenna has set up a chat group for volunteers so we can have online meetings. Thanks to the wonders of modern communication, I can totally boss the whole thing without getting out of bed. James tells us about the publicity materials he has designed; Shaun brings us up to date on the sneaky repairs he's carrying out backstage. Ted's job is to keep Dad occupied. There will be posters going up around town; there may even be local newspaper coverage if Daisy can charm the events editor. Somehow, Dad must be kept away from all this. Jenna has also set up a 'Save the Willow Tree' MySpace page, and filled it with photos of the theatre, which she took on a really overcast afternoon to make it look especially sad and pathetic. She wants to record a video of me asking people to come to the open day and then upload it to a bunch of web forums. 'You look sick, pale and gorgeous,' she said. 'That is viral gold dust. It'll be bigger than that *Star Wars* lightsaber boy'.

Jay and I are trying to pick up our friendship. A few days ago he just turned up at my door and I shrugged and let him in. That was that. School has begun again, but he comes round for his lunch every day and makes us sandwiches; he is back again as soon as lessons are over and I doze on the sofa while he sits on the floor playing video games. Sometimes I wake up and Jenna and Daisy are here too, and they're all squabbling with each other, and it makes me happy to hear them. I speak to Sally on the phone and she tells me things are tense as hell at home; she and Phil are either ignoring each other or arguing. That's when I realise – Jay isn't looking after me, I'm looking after him. He still hasn't managed to open up about what's happening at home. I hope he will.

I get a burst of energy in the evenings and that's when I write. I am all too aware that the grand finale of this whole dumb venture is down to me. I know the basic idea, I've just got to gather my thoughts into something that makes sense. I scrawl notes and plans on pieces of A4 paper, then bash it all into the computer. I don't really know what I'm doing. I email messy scenes and half-formed ideas to Sally and hope she can help craft them into some kind of order.

That's basically what Operation Willow is about: creating some kind of order out of chaos.

Tom

I returned from the meeting with Elizabeth still reeling from its twists and revelations, and threw myself into the weird palliative care of the theatre. Death, I discovered that month, inevitably brings two things to those left behind: grief and admin. If the Willow Tree was to shut, Ted and I would need to let everyone know, from box-office volunteers, to cleaning staff, to the touring theatre companies and stand-up comedians due to appear on our stage. We'd need to tell utility companies and catering suppliers, we'd need to return theatrical equipment to a host of hire companies. All the deals carefully put in place over many years, struck off with short, polite emails.

Ted, however, insisted that we put that all on hold for a while and instead focus on going through the office from top to bottom, carefully investigating every bulging lever-arch file, every creaking cabinet drawer, every over-stuffed storage container. 'The place needs a thorough sort-out anyway,' he kept saying. 'And you never know, we might find something that'll help us out of this mess.' Yes, I replied, maybe we'll finally locate that Ming Dynasty vase the previous manager misplaced in here; perhaps we should begin our tidying session with that box over there, labelled 'lost Picasso artworks'. He'd just handed me a shoebox of invoices and told me to get stuck in. In fact, he wouldn't let me out; I'd turn up in the mornings and be in the office all day. When I tried to walk into town to get some lunch, he'd quickly volunteer to get it for me. He was obviously trying to keep my mind occupied with mundane and pointless tasks, but I think he was also lonely.

'Angela has been spending a lot of time at her sister's home,' he said. I wanted to ask more, but he clearly didn't want to face it. As we went through all the artefacts of past productions, he would ask questions, trying to appeal to my innate sense of nostalgia.

This morning, for example:

'Do you remember the first production you put on as a manager?'

'It was Strindberg's *Miss Julie*,' I replied, slipping robotically into the anecdote. 'It was on the GCSE drama syllabus. I did an interview with the local paper and told them it was a naturalist classic, but they printed it as "naturist". We sold out in a day. I've never seen so many disappointed perverts.'

'What about *Lord of the Flies*?' said Ted. 'We had three tons of sand delivered.'

'And a real pig's head from the butcher. Hannah insisted it had to be free range.'

'By the time of the second performance, there was a swarm of real flies too. Looking back we should have kept the head in a fridge rather than a plastic bag in the props room.'

'You live and learn in the theatre.'

'Well, you live, anyway.'

We smiled together, but I felt there was a vast distance between myself and the expression on my face. If I were on stage, the audience would have been unconvinced. Eventually, I needed to get out of there. I needed to talk to someone who wouldn't try to console or coddle me.

'I'm going for a walk,' I said. 'I won't be long.'

'Where are you going?' asked Ted, his eyes strangely alert and urgent behind his old wire spectacles. 'If you need some lunch, *I'll* go into town.'

'I'm not going to town,' I said, pulling my long grey coat from the peg on the back of the office door and thrusting my arms into it with dramatic flourish.

'Then where—'

'Don't worry, I won't be long.'

'I'll come with you.'

'No,' I said, a little more abruptly than I meant to. 'No, thank you, Ted. I'm going to see someone, and I need to go alone.'

Hannah

James emails me the poster and it's amazing. He's made a sort of blocky image of the theatre in gorgeous pastel colours, with the words SAVE THE WILLOW TREE along the top in big chunky letters. It looks like a really cool art gallery poster. We're getting a hundred of them printed and then Daisy, Jenna and Jay are taking them around town. The box-office volunteers have set up a web page for information, so it's all official now; it's happening. I've got to finish this stupid play, and I have to do it fast because everyone needs time to learn their parts. I'm starting to feel the pressure, but I can't get stressed out, I'm supposed to be relaxed.

I got a letter from Great Ormond Street with all the details of my appointment, which takes place after the show, thank god. I will have to stay in London for three days. I need a chest x-ray, an ultrasound, a bunch of exercise and lung function tests, loads more blood tests – the usual fun stuff. I also have to speak to a psychologist and a transplant nurse who will tell me what I can expect from the procedure, and what things will be like afterwards. I know some of it already because I'm not stupid and the internet exists. I know if I do get a transplant, I'll carry the evidence on my body for ever. Sometimes, when I get out of the shower, I look in the mirror and trace a line from my neck to my belly button. That is how long the scar will be. I also know that a heart transplant means I won't be able to have children. The thought lurks at the edge of my brain like a sparring partner, like a secret enemy. One day, it will come at me and hit me hard.

On top of everything, I know my mum is at her parents' home, waiting for us to call, waiting for permission to make a personal appearance in my life. I don't know what to do about that. I'm certain Dad knows I've been talking to her on MSN. And it wasn't just talking. Sometimes she'd email me old photos of her and Dad together, when they were younger. I printed them out so I could study them. I hid them in my room. So much hiding.

I decide to go out for a walk – the first time I've left the house in three days. I should go to the theatre to see if there's anything that needs doing, or to the comic store so I can slump in a quiet corner and calmly read through the month's new releases. But I don't. I go somewhere else – and I have no idea what I'm going to do when I get there.

As usual, the curtains are drawn in the bedroom above Callum's front door. The street is quiet, apart from a small gang of children running about hitting each other with sticks; the unending drizzle has kept everyone else inside. As I approach the house I see Joe on the driveway, underneath another car. I quietly step over his legs to get to the door.

Before I ring the doorbell, I stop and try to regain my breath while thinking of something to say. But I've got nothing. I continually swap between anger and sympathy. Before this frantic indecision forces me to back away, I bang on the door. I hear the yapping dog, then Callum's mum shouting, 'Shut up, for fuck's sake!' Then the door swings open.

'Hello,' I say.

She looks older and more tired than the last time I was here, her eyes thick with yesterday's make-up; her frizzy hair has been badly dyed and is piled in a bun that slumps to the side of her head.

'I didn't expect to see you again,' she says.

'Is Callum here?'

'No, he's staying at his sister's in Bristol.'

'Oh.'

We stand in silence. She has a mug in one hand, which she's holding so loosely the coffee is about to pour out onto the Welcome mat. I'm waiting for her to say something, but instead she opens her mouth and suppresses a yawn behind her fist.

'Can you tell him I stopped by?'

She doesn't say anything, so I just nod like an idiot and turn away, ready to get out of there as fast as possible. But Joe is out from under the car, and now he's leaning on it, looking at me, wiping his hands on a rag. I hear the front door closing behind us.

'He told me it's like a darkness,' says Joe. 'The depression or whatever it is – it's like being trapped in the dark and he can't get out. He knows there are things he has to do, he knows it, but he can't find his way. It's like he's trapped. It's hard on him. It's hard on everyone.'

'I know,' I say. 'I'm worried about him.'

'He let you down, didn't he? He don't talk much to me, but he told me that. I try to help, but he's not having it. What can I do? I can't fix him with these.' And he kicks the toolbox beside him. 'You're sick too, ain't you?'

I nod silently.

'I'll tell him you were here,' he says. 'It's a shame. You two could have helped each other out. I never saw him smile the way he smiled when he talked about you.'

We wave goodbye to each other and I start the short walk back home, pulling up the hood of my anorak against the endless spray of rain. That's when I get the text message from Ted, telling me Dad has gone AWOL. I phone Sally, who is on her way to the theatre. She spots Dad leaving.

'I'll follow him,' she says. 'How are you?'

'I went for a walk, now I'm heading home. It's so boring. I'm always tired. I need to figure out what to do about Mum. And I should be doing more for the theatre.'

'You're doing amazingly well,' she says. 'Everything is fine. You're such a tough guy. I'm so proud of you.'

It is difficult to cross the road because suddenly the water has got into my eyes, and I have to keep wiping them so that I can see.

Tom

The cemetery is on the southern edge of town, a short walk along
a busy road lined with stately Georgian town houses. There was a
lazy drizzle in the air, the sort of rain that could conceivably last
for days, and it seemed to suggest that there would be no Indian
summer this year. I walked past the small industrial estate where
Shaun worked, and then along a small driveway that took me away
from the traffic, through a patch of scrappy woodland and towards
the expanse of gravestones.

It didn't take me long to find the small brass plaque I was
looking for. It was halfway along a narrow path lined with similar
memorials, beside a mossy bench and a pretty, well-tended flower-
bed; the scent of damp earth and buddleia hung in the air.

'Hello Margaret,' I said.

I first met her during my interview for the theatre manager job.
I was being shown around by Debbie, a volunteer front-of-house
assistant. 'What is the local drama group like?' I asked. 'Oh, they're
not a bunch of old luvvies, if that's what you're worried about,' she
laughed. Then she stopped dead as she noticed Margaret sitting
in the small café area in the foyer, a little yappy dog at her feet,

a bone china teapot and cup on the table in front of her. She was reading a biography of Lillie Langtry. 'She's always here,' Debbie whispered conspiratorially. 'She's been coming for as long as anyone can remember, but never seems to be with anyone. She brings the teapot and cup with her – she won't drink out of our mugs. She can be quite rude, so watch yourself.' Debbie introduced us and Margaret examined me with what appeared to be withering distaste.

'You look like the sort of young man who would put on subversive modern plays just to shock old curmudgeons like me,' she said.

'I'm afraid I probably am,' I smiled in return.

'In that case,' she said. 'I wish you all the best in your new job.'

She was around the building a lot in those days; she'd often sit with Hannah while I worked, reading fairy tales with her, or just slyly critiquing the clothes and manners of other theatre visitors. From the very beginning she treated Hannah as a friend and accomplice rather than a child – they had a connection, a mutual understanding that I couldn't really comprehend, and could never replicate. I bet Hannah told Margaret that she was in contact with Elizabeth.

In the cemetary, an elderly couple walked past, the woman holding a large bunch of white chrysanthemums. I wondered whose grave they were visiting. A friend? A sibling? A child? I watched them totter slowly and wordlessly along the path until they were out of earshot. Then I turned back to Margaret's plaque. I read the inscription out loud:

IN MEMORY OF MARGARET CHEVALIER WRIGHT,

1924–2005

A GREAT FRIEND AND PERFORMER, WHO
BRIGHTENED OUR LIVES AND IS NOW RESTING.

'WE ARE SUCH STUFF AS DREAMS ARE MADE ON.'

Standing in the rain, quoting Shakespeare, it felt like the end of *Withnail and I*, which I took Elizabeth to see and instantly regretted because she just kept saying 'It's you and your drama friends' all the way through. I remember making Hannah watch the DVD with me one Sunday afternoon. I was sure she'd identify with Paul McGann, the intelligent, talented one, but no, she fell for tragic, beautiful Richard E. Grant.

'What do I do now, Margaret?' I said. 'I have made quite a lot of mistakes recently.'

'I think her advice-dispensing days are over,' said a voice from behind me.

I spun around to find Sally standing a few feet away, dressed in a woollen hat, cardigan and jeans, watching me from under a large umbrella.

'What are *you* doing here?' I said.

'I was passing the entrance and saw you walk in. I figured this is who you'd be visiting.'

'I just needed some time to think.'

'Do you want me to go?'

'No.'

'Then maybe I can help? I have experience with making mistakes.'

She lifted her umbrella and stepped closer to me, so that we were both underneath, side by side, staring down at the long row of plaques.

'So how was it with Elizabeth?'

'Educational.'

'In what way?'

'Did you know Hannah was talking to her on the internet?'

Sally twirled the umbrella handle for a few seconds, creating a mist of droplets around us.

'I suspected as much.'

'How?'

'Little things she said or didn't say. I just picked up on them.'

'I didn't.'

'You've had a lot to deal with.'

'Do you think I was wrong – to keep Hannah away from her mum?'

'I think maybe Elizabeth has a bigger share of the blame in that respect, what with moving to Dubai and all.'

'But I could have taken Hannah to see her. Elizabeth was always offering to pay. I could have invited Elizabeth here?'

'Why didn't you?'

'I don't know. I thought I knew, but I don't. I always told myself it was for Hannah – that I was worried about her getting to know her mum then feeling hurt and abandoned. I thought she could maybe do without that added complication. But maybe I was just angry at Elizabeth. Maybe I wanted to punish her.'

'That's normal under the circumstances. It's normal to resent someone when this happens, to hate them even.'

'But that's the thing. I don't hate her, I never did. When things started to fall apart, she was apologetic, she was devastated. She said over and over again, she wanted to be a mum and a wife, but she couldn't do it. We came up with all sorts of plans: she'd commute to London, I'd look after Hannah, but we both realised that wasn't going to work. It just wasn't her. What she's doing now, building some massive internet business in the desert – *that* is her. She thought she was doing the right thing for all of us. She didn't know what was coming. And the weird thing is, there's still a part of me that feels frustrated we were unable to solve what was basically a logistical problem. That's another reason I was worried about seeing her. There's a part of me that thinks one day we'll figure it out.'

'You'd take her back? If she said she'd worked it out – that she could run her business from here?'

'That's not going to happen.'

'But if it did?'

I looked down and noticed that great puddles were starting to gather on the pathway. A stream was running down the little gulley between the tarmac and the row of plaques, carrying dead leaves like tiny boats.

'I don't know. I loved her. I loved her so much that I *wanted* her to leave – because it was the right thing for her. But it still left a giant hole in our lives. Maybe that's it. I wanted Hannah to feel completely safe, to feel wanted and secure, so I blotted Elizabeth out entirely.'

'Or at least you thought you did.'

'I don't know why Hannah couldn't tell me she was in touch with her mum.'

'Because she knew how you felt? Because she knew you wanted to protect her? Tom, you did what you thought was right. So did she.'

I nodded, and hung my head in silent acquiescence.

'Hannah is a grown-up now, isn't she?' I said.

'Oh yes, she certainly is.'

'Maybe I've been overprotective.'

'Maybe.'

'I think perhaps I have to let go.'

And I suddenly understood why Hannah was so furious at me during Margaret's funeral, when I gave that speech. There was something I didn't understand, but she did – she understood it very well. She didn't want to hear anecdotes; she wanted to mourn her friend. There comes a time when the stories have to end.

'I should tell her it's fine – it's fine for her to talk to her mum.

371

Maybe one day, I don't know, if everything works out, maybe one day she can go out and visit her.'

'One step at a time,' said Sally. 'But Tom . . .'

'Yes?'

'She'll always be your baby. That's just how it is.'

We started to walk away, back down the winding path towards the exit, silent for a while.

'What about you and Phil?' I asked.

She took a very long breath.

A fine mist was coming. It gathered in the distance, then rolled in over the gravestones like a rising tide. As we walked, the cemetery was being obliterated around us. In the absence of sight or sound, I suddenly became aware that Sally and I were holding hands. Quite possibly we had been for some time.

Tom

The entrance to Great Ormond Street Hospital, reached through an inauspicious covered walkway, was cavernous and noisy. There were children crying and laughing, running between the banks of low seats; there were paramedics speaking into walkie-talkies; there were nurses gathered in groups, chatting. Vast signs pointed in every direction. The tumult was bewildering. Somehow, I managed to communicate to a harried receptionist why I was there, and very quickly the cardiac support officer who had written to me weaved between the masses and introduced herself.

'You're Hannah's dad? I'm Pauline Croft, come this way.'

She took me away from the atrium, and down a corridor, passing more families and more rushing nurses. The sudden silence when we got into a lift was disconcerting.

'I'll take you up to paediatric cardiology,' she said, smiling broadly. And I guess my fear and confusion must have been obvious. 'It's a lot quieter up there,' she said. 'I'll give you a quick tour, and introduce you to the clinical support team and the cardiologist. If you have any questions at any time, just ask.'

From the moment the doors of the lift opened, to the moment

I was outside on the pavement again, everything was a surreal blur of information and images. I saw the ward itself, divided into cocoon-like bays; I saw children recovering from surgery, linked to machines. I saw laboratories and test rooms; I was shown medical equipment that I was familiar with, and some that I couldn't even pronounce, let alone understand. Everything was so white, clean and calm, it felt like being on some sort of space station.

I sat down with the consultant cardiologist, a wiry businesslike man with a surprisingly amiable smile. He explained, quietly and patiently, the likely course of Hannah's life from this point onwards. I had brought a notebook and pen with me, but for some reason I felt it would be rude to reach into my pocket for them. I felt hopelessly subservient; I felt like I was at the most important parents' evening in history.

After her three days of tests, Hannah would go on the transplant list. When a heart became available she would be contacted immediately and rushed to the hospital by a specialist transport firm. The surgery would probably last around six hours. The success rate on transplants was around 90 per cent, the cardiologist said. I nodded as though he had just told me a favourable football score. I listened carefully through all the assurances, I listened to him tell me that Hannah would be able to go to school, to exercise, to live normally. But then came the caveats. She would be in hospital for several weeks, they would need to monitor the organ very closely for signs that it was failing. She'd need to take immune suppressant drugs for the rest of her life.

'Now this is going to be difficult to hear,' the cardiologist said. 'That is why I asked you to come along without Hannah at first. A heart transplant is not a cure. It will last, on average, around fifteen years. I'm afraid it is very rare to receive a second transplant. Do you understand what I'm saying?'

'Yes,' I said. My voice was strangled and high pitched.

'Would you like a glass of water?' said a nurse. I hadn't realised she was in the room with us.

'No, it's fine. I'm fine.'

'Mr Rose,' continued the consultant. 'I know this is very difficult news, but it's best that you understand the limits of what we're able to do. No one gets any guarantees in life – none of us at all, so try not to fixate on the negatives. Hannah has a very good chance – she's young, she's fit and medical science is advancing all the time. There is lots of research into better immune suppressants, as well as new technologies and procedures. You never know what the future holds.'

I nodded again. I wished I had said yes to the water. I felt like I was acting very poorly in a scene that I should have been commanding. But the character I had decided on was Rational Guy. I would listen and understand, and nod sagely.

'I'll take Hannah through all of this when she comes in, but I always think it's a good idea to prepare the parents. Sometimes teenagers don't want to hear all this from a doctor; they need to hear it from Mum and Dad.'

I tried not to focus on the fact that he said 'Mum' first – Mum before Dad. Because when a child is hurt or scared, where do they run first? There were many more important things to be thinking about. What were they? What did I need to ask?

'Please could I have that water now?' I said.

Outside the hospital, the sun was glimpsing through great plateaus of steely grey cloud. I walked away, past an ice cream van, through Queen Square, with its little garden lined with wooden benches. I wondered how many parents had come to sit here and contemplate the lives of their children. Lives perhaps in peril. Lives perhaps lost. I cut down a side street and looked at my watch and realised there was a chance of catching an earlier train. I could get back to Hannah in time for dinner. We could order a pizza – we'd get her favourite, and we could sit cross-legged on the living-room floor and talk. A group of office workers walked past me and almost nudged me into the road. I saw a mother and son sitting at a small table outside an Italian café on the other side of the street; the woman was studying a newspaper, the boy had a comic and he was mimicking the way she turned the pages. When she realised, she laughed loudly and reached across to take his hand. Would they remember this moment when he was ten? Twenty? Forty? I staggered back a few steps, then made for a little alley beside a pub. I leaned against the dark brick wall, and I started to sob.

On the train journey home, I thought about how on earth I was going to explain all I had seen and learned to Hannah. The nurse had given me a support phone number, and told me to call them if either of us had any questions before Hannah's visit. 'There will always be someone here on the team to help you,' she said. Her kindness held within it a glimpse of the struggles to come, and the words stayed with me. I went to the buffet car and bought a gin and tonic but I left it untouched on the counter.

When I got home, I could hear voices as soon as I opened the front door. I thought perhaps Hannah had a friend round, or maybe it was Sally come to check up on her. I paused to collect my thoughts, then went through into the living room and was ready to greet them, but I stopped dead, my mouth agape.

'Hello Dad,' said Hannah.

'Hello Tom,' said Elizabeth.

Dearest Willow,

For my twelfth birthday I was starting to think that the annual plays, which had once meant so much, were now a little childish. I was falling into these dark moods and I couldn't get out of them. Teen angst and heart disease were a pretty troublesome combination. This, I thought, would be my last production.

I chose Little Red Riding Hood, one of the darkest fairy tales of them all. I felt like I was growing up and, you know, maturing as a writer and theatre director – so I told Dad I wanted to plan the play out alone. God, wasn't I a pretentious brat?! I remember Daisy and I had snuck into her dad's DVD collection and watched Company of Wolves, the surreal Neil Jordan movie about Red Riding Hood (Willow, you have to watch it, it's wonderful). We had to hide our eyes from the gory bits and it gave us nightmares for weeks, but at the time we were transfixed by its weird twisted vision of the old story. I was learning that the tales I'd always loved were allegories that weren't always about what we thought they were. I was learning that the world wasn't what it seemed.

Dressed in a flowing scarlet cloak and holding a basket full of delicious foods, Natasha crept into the forest on her way to grandmother's house. The trees around her, made of black-painted balsa wood, cast sinister shadows as she walked, and a smoke machine created a fine mist around her feet. Eyes like torch beams stared out at her from the darkness. I watched quietly with my friends – we usually chatted and joked as the plays went on, but this time we were all silent. It felt different somehow. There was a sense of peril.

Suddenly from the other side of the stage appeared the big bad wolf; the actor wore a black and grey wig, and plastic fangs. A long tail emerged from the back of his smart grey trousers. The audience screamed with shock and delight.

'It's the wolf!' they yelled. 'Run!'

But Little Red Riding Hood did not run.

'Where are you going, young lady?' said the wolf. 'And what do you have in that basket?'

'I'm going to my grandmother's house. She is sick and I'm taking her some bread and wine.'

'Delicious,' said the wolf. 'May I have some?'

He moved closer. Little Red Riding Hood stepped back.

'No, you can't have my food,' she said.

'Very well,' said the wolf. 'But we shall meet again this very day.' And with that he slunk from the stage.

Little Red Riding Hood continued to walk. She skipped between the trees, she turned back on herself and skipped some more. Kamil had built us a shed on casters so that it could be pulled onto the stage. It was decorated to resemble a small cottage with a chimney and thatched roof. Then, the front side of the shed opened completely to reveal the interior – and there, on a small camp bed, was Grandma, sound asleep.

'Oh Grandma, how pleased I am to see you,' said Little Red Riding Hood.

'It's the wolf,' shouted a child from the audience.

'Grandma is dead!' shouted another.

'Oh no, that can't be true,' said Little Red Riding Hood. 'But then, Grandma, what big eyes you have . . . '

378

'I don't have time for all that,' said the wolf, leaping from the bed wearing a long white nightdress. 'I'll just gobble you up now!'

Some children screamed; some laughed with delight. I just sat and quietly watched. In that moment, from the other side of the stage, the woodcutter arrived. It was Dad, wearing a checked shirt and braces.

'What's happening here?' he boomed.

'The wolf has eaten Grandmother and now he is coming for me.'

'Over my dead body!' shouted the woodcutter.

'In that case, I'll eat you both!' said the wolf. And with that he started to chase the woodcutter and Little Red Riding Hood around and around the shed. The children laughed and pointed as the actors ran.

But Red Riding Hood was not smiling and neither was I. I watched the wolf, running and running after Little Red Riding Hood, and I felt like I could hear the girl's heart beating faster and faster. Get away, I thought. Get away or you'll die. But the wolf kept chasing and the actors kept running and the children kept laughing, and the noise of the chase grew louder and louder. Thud-thud, thud-thud, thud-thud. With a shudder, I realised that it was my own heart I could hear. It was the noise that chased me all through my life.

One by one the other kids stood up on their chairs and they shouted, 'Kill the wolf! Kill the wolf!'

Little Red Riding Hood turned and so did the woodcutter.

'I can kill it,' he said. 'I can kill the beast for you.' And he drew from his backpack a glinting axe. The wolf reared up and howled; the woodcutter stood his ground.

'No!' said Red Riding Hood, and as the wolf began to run, she took the axe and pushed the woodcutter away. 'I have to do this.'

The wolf charged. The mist swirled up in his path. The noise in the auditorium dropped away. It felt like we were watching in slow motion. With a growl and a leap, he launched at the girl in the red hood, and they tussled and fought, and even though I had written the play and knew what was coming, I could still barely watch.

There was a yelp and the two crumpled in on each other and they fell to the ground. There were gasps from the audience. Then slowly, very, very slowly, one of them began to rise. There was so much smoke it was difficult to see – it was the perfect special effect. But then through the mist it became clear who was up. It was the wolf.

The children gasped again. Was Red Riding Hood dead? Had the wolf won?! But as he gradually turned, we saw the axe blade embedded in his side (or rather, supported between his arm and chest), and he whimpered and then scampered away. Red Riding Hood stood up, alone.

'You've beaten the wolf,' said the woodcutter.

The children cheered and laughed and clapped – all except me. Because I looked to the edge of the stage, beyond the curtain, and I could see the wolf, still there, still breathing. And though it was just an actor, I was filled with terror – because I was older now and I had come to a dark new realisation. Stories are just stories; they can't save us in the end. Some monsters can't be killed.

No, I thought to myself, Little Red Riding Hood would have to keep running. She would never be able to stop. The wolf would return and eventually, one day, it would catch her.

She knew it in her heart.

Hannah

I'm a mess. I am convulsing with nerves. Yesterday I sent an email to Mum. I wrote, 'Dad is going to London for the day tomorrow, you can come over if you like.' I just thought, look, if this is going to happen, if I'm going to see Mum for the first time in god knows how many years, I'd rather do it without Dad being around making everything even more weird and stressy. I didn't even think she'd see my message in time before giving up and sodding off back to Dubai. But two minutes after I hit send, my mobile phone starts buzzing and the display says unknown caller. It takes about fourteen rings before I get the courage to answer.

'H . . . Hello?' I say.

'Hannah?'

Oh shit. 'Yes?'

'It's Elizabeth . . . It's Mum.'

'Oh. Hi.'

'I got your email. I'd love to come. If you haven't changed your mind?'

'No, that's fine.'

'Are you sure? Are you really sure?'

*

People expect me to be angry. When I tell them what happened, how Mum left when I was little and never came back, they get really furious on my behalf. But I don't really know how I feel. I mean, I have no memories of her being around, and Dad always tried to explain everything so that she wasn't this wicked witch who abandoned her baby in a forest. He says she was never really meant to be in a family, she wanted to go somewhere exotic and challenging and make tons of money. That's fine, I guess, but wouldn't it have been better if she'd realised this *before* getting married and pregnant? Although then I wouldn't exist. I think this is what they call a paradox.

So much happened after that. Dad got the job at the theatre and I got sick, and those things were more important than resenting a person I never really knew. When I think about it, I've actually had loads of mums – Margaret, Sally, an entire succession of actors, volunteers and staff. I was never short of maternal understudies. I kind of convinced myself I wasn't angry – I was curious. That's why, when I was thirteen, I found Mum's company email address and added her on MSN. We chat once or twice a month. She tells me about Dubai and how they're creating this whole futuristic city out of nothing; her company is helping to build the telecommunications infrastructure. I kind of zone out on those bits. In return, I tell her about school, comics, acting and electrocardiograms. She has clearly done a lot of research into cardiomyopathy and it's sort of therapeutic to discuss it all with her on MSN because she's so detached and calm. As for family stuff, I just tell her about Dad and me and what we're doing. I don't ask her how she felt when she left us; she doesn't ask me about how Dad is coping without her, or why I never told him that we were in touch. The last time we chatted was on the day of Margaret's funeral. I told her all about Callum. She told me to be careful, and not to put too much trust in a boy. Ha! We've *definitely* got stuff to catch up on.

She arrives in the early afternoon. I see her pull up outside in a pristine white Range Rover – I see this because I've spent the last thirty minutes looking out of the window, then pacing around the living room, then looking out of the window again. I recognise her from photos she's emailed me, but when I open the door and see her for the first time in the flesh, I have this weird internal earthquake of recognition – this is clearly *my mum*. We have the same eyes, the same cheekbones, the same wild hair (although hers is barely shoulder length and beautifully cut). Apart from the age gap, the major difference between us is that I'm wearing a gawky Akira T-shirt and torn skinny jeans, while she is in a long woollen skirt and an Argyle sweater over a pristine white shirt. She strides down the path like a catwalk model. I feel weirdly intimidated – I even wonder if she's *trying* to intimidate me, but that's a totally random idea. I feel stupid. My stomach is a broken washing machine on spin cycle.

'Hello Hannah,' she says.

'Hi Elizabeth,' I reply.

I show her in. We don't hug.

We go through to the living room and she sits down (in Dad's chair) while I head to the kitchen to make some tea. I hold the kettle under the tap but it shakes so much water sprays everywhere. I hold on to the side of the sink and take some deep breaths. I tell myself this is just a woman my dad once knew. But I feel emotions swirling around and I don't know what they are.

'This is a lovely house,' she shouts through.

Of course, she's never seen it before. We moved here after she left.

'I'll show you around in a bit.'

383

'So many books piled everywhere,' she says. 'Some things never change.' I don't know if she's saying that Dad has always read a lot or that Dad has always been messy, but the comment makes me feel even more freaked out.

I come back in with two mugs of tea and a packet of chocolate digestives, and there's all this awkward silence where we're just sort of sitting there looking around. The tension is surreal. I dunk a biscuit but leave it in too long while trying to think of something to say and half of it breaks off and sinks into my drink – me and Dad's pet hate.

'So how is everything?' she says brightly. 'Are you back at school?'

'No, I've been signed off.'

'So I guess you won't see your boyfriend as much?'

'We split up.'

'Oh god, I'm sorry. How do you feel?'

'I'm too tired to think about him. I'm really, really tired all the time. If I walk for longer than about ten steps I need a rest. It's crappy because we're putting on this whole Save the Theatre event and I'm stuck trying to help out from here.'

'Your dad told me about the theatre closing. I didn't know he was planning an event.'

'Oh he isn't,' I say. 'I am. He doesn't know anything about it.' And now I realise this is another secret we're keeping from him.

'Why?'

'Because he's given up a little bit. His heart's not in it.'

She nods and smiles in a way that makes me cross but I can't identify why. I grip the mug so hard there's a chance it could explode and cover me in tea and disintegrated biscuit.

'It's something we're doing *for* him,' I continue. 'I didn't want him to know because it might not work. People might not come. Also, we don't have an entertainment licence. It's technically illegal. We'll probably be thrown in jail.'

'Haven't you got enough to deal with?'

I choose not to respond. Instead, I become obsessed with my biscuit. I make the decision to retrieve it from my tea and then try to discreetly cram it into my mouth, but she's watching me really closely.

'How are you coping?' she says.

I start saying, 'There are times when . . .' but I have to stop and think, because I don't know how to describe this to a stranger – a *stranger*. 'There are times when I just lie in my bed completely bawling my guts out, going through all that "Why me, God?" stuff. I get these waves of terror, just sheer terror and dread, about what's happening. I mean, I'm going to have a huge, life-changing operation. That's what I'm dealing with. It's big and it's fucking . . . sorry . . . it's really scary. But I realised, I physically can't spend the next week, or month, or year, being constantly scared out of my mind and crying. There are some days, well, life just goes on, you know? You wake up, you have stuff to do, you eat, you go to bed. Sometimes I want to fall apart, sometimes I want to go shopping with my friends.'

'Well I can at least take you shopping,' she says. 'Although I can't imagine there's much choice around here. Come to Dubai – they're building the biggest malls in the world.'

'I don't know,' I say. 'I'm not sure how it will work – with flights and stuff.' And I instinctively put my hand over my heart.

'Oh,' she says.

'Do you think you're going to stay out there?'

'I've been there almost ten years and it's an incredible place, but after a while, you start to see . . . it's all surface, it's all about money and image. I'm thinking of a new challenge. There are lots of interesting things going on with the internet right now. The whole Web 2.0 revolution; video sharing, podcasting, Wi-Fi hotspots everywhere. Silicon Valley is buzzing. London is always interesting.'

'You might come back to Britain?'

'I don't know. It depends on ... a lot of factors.'

This is maybe a little too close to the bone, because for a while she goes quiet again, and I see her eyes scanning the room. Finally, she spots a photo on the mantelpiece – it's of her and Dad, before I was born. They look very happy. She's wearing an anorak, but somehow still looks cool and immaculate. Dad is dressed as a pirate. She sees that I'm looking at it too.

'That's us at the Edinburgh Festival in 1986,' she says. 'Has he told you about it? It was the year after we finished university. Tom ... I mean your dad ... was taking a show up there with a bunch of his drama friends; we all shared this tiny flat in Leith, sleeping eight to a room. We had no money and it rained constantly.'

'Oh dude, that sounds miserable,' I say.

'It should have been,' she replies with a sort of wistful faraway expression. 'But your dad ... he just had this way of turning everything into an adventure. He found all the best shows, all the best bars and parties. We went salsa dancing, we drank absinthe, we made friends with a Finnish mime troupe. We traipsed up and down the Royal Mile giving out flyers for his pirate version of *Doctor Faustus*. The air smelled of rain and hops from the Caledonian brewery. It was just ... Sometimes, when we were together, it felt like anything could happen.'

For a moment, everything feels much calmer. We're both lost in this nice memory.

'But he never grew out of that. His friends were getting plays produced at the Royal Court, the Old Vic, the Lyric. He was happy messing about with little shows here and there. He still is, it seems.

I mean, he has it in him to be amazing – he could be running the National Theatre, I really believe that. I just wish he'd see that potential in himself.'

For some reason, that gets to me. It really gets to me. Some switch in my head flips straight from anxious to meltdown.

'That's not how it is,' I say in a mega-loud and abrupt voice. 'He works really hard at the theatre! Ask anyone!'

'I didn't mean—'

'You make it sound like he can't be bothered, but that's not it! He loves that place. It's not his fault it's closing.'

'Hannah, that's not what I meant.'

'Yes it is! You don't know how hard it's been. You look down on him, but what do you know about anything? You left us!'

'Let me explain . . .'

There's no turning back. 'How could you?!'

She is actually panicking now, it's in her voice. 'Your dad must have told you. It wasn't working.'

'It wasn't working for you! For *you*!'

'Hannah, please, let me explain. I was in love with your father, I thought it was what I wanted, but I couldn't do it. After you were born, I just . . . I'm so sorry Hannah, I felt trapped and empty, and I couldn't do it. Everyone said it was post-natal depression. I went to a therapist, I took the drugs they gave me, I did everything I could.'

'But you still didn't want me.'

'I did! I did! But I couldn't . . . it wasn't in me, the thing you need to be a parent, it didn't come like everyone said it would. But, oh Hannah, I wanted you. And when I left I ached for you, it was physical pain, the worst I've ever known.'

'Then why didn't you come back?'

'Because you were both better off without me.'

'No! Don't you see? When you left, it destroyed him! He never got over it! You're a bitch. You left him alone, and when I die, he'll be alone again!'

There.

I said it.

When I die.

Because I might not get the operation. Because people die on the waiting list. Because my body may reject the heart.

My words echo around the room and then there is a silence so deep it feels nothing will ever be said again. We both look at each other in shock. That's when I hear the keys in the door.

Dad always did have impeccable comic timing.

Tom

There was a game we used to play on my university drama course. Two students would begin an improvised scene, and then at a certain point, a third participant would be brought in from another room who would then have to pick up on the context and narrative, and seamlessly join in. This was fun in the context of acting classes; it is not fun when it's happening in your living room and the characters are your daughter and your estranged wife.

The scene as I found it: Hannah was standing, looking upset and angry, Elizabeth was in the armchair, sitting forward, seemingly alarmed. Amid the silence, there was an unmistakable atmosphere of confrontation in the air. When you've seen *Look Back In Anger* as many times as I have, you can spot it a mile off.

'Hello Dad,' said Hannah.

'Hello Tom,' said Elizabeth.

And for a few seconds that's all any of us could manage. We simply held position as traffic swooped by on the road outside. Eventually, one of us had to speak.

'I asked you not to just turn up at our house,' I said to Elizabeth.

'I invited her,' replied Hannah. 'I'm sorry.'

'It's fine,' I said.

'No it isn't,' said Hannah, her eyes flicking to her mother.

'Well,' I said. 'Shall I put the kettle on?'

'We've just had a cup,' said Elizabeth.

'I'll do it,' Hannah countered, and then she paced through to the kitchen.

I moved a bunch of comics from the sofa and sat down, trying to look calm and amenable.

'So what's going on?' I said.

'I should have told you I was coming. I got an email from Hannah, and I just . . . I just thought that I really had to see her; I thought I might not get another chance for a while. I borrowed my parents' car and drove up before I'd considered it properly. Oh god, I've made a complete mess of this.'

She put her hand to her forehead in a dramatic gesture of despair.

'This is a nice house,' she said. 'Lovely views.'

'It gets cold in the winter.'

'That's the one thing I don't miss about Britain.'

'The only thing?'

After centuries of uncomfortable silence, Hannah returned holding three steaming mugs, which she abandoned on the coffee table, next to a plate piled high with chocolate digestives. The awkward, stilted scene could not be more British. I had pictured this reunion so many times over the last decade. I thought perhaps we'd meet in a country café or at a beautiful beach in Devon, or some lush London hotel; in my admittedly unrealistic fantasy, we'd put aside the whole abandonment issue and just chat – like an actual family. I did not expect a surprise get-together in my own living room over a plate of biscuits. I wanted to try to see the funny side, to puncture the mood of foreboding.

'So,' I began. 'What have I missed?'

'Elizabeth was explaining how it was for everyone's good that she left,' said Hannah with controlled spite.

I glanced from her to Elizabeth, who in turn was looking at me, then Hannah. The ridiculous thought that popped into my head was that this felt like the shootout scene at the end of *The Good, the Bad and the Ugly*.

'She's right,' I said quietly. 'It broke me into smithereens, but she's right. For two years we tried everything to make it work, but it felt like she was slipping away. Then it came to me in a flash of inspiration; it was clear what had to happen. She had to go.'

'So she got to travel the world and you were stuck here with a baby?'

'No, that's not it. I wasn't stuck here with a baby; I was with you. I got to see my daughter grow up, I got to be with you. It was wonderful.'

'But Elizabeth said there were acting jobs in London.'

'There probably were, but I didn't miss out on them because of you. I didn't miss out at all – it wasn't what I wanted. I wanted this.'

And I held out my hands to draw in the whole room, with its books and play texts and photos and framed posters of old productions, and its little open fire and its grubby windows looking out onto the fields beyond.

'Look,' said Elizabeth with a decisive air. 'I said something just before you arrived. We were talking about that photo of us on your mantelpiece. I made it sound like you'd not lived up to your potential, that you'd not been as ambitious as your friends. That was wrong. That was very wrong, Hannah.'

'No, you are right.' I shrugged. 'I wasn't as driven as my friends, not in that way. I never was.'

'Dad!' protested Hannah. 'Stop defending her!'

'But it's true. I could have pushed harder, I could have packed us off to London, made a dent on the fringe. Instead, I came here to run the Willow Tree.'

'But there's nothing wrong with that!' said Elizabeth. 'You wrote and performed in brilliant plays, and then you came here and you ran an actual bloody theatre! And you've put on great shows and supported people and you've given this little town, whatever the hell it is, some culture.'

'Oh not really.' I said. 'You don't know the kind of thing we put on here.'

'I do,' she said. 'I know all about it,' and she paused for a second, glancing away from me towards our daughter. 'Hannah told me.'

Hannah looked down at her feet.

'She has told me everything about the Willow Tree and what it means to her and to everyone who performs there. It sounds like a wonderful place.'

'It is,' I said. 'It was. It's a pity you'll never see it.'

Sometimes, when you look at someone you love, or once loved very much, the years fall away like cobwebs; you see the person as you once did, in the first real flush of it; the feelings fresh and somehow new; like the way the smell of cut grass takes you back to some glorious ideal of summer, to ice creams and picnics, to parks and paddling pools, light rippling on the water. I looked at Lizzie, in our living room, in the golden sun, and for an instant I saw the fierce brilliant student, I saw my girlfriend, my life. When she left a decade ago, I was stranded in sorrow. Days of nothing. Days upon days of it. She tried to contact me – for months, she phoned but I didn't answer; she wrote but I didn't reply. That was how I got through. That, and our daughter. At first, Hannah was too young to really understand, and when we talked about it later, I always hid the worst of how I felt. I couldn't explain it. Everyone wanted me to be angry, to hate Elizabeth, and they were furious that I didn't. People saw her as cruel – inhuman even. That made everything harder. Life is short and precious and you don't have the right to imprison anyone else in your expectations. That is the real cruelty. And then a thought hits me. Something so shocking but yet so obvious. The birthday plays, the Days of Wonder, as I called them – I always thought they were a distraction for Hannah, something fun to take her mind off everything. But maybe it wasn't that at all. It felt like the room was cracking up, like the house was collapsing into rubble. Because maybe the birthday plays were for me – they were *my* distraction. What did it say about me?

Hannah must have seen my anxiety. She saw it, but she misread it.

'Are you angry that I contacted Mum?' she said. 'Are you angry with me?'

'Oh, Hannah, no. That's not it. That's not it at all. I shouldn't have made you feel like it was the wrong thing to do.'

'I just needed to understand,' she said. 'I needed to know who she was. But I didn't . . . I couldn't do that really, not until we met. I couldn't say what I wanted to say.'

'And you've said it now?'

Hannah looked towards Elizabeth and was perhaps trying to think of some conciliatory gesture, but it wouldn't come.

'Can we go out? I need some air,' said Hannah.

I looked at Elizabeth and, unable to gauge her response, I nodded. 'We could head into town, there are lots of nice cafés, and—'

'No,' said Hannah. 'Let's walk to the woods.'

'That sounds nice,' Elizabeth agreed.

The three of us strolled over the road and across the meadow, the sun dipping between the low hills on the horizon. There was a bonfire smell in the air, but it wasn't cold. We walked all together until we reached the narrow track leading into the trees, then Hannah fell slightly behind, checking her phone, holding it out to find a signal.

'Is this what teenagers are like now?' said Lizzie.

'I'm afraid so,' I replied. I turned back to my daughter. 'Put that thing away or I'm going to throw it in a cow pat.'

Freed from the claustrophobia of the house, we seemed to brighten. Lizzie and I swapped stories about old times and old friends; the houses we lived in as students, the battered broken hovels with thick mould edging up the walls devouring our clothes and records. Hannah joined in, asking questions, laughing at the tales of ill-advised fashion statements and crap indie nightclubs. For a few minutes, we escaped the reality bearing down on us – the theatre, the wrecked marriage, the transplant. The cardiologist's words lurked at the back of my mind, his gentle assurances, his careful warnings. I would have to sit down with Hannah and we would have to find a way to cope. But for a few minutes, the three of us put aside our differences, our battles, and made each other feel better. Like a real family.

Back home, Hannah begged Elizabeth to stay for hot chocolate. While I prepared it, the two of them huddled together on the sofa, looking through photos and videos on Elizabeth's fancy mobile phone. I strolled back into the room and found them watching a clip Elizabeth had taken at a fashion show in Dubai – all glitz and marble and beautiful women and flashing cameras.

'Oh my god, look at that dress!' exclaimed Hannah. A pouting model was slinking past the camera wearing a silvery slip of material covered in sequins. As she walked, ripples of light cascaded along the fabric like sunbeams filtering through a waterfall.

'You would look astonishing in it,' said Lizzie.

'Oh shut *up*.' Hannah blushed. 'Anyway, where the hell would I wear it? The school disco? The local nightclub? The comic shop?'

'Come to Dubai,' was the predictable response. 'There are a dozen places you could wear it – and if you did, believe me, you'd silence the whole room.'

When the time came for Lizzie to leave, we all stood in the porch together, buffeted by a wintry gale blowing along the road, awkwardly uncertain of how to see her off. I'm sure we were all thinking, though none of us said it, about the last time this had happened.

'So, are you heading back to the desert soon?' I asked her.

'For a while, but I don't know how long I'll stay. I'm looking for something else.'

It may have been the fresh air playing havoc with my senses, but it felt as though there was a script developing here that could pull us back towards each other. The thought of it made me slightly giddy for a second, as though the years of missing her were just silly moments of doubt. I was certain that if I said the right things, in the right order, something would happen.

But something else held me back. It wasn't fear or good sense (admittedly, the first had stopped me in my tracks before, but the second certainly hadn't). I couldn't quite place what I was feeling, I just got a brief glimpse of a recent memory – only the slightest impression – but it was enough to throw me off balance. It was enough to make me think about someone else.

Hannah

The theatre is coming back to life – just like Professor Xavier's mansion in *Uncanny X-Men* after it's been destroyed by an extra-terrestrial supervillain. Ted has organised a bunch of volunteers to come in and clean up; Shaun and some friends are fixing the electrics or whatever; the bar and café have been restocked (using some shadowy emergency fund that Ted had tucked away in a hidden bank account), and the local WI is baking cakes for us to sell. Apparently there's been no word from the council. Surely they must have seen the posters? They must be aware that we're running a completely unofficial event? People are a bit worried the show could be shut down by environmental health officers or something, but none of us are really dealing with that scenario. I have some experience in filtering out terrifying possibilities.

After working on the script for a few days, Sally managed to assemble a cast for the play, and to arrange for rehearsals in the scout hut down the road. Without a budget, Kamil has been working on a set using offcuts from the timber yard that his brother-in-law manages, as well as recycled odds and ends from the props room. 'It will be my masterpiece,' he says. This is what I've always understood about the theatre – it is a place of possibilities, of magic – it is not bound by the rules the rest of the world has to follow. I've sat in the stalls my whole life, watching quietly through the twilight gloom as sets were assembled and scenes rehearsed. You see how fragile everything is: the walls of a prison held together with gaffer tape; the costumes pinned and clutched at the back with crocodile clips; the actors nervous and spotty under the house lights. But for the performance, there is a transformation – the shapes align, the signs are read, and bare stages become battlefields and bedrooms. If anyone does come to our open day, that's what I want them to understand – that life always seeks to limit you, but it can't do that here. The world is as big as you want it to be and it lasts as long as memory. Things happen on the stage that can't happen anywhere else, because it's not really a physical space – it exists in something shared between the actors and an audience.

We've managed to keep Dad completely away from the building for this last week. A big part of me feels guilty for hiding it all, but then I tell myself it wouldn't be happening if I'd come clean. And it has to happen. When he sees the play – if it goes ahead – I need him to know we'll always have this. It cannot be taken from us. Even when I leave for ever, we'll always be here.

Two days before the show, I manage to walk into the theatre. The five-minute journey takes me an hour, with loads of stops so I can breathe. I feel kind of euphoric when I make it, but in the auditorium I find Sally, Jay, Ted and Shaun, and a smattering of the actors, standing about looking sullen.

'They've taken the lights,' says Ted.

'What? Who has?'

'We had all the equipment on long-term loan,' says Sally. 'The hire company heard from the council that the theatre was closing so they turned up to collect. They were worried it would all get looted.'

'So there are no lights?' I say dumbly. I look up and see the rigs bare, apart from a couple of old spots we've had for years. 'But how can we . . . ?'

'Exactly,' says Sally. 'I mean, we can put the play on with the house lights up, but it's pretty gloomy on stage. Most of the audience won't be able to see much.'

'Can't we ring another theatre nearby and borrow theirs?'

'They've all got productions on. It's too late to source anything else now.'

'Could we use, like, hundreds of candles?' says Jay.

'We've already flooded the theatre,' Sally replies. 'I'm not sure we should set fire to it as well.'

Our upbeat chatter is interrupted by an electrical drill noise coming from the stage. We turn and see Kamil in the midst of constructing some sort of large circular platform.

'He's been here since 6 a.m.,' says Shaun. 'Now we'll have to tell him no one will be able to see his magnificent creation.'

'If Margaret were here, she'd tell us about the time this happened to her at some famous London theatre in the sixties,' Ted adds in a wistful tone. 'She'd tell us to make do and mend.' The thought is enough to silence us all for a second. Then Jay gets this look on his face as though he's just realised the meaning of life.

'I think I've got an idea,' he says, checking his mobile. But no one hears apart from me, because Kamil has started his drill again. Sally only looks around when she notices her son jogging off up the sloped aisle towards the exit.

'Where's he off to?' she says.

I shrug, doubtful that among Jay's phone contacts is a kindly theatrical lighting supplier.

We sit around for a while in the front row of the stalls, watching Kamil and his brother working on the stage. James arrives with two paper bags filled with warm croissants, which he hands out like he's at some kind of middle-class soup kitchen. When he sits down next to Shaun he wordlessly hands over a separate bag, which contains a jumbo sausage roll – much to Shaun's obvious delight.

Just as I'm watching these two guys being cute with each other, the exit door bursts open and shudders against the wall. The noise is loud enough to stop Kamil drilling for a second. Even before anyone looks up we know who it is. There's only one person who barges into the room like this.

Phil looks wild-eyed and scary, his face unshaven and stretched into this horrible expression of anger.

'I knew it,' he says, in a seething, rasping voice. 'I fucking knew it. The place is falling apart and you'd still rather be here than at home.'

Sally looks at him for a while, her expression blank, but I see that she's shaking. 'Phil, please,' she says. 'Calm down.'

'Don't tell me to calm down,' he yells, jabbing a finger in her direction. 'You've been hanging around this bloody place for the whole week, and now you're here all day Saturday? You're taking the piss.'

'Phil, please go.' Sally's voice is calm and measured.

'No,' he says. He sounds like a small boy. 'You're coming with me, right now. You're coming home and we're going to discuss this.'

Ted, James and Shaun subtly realign so that they are beside her.

'I'm staying here,' she says. 'You're embarrassing me.'

'I'm embarrassing you?! Get out now, you stupid bitch.'

'That's enough,' says Ted. 'I don't know what's going on here, but you can't talk to Sally like that.'

'Oh piss off, you old fart. I'll talk to my wife how I want. Maybe when this fucking place closes, you'll leave us alone.'

Sally looks up towards Phil and her mouth is wide open in shock, like she's just suddenly figured something out.

'It was you,' she says. Her voice is so quiet it's almost a whisper. 'It was you who smashed up the boiler.'

'Oh give me a break,' says Phil.

'The night of the play, you came to the green room and we had an argument. You stormed out. I thought you'd gone home but ... Margaret saw you, didn't she? Did you threaten her?'

'Oh Christ, I don't have to stand here and listen to this shit.'

'Why, Phil? Why did you do it? This place might close down because of you, because of what you've done! Is that what you wanted?'

'No! I didn't mean to break the boiler. But you're always here, I was pissed off! I lost it. I'll pay for the fucking damage, all right?'

'Get out,' says Sally. 'You're a monster. I'm sick of the sight of you.'

It's a stalemate now and the tension is crushing. We're all in this, we're all actors and audience at the same time, trying to figure out what comes next. It's James who breaks out of the hold. He walks slowly towards Phil. 'Come on,' he says. 'Let's go outside, let's just back away and ...'

James puts his arms out in a calming gesture, just inches from Phil. It looks like he's trying to deal with an angry dog.

'Fuck off!' yells Phil. He pushes James away and then makes a sort of random flailing movement. James spins away, his hands to his nose. It is not like the violence you see in films – there's no sound effect, no slow-motion reaction. It looks like nothing. But then we see blood coming out from between James's fingers. A lot of it. He slumps down on one of the seats in the closest aisle.

Immediately, Shaun is storming towards Phil, looking

completely fucking terrifying. He passes Sally and, holy shit, she makes no effort to hold him back; she just watches him. This seems big and important, because there is only one thing Shaun is going to do when he reaches her husband.

Phil looks small and deflated all of a sudden. He takes a few long steps backwards.

'Now look,' he says in a very different voice. 'I've got no trouble with you, mate.'

Phil has always tried to get on with Shaun, always tried to joke with him, like old pals together. Shaun used to humour him. Not today, not right now.

'Oh yes you have,' he says and his eyes move to James. Phil's follow.

'I hardly touched him,' he jokes, making a horrible leering smile. 'The stupid twat shouldn't have tried to grab me.'

'That stupid twat is my boyfriend.'

Shaun draws his right arm back, his whole body leaning into the movement. Right, *this* is what a movie punch looks like. Something terrible and decisive is about to happen, something shattering. It feels like all of us are bracing for impact.

'No!' comes a voice, loud enough to stop the punch in mid-air. 'Shaun, please don't hit my dad.'

Jay is in the exit doorway in his dumb baseball cap. For a few seconds, Shaun's fist is still raised, still ready to strike. But as Jay's arrival filters in, he drops it.

'Get out,' he says to Phil. 'Now.'

Phil straightens up, clearly desperate to garner some status in front of Jay. It's almost tragic. Ted puts his arm around Sally, who now looks like she's in shock.

'If you don't come with me now, it's over,' Phil says to her. 'It's fucking over!'

Sally takes a step forward, and it looks like Ted almost wants to hold her back, but then thinks better of it. His arm slips away. I'm screaming, 'No! Don't go with him!' in my head. But she's walking and she's looking at this awful guy with a sympathetic smile on her face.

She stops a few feet away from him. 'Oh Phil,' she says, her tone almost sweet, almost affectionate. 'It was over a long time ago.'

He stares at her in horror. Sheer horror. It hits him harder than Shaun ever could.

'Right,' he says, jerking himself into action. 'Come on, Jay.'

And he walks towards the exit, putting his hand up to place on his son's shoulder. His son. The one person he can rely on.

But this time Jay doesn't move. He closes in on himself, his shoulders hunched, his face away.

'Come ON, son!' yells Phil, and once again he puts his hand up to Jay's shoulder. Jay in one floundering move pushes it away, sending his father staggering into the foyer.

'Fuck off,' says Jay. 'I'm ashamed of you!'

We do not see Phil's reaction. We just hear the front doors swishing open and then closing.

As Sally rushes to her son, I sit down in front of James and hand over a wad of tissues from my pocket. He puts them up to his nose. Gently Shaun sits next to him and puts his arm across James's shoulder.

'Keep your head down,' he says.

'I could have done with that advice a few minutes ago,' says James. 'Do you think it's broken?'

Shaun takes the tissues away and looks at James. His nose is red and streaming with blood, but it's not exactly squashed over his face.

'No,' says Shaun. 'You're still beautiful, don't worry.' And he kisses James on the forehead.

James looks away and laughs to himself.

'Trust you,' he says, shaking his head.

'What?' says Shaun.

'"That stupid twat is my boyfriend"? Only *you* could come out immediately after a fist fight.'

Sally is hugging Jay, and speaking to him quietly, working through what is going on in their lives. We're staring at them with looks of utter confusion on our faces. Oh god, this is so random.

'I didn't realise,' says Ted. 'How did we not realise?'

He walks over to Sally and her son, and without saying a word, James and Shaun follow him. They huddle around protectively.

There, crystallised for me in one second, is why the theatre is worth saving.

Hannah

It's the big day. Well, it's either the big day or a gigantic mega disaster – I guess we'll find out which in a few hours. I start texting Sally at 9 a.m., asking if she's at the theatre, what's going on, are the actors there, are they rehearsing? She texts me back and says calm down, everything is in hand. I try to find a calming comic book to read – I've been meaning to start Craig Thompson's *Blankets* for ages – but it doesn't help. I text Jenna and Daisy and ask how things are going with them – has there been any interest in the event online? Does anyone care? They both text back and tell me to chillax. They say they'll see me at the theatre later. How can I not worry? This is everything.

Ted says there's still been no word from the council, so at least there's that. Maybe they will just let us have our fun and then bulldoze the theatre anyway. Maybe we'll get there just in time to see the place collapse into a pile of rubble.

I feel completely minging. I feel sick with nerves. And then I *am* sick, crawling to the bathroom, and chucking my empty guts into the pan. Dad is immediately frantic. In the world of cardiomyopathy, nausea is not a good sign. Well I'm sorry, heart, you saggy shitbag, I don't have time for your arrhythmic crap today.

'Shall I phone the hospital?' Dad says, fussing, kneeling beside me on the floor.

'No, it's fine,' I lie. 'I'm just worried about school stuff.'

Honestly, I'm getting used to the ever-growing exhaustion blotting out the edges of the day. I'm getting used to not being able to wake up; I don't mind that it takes me three hours to get out of bed. I've started to plan shortcuts around the house, working out the least tiring route to the microwave. If I go out, I go out in the mid-morning and mid-afternoon, when things will be less busy; I pace myself.

But today, I want to be on it. I want to be awake and strong. I want to be there. We've made this huge gamble on the theatre and how much it means to people, and I need to see it through. I want to make sure I'm there with Dad when we find out whatever it is we're going to find out. I get up and wash my face and tell Dad to go down and make me a cup of tea. Then I sit on my bed and think about the play, and how Sally will have planned it all out. I suddenly remember about the lights. I made lots of stage directions and they won't work without good lights, working theatre lights. I text her again, and again she gets back to me almost immediately.

'I told you not to worry,' her message says. 'Something has come up. Wait and see.'

405

Tom

It was a crisp sunny Saturday morning – the sort of day we would have once adored and made good use of. We'd have been out of the house and down into town, for warm croissants and tea, and newspapers and comics. We could spend whole days in the café, dropping in and out of each other's company. I'd whizz off to the theatre to check on the box office; she'd head out with Jenna or Jay or some other friend, doing a circuit of the shops, or sitting around shivering in the park. Sometimes we'd reconvene later at the Willow Tree, if there was work to do, or an interesting performance to see. Those were dream days.

This morning, I was crouching with Hannah as she threw up, the first time she had left her room for many hours. She was pale; her wild hair tied up, limp and greasy. When I helped her up I felt the bones in her back. I wanted to ring the hospital but she said it was nothing; I felt trapped between being desperate to take over, to do *something*, and respecting her right to manage her health. I went into her room to clear up a bit for her, and almost instinctively checked the wastepaper basket. The questionnaire was in there. I sat on the bed with my head in my hands and I looked at it for a long time. I stretched my arm out towards it, but stopped and drew back. This time, though the pain of it wrenched at my insides, I left it where she had thrown it.

There was of course something else to contend with. Hannah told me about Phil. He and Sally had argued on the day of the seventies farce; he'd stormed off, into the boiler room, picked up a piece of scaffolding and smashed the place up. I thought Phil was jealous of our friendship, but he was just jealous of anything she owned that he hadn't given her. He had been sabotaging their relationship for years. In the end he destroyed it and took the theatre as well. There was no way we could report the damage to the police now. What effect would that have on Sally? On Jay? The insurance money was lost. I berated myself for my selfishness. What did that place matter in the midst of everything else? Everything was crumbling.

When the doorbell rang that evening, I was not surprised to see that it was Sally.

'Hey Tom,' she said. 'Are you busy?'

'Sally! Hannah, told me about everything. I'm so sorry, I—'

'Phil has gone. Packed a bag and left.'

'Oh god.'

'I feel weirdly calm.'

And the strange thing was, she did look calm. She looked serene.

'How is Jay?' I asked.

'I don't know. We haven't talked much. But we will.'

'If you need company, if you need somewhere to stay . . .'

Sally put a finger to her lips. 'Another time,' she said. 'Can you come to the Willow Tree? Straight away?'

'Oh, Sally, don't worry about the theatre.'

'It's important. I promise you. Ted is there, so are the others.'

'I don't understand what's going on, but I can't,' I said. 'Hannah is ill upstairs and—'

'*Who* is ill upstairs?' said a voice from behind me.

I turned and there was Hannah, four steps up, fully dressed in jeans and a sloppy black jumper, her pillar-box-red lipstick glistening beneath the bare hallway bulb.

'Are we all set?' she said to Sally.

Very subtly, Sally gestured something affirmative.

'What . . . what are you doing?' I said, as Hannah walked forward to the coat pegs to collect her leather jacket.

'I'm coming to the theatre,' she said.

'But, I mean, I think Sally just needs me to come in and see Ted. I expect something about clearing everything out? Though I'm not sure why it can't wait until Monday.'

'It can't,' said Sally, calmly. 'Something has happened and you need to see. Both of you.'

I just stood there looking at Sally, then at Hannah who was busy pulling on a pair of trainers. I couldn't quite work out what was happening; my mind grasped for explanations but they were all quickly wrenched into a sort of swirling mental washing machine. Was Hannah using this as an excuse to escape the house and meet her friends? Was Sally having some sort of breakdown? Was I?

'Come on, Dad,' said Hannah, taking my hand. 'You'll see when we get there.'

We clambered into Sally's tiny Ford Ka and set off on our bizarre Saturday evening trip to the shuttered theatre, Hannah in the back, furiously tapping away on her phone. I kept looking at Sally, trying to think of things to say, but coming up short – mostly because I didn't know what the hell was happening and kept thinking there was a chance I'd knocked myself unconscious in the kitchen and this was all a detailed hallucination.

'So, how are you doing?' I managed finally.

'Phil is staying with his brother in Radstock,' she said. 'I don't know where he goes after that and I don't really care.'

'Is there a chance you'll get back to—'

'No,' she says quickly. 'This is going to sound stupid, but what's happened with the theatre over the past few months, what's happened with all of us, with everything ... it's just, I'm a different person now. Sometimes you have to let it go.'

I nodded, as the car turned out onto the main road, and I thought about her words as we drove on past the familiar rows of neat old houses, windows dotted with lights. I thought of Hannah, in the back seat, and how she looked so grown up tonight, and how the big decisions that were to come were hers to make, not mine. Not mine any more.

'*Sometimes* you have to let go ...' Sally repeated, almost to herself as we approached the theatre. The building was just coming into sight beyond the end of the terrace. Then she turned briefly to me.

'But sometimes you don't.' Her smile was bright in the darkened interior of the car. 'Sometimes you stay, and you fight.'

There were people outside. That was the first thing I noticed as we approached. There were people milling about, lots of them, I don't know how many. I thought at first it was just some sort of random crowd, a strange spontaneous gathering, shoppers heading home, drinkers heading out, the groups colliding in this one space. But it wasn't that. It wasn't a crowd.

It was a queue.

It was a somewhat chaotic queue, starting on the main road and snaking up towards the theatre and into the car park – which I then comprehended was full. There were families – fathers, mothers and children – in coats and anoraks, shuffling and laughing in the afternoon gloom. There were people in high-visibility jackets who seemed to be ushering others along, talking to them and laughing. I thought I recognised one or two as theatre volunteers. We drove slowly on, and my eyes followed the line to its end point. I was almost unable to comprehend it, my senses hopelessly blurred. The line was leading to the front entrance of the theatre.

'What's going on?' I said.

I could hear music, a fiddle, a flute, some drums. I scanned the crowd until I could make out, yes, a folk group, beside the main doors, all dressed for some reason in olde worlde garb, like players at some fairy-tale pageant. I saw two theatre staff walking slowly along the line, handing something out to the children. When they drew away, a dim light followed them, and I realised with a swoop of emotion and recognition that they were giving out little lanterns. The queue had become a glowing procession.

Someone ushered Sally's car into the last free space right in front of the building. She pulled up and yanked the handbrake and we sat in silence for a few seconds. I turned around to Hannah and saw that she, too, was scanning the throng with astonishment, the phone forgotten in her lap.

'We did it,' she said.

'Did what?' I replied.

She looked outside.

'This.'

'Come on, Tom,' said Sally. 'Let's get out then, see what's going on.'

I opened the car door and waited for a few seconds as a couple of children ran past, before climbing out and into the weird unfolding scene. Sally stood next to me, took out her phone and dialled. I heard someone answer, and then she nudged me, nodding her head up towards the front of the building.

'Now,' she said.

*

Two large floodlights, placed on tripods either side of the main entrance, sparked into life, their blinding beams converging on the face of the theatre. What they pointed at was the blank expanse of concrete above the doors, only now it wasn't blank. There was a large sign, taking up almost the entire frontage, its bright white background contrasting with the grey edifice around it. Along the top were the words, 'Save the Willow Tree presents . . .' And beneath them, in a larger text, a beautiful swirling calligraphy:

Days of Wonder,
a play by Hannah Rose

I stared at it for several long seconds, trying to give my mind time to unscramble.

'If I'd told you, you wouldn't have let us do it,' said Hannah, standing at my side, looking up at me, hopefully and a little cautiously.

'You've written a play?' is all I could manage.

'Kind of. Sally helped. But a lot of it was already written.'

'But the council . . .'

'Screw the council,' said Sally. 'Read the sign. We've set up a community group to save the theatre. We're going to fight, Tom. We're going to fight them.'

Through the zombified daze, I was beginning to get a sense of what was happening. My colleagues, my friends, my daughter – they kept the faith. They kept believing.

'How . . . how did you even do this?' I stumbled.

'Come on,' said Sally. 'We're just about to open up. And as

theatre manager, you have to stand at the door and welcome our guests.'

She took my elbow and guided me forward, towards the glass doors. On the other side I could see Ted, waving furiously from the darkened foyer. I gave him an apprehensive wave back.

'Just stand there,' said Sally, 'and say hello as people come in. Everything else is covered.'

'I can't quite believe any of this. Am I dreaming?'

'Get used to it,' she smiled. 'I think there will be more surprises tonight.'

With that, the doors parted and she walked in.

There was some mumbling and forward momentum from the crowd. I gathered myself, the innate showman in me waking up. There is an audience waiting, they come first.

'Are you open, then?' a woman said.

'Yes. Yes we are,' I replied. 'Welcome to the Willow Tree.'

They filed in, couple by couple, family by family. Hannah stood beside me, welcoming her friends, many of whom I suspect had never been to a theatre, or at least hadn't been for years. 'I used to come to the pantomime with my nan,' one of Jay's friends said as he passed, his jeans halfway down his arse, his boxer shorts exposed. He eyed the foyer suspiciously as though entering a police station. Shaun's extended family arrived, Natasha's husband and his mother, the couple who run the comic store, who spent a long time talking to and hugging Hannah. I saw Daisy and Jenna and, surprisingly, Jenna's parents.

'They let me out for the night, Mr Rose,' she yelled. 'So this had better be good or I'll be banned from the theatre as well as everything else.'

She ran off to greet Hannah and her father watched her go.

'She thinks we're ogres,' he said. 'But we're just trying to keep her on track – if only for another three years. After that ... Well, she's a whirlwind, she'll go where she wants. We love her so much. You do what you can, don't you?'

Further into the queue, I was confronted by the ghosts of internet dating past. Jocasta the environmentalist, Oregon the childcare guru with the amazing celebrity gossip, and Karen, that first disastrous date in the Italian restaurant. She was with her children and, I'm guessing, her mother. She looked happy and confident.

'I'm sorry for running out on you, and spilling the wine,' she said, offering her hand to shake. 'I was not in a good place. I'm much better now.'

'That's good. So am I.'

'It takes time doesn't it? To move on, to just let someone go out of your life. It's a skill you have to practise. Like basket weaving.'

'Yes, it's exactly the same as basket weaving.'

I did not see Vanessa, though from that moment I was looking out for her.

After about twenty people, an old couple, well into their eighties, shuffled forward.

'This takes me back,' the woman said, before pulling me into a conspiratorial embrace. 'I was here on the opening night in 1974. *The King and I*. Lovely sets, very nice king. We came a lot then, didn't we, Brian?'

Her husband, stooped and silent, nodded from beneath a well-worn flat cap.

'I don't know why we stopped,' she continued. 'My legs are bad, Brian has his back problems. It's easier to stay in and watch TV. But then when I heard it might close ... Well, we had to struggle in, didn't we? We had to show our support. Good luck to you.'

We shook hands and they passed by, into the now lit entrance. I saw that inside there were large trestle tables laid out with cakes and biscuits, and cups of squash for the kids. The bar was open and crowded with customers. It was as though we'd never been closed.

With almost everyone inside, I decided to follow the crowd, eager to see the play Hannah had concocted. I took one last look around. Outside the halo of light that encircled the theatre, the cool evening was drawing in. Traffic passed by oblivious, as though nothing incredible was happening here. Just before I turned away, I saw a car parked on the opposite side of the road, and for a second my blood turned icy. It was Phil. He was slumped in the driver's seat, looking across at the building. His unshaven face, silhouetted in the gloom, looked sunken and pitiful. For a moment, our eyes met and he made a sudden movement. I briefly thought he might be getting out to confront me, but in fact he was reaching for the key in the ignition. The car started and he drove away slowly, as slow as a hearse, a billow of dust and rubbish swirling in his wake.

'Don't ever come back,' I said.

Hannah

I leave Dad to the introductions and head inside, wondering if I should go down to the green room and make sure all the actors are ready. Is it bad luck to see the writer before the first performance? Probably. I still can't believe I've written something that people are going to watch.

I also want to find out how Sally has solved the issue with the lighting, because if it's too bright in there it'll be rubbish and soulless, but if we're relying on the auditorium lights, it'll be way too dark. I need to stay calm, because Sally said I should go up and say a few words before the play and I don't want to pass out again. Once is funny, twice is just desperate, let's face it. Although maybe it would help with the fund-raising?

These thoughts are whizzing around my brain as I wind through the crowd, squeezing between the queue for the bar and a group of children wrestling on the floor. I spot James rushing past towards the green room and I wave, but then I catch a glimpse of someone else, someone I was half expecting, but also not expecting. Does that make any sense? Oh my god, I'm all over the place.

'Hi Hannah,' she says.

'Hi Mum.'

Mum? Will I ever get used to saying that?

She looks amazing. She's wearing a beautiful short black sleeveless dress and her hair is elaborately styled, like she's going to the Royal Opera House rather than a local theatre. Seeing her here, like this, just kind of knocks everything else out of my head for a second.

'I . . . um. This is a surprise.'

'I was just in the neighbourhood. Sorry, stupid joke. I'm nervous. I don't know how welcome I am. Am I welcome?'

'Yes. Yes, sure. Of course. Thank you for coming. Has Dad seen you?'

'Not yet. I managed to sneak in without him spotting me.'

'Looking like that?!'

She smiles for the first time.

'Hannah. I know I will never . . . I can never make up for what I've done. For the decision I made. It will never—'

'Mum, look, not now. Tonight is about the future, not the past. I don't have the strength to deal with both at the same time. I'm not a time lord. I'm really glad you're here, honestly I am. Just . . . enjoy it. Have a drink, donate some money. I'll see you afterwards, all right? I just need to prepare myself. I've got to go up on stage and I'm freaking out about that right now.'

'You're going up on stage, in front of all those people – dressed like that?'

I look at her in disbelief, suddenly sort of speechless with shock. 'What's wrong with it?'

She looks at me for a second as though summoning the courage to say something else. Then from behind her back she takes a very large, very posh-looking paper bag – the handles tied with a beautiful red silk ribbon.

'I was going to give you this as a present,' she says. 'But now I'm thinking it's an absolute wardrobe essential.'

I take the bag from her in a sort of confused trance. I only need one brief peek inside to know what it is. I see the twinkle from the sequins; like a pool of diamonds. I undo the bow, and open the bag wider. I lift the dress and it drips through my fingers.

'It isn't prêt-à-porter, it's made to measure,' she says. Her voice cracks. She really is nervous. 'I had to guess your size. There were a lot of phone calls with the store. I hope I've got it right.'

'Oh my god,' I whisper, shaking my head. 'I love it. Oh Mum. I love it.'

Something in my reaction emboldens her and the tension seems to break in her expression. She leans forward and kisses me on the forehead, her confidence restored.

'You *shall* go to the ball,' she says.

I let her hold me and I hold her back.

And suddenly I feel like sobbing; full-on sobbing; the sort of sobbing we only ever do in our worst dreams. It's not gratitude, it's not surprise, and it's nothing to do with the hundreds of other things going on in my life tonight. It's because I suddenly remember something from long ago. That day when the taxi came to take her to the airport and someone was saying 'I'm sorry' over and over again. It hits me with one-million-watt clarity. It was me. It was *me*. I was saying sorry to her. I was saying sorry to my mum. Because it was all my fault.

'I held you back,' I say.

'No,' she says, and she takes me by the shoulders, and her grip is really strong. 'No. Never. We should have worked it out better, your dad and I. We made a mistake. *I* made a mistake.'

'Mum,' I say. 'Don't break his heart again.'

She looks at me, her hands still on my shoulders. Her expression gradually fades into an emotion I can't recognise.

Tom

I stepped inside the foyer and, through the bustling crowd, I saw Hannah and Elizabeth hugging. This was becoming an evening of complicated feelings. My overriding thought wasn't 'What the hell is *she* doing here?' Instead, I thought I saw something in their embrace that I'd never seen before. They looked like a mother and daughter. At last, they looked like part of a family. I wondered, for a split second, if this was an occurrence I would see more of. I could not place what I was feeling. I started forward to see them, but as I did, Hannah stepped away through a group of jabbering parents towards the green room.

'I wasn't expecting to see you,' I said to Elizabeth.

'I had to come, I hope you don't mind.'

'Of course not. I saw you two ... you and Hannah ...'

'She's such an intelligent girl.'

'I know. When I told her you were coming back to Britain, she said I had to give you a chance. She said everyone deserves that. She was right.'

Elizabeth looked down, her fingers fumbling with a ridiculously expensive-looking clutch bag. When she looked up her eyes were wet. She said something quietly, too quiet amid the hubbub around us.

'Sorry?' I said.

'My flight back to Dubai,' she repeated. 'It's booked for tomorrow afternoon. But, I can cancel it, if . . . '

She trailed off, looking at me.

We were silent for a second and I felt the groups of people bustle and bump around me, laughing and talking. I caught snippets of other conversations. I heard one of the volunteers explaining, 'Oh no, we do all sorts here: music, comedy, dance . . . ' I heard Ted reminiscing with the theatre critic from the local newspaper. I saw Janice chatting to a friend, or perhaps a family member, a glass of wine in one hand, her grandchildren tugging at the other. It took an age to gather myself for what I needed to ask.

'Just tell me this,' I said, feeling a lump forming in my throat. 'Did you come back because . . . ' I needed to take a breath. 'Did you come back because you thought this might be the last chance to see her?'

Lizzie looked at me, her eyes and expression unswerving – like the times in the university library long ago, when she knew exactly why I wanted to sit at her table. She always saw through my every diversion and dalliance; she was always able to correct the course.

'No,' she said. 'I came back because I know she's going to live – I know it. I can feel it to my very core. I wanted to see you both now, so that when things get better, we'll already have the foundations of something. We can make a proper start. In business, you invest *before* the upturn, not afterwards. By then, it's too late.'

I look at her, unable to hide my astonishment at her analogy.

'Jesus, Lizzie, that is the most "you" thing you've ever said.'

'Tom, if there's a chance we could . . . '

419

Before she could finish, the PA system buzzed into loud crackly life.

'Ladies and gentlemen, the show will begin in twenty minutes.'

I looked back at Elizabeth. 'Let's talk afterwards,' I said.

Hannah

The women's dressing room is full of life when I arrive. Natasha is busily dressing Ashley, actually enjoying their shared endeavour; Rachel and some of the other actors from the drama group are sitting at the mirrors lining one of the long bare walls, laughing and putting on make-up. There is a clothes rail loaded with costumes, and the torn old sofa in the corner is piled high with bags and discarded clothes.

'Hannah!' says Natasha. 'How are you feeling? You must be shitting it! Do you want some Pinot?'

'Thank you,' I say. 'Is it okay having Ashley here?'

'Do you know what? It is. She's sort of this funny little person with a weird, completely innocent view of the world, just running around doing things. Like an intern, but less useful. I might take her out more. I mean, I'm never going to win parent of the year, but . . . I'm starting to get it.'

She fills a plastic cup from a wine box and thrusts it in my direction.

'What's in the bag?' she says.

'A dress for tonight,' I say. 'My mum bought it for me, but . . .'

421

Natasha is already investigating the contents. 'Jesus Christ, Hannah, it's amazing.'

'I know, but I don't know if I should wear it.'

Natasha takes it out of the bag and puts it up to me. The others have turned towards us. The sequins catch the light from the bare bulbs around the mirrors and almost glow.

'Shit, you *have* to wear it,' someone says.

'If you don't I will,' says Rachel.

And then they're crowding around me, pleading with me. And I just think, fuck it, if I'm going on that stage for perhaps the last time, I may as well make an impression. Then I am undressing, and they're helping me, taking my clothes and lobbing them at the sofa, guiding me into my exotic costume like handmaids around a storybook princess. I expect it to feel scratchy and uncomfortable, but the lining is so soft, the dress slips on like a silk glove.

'Now, you can get away without wearing tights, but you need shoes,' says Natasha. 'What size are you?'

'Um, seven.'

There is much digging into bags and suitcases and the dressing room store cupboard is well and truly rifled until someone launches a pair of black kitten-heel pumps at me. It's a squeeze, but they fit. When my makeover crew are done, they step back and look at me; their eyes travelling up and down. I feel utterly selfconscious, like all those times I ended up in a hospital gown being prodded by nurses – but a bit more glamorous. I don't know what to do with my arms.

'So you won't believe what's happened now, Nat—' Sally bundles into the room, holding her phone. She looks at me and stops dead, her mouth dropping in a ludicrous pantomime of surprise.

'Excuse my language, but fucking hell, Hannah!'

'Are you sure?' I say. 'The neckline feels a bit low, and . . .'

'You look amazing.' She walks over and puts her arms around me. 'You look amazing,' she repeats. 'Are you ready for this?'

'Yeah, I think so.'

'You don't have to go on you know, I can introduce it if you like?'

'No, I can do it. I have a sort of speech ready. Sort of. I need to do this.'

'Is it all right for me to tell you I'm proud of you?'

'Yes.'

'Then I'm proud of you, girl.'

There is a knock at the door.

'Is everyone decent?' shouts Ted.

'No! Come in!' shouts Natasha. There is worryingly drunken laughter from the others.

'I'm just going up to make the announcement that we're start-ing,' he says, still cowering behind the door.

'Is your wife here yet?' says Sally.

'Yes, she's in rather a strange mood. She says she's got something to show me afterwards.'

Natasha and the others giggle into their wine. Ted self-consciously slips from the room, his walkie-talkie clasped in his hand.

'You better tell our lighting crew to get ready,' says Sally.

'Lighting crew?' I say. I'd forgotten all about the lights. I am suddenly swamped with worry again. 'Who is it?'

'Well, I . . .' but before Sally can finish, the speaker in the corner of the room blasts into life.

'Ladies and gentleman,' says Ted. 'Please make your way into the auditorium. The show is about to start.'

Tom

I didn't know whether to head into the auditorium or check on things backstage. Events and emotions were reeling out beyond my control. I was trapped in my own Restoration drama. I decided I should go in and find Hannah – tell her good luck. I had no idea what was going to happen on stage, but I wanted at least to see her before it began. I started toward the corridor, when I felt someone tap my shoulder.

'Mr Rose?'

The voice was thin, officious and vaguely reproachful. I spun around, almost expecting to see a police officer. But this was a different sort of authority figure – I recognised him straight away. It was Bob Jenkins from the council planning committee. Sally was right about this being a night of surprises. At first my heart sank into the floor. Was he here to shut us down? Could he really be so cruel? But something about his self-satisfied expression suggested otherwise.

'I see you've put on quite an event,' he said. 'I'm surprised we did not hear about it sooner.'

'Well, I . . . '

He made a sort of toothy grimace, and it took me a moment to recognise it as a smile.

'We're going to contest the closure,' I said, steeling myself.

'That much is clear.'

'We'll do everything we can. This is just the start. I know we'll have a fight on our hands.'

'We'll see,' he said in a cryptic tone.

He was just about to move on when I caught him by the arm. 'Is Vanessa here too?' I asked.

'I don't know but I expect she is, considering the sacrifice she made for this place.'

'Sacrifice?'

'Yes. Didn't you know? When she put a case forward in the theatre's defence, it was considered ... inappropriate by some of the council officials. They cancelled her contract.'

'They fired her?'

'Not technically. She was a contractor rather than an employee. But yes, to all intents and purposes, they fired her. She made a few people think that evening, though. If you do see her, you ought to thank her. She paid quite a price.'

'So you're not going to shut us down tonight?'

'Not tonight, Mr Rose. This is actually very useful – to gauge how invested a community is in a building. Very useful indeed. If everyone leaves here stony-faced, if the local newspaper decides not to print a story, if no one signs up to your little protest group ... well, let's say some of my more determined colleagues on the buildings committee will be very steeled by such a public show of indifference.'

And with that, he loosened himself from my grip and sloped away into the crowd. I watched him for a while. The noise of the room melted. It wasn't his parting threat that stayed with me. It was what he said about Vanessa. I thought of that morning outside the theatre – why didn't she tell me? I had been secretly disappointed in her, disappointed that she hadn't done more. What an idiot.

I resolved to thank her properly when I saw her – that was all I had to do. I mean, we'd only been on two dates really. It meant nothing. Nothing at all.

I looked around, trying to spot Hannah. Once again I found myself trying to get a hold on the evening, trying to make sense of it. What next? I thought. What next? There was a whine and an explosion of static from the PA system.

'Ladies and gentlemen,' Ted's voice announced. 'Please make your way into the auditorium. The show is about to start.'

People began to bustle towards the auditorium door. I was caught in the tide. I felt confused and disorientated as the current pushed me onwards, but the moment I passed the threshold of the theatre, I knew that only one thing mattered. I saw Ted in front of the stage with a man I hadn't seen before who looked like some sort of mechanic. Ted noticed me and swerved through the incoming masses in my direction.

'How are you feeling?' he said.

'I don't know.' I laughed. 'How are you?'

'I'm very good. Excited, nervous.'

I didn't really hear his words. I was looking around, staring in disbelief as the seats quickly filled. Whole extended families were here, whole neighbourhoods it seemed. Kids rushed up and down the aisles, older folk quietly took spaces at the ends of rows, happily heaving themselves up to let children snake past. I tried to spot Vanessa, but couldn't. The air buzzed with conversation.

I turned to Ted. 'It's ... Wow, it's so much to take in.'

'Just wait until you see your daughter,' he replied. 'Right, I'd better go and get changed.'

I edged forward, down the sloping steps towards the front row. There were two empty seats next to Jay, who was gesturing towards them, and when I sat down next to him, I turned round to take in the room and saw Elizabeth smiling at me from two rows back. I waved and she did too, then crossed her fingers. On cue – just as everything else had been tonight – the house lights went down. The chatter lowered to a murmur and then to silence.

Two rows of spots went up, illuminating a beautiful woman I didn't recognise, standing alone at centre stage. In the following seconds I realised two things. First, the lights weren't theatre lights. At either side of the stage there were scaffolding towers rigged with the rugged lamps you'd find on top of off-road vehicles, while along the back of the stage there were industrial floodlights – the sort they use in car garages.

Secondly, the beautiful woman was Hannah.

Hannah

Sally whispers good luck. I walk along the stark corridor towards the stage, and then I am on. My mind does a flashback to the seventies farce, and how I felt that night – the electricity all over my skin. I want to know how many people are in the crowd but it's hard to see because there are banks of blinding lamps at either side. At least I know this definitely got sorted out, but I don't understand how. Not until I walk slowly to the centre of the stage and glance down over the edge does it all click into place. From there I see a makeshift lighting desk, cobbled together just off to the side, with cables snaking out in all directions. Standing behind it are Callum and his mum's boyfriend, Joe. Our show, it seems, is going to be lit by the contents of Joe's garage and workshop.

I'm at the front of the stage. Alone. There are whispers from the darkness in front of me, a few cries and yelps from bored toddlers. I can feel my heart, a pathetic, wheezing thud against my chest; a baby's punch. I just need to get through the next few moments. I clear my throat.

'Welcome to the Willow Tree Theatre,' I say. My voice is a little broken and husky. I need to breathe. I wonder how much lung capacity I have left to call on. 'Thank you for coming. The theatre was built in 1974. It is not a beautiful building, but it does its job. My dad has been managing it for a decade – he's there in the front row. He didn't know about tonight. I'm sorry, Dad, but someone had to do something.'

A polite smattering of laughter.

'I hope some of you have been here before, to see a play, or a show or a comedian. Maybe you've come for the over thirty-fives breakdancing classes? Maybe you just pass by sometimes and look up and think about coming along one day. And now you're here – you're here for the most important night we've ever had.

'A few weeks ago, there was a flood backstage and it looked like everything was over. The council wanted to shut us down. But we don't think that's a good idea; we think this place is important. You're here so I guess you agree. For me, the Willow Tree isn't just a place my dad worked; it was my home, this was where I grew up; I played on the seats you're sitting on; I learned how to read on this stage. This is where I learned to love stories.

'I'm not sure I can communicate how important stories have been to me. When I was five I was diagnosed with a serious heart condition. Recently, it has got worse – a lot worse. I've always had this knowledge – that things were going to be difficult, that I might not make it. I should have been scared my whole life, but I wasn't and I'm still not. The play we're going to perform for you this evening is about why.

'I hope you like it. We're asking for donations at the end. We have volunteers with buckets just by the door. If you could sign up to be a member of the Save the Willow Tree Committee, that would be amazing. And now, for hopefully not the last time, we have a story to tell you.'

*

The night after visiting Margaret's house and unlocking the green room, I sat and read through the scripts she had left for us. Something struck me about them as the memories flooded back – whichever fairy tale we were telling, whichever fantastical illusions we conjured, they were really all about the same thing. When I told Sally, she knew this is what we had to try to communicate.

I climbed down from the stage and took the seat next to my dad.

Tom

The workshop floodlights rose on a simple scene, the panels of Kamil's revolving set decorated with painted sheets resembling thick stone walls. In front of this was Ted, in fairy-tale regal garb – flowing cloak, a crown – sitting beside a bed, where Natasha's daughter Ashley lay. Sally walked on to the stage and stood at a podium on the far left.

'A king and his daughter lived in a beautiful castle,' she said. 'They were happy and carefree until one day the daughter fell gravely ill ...'

Memories surrounded me like silvery planets. I recalled a time when Hannah was seven, sitting in the stalls, sketching a theatre set with felt-tip pens and a pad of paper. 'Will you be a set designer when you grow up?' I said to her. 'Daddy, I won't grow up,' she replied.

But she did.

I looked at Hannah. She took my hand.

'The king resolved to find a cure, no matter how long it took, no matter how far and wide he would have to travel,' said Sally. 'But his daughter begged him not to leave her in the gloomy castle.'

'I'll die of being lonely and bored,' wailed Ashley.

She overplayed it beautifully, and there was laughter from the audience. I looked around and saw row upon row of families, messy chaotic groups, with their coats and gloves and hats spilling out onto the auditorium floor, cast aside for now. Some children snuggled under the arms of mums and dads, thumbs in mouths, some stood on chairs, some sat cross-legged in the aisles. A minute ago they had been yelling and shouting, now they were watching. I saw Elizabeth, gazing at the stage, the lamplight glistening in her eyes.

'The distraught king had an idea,' said Sally. 'There was a troupe of actors at his royal theatre, a merry band of rascals and misfits, who could surely keep the princess company while he was away.'

And now the rest of the drama club players were on stage – Shaun, James, Natasha, a few others – dressed gaudily as jesters and acrobats, gambolling across the space like circus performers. They were accompanied by the small folk band from the theatre entrance, playing slightly out of tune and lending a Pythonesque tone. Children in the audience laughed and pointed, especially when Shaun attempted a cartwheel and almost fell off the stage. James grabbed him of course.

'Will you visit the princess as much as possible?' Ted asked. 'Will you make up plays and diversions for her?'

The actors agreed with relish. And I saw in my head my little girl running to the bedroom window, throwing open the curtains, the caravan of fairies outside. It was cold that night, but they all turned up. My friends. Oh my friends, we couldn't have got through without you. My throat felt thick. Hannah looked at me and squeezed my hand.

'I'm thinking of that night with the fairy train,' I whispered.

'I know.'

'When I asked them all, I didn't think anyone—'

'I know, Dad. Just watch.'

'When the king left, the actors kept their word,' said Sally. 'The next day, they visited the princess in the castle, and asked what they should perform.'

'*The Little Mermaid*,' shouted Ashley from her bed.

And with a loud creak, Kamil's revolving structure turned. He had triumphed again. Now, we saw an undersea setting, the walls draped with sheets of shimmering blue organza. As the cast began to perform the old tale, it all looked so familiar. Where had I seen this? Where? The cast wheeled on the wooden replica of an old ship bow; at its helm, a young prince.

And then, in a phosphorous flash of memory, I understood. This was *our* version of *The Little Mermaid* from all those years ago, the version Hannah and I planned and then lost with all the others. I turned to her, astonished.

'How?' I said.

'Margaret wrote it down,' she replied. 'She memorised them all.'

There were mermaids in their sparkly tails, there was the sea witch, now played not by Margaret, but by Natasha (Hannah wiped away a tear). The years rolled back. Wherever I looked on stage, from the curtains to the lighting rigs, to the flats, to the exits, I remembered moments from plays we'd put on. Glimpses of actors, singers, clowns and comedians. But more than that, I thought of the audiences. Laughing, crying, shouting. I once said to Hannah that what you see on stage is yours alone – because everyone sees something different. The important thing is, everyone sees it together.

'The princess watched in delight,' said Sally. 'And as she watched, she felt a little better, and sat up just a tiny bit in her bed.'

No movement from Ashley. She was too busy admiring the mermaid outfits.

'As she watched,' repeated Sally, 'she felt a little better, and *sat up* just a tiny bit in her bed.'

Eventually someone prodded Ashley and she sprang up, to general amusement. Sally cleared her throat and began again.

'But when the king returned, he was dejected.'

'I have not found a cure,' said Ted. 'I must leave again at dawn.'

'And again, he set off alone,' read Sally. 'And again he asked the actors to come to the castle and entertain the princess.'

This time, the set revolved to an icy wasteland, to our *Snow Queen*, the story Hannah had loved when she was eight years old. I always remembered it as Ted's play, and when he was on the stage as the robber chief, I thought of how he came here certain he'd have nothing to offer, and I thought about how wrong he was. I could not have managed without him.

'The heroism shown by Gerda made the princess a little stronger,' said Sally. 'The colour began to return to her cheeks. She sat straight up in her bed.'

With the structure established, the play continued. Each time the king went away, the actors put on another of our old birthday productions, and the princess improved. With each scene, things I'd forgotten came back to me. The hull of that ship, the glitter of the Northern Lights, the princess fighting her way to Sleeping Beauty.

'Finally, the actors put on a production of *Little Red Riding Hood* for the little princess,' read Sally.

The lights fell a little, and the revolving stage turned to show a forest of blackened balsa-wood trees. Vapour flooded in from a machine at the rear, forming a low mist around Ashley's bed. She cowered theatrically beneath the bed sheets as the wolf crept in. There was a loud chorus of boos from the children in the audience.

'This time the princess was not delighted, she was afraid; she saw in the wolf the shadow of her illness. She knew in that moment she could not get away; she knew her father would never find a cure.

'But here was the thing. The actors had shown her such delights that she felt sure she had the strength to survive, whatever happened.'

With the help of the cast, Ashley lifted back the blankets and stepped onto the cold stone floor. I looked across at Callum, his face taut with concentration at the rickety lighting desk he had clearly constructed himself. I did not know how he had been lured into this collective effort, but I knew why. Hannah had seen something in him, and now he had seen it too. He looked up at the stage, just as Ashley stood up.

'It was the stories,' said Sally. 'The stories made her strong.'

Callum pressed a button and the trees began to turn around. As they did, we saw that on the other side, they were covered with tiny reflective mirrors. In that moment, as though suspended in time, Hannah leaned closer to me, and whispered into my ear.

'Thank you,' she said. 'There was always magic and wonder in my life.'

A powerful theatre spot – clearly the last we had left – turned on. It sent a beam directly at the trees. The audience gasped.

The light caught and reflected a thousand times, it ricocheted from surface to surface. It shone in our eyes; it cast rainbows through the dusty air.

This was always Hannah's gift to me. Over the last few weeks I'd started blotting out the past; the past was where my daughter became sick. But that wasn't the whole story. There was light all along. It was there with us on the way, it was there in everything we did together – every play, every silly escapade. We had love and fun, and the fear on the horizon, the darkness on the edge of town, only made it more vibrant and more precious.

My sight was blurred, and I thought it was light, but it was tears. I saw the stage through the prism of our lives – an immense jewel.

'Blinded by the light, the wolf skulked away,' read Sally. 'When the father returned, he found his daughter awake and standing. She looked as well as he had seen her in years.'

'But I failed,' said the king. 'I failed to find you the cure you needed.'

'No,' says the princess. 'You brought me the cure. You brought me the cure many years ago. You just didn't know it.'

'I don't understand,' said the king.

'Well then, as the narrator of this tale, let me explain,' said Sally to the king. 'Whichever fairy tales the actors told, whichever fantastical illusions they conjured, they were all about the same thing; they were about a father who saved his girl with stories.'

And with that, the lamps faded. The stage was dark.

When the house lights came up, the cast formed a line and bowed. There was that moment of silence; the moment of reckoning every actor knows. You wait and you hope.

There was a ripple of applause across the front row – almost cautious, almost timid. But then it spread backwards, like a wave, gathering force. Pockets were breaking out around the auditorium. The noise grew louder and then seemed to explode. There were whistles, there were cheers; I looked around and some people were standing; a few at first, but more and more, until it seemed everyone was up. I saw Bob Jenkins get to his feet. I thought he was going to leave, but no, he was clapping. He was clapping too. I had never heard it so loud. I turned to my girl. 'I'm so proud,' I told her. 'Oh my baby, I'm so proud of you.' I wrapped my arms around her, and I was crying, and she said, 'Shhh, Daddy. We're not done yet.'

Sally came to the front and gestured for silence. It took a long time.

'Thank you so much, I hope you enjoyed our play. I guess all of us on this stage have been transformed by this place – myself included. Ten years ago I had no confidence, I was shy and quiet and a bit broken. But the drama club took me in as a set designer, then a stage manager and finally creative director, and they trusted and believed in me. Do you know what that's like? To have someone believe in you when no one else does? It changes your life. It gives you the strength to move forward. The Willow Tree saved me.

'But I think the final word should go to Hannah, who organised this whole event and is perhaps closer to the Willow Tree than anyone else. Hannah?'

Hannah got up and with the help of James and Shaun, swung onto the stage. My daughter took out a piece of crumpled newspaper from her pocket and faced the audience.

'Recently, the theatre group lost one of its veterans, Margaret Chevalier – the best actor and friend I ever knew.' She paused for a few seconds, breathing heavily. Sally put an arm around her. 'I've spent some time looking through her belongings – she'd asked me to, by the way, I haven't just been ransacking her house – and I found a clipping from an old theatre newspaper that I want to share with you. It is an interview with Margaret about a role she was playing somewhere. It was mostly a lot of luvvy anecdotes and stories – Margaret was good at those. But when the interviewer asked something about the meaning of the play, this is what she said: "Darling, here is a thing I have learned; I learned it through my whole life as a struggling student, as a lover, as a wife, as a television actor. All stories are true. They are the way we make sense of the world, the way we remember and communicate the things that happen to us. We keep them safe and pass them between us like gifts. They are recipes. They are spells. Stories are about survival. And where there is life, my dear, there are stories."

'Please help us keep this building safe so that stories can live here for ever.'

Applause again. It began to feel like a celebration, not just of the play, but of the theatre itself. It felt defiant. James hugged Shaun, Natasha hugged Ashley, Ted hugged Sally.

I looked to my daughter. I managed this place for a decade, but she might just have saved it. If it's still here in a decade, in a hundred years, it will be because of her. I stood too and I clapped; she saw me and waved. She mimed fainting but didn't faint. Cruel to the very last, that girl. People were gathering around me; there was a semicircular crowd, hugging me, shaking my hand. I wanted to get to the stage, to reach Hannah. But I couldn't make it. She was already heading towards the corner, towards the lighting desk. I wanted to tell her she had the story reversed.

It wasn't the king who saved the girl with stories – it was the girl who saved the king.

Hannah

Amid the noise and excitement and confusion, while Dad is surrounded by people, I know exactly who I need to see first. I step carefully down the stairs at the side of the stage, into the auditorium.

People clear a passageway for me, but I don't see him at first. Instead, I see Joe pulling plugs and leads out of the improvised lighting rig. As I approach, he drops a length of cabling onto the floor so he can offer me his hand. I shake it bashfully.

'Hi Joe. I don't know what to say about all this. I mean ... how did you? Why did you?'

He grins at me. 'These are all lights from the shop,' he says. 'They're not as powerful as theatre ones apparently, but they did the job.'

'But why? Why did you do this? You're not ...'

'A fan of the theatre? I saw some comedian here a few years back, I'm not a total idiot. But yeah, it's not really my scene, if I'm honest.'

'So why? Why did you do this?'

He sighs and leans on the desk. 'Because Callum asked for my help,' he says. 'It's the first time that lad ever asked me for anything.

I had to step up, didn't I? Have you met his dad? Not Kerry's ex-husband, his actual dad?'

I shake my head.

'Well don't. He's a tosser. So is Kerry's ex, but don't tell her I said so. That boy has been surrounded by tossers all his life. He doesn't need another one. I don't know much about what's wrong with him, but I know it breaks his mum's heart. And he's a good kid – even if he does know fuck all about cars. Did he tell you he got an email from some comic book bloke he met at that thing in Bristol? Apparently, this guy's setting up his own company – he wanted Callum to send him a proper sample of his art, with a decent story.'

'Shit,' I say. 'Callum wanted me to write it.'

'He's blown that, hasn't he?'

'Uh-huh.'

'That lad – everything is such a struggle with him. He doesn't think he fits in anywhere. Maybe he doesn't. But that's a good thing, ain't it? If you look at where the world is going, it's the people who don't fit in who are going to do well, not thick twats like me.'

'I don't think you're thick, I think you're wonderful,' I say. 'Thank you for helping us.'

'It's nothing. I hope it does the job. Keep fighting.'

'I will. I mean, I have to.'

I see Callum approaching. He is holding two huge floodlights, his T-shirt is flecked with oil and grime and his hair is all messy. He looks like a boy band photoshoot come to life. Joe smiles and subtly moves away, ducking beneath the table and pretending to root through a large toolbox. I step towards Callum and he looks at me with those big glum eyes.

'Hey,' he says

'Hi.'

'I'm sorry,' he says. 'I'm sorry for what I did.'

'What you did?' I say. 'You mean finishing with me with a text message? Just when I needed you most?'

He looks down and nods. His face is so full of shame, it actually hurts to see him.

'Why? Why did you do it?'

'I don't know. I . . . I was scared. And I didn't think you needed my shit to deal with, as well as your own.'

'That was my decision to make, wasn't it?'

'I don't know. I suppose. You just . . .'

'Go on.'

'You deserve better. You deserve someone strong enough to help you. I couldn't face watching you get worse and not knowing if I'd be able to help. But that was selfish and weak and shitty. I know there's nothing I can do now to make it right.'

I look at him and I *do* think about what is coming, I do think about what I'm going to need. I think about how I felt uncertain for the whole summer. All the time we spent together, I wondered why I was spending time with him and if it was worth anything. But then I remember the comic exhibition, and how we helped each other. It felt natural. It was not an effort. The things we needed, we just gave them to each other. The things keeping us apart are the same things trying to destroy us both. In this moment, amid the traffic of friendly people, under sparkling car headlights, I think that maybe it'll take both of us to defeat them.

'So why did you do all this?' I say. 'If you thought it was hopeless. Why bother?'

Finally, he puts the lights down, and he steps a little closer to me.

'I'm not good enough,' he says. 'But you are. You're good enough. You're the best person I ever met, or am ever going to meet. I'll never forget this summer. I don't have much, but I have that. At least I've shown you one thing tonight. Hannah, when you need help, I can stand in the darkness and shine a light. I can do that much.'

There is the faint noise of music coming from the foyer. It is almost imperceptible beneath the bustle in the auditorium and I can't recognise what it is. But there is a driving beat. A heavy beat. Bomp, bomp, bomp. The bass is so low I feel it in my chest. I feel it rather than hear it.

'You're an idiot,' I tell him. 'Have you been practising that speech?'

'Yes,' he says. 'For about three days. I had others ready; that was the best.'

'Really? *That* was the best?'

'I'm not a writer,' he says.

He looks away for a minute, abashed by the intimacy we are making. But he's still sad, so sad and lost. And also annoyingly cute. Stupidly cute.

'You need an inciting incident,' I say.

'Huh?'

'An inciting incident. Your character – she can't just get depressed for no reason. Not in a comic anyway. Something has to happen to her. Some terrible crime. You know, Batman and his parents, Daredevil and his sight. She needs to be looking for revenge.'

'Right,' he says. 'I should have thought of that.'

'You should have.'

'That guy from DC . . .'

'I know, Joe told me.'

'Oh.'

'Is that why you did all this? Because you wanted me to write your damn comic?'

He looks stunned for a second, truly horrified, like the whole theatre is collapsing, as well as the world around it. But then, I can't stop the sly smile that's spreading across my face. I never could help smiling at him.

'Yes,' he says, catching on. 'I admit it. I did this because I need you to make me famous.'

'Callum, I have real trouble thinking about the future.'

'I've noticed.'

'It's a defence mechanism. Against, you know, death.'

'It's not a very good one.'

'Just . . . just bear with me? I'm learning to look beyond the next two weeks, but it's hard.'

'If you can put up with me falling apart once in a while, I can put up with you being obsessed with your own death.'

'In that case,' I say, 'I'm in.'

And I put my arm out for the second handshake of the evening.

'By the way,' he says. 'I liked that bit at the end of your play – where the trees turn and the light blinds the whole audience. Where would you get an idea like that?'

'Oh, you know, just some dude. His idea was a bit raw. He needed a lot of help.'

'I know how he feels.'

We hear someone loudly clear their throat and both of us swivel around to face them.

'Ah, so you two have finally made up.'

Jay is standing a few feet away in the now almost deserted auditorium, looking as gangly and awkward as ever.

'I'd better help Joe take the rest of these lights down,' says Callum, and he wanders off towards the stage.

'You told Callum about the theatre lights,' I say.

'Yeah,' says Jay. 'Someone had to save the day.'

'You're a good guy, Jay. No matter what everyone else says.'

Suddenly everything is quiet. The crowds have moved through

443

at last, out into the foyer, out onto the streets, away towards their lives and homes. We're still standing here, Jay and I, where we grew up, where we played together as kids. He clears his throat again, as though to call me back from the memories that whirl around this space.

'I'm not,' he says. 'I'm not a good guy. Mum threw Dad out. There was a lot going on. I'm so fucking dumb, Hannah.'

'It's not your fault. You didn't know.'

'But I did. I heard them lots of times. I heard him shouting when he thought I was in bed asleep. Now, all I can think is, I should have done something. But I did fuck all.'

'What could you have done?'

'I'm not like him, am I? Please tell me, I'm not like him.'

'Would I be your friend if you were?'

'Are you my friend?'

'Of course, you prat.'

'Do you think my mum will forgive me?'

'She doesn't blame you, Jay.'

'I don't know what's going to happen.'

'Believe me, I know that feeling. So we've got to help each other. Like we always did.'

He nods slowly. 'In the comic shop, when you said I had to talk to you when things felt wrong,' he says. 'Sometime soon, I want to talk, if you do. If you still want to.'

'Jay, yes. Yes I do.'

Clearly, he knew more about the troubles in his parents' lives than anyone realised. He just didn't know how to deal with it. He's always been such a big puppy of a boy, bounding around the place, getting into trouble. Now, tonight, this minute, there is something I catch in his expression, something in his posture and bearing, that looks very different, that looks older.

'Things are going to be tough, aren't they?' he says.

'They really are. But hey, that's what comics and video games are for.'

I smile and look into his eyes and I see that old glint – I see the boy I played tag with, and fought with and hid with between the seats and through the corridors of this theatre. I am so relieved, I almost cry. Because I'm going to need him. I'm going to need him and Jenna and Daisy and Callum. I'm going to need them to make it feel like everything is functioning, that I'm part of their world, that I can help them. Even if it is a lie. Even if it is just theatre.

Tom

I was caught in the surge as people jostled towards the donation buckets, and I was half spat out into the foyer as they burst through to sign the petition. Here, finally, I caught sight of Sally and Ted, emerging with the rest of the actors from the backstage corridor.

'I don't know what to say,' I told them, my arms aloft in a gesture of bewildered surrender. 'There aren't the words to express how I feel. What you've done here – it's a miracle.'

'I'm sorry for the subterfuge,' said Ted. 'It's just, if the council got wind of it, if they reported us or shut us down, we didn't want you to be implicated. You've got enough to deal with, old friend. We just wanted to try and save this place. If I'm honest, at the time, it looked pretty hopeless. But now . . .'

'It's got to work,' said Sally. 'Apart from everything else, I want Phil to see that everything is going to carry on – in spite of him.'

'Have you seen how many people are donating?' I said. 'I mean, it may not be enough to pay for the repairs, but Ted, perhaps it can secure us a loan or something?'

'I'll get on it on Monday morning.'

We were all standing in silence, reflecting on the wild swing in our fortunes, when Shaun and James bounded out, their faces still smudged with stage make-up. They both had open bottles of cava in their hands, the contents frothing over their fingers.

'Jesus, what's with you lot?' said Shaun. 'Haven't we just saved the theatre?'

'Well, we've still got to wait on what the council makes of all this, and—'

'Oh screw the council,' slurred Shaun. 'Look over there.'

Amidst the crowds still hanging around, unwilling to part from the warmth of the evening, we saw a woman with a voice recorder aimed at a group of people near the bar. Behind her a photographer was taking pictures of the smiling group.

'The county newspaper,' said James. 'What a story, eh? "Local community rallies around threatened theatre"? Jesus, it almost writes itself. She'll be after a Pulitzer. The council won't be able to touch us after that.'

'Come on, we've got to go,' said Shaun, his arm slapped around James's back. 'We're going for pizza. Our families are meeting for the first time. It's going to be a fucking nightmare.'

James shuddered with histrionic force. 'The play may be over, but for us, the drama has just begun,' he said. 'The things we must do for love ... Oh Tom, someone called Vanessa was looking for you earlier.'

'She was here?'

'Yes somewhere. I don't know if she still is.'

'We're always here for you,' said Shaun. 'If you need dating advice.'

He took James by the lapel of his expensive coat, shouted 'Once more unto the breach dear friend,' and dragged him out through the sliding doors and into the night. The gap they left in the close little circle was quickly filled by Jay, coming out from the auditorium. Sally welcomed him in, putting her arm around him, and he returned the gesture.

'I need a beer,' he said.

'You're fifteen!' said Sally. 'But you know what? You're right. We both need one. Come on, let's get home. I think there are some cans in the fridge. We've got some stuff to talk about.'

She turned to Ted and me. 'I'll see you both on Monday? We have a lot of planning to do.'

'I'll bring the biscuits,' said Ted. 'Maybe even cake. We'll see.'

'Look at him,' said Sally. 'Spending our "save the theatre" fund already. And now he's on his phone. Who are you texting, Ted? Your bank manager?'

'No sorry, I've just got a message from Angela, telling me to meet her outside right now.' He shrugged and put the phone back in his pocket.

'Thank you,' I said to Sally one last time. 'I can never repay you. Either of you.'

'There are no debts,' she said. 'That was the moral of our story tonight, wasn't it? If you owe everything to each other, there are no debts to clear. Right, come on Jay-boy, let's get a pizza on the way home.'

As we watched them leave, I was about to excuse myself so that I could finally find Hannah – but before I could speak, there was an almighty roar from the car park, the unmistakable noise of an approaching motorcycle.

'My goodness,' I said. 'Have the Hells Angels shown up to support us now? Does Somerset have a theatre-loving biker gang I didn't know about?'

I turned to Ted, but he wasn't looking at me; he was staring goggle-eyed out of the door. 'That's not a biker gang,' he said. 'That's Angela.'

For a few seconds the words made no sense whatsoever, until the doors slid open once again, and Ted's wife walked in wearing a battered leather jacket over her floral dress. And also a motorcycle helmet. It took her a few seconds of fiddling with the chinstrap to remove it. Her hair was wild, face flushed.

'You're supposed to be outside,' she said.

'I ... I ...' responded Ted. He looked at his wife, and then outside at the dented, rusting but apparently roadworthy Triumph Bonneville motorcycle and sidecar, resting just beyond the doors.

'Oh *that*,' she said. 'I got talking to one of the nurses caring for my sister; turns out he's a motorcycle enthusiast. He offered to help with the repairs when he heard it was an old Bonneville. It's in good shape, apparently, most of the work was cosmetic, you daft old thing.'

'You ... you fixed my motorbike?'

'*Our* motorbike. It's still a little leaky and the gearing is loose. Some of the bodywork is beyond repair apparently. But it goes. Anyway, I took one of those intensive motorcycle training courses. It's been quite handy, this business with the theatre, kept you occupied while I snuck about. I was going to unveil it for your birthday next week, but I couldn't resist bringing it tonight. Thought I might cash in on all the drama. Why did you never tell me what it felt like to ride it?'

'I didn't think you were interested.'

'Maybe I wasn't. But I am now. Come on, do you want to take the old girl for a spin? I have your helmet out there. Maybe we could go touring. I've heard Scandinavia has some wonderful routes. Lapland is beautiful, they say.'

'I'd like that very much. But Angela, your sister?'

'She's safe, she's being looked after. Not long ago, a very clever young woman told me that the Julia I knew would want me to live,

449

to be happy. She's right. I owe it to my sister to use the time I have, and not to waste a second more of it. Ted, we have each other, we have our health, and now we have a motorbike with a full tank of petrol. Let's just hit the road and see where it takes us. Tonight, I'm guessing that'll be the fish and chip shop and then home.'

Without saying anything else, Ted walked to his wife and kissed her, and they strolled together, arm in arm, out of the building. I heard the motorbike start up and tear away into the night, but I did not see who was riding and who was in the sidecar. I turned around, and looked for Elizabeth, because I knew what I had to do.

The theatre was emptying. Family by family, couple by couple. The tables put out for the cakes were empty, the volunteers were clearing up around the bar. I helped Natasha and Seb drag the donation buckets into my office; they were filled with notes as well as coins. We had eight pages of names and addresses on our forms. We would have a strong story to take to the council; we would have the local community and media on our side. But that was a thought for another day. I closed the office door and locked it behind me. Back in the foyer, only a few stragglers remained. And of course, this being the theatre, a place of drama, of surprise, of revelation – there were just two people I recognised at the bar. Elizabeth was there, looking cool and detached and slightly out of place. And nearby, with a pint in her hand, was Vanessa. I walked over. Here we go, I thought. Moment of truth.

'Hello,' I said. 'Thank you for coming. I wasn't sure you would, but it means a hell of a lot that you did. I mean that.'

'I'm really glad I did – it's been amazing,' said Elizabeth.

'When I came to see you at Gatwick, I mean, I thought it was going to be a complete disaster. It's been so long, Lizzie.'

'I know.'

'So much has happened.'

'I know.'

'That day when you came to the house, and we went for a walk … suddenly, it felt like … it felt like a family. It sounds so silly, but that's what I felt.'

She paused for a second. Just a second. 'I felt it too.'

The sun through the trees, the orange tint in the light; the leaves at our feet. The three of us walking in a line.

'Elizabeth,' I said.

Not all stories are linear. A beginning, a middle, an end, but not necessarily in that order; sometimes they swirl in on themselves like a whirlpool.

'Yes?' Her smile was as familiar to me as my own.

'You and me,' I said. 'You, me and Hannah. It will never work again.'

The front door. The taxi. It was Hannah who said sorry. My baby girl.

'Lizzie, you could walk into any meeting room, anywhere in the world – Dubai, Shanghai, San Francisco – and within thirty seconds, you'll know who is important and who isn't, who has things to contribute, who the deadweight is, and how to deal with every single person around you. But you walked into our house and you were lost. You didn't know what to do or who you were, or how to do or say the right thing. It's been so emotional, it's been so intense, but this isn't where you belong. You don't have to be sorry, you don't have to make it up to us. You need to be you. We've got to move on.'

She looked down at her purse, then her watch.

'Have you … is there someone else?' she said. She said it almost casually, like she was enquiring about a minor household chore.

I glanced up and further along the bar, there was Vanessa,

451

talking to Bob Jenkins. He was saying something; she was shaking her head. She turned away, leaned up against the bar and looked at me.

I can't explain, but it was like a hundred spotlights hitting me at once, a supernova of light. The static buzzed in the air. It felt like the static between the end of the performance and the applause.

'There is someone, yes. But I don't know. It's very early. It might be nothing. I have to speak to her. I have to find out. I really have to find out.'

Lizzie smiled her broad, wise smile. 'Well,' she said. 'I'd better go. Early flight tomorrow. Lots to do.'

'Goodbye,' I said.

We hugged, her hair in my face.

'Tom, take good care of our girl.'

'I always have.'

'I know, I know. But, if you'll let me give you one piece of advice: please listen to her; let her tell you what she needs. It might not be what you think.'

With that, she walked away. I watched her go. Out of the sliding doors, into the dark. Then I looked back to the bar, to where Vanessa was.

But she was gone.

That was so typical of us. Just when I thought I had it worked out, I hadn't.

I pushed open the doors into the auditorium, where I knew I'd finally find Hannah.

She was sitting at the front of the stage, legs dangling over, watching Callum pack up cables and equipment. She was dressed in her jeans and jumper again, the dress folded over her lap, the sequins still catching the lights and reflecting them across the floor around her. She looked pale, almost translucent, her hair messily tied up. I would never know what it took out of her, those weeks of planning and organising. I had given up the fight, but she wouldn't or couldn't. In the midst of everything else, she was determined to save this place, or – as the saying cruelly has it – die trying. It was only when the door closed behind me that the two occupants looked up.

'Do I need to fight this young man, or have we forgiven him?' I said.

'Hmm, I think he's suffered enough,' said Hannah. 'Getting beaten up by you would be an indignity too far.'

'I'll, um, take some of this stuff out to the van,' said Callum, quickly grabbing a plastic crate loaded with car lights and tools.

He scurried away, up the steps and onto the stage, towards the side entrance.

'Callum,' I shouted. He stopped and turned guiltily, like an actor cued in for a line he had forgotten. 'Thank you,' I said in a more placatory tone. 'You did a good job tonight.'

He nodded and rushed away.

I walked down the sloped steps towards the stage. And with every step, the pictures played out in my head, of the little girl I brought here day after day; of the times we came after hospital appointments, and of course, of the plays we put on for her birthdays – the plays that were joyous but also defiant – because they were designed to challenge the memory of that diagnosis and what it threatened. It occurred to me so clearly, so brightly, in the semi-darkness of the auditorium, that our days together had been wondrous and full, because we understood the fragility of it all, even if we never acknowledged it. But time forces you to acknowledge everything in the end. The brightest sun casts the blackest shadows and as I walked towards Hannah, I feared the future more than I ever had. As well as incalculable love, I felt the darkness upon me – and I knew why.

'Did I tell you how proud I am?' I managed to say finally.

Hannah shrugged. 'I just took the old plays and put them together. Sally helped. Sally did most of it.'

'I don't mean the play. It was beautiful, of course, it was an amazing surprise – I'll never forget it. But this place, as important as it is, it was only ever the venue, it was the set. The magic was you. From the moment you were born, it was always you. I'm so grateful and astonished that you've done this, but you didn't have to risk your health to save this place.'

'Yes, I did,' said Hannah. And she slid slowly down off the stage. 'I did have to save it.'

'Why?'

'Because you'll need it, you'll need something.'

'Hannah . . .'

'Dad, listen – whatever happens, you have to let go of me. Just a little.'

'I can't, baby.'

'You have to. This whole summer, I've been trying to . . . I've been trying to tell you. When I fainted and fell down the stairs, the morning after, I was in the hospital and I knew that, oh god, I knew I couldn't do this to you any more.'

'Do what?'

'Rely on you to keep us safe, to keep everything away. But the thing we were running from, it's here now, and I have to face it. You have to step away. It's my scene, it's my soliloquy.'

'I don't understand,' I said. But I did. Underneath it all, I did.

'I can't think of the right words, so I'm just going to come out with it,' she said. 'I've got a fight coming, the biggest fight I'll ever face. If I'm going to win, I need everything around me

454

to be normal – or at least our version of normal. I need life to go on – because that's what life does. Don't take this the wrong way, but sometimes, I need you not to be there. I need you to tell me: Hannah, I can't sit and watch crappy DVDs with you today because I've got a date, or I've got work, or I'm driving the theatre group to a really shit arts festival in a godforsaken field somewhere. Because that's *you*. I don't want to lose who you are, Dad. I don't want you to put everything on hold for me, I don't want you to hover over me like the grim reaper. I need you to be you. That's how we're going to win. Do you understand? We win by living.'

'Come here,' I said.

We hugged, and she felt light and tired in my arms. But I knew she was strong enough.

'Promise me,' she said. 'Promise me, if anything happens, you won't just sit around at home looking at old photo albums, like a complete loser. You'll get out there, you'll put on plays, you'll live.'

'I promise,' I said.

'Good,' she said. 'Now I'm going to find my boyfriend, and you're not coming.'

'Hannah, I . . . Be home by ten-thirty or you're grounded.'

She climbed back on the stage and past the set. I heard her footsteps recede down the passage to the changing rooms and the stage door.

Alone in the theatre again, the silence was palpable – although of course, there is never really silence here. The air in a theatre auditorium has a buzz, a charge; it carries every moment of tension, every burst of laughter that's ever played out – these moments stay forever like static, like memories. Somewhere in the perpetual buzz are the sounds of Hannah as a toddler, running along the aisles and down the slope. The sound would be here as long as the building. It would always play. All I'd have to do was listen very hard.

I started back up the long walkway to the doors at the rear, and I thought, if we have truly been granted a reprieve here, we should do something about it. We should put on new plays, challenging plays, we should provide something else alongside the musicals, the bedroom farces, the GCSE set texts and the stand-up comedians. Everything is changing; the internet will cause a revolution in the way people watch things, the way they experience stories. I thought to myself, the person in charge of the theatre should understand where all this is going, so that we can keep up.

I switched off the house lights and walked through into the foyer. One of the volunteers would lock up tonight. The glass doors swished open and I set foot into the enveloping night. The crowds had long since left, the car park emptied. Clouds hung over the moon like great proscenium curtains. I looked back at the sign above the entrance. A play by Hannah Rose. Would there be more?

When the voice came, it startled me.

'Have you forgotten where you parked your car?'

She was wearing the same dress she wore on our first date, paired with a long elegant raincoat. Her face, bathed in the after-glow of the spotlights, was starkly beautiful.

'Vanessa,' I said dumbly. I had so much to say – thank you for coming, thank you for your help, thank you for taking me out of myself for a few hours one sultry August night. None of it managed to make it out of my mouth, though Vanessa nodded anyway, seemingly able to read my garbled thoughts.

'So there's a new theme restaurant opening up near the cinema,' she said. 'It's called Go Go Sushi. Apparently the dishes whizz around on a little conveyor belt and you have to try and grab them as they pass. I figured, if we were to go and eat there together – what could possibly go wrong?'

'I can't conceive of anything that would lead to us fleeing such an establishment,' I replied.

'I am available this Friday – it would be a pleasant way to end the first week of my new job.'

'Then it's a date,' I said.

We stood awkwardly for a few seconds, which was probably a good preview of what was to come on Friday.

'How is the theatre?' she asked. 'How is Hannah?'

I smiled. 'There's a battle coming,' I said. 'We'll fight, and we'll win. One way or another, we'll win.'

Hannah

When I get home that night, I lie on my bed and check my phone; there are dozens of texts from people at school, saying nice things about tonight. The best is from Jenna: OMG! ma and da so moved by play they're letting me join drama club! Might evn let me take an arty a-level. Yr a star xxx

Maybe this is how life works. Little acts of love ripple outwards. They tell people it is acceptable to hope for things. I take the A-level questionnaire out of the bin. I put it on my desk and smooth it out as well as I can. I take a pen. On the line where it asks what subjects I want to take, I write English, Drama and Psychology. Then I look at the question underneath: where will you be in five years?

For a few seconds, I think about that, and it reminds me of something else, something I once learned.

In a transplant situation, the surgical team must get the heart from the donor to the recipient within four hours. Four hours. When the time comes, they don't transport the organ in some fancy high-tech receptacle – it goes in a container full of ice. A picnic coolbox. It is rushed to the hospital on a motorbike or a plane, and then it has to be teased back to life at the other end. Venkman told me all this years ago, before it ever looked like I'd need a transplant myself. I remember the conversation we had.

'Why does it start beating again?' I said to him.

'Well, they pass an electrical current through the—'

'No, I don't mean how – I know the medical process. I mean why? It's just this piece of meat that's been ripped from a body, shoved in an icebox and then zapped with a cattle prod. It's totally broken and . . . alone. So why does it come back? Why does it even bother?'

Venkman thought about this for much longer than I expected. He tapped his pen against his clipboard; he stared glassily out of the window. Finally, he turned and looked me straight in the eye.

'Everything wants to be alive,' he said.

And that's it, that's really it. Margaret told me that you must measure life in moments – because unlike hours or days or weeks or years, moments last for ever. I want more of them. I am determined. I will steal as many as I can.

'Where will you be in five years?' the paper asks. I put my pen to the paper and I write 'alive'.

Dearest Willow,

I promised you that one day I would tell you what happened at the end of The Little Mermaid, *the play we put on for my sixth birthday. Well, here we go.*

You remember that, in the story, the Little Mermaid had a choice: she could kill the prince, or allow his marriage to go ahead and then die herself. As much as she wanted to live, the mermaid could not bring herself to hurt the man she loved; instead, she dived into the organza waves, drifting to the bottom of the ocean.

And there was Rachel, lying on the stage in her beautiful costume, her eyes closed, the whole place silent. But suddenly, something about that didn't seem right to me. It was not how it ought to be.

'No,' I yelled. And I pushed away from my friends, and before anyone could stop me I was running up onto the stage, towards the Little Mermaid. Because it wasn't a play any more, not in my head. It was something else – I think the shock and worry of my diagnosis had come back to me all of a sudden. I dropped at Rachel's side.

'You can beat the witch's curse, you can stay alive,' I said.

Rachel opened one eye and looked at me and then all around, clearly thinking, 'Oh god, what the heck do I do now?' But to her credit she stayed in character. She saw I was crying, because I was actually crying now, and she stayed with it.

'Do you really think I can live?' said the mermaid.

'Yes,' I said. 'You can live. You can do it.'

'But . . . but my heart is broken.'

I put my arm around her.

'It's all right,' I said. 'So is mine.'

And now Rachel had tears in her eyes. I remember her make-up was running, and the glitter from her eyeliner was sparkling under the lights. Then I leaned down close to her and I said, 'But I'm going to live.'

As I recall, the other mermaids heard this, and they gathered about their friend. They took her arms, and lifted her; they lifted her from the ocean floor. They whispered encouraging words. Uncertain and unsure at first, weakened by her weeks of torment, she began to move her tail. Gently and slowly, her friends let her go, and then with one strong swish of her tail she was swimming again. That was how it appeared to me anyway.

Willow, one day you may feel lost, you may feel broken-hearted – it can happen, no matter how careful we are. People can be cruel, life can be hard. But there will always be somewhere you can escape to; it may be music, or art, or comic books or fairy tales; it may be a city, it may be a friend. But remember, you are the author of your life, you choose the setting and the script. Let no one else tell it.

Through the thorns, through the shadowy forest, through the swirling seas, through the wolves and witches, there is a place for you. The story is how you find it.

Epilogue

27 September 2025

It's hard to believe it was twenty years ago today, the night Hannah and Ted and Sally saved the old Willow Tree Theatre from redevelopment. Everything was so uncertain, so bewildering, my memories of that time are still hazy and ill formed – I pluck at them but they evade me. We didn't know that night that the local newspaper would start a campaign to support the building, that Margaret would leave in her will a sum of money for the theatre – as well as for Hannah. We didn't know its future was assured – even beyond the recession and the Arts Council cuts that would come barely five years afterwards.

We didn't know that within six months, on one fine spring morning, Hannah would get a call from the hospital – a donor heart was available. We were driven to Bristol airport and then taken by private plane to London. Callum followed by car. Joe drove him. The operation took six and a half hours, and for days afterwards Hannah was a groggy presence amid machines and tubes. But she pulled through. She leaped through. Barely two weeks afterwards, she was out of intensive care and then out of the ward and home. Her colour and strength returned. She was formidable. We could barely keep up. I don't think I ever kept up again.

She passed her A Levels; she took a gap year and visited her mother; she studied English and Drama at Queen Mary University in London. She and Callum wrote their comic. A

Darkness was released on a small print run, to critical acclaim. Callum struck up a partnership with a well-known Marvel writer; he has become something of a star. Hannah wrote plays – dark, funny, weird, thrilling plays about mythology and heroism. I came to see her professional premiere at a pub theatre in London. Several months later it hit a major fringe venue. I wrote plays too, but never as good.

I left the theatre soon after that night; Sally took over. I had other things to see and do. I wrote, I acted, I toured again. I took a show to Edinburgh – I met Ted and Angela there one last time. Vanessa even persuaded me to take a modest Shakespeare production to a festival in Thailand – then her son and daughter stayed with me while she spent some time travelling. When she got back she was able to remove sixteen pins from her world map.

Ten years later, there was a health scare for Hannah, a tortuous month, but once again she pulled through. She decided that she should marry Callum. It was another milestone we'd dared not hope to see. The reception was at the Willow Tree of course. Vanessa and I managed not to get thrown out.

Time expanded, we took all the opportunities given to us, we let the days pass; languid summers into long crisp winters. We were thankful for every moment. We were patient, we were lucky. It took many months, but Callum and Hannah adopted a baby daughter. An astonishing gift. Naturally, they called her Willow.

The night of the play, the play that saved the theatre, Hannah had told me there was a fight coming, and that we would win by living. She lived for eighteen more years. She passed in the night, 12 July 2024. The windows were open, a soft breeze brought in the scent of jasmine from the garden below. Callum says he heard her whisper something to him, her lips on his ear. 'Steal the future,' she sighed, and then sighed no more.

Hannah had read to Willow every night of her life; she took the fairy stories from her own shelf, one at a time, and worked through them. Nobody could tell them like her. It drew the two of them together. Throughout Hannah's life, she also wrote letters to Willow about her own childhood. She didn't know how long she'd have to tell the story. She hid the letters away in a folder; we found them just after she died. The folder also contained a sapphire engagement ring.

And now Willow is staying with me for the weekend – in her mum's old room. Earlier, I read to her and she sat up in bed and asked questions I have heard before, questions I answered for someone else a long time ago. Once again, I was ready.

'Is magic real, Grandad?'

'Yes, of course. It's not like it is in the books, but it is real.'

'Are fairies real?'

'Shhhh, it's a secret and not everyone can see them.'

'Who can?'

'Special people.'

'Am I special?'

'Oh yes, definitely.'

'Can I see them?'

'I don't know. If you look out of your window later, maybe you will. If you're very lucky.'

I kissed her goodnight and crept to the door. But I did not go out. I waited quietly, because I knew what was to come. It was difficult to hold myself together; the memories still made me sob sometimes. All good memories contain sadness within them – they only ever give us a glimpse of what we once had, but if you are prepared to grasp wondrous moments when they come, there is always the chance to make more.

So there I stood, halfway between the bedroom and the hall, as a soft glow of light appeared at the very edge of the bedroom window, and the sound of distant music grew louder and louder.

Acknowledgements

Writing a book with a rare medical condition at its core is a complicated and intimidating endeavour. Thankfully, I received utterly invaluable assistance from the cardiology staff at Great Ormond Street Hospital. I would especially like to thank consultant cardiologist Dr Matthew Fenton who has been involved from the very beginning of this project, giving me detailed medical information, showing me around the ward and answering hundreds of questions about heart disease. Thank you so, so much, Matthew, you have been a huge inspiration to me. I would also like to thank clinical nurse specialist Jane Crook, who gave me crucial insight into the emotional and psychological effects of heart disease, as well as endless information about medication and myriad other aspects of cardiology. My sister Catherine, a matron at GOSH, also helped enormously, connecting me with staff at the hospital and meeting me for coffee afterwards. So much coffee.

Thank you to Sarah Ryrie who sat down with me and told me about her own experience of living with a heart condition. Thank you Pippa Goldfinger who gave me very useful information about the infrastructure and machinations of local councils; thank you Claudia Pepler who explained to me how she runs the Merlin Theatre in Frome. The experienced lighting director Malcolm Rippeth guided my understanding of stage lighting. Kieron Gillen, Emma Vieceli and Kev Sutherland were hugely generous with their knowledge of comics, comic book history and comic book events.

Thank you so much to Chris and Caitlin Mosler, to Ruth Price and Poppy Andrews, and to Harris West, who all helped me to understand the lives of young women and their parents in the twenty-first century. Lisa Merryweather-Millard showed me around Frome College and answered lots of questions about modern teenagers.

Thank you to my *Guardian* colleagues Jonathan Haynes, Alex Hern and Samuel Gibbs. Thank you to my pal Ann Scantlebury who read a very early synopsis of the book and had great ideas about it. Thank you to my wonderful friends Simon Parkin, Will Porter, Christian Donlan, João Diniz Sanches, Simon Attfield and Kat Brewster. Special thanks to my partner in crime, Jordan Erica Webber, for her help, wisdom, guidance and friendship. Thank you to Jules May-Brown and Brigid Moss, for our regular and highly inspirational writing club meetings.

Much of this book was written in pubs and cafés in the Frome area. I would really like to thank the staff at the River House café, the Talbot Inn, Sam's Deli and Babington House for being so welcoming and patient.

I cannot stress enough how thankful I am to the wonderful, passionate staff at Little, Brown, especially my editor Ed Wood, my publisher Cath Burke, my desk editor Thalia Proctor, publicist Clara Diaz and foreign rights stars Andy Hine, Kate Hibbert, Sarah Birdsey and Joe Dowley.

Thank you to the most important people in my life: my sons Zac and Albie, and my wife Morag, who read every word of this book as it was written, who advised me, who had brilliant ideas and who made me believe I could do this even when it seemed as though I couldn't. Thank you for everything.

Now read on for the beginning of
Keith Stuart's heartwarming next book,
The Vanishing of Elsa Klein

Prologue

Will, Bath, 26 April 1942

The sirens woke Elsa but not me. I'd crawled into bed only an hour or so before, exhausted, bruised, desperate to blot out the memories of the previous day; the awful things I'd seen. She was shaking me, harder and harder, and even then sleep would not relinquish me. Finally she shouted, 'Will! Will! Wake up! Will, darling!'

'What is it?' I groaned, turning away from her, pulling the blankets up and over my head. She switched on her bedside lamp.

'Will, we have to go. They're back. They're coming back.'

For several seconds, I still couldn't understand her, desperate to return to the peace of unconsciousness. But then I heard for myself. The undulating wail of the sirens – and beneath them, the sound like rolling thunder.

The bombers. The bombers had returned.

Elsa was up and out of bed, pulling on her thick dressing gown, bumping against furniture in the darkness, a growing frenzy of movement and panic. I sat up, rubbing my eyes, and for a few seconds I entertained the possibility that the noise would pass – as it had done every night before yesterday. But just as I was about to reassure Elsa (more prone to panic than I for understandable reasons), we heard the unmistakable high-pitched whistling sound of bombs being dropped, dozens of them – a horrible choir. Then multiple impacts, low and distant.

We looked at each other.

'I'll need to get dressed,' I said. 'I have to report in.'

'You can't, you were out all day yesterday. For God's sake, let someone else go.'

'It's my duty.'

As I dressed, Elsa peeled back a little of the black curtain and looked out of the window. From here, we had a panoramic view over the city; it was one of the reasons my parents had bought the house. How lovely, my mother often said, to see all of Bath laid out before us like a picture postcard. Last night, we'd seen a very different prospect: vast areas on fire, like some awful vision of the apocalypse.

I was struggling with my shirt when Elsa spotted something that made her open the curtain a little wider.

'Will,' she said. 'There's someone in your workshop.'

A cold chill went up my spine.

'What? Are you sure?'

My shirt still unbuttoned, I joined her at the window and looked out toward the end of the garden. Sure enough, there was light seeping from beneath the workshop door. A shadow passed across it from inside.

'Looters?' said Elsa.

'Surely not, we haven't even been hit yet. I'll go and see.'

'No, Will – we have to get to the cellar!'

There were more long droning whines, seemingly nearer now, and then three massive impacts, loud enough to shake the house. Outside, someone very nearby was screaming. The sound jolted me back to yesterday; the houses on the Lower Bristol Road, all obliterated, like a row of grotesque blackened skeletons. Bodies in the soot.

'You go,' I said. 'I'll have a quick look, there's a lot of equipment in there that—'

'Oh forget your damn contraptions, Will, come with me. *Bitte!*'

'I'll only be a moment, darling. I promise.'

I opened the back door and the horror of it all hit me again. From further down the hill the gut-crunching sound of another explosion, then cries from God knows where; the rumble of falling masonry; a smell in the air like tar. Another wave of bombers was coming in for its turn at the city, untroubled by the pathetic patter of distant anti-aircraft fire. Bath had no guns of its own.

'Go to the cellar,' I said, and I stepped forward and kissed her.

When I broke away, she looked at me desperately, but started to step back for the cellar door. I scrambled out onto the steep path leading down toward the workshop. My father had built it many years ago; my brother and I helped him, carrying bricks along the garden in a rusty old wheelbarrow. There had once been an orchard down there, he told us. As I got closer to the door, I could hear someone speaking inside; instinctively, I looked around for a weapon, a spade or pitchfork, anything. But then as my senses gathered, I realised with a start that I recognised the voice. I wasn't sure whether to feel shocked or relieved. I opened the door very slowly.

The interior was mostly lost in shadow, but a single lamp illuminated the large worktable in the centre of the room, crammed with half-built wirelesses, tools and components. At the rear, a window overlooking the city let in a little more light, revealing the metal shelves lining the walls, loaded with more tools and parts. My father had tinkered with his car in here, but for me it was always the wireless; there were several models I had bought or scrounged from work, several more I had made myself. And there, sitting at the desk with his back to me, one hand desperately fumbling with the dials on my home-built radio transmitter, was a small boy, dressed in striped pyjamas.

'David,' I said. I spoke quietly, calmly, so as not to startle the lad, but I was aware we had to get out, to get to safety. 'David, what on Earth are you doing here?'

Before he could answer there was a series of loud blasts, not far from us, perhaps up the road toward Camden Crescent. The whole building shook, releasing a shower of dust from the low rafters.

'David,' I said again, gritting my teeth to stop myself from yelling.

'I have to call Papa,' he said. 'He has to come and rescue us.'

'David, I'm sure your father is on his way, but we have to get to safety. Does your mother know you're here? She must be frantic.'

Through the grimy window, an unknowable distance away, I could see flames, or more like one giant flame. Something vast was on fire down there – perhaps the whole city this time, perhaps everything. And then my eyes rose slowly, attracted by an all-too familiar noise: high up, but caught unmistakably in the bright moonlight, there were three bombers, heading in our direction like a flock of dragons.

'Oh Jesus,' I whispered.

Without thinking I leapt forward and grabbed the boy, knocking the chair from under him. He screamed and grasped at the radio microphone, but I had him in my arms. What now? I was terrified his mother would be out looking for him, combing the streets – if I took him to our cellar, would she still be out there searching when the bombs hit? Should I take him home? He lived only five houses along from us, but there was no time now, and the noise was getting louder. *This is it*, I thought.

The boy was screaming and punching me with his little fists as I struggled back toward the door. I stopped and looked at him. I could smell smoke from somewhere and the sound of a motor vehicle, perhaps a fire engine, in a street very nearby.

'David, please – I'm going to take you to our cellar, you'll be safe with us. I'm sure Elsa will sing to you. Some of the songs she has been teaching you on the piano, perhaps?'

He stopped struggling.

'The Grand Old Duke of York?' he asked.

'Yes, of course.'

'But my papa . . .'

'Your papa will know we are in trouble. He'll fly in his plane and he'll shoot the Germans down, I'm sure of it. But for now, we have to get inside.'

'But how will he know?'

'The RAF has lots of technology to let them know what is happening in the war. Come on let's get inside, I'll tell you more about it.'

I wished I'd never taken him out to see the workshop; a few weeks ago he'd been over for his weekly music lesson, talking about his father and his Spitfire and I'd told him about how pilots used radios to talk to each other. 'Come and see,' I said. I showed him the transmitter and explained how it worked. He had asked, 'Could I talk to Papa on that?'

With the boy in my arms I kicked open the door and made to go outside. It was a steep climb back up the garden to the house and after all that had happened yesterday I was worn out, my muscles ached. But I had to be fast.

'Here we go, old boy,' I said.

And I started to run, out onto the path, stumbling for a second as a gust of smoky wind hit me, then regaining my balance. I looked up and saw that the sky was molten, the glow of fire reflecting from the clouds; everything throbbed with the sound of aircraft engines. I thought my eardrums would burst with the noise of it all.

But then, the strangest thing.

All of a sudden, everything seemed to stop. The screams, the rumbling, the crashing. It was as though a great peace had descended. I looked up again, and there was a blinding light seemingly focused on us from somewhere very high up, as though we had been picked out by a theatrical spotlight. I saw raindrops swirling in the vortex like jewels. I was enraptured, frozen to the spot. Then I heard a voice calling from a long way off and I recognised it. With a great effort, I looked toward the house. It took my eyes a few seconds to adjust, but it was Elsa, calling for me from the back door. I smiled at her, but she wasn't smiling. It was somehow disconcerting, almost irritating in fact, to see that her face was distorted into a look of pure, undiluted terror. I thought she had been saying 'love', 'love'. But I was wrong. It was 'run'. She was screaming 'run'.

I looked up again through the light and the whirling rain, and I was aware of a strange whooshing sensation that seemed to herald something approaching very fast. And I knew. I knew in a second of calm clarity what it was. I held the boy close to me and bent over him as though shielding him from a sudden storm.

'David,' I whispered. 'Hold tight, son.'

I'd been told that the survivors of the London Blitz had a saying: you don't hear the bomb that's coming for you. I was surprised, in those final seconds, to discover it was true.

Chapter One

Laura, Bath, 23 October 2018

Standing outside the decrepit house in the lashing Autumn rain, I am struck with the certain knowledge that I'm in completely the wrong place – and also, if I am being honest with myself, the wrong life.

I check my watch. It is 9.47am. I am having my first major existential crisis of the day. That seems about right.

After leaning my old Raleigh bike against the garden wall, I push my glasses back up, then drag my Filofax out of the saddle bag, flipping to the page where I'd scrawled down the address. No, this is it: this is Avon Lodge. I look up again and stare at the large, dark Victorian house in front of me.

It probably would have been beautiful once, with its bath stone exterior and bulging bay windows, and the two ornamental turrets above the attic rooms, which give it a sort of fairy tale grandeur. On the roof, the slate tiles look glossy beneath the deluge. But it's clear the building has seen much better days. The façade is blackened and pockmarked, and there are huge cracks in the stonework around the windows – which are themselves spotted with mould. Rain is streaming down the wall from a vast fissure in the iron guttering. The front door is missing a glass pane and seems to sag with age and damp. It is set back from the road, separate from both a smart row of houses on one side and some sort of vast building site on the other, as though quarantined with some horrible contagion.

Surely no one could actually live here? Especially not a ninety-eight-year-old man?

I check the address again, looking down at the paper, then up at the house. I do this several times, but it still feels like something is wrong. Actually, it feels like *everything* is wrong. Here, now, yesterday, the day before. I just have to breathe deeply. In through the nose, out through the mouth. *I'm in the right place. I'm in the right place.* It might not be the place I want to be, but that's okay.

I am used to feeling like this, like I am suddenly being ambushed by reality. Sometimes, I am having tea with my mum, or walking down the street, or browsing the pasta aisle in the supermarket, and The Banality of My Existence will suddenly leap out at me from behind a lamp post, or sofa, or display of breakfast cereal boxes. It will slap me in the face with familiar accusations: Laura James, you messed up and that's why you're here. You messed up, you gave in, you dropped out, but hey, while you're in Tescos, could you get a pair of washing up gloves and some refuse sacks? The ones with the tie-up handles? Thanks.

My self-loathing internal monologue is really great with shopping lists.

I decide I should walk up to the house and try to peep in through one of the windows, but when I push the garden gate it collapses from its rusty hinges and falls to the path with an almighty clang.

Once I've recovered from the shock, I try to lift it back up, but it is too heavy and wet, and it falls from my grip, landing noisily once again only millimetres from my feet. Deep breaths. I nudge my glasses up again and then check my hands for injuries because I don't want to get tetanus and die in hideous convulsions. I examine them at some length, turning them over, letting the rainwater wash off the mud and rust. They seem fine. When I eventually look up again I realise with a start that the porch door is now open and a very old man is standing there staring at me.

'Can I help you?' he says.

This all started on Monday. I had been called in to see my boss Jane at the Shady Oak home care agency, which sounds idyllic and pastoral but is in fact housed on the second floor of the ugliest 1960s office block in Bath town centre. Jane explained she'd received a call from a friend of hers in social services – they were concerned about an old gentleman in a house next to a property development on Lansdown Road. There had been some sort of accident at the site, an exploding gas canister. The police had checked in with neighbours and found him lying in his back garden in some sort of hysterical state.

'Social services were called but the old bugger refused to talk to them,' said Jane in her thick, fruity Somerset accent, which always made her sound like she was in an advert for cake or cider. She was wearing a Marks & Spencer blouse that had so many jazzy patterns going on at once I was worried that if I looked at it for too long I would trip out. 'They thought perhaps the agency could send someone to assess him. I asked Bob to pop over yesterday, but the chap told him to bugger off – he was very odd and aggressive apparently. I thought you'd have a better chance, love.'

A tinge of anxiety. I didn't want any new clients, I wasn't ready, everything was only just about manageable as it was. Now, there was someone new, someone who clearly did not want help.

'Why?' I managed. 'Why me?'

Jane looked at me conspiratorially.

'You're a young girl and a bit, you know ... he might fancy you enough to let you in. It's worth a shot, look.'

I just started at her, shocked and uncomprehending. I couldn't quite to process what was happening. Jane saw the look on my face then laughed uproariously, wriggling her giant bottom in the chair. Her face straightened out into a look of cloying sympathy. She leaned across her desk and gently grabbed my arm with her great fleshy fingers.

'You'll be *fine*,' she said. 'He's ninety-eight years old, he's not exactly dangerous. It'll do you good – a nice little challenge.' Her fingers gripped my arm a little harder. 'Your mum told me what you're going through right now. It's tough, I know.'

I looked down and picked at my fingernails. Of course Mum had told Jane – the two of them are lifelong friends. It was Mum who got me this job in the first place. I could imagine the conversation: *Please help my useless daughter, her life's a gigantic mess, but she's a good listener and very diligent.*

Jane drew her hand away and smiled warmly. 'If it doesn't work out, we can just get back to social services and tell 'em he's unstable and needs a social worker,' she said. 'You'll be done with it. But if he lets you in, well, maybe you can charm him into signing up. I'll add him to your roster. It's more money for you.'

Laura James, care assistant. This has never been my great ambition, but here I am, spending the week visiting old people; travelling from one sad home to another, sorting their meds, making them lunch, taking them shopping, talking to them. Jane told me that I made them feel safe, which is ironic because I never feel safe. That's why I'm here in this job. I tell myself this is just temporary, something quiet and non-stressful while I am recovering, while I'm beginning my big year of change, but after two weeks of training and a month on the job I can already see how quickly time is slipping by. There are moments I think, *hang on, what the fuck am I doing? How did I get here?* And then I remember how and I always really wish I hadn't. I am also back living with my mum. So yes, things are really working out for me on every conceivable level. Oh, and I am also standing on this old man's path staring at him.

'I said, can I help you?'

It strikes me immediately that he doesn't look ninety-eight. I don't know what ninety-eight is supposed to look like, but this tall, thin man with only the slightest stoop is not it. His face is craggy but alert, his eyes a glinting steely grey within their deep sockets. His hair, a shock of white, is almost trendily styled into a messy crop. He reminds me of a big poster of Samuel Beckett our English teacher put on the classroom wall – his face hewn out of angles and deep lines like canyons. He wears thick corduroy trousers, a striped shirt and a dark green cardigan with patches on the elbows. It is an eccentric, old-fashioned look, but it is definitely a 'look' rather than something wrangled onto him by a carer. He seems fitter and sharper than the men I am caring for in their late seventies, but at the same time, there is something off, something not quite 'there' about him. He doesn't have that dour, droopy absence that dementia usually brings with it – I have seen that enough to recognise it immediately; it's something else, like there is some aspect of inner life that has been taken from him. His eyes lead nowhere.

'Hi, are you Will?' I shout through the downfall. I look at my Filofax again, but the ink is running away. 'Will Davidson?'

He glares at me. 'Emerson,' he snaps. 'Who are *you*?'

'My name's Laura James, I'm from the Shady Oak home care agency.' I pull my hood back from my head to show my face so that he can see that I am not a psychopath. Immediately, I feel the driving rain trickling into my mouth. It is not a pleasant sensation. 'We phoned you last week to arrange a visit? My colleague Bob—'

'I told that gentleman I would not require another visit,' he says, more sternly now. 'Good day to you.'

He starts to close the door, and usually I would have just let him, but something compels me to actually make an effort.

'Mr Emerson,' I say stepping forward. 'I won't take up much of your time . . .'

'You are quite correct,' he says. 'In fact, you won't take up any.'

'But it's very wet out here, it would be lovely to . . .'

'To get home, I suspect. Don't let me stop you.'

'If you would just let me in for a few minutes, I could take my clothes off and . . .' What the fuck. 'I mean my coat, my wet coat.'

He stops closing the door and stands looking at me for a second. I can feel my face reddening. God knows what I look like, bedraggled and be-anoraked on his doorstep like a lost child. And now I have also offered to strip naked in his lounge.

'I'm sorry,' I clarify. 'I didn't actually mean I was going to take my clothes off.'

'I see,' he says. 'I thought perhaps private home care provision had changed rather a lot in the modern era.'

There is a pause, the only sound coming from the rain battering at the roof of the porch. This is getting incredibly tense and awkward and wet and cold.

'Well, I'll go,' I say. 'I'm sorry to have bothered you. Also I have sort of wrenched your gate off its hinges.'

'Yes, I see that.'

'I could try and move it off the path?'

'I think you've done enough.'

'I'm sorry. I'll ... I'll go.'

Without thinking, I pull the hood back onto my head, but it has filled with rain and a tidal wave pours over my face and down the back of my neck.

'That was really cold,' I say. I look up at the old man pathetically. There is no expression on his face, not even a pitying smile. I turn away and start back up the path, desperate to escape this fun new lesson in discomfort and rejection.

'I'm just making some tea,' he says. He shouts it loudly so I can hear through the rain. 'Why don't you join me? We could hang up your coat next to the fire to dry – although what sort of man-made material is that? It will probably ignite.'

I turn back to him.

'Tea would be nice,' I say.

He grunts and walks back inside, leaving the door open, clearly expecting me to follow him. I look around again. The house is just past the really posh part of Lansdown Road, the long, steep thoroughfare winding out of the city toward Bath's northern suburbs. Avon Lodge was perhaps once part of a grand little terrace, but now, divorced from its era, the house looks out of place and ghostly, crumbling into its own untended grave.

The thought makes me shiver and I step into the hallway, discovering that the theme of decayed grandeur is very much continued inside. The parquet floor is chipped and faded and the thick pattered wallpaper is peeling away, exposing large sections of blackish plaster. Ahead, there is a narrow staircase, its painted handrail now chipped and rotten, and beside it, the hall narrows into a shadowy passage leading toward the rear of the house. It reminds me of all the student hovels and shitty flatshares I've lived in, minus the stench of dope and vegan curries.

'Give me your coat, I'll hang it by the Aga, it'll dry faster out there.'

I take it off and hand it to him.

'Please, go into the parlour,' he says, pointing at a door. 'I'll make some tea.'

I always dread going into their houses for the first time – I never know what I'm going to find. I've seen my fair share of scary stuff: massive collections of creepy china dolls; giant moth-eaten moose heads mounted above fireplaces. Also, with old people there is always the chance of cat shit. Cat shit on the rug, on the sofa, and once, on a dining table, like a decorative centrepiece. But the hardest things are the always-present photos of lost husbands and wives – their young faces black and white and hopeful, their whole lives ahead of them. They make me really sad. So before I walk into the front room, I steel myself for the worst – and when I see inside, I almost gasp out loud.

It looks like some kind of 1940s museum, like a National Trust property that has been intricately dressed to give an authentic sense of the past. The wallpaper, a garish maze of now faded pink and blue blooms, clashes dramatically with a burgundy rug that takes up most of the floor space and is also decorated with flowers that are now almost lost to age. A matching sofa and armchair are both heavily upholstered in the same sickly olive-green material, which is dotted with dark stains. There is a small fireplace and a carriage clock on the mantelpiece, which is ticking loudly. On one side of the chimney breast a set of shelves holds a row of musty hardback books and a vintage wireless, on the other there is an ancient record player in a large wooden cabinet. In the middle of the room a walnut coffee table has a vast newspaper spread across it – the old man was clearly reading before I wrenched his gate off the wall. I don't really keep up to date with current affairs, so when I see a headline mentioning some kind of war in Europe, I am a little alarmed. Then I notice the date at the top of the page – October 23, 1944. Okay, that's fine, he's reading a paper that is exactly seventy-two years old. That's not strange at all. Maybe he's a history buff.

I sit down on the sofa, beside a floor lamp with an extravagant orange shade. Will Emerson is taking his time. There is a smell of something old in the air, something like pipe tobacco or the polish my gran used to rub on her brass ornaments, and beneath that, an unsettling stillness. I get this sudden weird sense that something once happened here, something immense – like a furious, horrible row – and that the dust still hasn't resettled. I realise I am biting my nails and I know this means I have to be calm. There are no dolls in here, at least. I hear a drawer being pulled open in the kitchen and a lot of clattering, which leads to a brief ridiculous thought: what would I do if he suddenly came at me brandishing a knife? Was it possible to be murderously attacked by someone in their late nineties? It is the sort of thing that would happen to me. But no, he comes in holding a tray loaded with china cups, a teapot, and a small jar filled with sugar cubes. He places his load down top of the newspaper.

'So you live here alone?' I ask as he busies himself with pouring the tea.

'Yes,' he says. 'I have for a long time. Which does make me rather curious as to why I am suddenly receiving all this attention.'

He passes a cup of tea to me, his hands trembling with the effort. I take it, wondering how I should explain.

'We were asked by social services to come and see you,' I say. 'They were worried. You had a fall in the garden last week?'

Silence. He looks at me in bewilderment. Does he remember?

'Do you have any friends in the street?' I ask. 'Any neighbours who visit you?'

'I do not get on with my neighbours,' he says. 'They are busybodies.'

'How about friends or relatives?'

He shakes his head then sits down slowly and heavily in the armchair.

'It is just me,' he says. 'By the time you get to my age, everybody you ever knew or loved is a memory.'

This is not going to be a life-affirming conversation. He goes silent again and out of the corner of my eye, I can see him staring at me. Just staring. His face is quizzical and angry. The sound of the clock echoes around the room.

'You look familiar,' he says. 'Do you live around here?'

'No, I live in Bear Flat.'

'You lived here in the past? Many years ago? I've seen you, I'm sure.'

I shake my head. Many years ago? How old does he think I am? Maybe he *is* losing it. I can't think of anything to say so I take big gulps of the scorching tea and look around the room for inspiration. There *must* be some sad photographs – family, friends, a spouse, a lover – anything to get a grip on this man and his life. But there are none. None at all.

It is only then that notice it – on the wall above the record player. A large modernist painting within a simple wooden frame depicting a naked woman curled up on herself, her eyes closed, her red hair splayed out around her shoulders. Amid the staid, old-fashioned clutter of the room the picture stands out sharply, like something from another universe. I feel myself blushing and quickly look back to the bookshelf, but the old guy has spotted my reaction.

'Do you recognise it?' he says. 'The painting? It is only a print, of course.'

This feels like a test. I stare at it again, trying to access the memories of my Art History A-level; I recognise the style – the rich, almost golden colours, the wan expression on the model's face, the soft tones of her flesh. I just have to remember the name ... I catch an image of myself at seventeen, sitting on the hill beside the school field, reading Gombrich, feeling the sun on my face, feeling almost happy.

'It's Klimt, isn't it?' I look back to Will with a hopeful expression.

He nods joylessly, walking slowly over to the painting and studying it. 'At the time, people thought his work was pornographic.'

'Right,' I say. I am very unsure about the conversational route this could lead us down – it may take me somewhere incredibly uncomfortable. Time to change direction.

'So, social services think you may benefit from a little ... assistance. Is that something you'd be interested in?'

No reply. He is now just staring languidly at the painting. Lost in it.

'We could help with medication or shopping. There may be funds available to help pay, if you can't afford it?'

'Do *you* think this picture is pornographic?' he asks.

Oh God, I was right. Here we go.

I do not need this. I do not need to be made to feel weird and uncomfortable. Not right now. Something starts bubbling inside me, like volatile chemicals being poured together. It doesn't take long these days, to go from nought to completely stressed out. I know why.

I stand up quickly – quickly enough to make the old man jump a little.

'I'd better go,' I say, putting my teacup back on the tray. 'I've got another meeting soon, I can't be late. If you don't want us to visit, it's fine, I can tell the company you're okay. You look okay to me. Are you okay?'

Finally he is drawn away from the painting and he stares at me again.

'Apparently, *you're* the professional,' he says. 'Shouldn't you know?'

I don't say anything and he tuts loudly at me. He clearly hates my guts. 'I'll fetch your coat,' he sneers.

He walks slowly out of the room and I take one last look around. I have that strong feeling again, of something being present, some atmosphere, some jolt of tension. Even though the fire is crackling away, I feel something icy. I've had feelings like this for several days – weird twinges of cold and paranoia – my GP told me it might happen, but this is the worst it's been. I pull my hands up into the sleeves of my jumper, bunching the thick fabric into my fists. Keen, now, just to be out of there, I turn to walk through into the hallway. But to my shock, Mr Emerson is standing right there, watching me, holding my anorak. I gasp involuntarily, and suddenly want to grab the coat from him and run, but instead he holds it open, clearly expecting to put it on for me. Begrudgingly I walk over, turn my back and let him. Okay, *this* is where he stabs me, I think. But to my faint surprise, he just puts the coat on.

I open the door, noticing the rain has softened to a drizzle, and walk out.

'Goodbye,' I offer. He doesn't say anything until I have stepped over the gate and out of his garden.

'You didn't answer my question,' he shouts after me.

I stop and turn back, confused.

'The painting,' he says. 'Do you think it is indecent?'

I look at him, slowly raising my hood over my head once again.

'No,' I say. 'I think it's beautiful.'

For a second, he stands in the doorway scowling, his eyes offering nothing at all in the way of recognition. And then he slams the door shut. God, he detests me.

Right, I think, that is the last time I'll see *him*. And I take my Filofax out of my pocket, turn to my 'to do' list for the day and put a line through the visit. Then I pop it back in the saddlebag. Just as I am removing the bike lock (as if anyone would steal this thing anyway), a young woman approaches on the pavement, pushing a buggy.

'Have you just come out of that house?' she asks, jabbing an e-cigarette toward Avon Lodge.

I nod.' I'm a carer. Do you know him?'

'Stay clear of him, love,' she says. 'He's a fucking old weirdo.'

With that, she yanks the buggy forward and strolls casually past.

I sit on my bike watching the woman veer off toward the sixties flats further down the road. What the hell was that about? I take a last look at the house. It turns out I am already wrong about never seeing Will Emerson again, because there he is in his front room, just visible through the musty window. He is standing very still, and he is staring at the painting.

Read Keith Stuart's inspiring debut

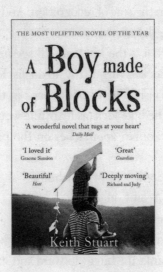

THE RICHARD AND JUDY BOOK CLUB 2017 BESTSELLER
and NUMBER ONE AMAZON BESTSELLER

A *Boy Made of Blocks* is a funny, heartwarming story of family and love inspired by the author's own experiences with his son, the perfect latest obsession for fans of *The Rosie Project*, David Nicholls and Jojo Moyes.

A father who rediscovers love

Alex loves his wife Jody, but has forgotten how to show it. He loves his son Sam, but doesn't understand him. He needs a reason to grab his future with both hands.

A son who shows him how to live

Meet eight-year-old Sam: beautiful, surprising – and different. To him the world is a frightening mystery. But as his imagination comes to life, his family will be changed ... for good.